Love Is a Canoe

Center Point
Large Print

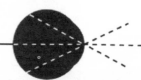

**This Large Print Book carries the
Seal of Approval of N.A.V.H.**

Love Is
a Canoe

BEN SCHRANK

CENTER POINT LARGE PRINT
THORNDIKE, MAINE

This Center Point Large Print edition
is published in the year 2013 by arrangement with
Sara Crichton Books,
an imprint of Farrar, Straus and Giroux, LLC.

The text of this Large Print edition is unabridged.
In other aspects, this book may vary
from the original edition.
Printed in the United States of America
on permanent paper.
Set in 16-point Times New Roman type.

ISBN: 978-1-61173-695-3

Library of Congress Cataloging-in-Publication Data

Schrank, Ben.
  Love is a canoe / Ben Schrank.
  pages ; cm.
  ISBN 978-1-61173-695-3 (library binding : alk. paper)
  1. Authors—Fiction. 2. Bereavement—Fiction.
    3. Self-help techniques—Fiction. 4. Loss (Psychology)—Fiction.
    5. Large type books. I. Title.
PS3569.C52913L68 2013b
813′.54—dc23
                                        2012046410

For Lauren, who helped

Love Is
a Canoe

Introduction to *Marriage Is a Canoe*
by Peter Herman, published
by Ladder & Rake Books, October 1971

Dear Reader:

In this brief volume I will share some stories that were told to me ten years ago during the summer of 1961, when I was twelve. The stories are meant to entertain. But they are also life lessons.

In that summer of 1961, my parents divorced. I was bewildered and lonely. During those July and August weeks, while my parents spent each night fighting over their possessions, I was sent to stay with my grandparents Hank and Bess Latham. They lived in a grand old cabin on the shore of Lake Okabye, in Millerton, New York.

Over the course of our days together, we took long walks around the lake and I learned the proper names for the many things found in nature that had been, before then, unfamiliar to a city boy like me. We enjoyed picnic dinners of fried chicken and lemonade at dusk on the lawn that rolled down from their cabin's back porch to the shore of the lake. I played baseball and went to square dances with the local children. And just about every day, Pop and I went fishing on Lake Okabye in his Old Town canoe.

The stories my grandparents told me have become the lessons and guideposts that I return to as I go about the happy business of being a hardworking man, a kind neighbor, and an honest citizen. But what I remember best, and what I'll share in these pages, is all that my grandparents showed me about how to be a good husband and lover.

Though they would never come right out and say it, my grandparents were eager to share their philosophy of love. They were terribly upset at my parents because of how badly they mishandled their marriage. And I believe they wanted to keep me from following in their footsteps. My grandparents did something unusual: they brought me, an unhappy young boy about to enter adolescence, inside their world and they talked to me about their marriage. They showed me how to nurture a truly loving relationship.

I am sorry you weren't there with us that summer. But the wonder of all that happened then and my need to share it is what compelled me to write this book. I have done my best to fill this volume with all the lessons I learned about love from my grandparents. Their stories are meant for whoever might care to read them. Because I believe anyone who does, will benefit.

Peter Herman, April 12, 1971, New York

Emily Babson, July 2010

"I got everything," Eli called out. He carried his bike in one hand so its top tube was level with his ear and he swung a canvas bag full of groceries in the other hand.

Emily smiled at him from the middle of their apartment, where she stood next to the kitchen island. She had been examining a defrosting piecrust.

"Did you get cornstarch?" she asked.

Eli let their front door slam behind him, dropped the bike so it bounced once before coming to a lean against the wall, and came through the big parlor and into the kitchen. He kissed her. He smelled like iron and oil from his bicycle factory and then underneath that, the smell she'd given up trying to properly name and now just thought of as green olives, which made no sense. She loved his smell. He had dark hair that he wore a little long and his eyes were brown but sometimes she saw them flash violet. She let go of the piecrust and put a hand on his chest.

"I forgot that. I got everything else, though."

"Blueberry pie won't work without it."

"Sure it will. It should. Anyway, we must have some." He kissed her again. Eli Corelli was as tall as his wife, though he was thicker, so in photographs he looked shorter. When Emily first met him after a lecture he'd given at the New School, she thought he had legs like tree trunks and she loved that about him immediately, that he was so solid that if she were ever inclined to throw herself at him, he could catch her.

Though it was Saturday, they'd both been working all morning and now they planned to spend the rest of the day making a pie for a contest held by Emily's sister, Sherry. Emily didn't often go to Sherry's parties, which Sherry threw when she was between acting jobs, but she liked the theme of this one.

"I called her and got the scoop," Emily said. "There's two categories, sweet and savory. And then a final big winner at the end. So our blueberry could go up against chicken potpie. Though it's too hot for that."

"I hope going sweet was the right move." Eli slipped his hands around Emily's waist.

Emily pushed the piecrust around on the counter. She'd bought it yesterday and it would take at least another hour to thaw. She'd said yes to her little sister's pie party on Monday before her shyness held her back and now she was nervous. Emily had long ago accepted that Sherry was social and she was not. Sherry was striking to look at. She had black hair while Emily's was only very dark brown. And Sherry's face was all angles so her photographer friends loved to take her picture because of all the shadows they could find when they lit her. Emily's face was softer and rounder and she was quicker to tan. Most of the time she had a spray of freckles over her nose and cheeks. She had her hair cut in bangs to contrast with her features. The sisters weren't best friends—Sherry's best friends were actors like her, and they changed every year or two. Emily was just three years older than Sherry. They were equally protective of each other. And if Emily was being honest, she would have to admit that she was closer to Sherry than anyone else in New York. Emily had been too shy in her twenties and then she'd surprised herself and everyone else when she met Eli and married him. But instead of becoming more confident because she had a husband who everyone loved, she had come to live too much inside their marriage. She beat herself up about this situation and often thought up schemes that would change the dynamic before it solidified and she completely lost her identity to their coupledom. Before she was with Eli, she had trained herself to love to go to yoga at least a few times a week, to switch to merlot after a Manhattan or to just start with merlot, to not feel remorseful when she went shopping for clothes and brought home the same charcoal cashmere cardigan over and over again. She had learned to care for herself. Now she was sure she could work herself out of this newish state, and she believed that she absolutely had to before they had children. Emily was aware of the calculation that went into her decision to go to this party, aware of how purposeful she was and how she was bothered by it, but she was determined to go anyway. Eli never seemed to tear himself up the way she did. She loved Eli. But she was often frustrated with herself and jealous of her husband.

"The more I think about it, the more I don't see how we'll win with straight-ahead blueberry." Eli opened some cabinets. "Blueberries are in season. Everybody is going to show up with the same pie."

"We don't have to win. We just want to make a yummy pie, that's all. Not some avant-garde bacon and peach monstrosity. I want ours to be liked."

"Liked? No, baby. It's easy to make a likable pie. I want to see people fucking love whatever we make. I want to see forks go in mouths and swoons happen. I want to see finger licking, not liking." Eli wouldn't stop moving around the kitchen. He frowned. "I want to help you cook this thing, but what's always weird about Saturday afternoons is that I need a nap."

"I won't sleep, but I'll go in there with you."

They held hands and walked into their bedroom. They rented the parlor floor of an oversize limestone town house on Clinton Street in Carroll

Gardens, in Brooklyn. The tall front windows were near exactly like the ones Emily had dreamed of when she first came to New York a decade earlier. Emily had repainted and washed those windows when they moved in. The rest of the place was good, though unloved around its edges, with a noisy refrigerator and a parquet floor that would be amazing if their landlord would just sand and polish and care for it. They did their best to keep everything clean and bright, except for the bedroom, which had chocolate-brown carpet and blackout shades. Eli had painted the room a deep red when they moved in two years earlier, just a few months after they were married. It was a much sexier color than Emily would have ever thought she would like in a bedroom. When her mother had come down for a conference and stayed on their couch, Emily had kept the door to their bedroom shut.

They lay down on the bed, over the sheets.

"Did you get enough done today?" Emily asked.

"Nope. The boys in Japan want eighteen more bikes. And I'm falling behind schedule. I don't love the stress."

"Send them a pie." She laughed and her eyes crinkled. She knew he liked seeing her laugh. He brushed back her bangs and kissed her.

"Maybe I will if we can make one worthy of their undying love . . ."

Eli kept talking about work. His six-year-old

company, Roman Street Bicycles, made single-speed bike frames that were in demand all over the world. Eli was having trouble managing growth. He was determined to touch each frame and get involved with every build, and if he kept meeting demand, soon that wouldn't be possible. Emily was thinking about work, too, about a proposal she was doing for a company that wanted to re-brand a line of cotton blankets.

"What's a good name for a blanket?" she wondered aloud.

"I knew you weren't listening." Eli buried his face in her neck. Warm blanket, she thought. Soft blanket. There are so many things, Emily thought, that gain nothing from being reconsidered. Her group had been paid well a few times for suggesting that a company not change a thing. But a good brand consultant couldn't do that every time. Eli threw an arm over her. His hand slipped behind her back. It amazed her that after four years together, they could fall asleep intertwined. She thought she would need an abstract word in front of blanket, *Moomja* or something. *Eli*. The Eli blanket . . .

"Kiss me," she said. "Kiss me for one minute before you fall asleep." He did and she was happy that she knew what to ask for from Eli. She would make that trade and stay too prim with everyone else but never with him. To be too ensconced in your marriage? Why was that bad? Emily did not

16

consider herself a dreamy person. She believed life was made up of trade-offs and this was surely a fair one.

She woke up an hour later with her brow sweaty. She wiped her forehead and blew out air a few times, opened her eyes wide to see in that dark room. She smelled onions frying. She pulled her hair back and went into the kitchen. Eli was mixing something in a little bowl. He was in a pair of khaki shorts and nothing else. The Roman Street Bicycles logo, made up of the letters *RSB* wound through the spokes of a bicycle wheel, was tattooed on his left shoulder blade. Sometimes she scratched at it, as if she could take it off with her nails. Eli didn't like it when she did that. Now she touched his back without scratching him and looked around the messy kitchen.

"What happened?" she asked. "What'd you do to my piecrust?"

Eli was looking into a glass bowl. Bits of egg bobbed in a green sauce that didn't seem like it could possibly set. There were mounds of vegetables on cutting boards and spices everywhere. Butter was smeared in pie plates. Though she didn't see anything cooking in a pan, the smell was now more complex than just onions.

"I had an idea," Eli said.

"This is not blueberry pie. I love you, Eli. But this doesn't look like a winner."

"No it is, don't worry. I saw eggs in the fridge and we have potatoes and there's prosciutto that I bought with that old Staubitz gift certificate. But the green sauce is the key. That's our secret weapon. I called my uncle Frito. We'll go savory with a breakfast pie for dinner that's actually like a timbale and we'll win. I'm going to get the male vote. You watch."

"Uncle Frito?"

"Uncle Frito, in Mexico, who created the Frito pie. He had a good pointer for me so I'm glad I called."

"I don't get how just because your mother is from Chile it allows you to both claim and denigrate all of South America," Emily said. She was Jewish and had grown up in Milton, outside Boston. And then her parents divorced when she and Sherry were still in middle school and their mother had gone to Maine to teach at Bates. So Emily felt strictly Northeastern and was even a little proud of it.

"Take it easy, Mrs. Laid-back. This pie is initially subtle and then studded with fire. Or it will be if I can get it to set right." Eli stroked his chin. "You go take a shower. Let me do a few more secret South American things."

"This isn't very team," Emily said.

"Sometimes one member of a team needs blind support and then the whole team ends up winning," Eli said. "Actually, it's like that a lot.

Look at Lance Armstrong." He grabbed a spoon and dipped it into the bowl. "Taste."

"No. If you expect blind support, I won't. What illegal something extra did you put in there, Lance?"

"Taste."

So she did and the sauce was smoky and fiery and everything Eli said it would be.

"It's delicious," she said. "I guess I'll get dressed. You'll get the male and the female vote."

When Emily came out of their bedroom she was in a dark blue summer dress with white polka dots.

"You look hot," Eli said. "Later you'll pull that dress up around your thighs and we'll do our victory dance on a tabletop. You can flash your underpants at the boys."

There were two big paper bags on the kitchen counter. Tomorrow she'd bake a pie with the blueberries and bring it to work on Monday.

"How about clothes for you?" she asked.

"Oh, yeah." Eli threw on a shirt and found his flip-flops by the door. "Also, I need your help with the speech."

"Speech?"

"I don't want to be at a loss for words when we win."

Sherry lived on Lorimer Street in Williamsburg above a recently shut-down restaurant called Baba.

She had briefly dated Nicola, the restaurant's owner. Sherry mostly appeared in productions at Playwrights Horizons and in new plays by Kenneth Lonergan and Annie Baker. Because she was intermittently funny and conventionally beautiful, she occasionally flew out to Hollywood or Vancouver for supporting roles in movies starring Anna Faris.

"I know," Sherry said to Emily once Eli had gone off to set out their pies. "I'm all sweaty."

"Don't be dumb. You look like somebody's dream come true," Emily said.

Sherry was in a black dress with a thick white sash across the middle. Her lipstick was bright red. She had a habit of biting her lower lip and she did that now.

"You do get that I'm a truck-stop waitress?"

"I do," Emily said. "It works."

Baba had been a bodega before becoming Baba, a wine-and-small-plates place, and then Nicola gave up on it and went down to Miami to run a catering business. But Sherry had a key and was friendly with the landlord. Now the small room was filled with round café tables with a pie stuck with a numbered flag on each one. The place smelled like spilled wine and it was noisy.

"You told me twenty people," Emily said. "This is more like forty."

"Micky's friend is coming with his klezmer band," a voice called out, close to Emily's ear.

"I'm hearing that savory is the true challenge category," Eli said, joining them. "Somebody actually did mince. Is it secret ballot or a panel of judges?"

"Bits of paper with numbers in a hat and then we count them and see which pie got the most votes," Sherry said.

"I'm going to eat." Eli found a paper plate. "Secret ballot. I like that."

Sherry and Emily exchanged a smile. The other thing about Eli was that, at thirty-seven, he was still kind of a big kid. Though Emily was only thirty-two, she never felt younger than him. Sherry went away and Emily watched Eli spy on people as they tried out the pies. He was never far from her, and not more than a minute went by when he didn't at least have one arm around her. He liked to hold her high, his hand covering her ribs just below her breast. Or he would slide his hand low on her back. They could easily have gotten pulled away from each other. But it didn't happen. Instead, he knew her shyness and by staying where she could see him, he kept it from overwhelming her. He was there, guiding her, keeping her fresh and near and safe and happy. He didn't talk about it with her. He just knew.

Though people kept threatening that the klezmer band was minutes away, it hadn't yet arrived, so Sherry brought a speaker dock down from her apartment and someone plugged their phone into it. An old Neil Young song came on: "Sugar Mountain." Emily strained to listen to it. Outside, it had begun to rain and the sudden summer shower made the people standing by the open windows laugh and show off their wet shoulders. Emily told herself that Eli was like a Neil Young song she wanted to hear over and over again. People were still coming in. A short young woman with dark hair yanked the door open and threw herself inside. She had just the sort of long loose ringlets Emily didn't care for. Untamable creature, Emily thought, as the woman shook the water out of her hair and looked around. But that wasn't fair. The woman was beautiful, a beautiful mess. Emily tried to feel sympathetic. It would have been unbearable for her to arrive late and wet and empty-handed and have people look her over. The woman threw down a camouflage-patterned duffel bag and smiled wide at no one. Emily resisted an urge to tell her to put her bag some-where farther from the door, so no stranger lurking on the street just outside the party would take the opportunity to reach a hand inside and steal it.

"Jenny?" Sherry called out. "Hi!" Sherry went over and hugged the woman, who was wearing a denim skirt and flip-flops and a billowy blue-and-white-striped sleeveless top that showed off her jangly breasts.

"Hey. I didn't bake anything. I literally just got

out of a cab from Kennedy is why. But I am sure ready to chow down on some pie!"

"Jenny, this is my sister, Emily. Jenny's moving back from L.A. soon and this is, like, her scouting trip."

"Yeah, you know, like where I look for an apartment and a job." Jenny made a bummer face by rolling her eyes and frowning. Emily saw Eli come back toward them. He'd been pushing people to vote for his pie. There had been a lot of jokes about electioneering too near a polling place.

"We are looking good," he said. "Great feedback. I love that the chiles are making people sweat."

"And this is Eli Corelli, my brother-in-law."

Jenny raised her eyebrows. She'd already grabbed a plate and scooped up a piece of someone's pistachio-currant pie—a pie that had barely been touched.

"Roman Street Bicycles, right?" Jenny spoke with her mouth full. "I've totally heard of you. I've ridden your bikes."

"You have one?"

"No. I have an old beater I never use. In L.A. we don't get to ride enough to justify buying an RSB bike. I'm excited to start biking again."

"Who made the pie called Uncle Frito's Special?" someone called out. "We're ready to vote!"

"Excuse me." Eli smiled. "I need to make myself available for last-minute questions."

"Even though nobody is supposed to know who made what," Sherry called after him.

"I better get my eat on before it's all gone." Jenny gave Sherry a quick hug. "You look super-hot, by the way. I'd take an extra cup of joe from you for sure."

"Where do you know her from?" Emily watched Jenny use her fingers to pull bits of crust off someone's imitation of a Momofuku crack pie.

"College. She's funny. She has a million weird hobbies so she's really adaptable to scenes. She was always like that."

"Scenes?" Emily smiled. "Is she an actress, too?"

"No—like you and the industrial design scene. Don't be fake-naive. You know what I mean," Sherry said. "Drink this wine. That rich guy over there brought it so it must be good. Jenny should call Eli," Sherry said.

"Why?"

"She managed some photographers in L.A. and that went really well. I'm sure she can help with Eli's company. You know, help figure out how to grow the business. Isn't that the thing he's always whining about?"

Emily nodded a yes. Eli was close again. She reached out with her hand and Eli slipped his arm around her waist.

"What are we talking about?" Eli asked. "That guy was really critical of my pie."

"Don't worry," Sherry said. "In my experience sweet never beats savory. But at the same time, yours is maybe a little out there."

"Whatever. My genius is misunderstood."

"We were just saying it would be great if you hooked Jenny up with a job. She's amazing once she gets focused. She totally knows how to run a business."

"Does she? Maybe we can set something up," Eli said. "I definitely need help." He took a long pull on his beer.

Emily looked around her at the field of little tables, some with nothing but an empty pie plate in the middle, picked clean and scarred with knife cuts, and others with barely touched pies that were beginning to break down at the seams, pies that had turned someone off too early and that nobody was willing to touch now.

"Don't worry," Emily said. "I'll help you clean up. And you're right. If she's good at organizing, Eli should hire her. He needs that."

Sherry smiled. She said, "About the mess? I wasn't worried. If this thing with Jenny works, we totally did a mitzvah. I'll tell Mom."

"She only cares if it makes you happy," Emily said.

"Well, if Jenny helps Eli and makes him more successful and that's good for you, then that does make me happy. So I'll tell Mom, okay?" Sherry winked at some late arrivals. "I'm sure I'll talk to her tomorrow and she'll ask about tonight and whether you had a good time and were social and fun—which is hilarious since how social is she? Not very. I am going to call her out on that tomorrow. Maybe."

"I am social!" Emily said, too loud. "How big of a problem is that, anyway? It is not a problem, actually."

Sherry raised an eyebrow at Emily. "It kind of is. You're definitely defensive about it."

"Emily is a sensitive soul." Eli pulled Emily in and tried to kiss the top of her head, but she squirmed away. "And I love her for it."

"Thank you very much," Emily said. "I love being labeled. Now can we move off the subject of me right now, please?"

Peter Herman, July 2010

"Lisa?" Peter called out to his wife. She was in the bathroom and he didn't want to interrupt her, but he would if he didn't hear from her in another moment. "Are you all right?"

He stood up to go to her. The phone rang.

Peter stared at it. Generally it was Henry calling to give him an update about what was going on at the inn. Henry loved to call and discuss the problems that made good stories—drug-addled cooks and pregnant maids and missing wedding rings. There would always be empty rooms and young employees who could not resist putting those overstuffed mattresses to good use. And then there were fights and missed workdays and inevitably, someone had to go. The day-to-day life of the inn could be overwhelming. For most of his working life, Peter had been the one who was best able to manage the human element. He had done a fine job, with his cool head and a charm he'd acquired in his early twenties, when he'd moved to Millerton soon after he published his little book, *Marriage Is a Canoe*. Though Peter's relationship to the inn had grown tenuous now that Lisa was so ill, Henry still called to get his help.

The phone kept ringing. Peter picked up a handset from the bedside table where it sat next to a stack of *Poughkeepsie Journal*s and *The New York Times*, both of which Lisa still liked to have within reach even though she no longer bothered to even pretend she was able to read.

"Yes?"

"Hello, may I speak to Peter Herman?"

"This is Peter."

Lisa returned from the bathroom. She stood in the doorway, her graying auburn hair pulled back badly in the braid Peter had learned to make just a few months earlier. Her face had turned pale over the years and the blue in her eyes had grown lighter, too. Just the sight of her wearing her purple robe leavened him. Though he'd been frowning at the phone, now he smiled. Eleven in the morning and she thought she should be getting ready for bed. He beckoned her to him. But she remained in the doorway.

"My name is Katherine and I'm calling because of your book."

"You'd be better served by sending a letter to me care of Ladder & Rake. I can't take calls."

"I'm sorry—I do understand and I don't want to take up too much of your time, but your book means so much to me. There's a passage in the beginning, after you explain how marriage is a canoe and then later when you say the voyage you take in it is driven by passion—let me find it—

anyway, I'm having trouble with passion and how it relates to staying in the canoe and—"

"Listen, listen now, Katherine, is it? Here's the thing. You've called my home. And my wife is ill. So you can see how this call is an intrusion."

"Of course. But Peter, now that I've reached you—"

"Goodbye." He pressed OFF and threw the handset on the rug. He caught his breath and put his hands on his lower back. He weighed less than a dozen pounds more than he had in college. He had a couple of blazers from back then that still fit, and though now he had a visible belly, he could get into the Levi's he wore in the mid-seventies, when their daughter, Belinda, was born. His spine had begun to bend, so he'd lost the couple of inches that had put him above six feet. But the mornings when he woke up and had to roll rather than spring out of bed were still blessedly rare.

He spread his arms wide and waited. Lisa padded toward him.

"Who was that?" Lisa's voice contained a glimmer of her old jealousy. She didn't mind sharing him with Millerton. But over the years she had come to hate when he was asked to go away, down to New York or to do a talk somewhere. He had begun to live his life much closer to home because of her preference, and that didn't bother him at all.

"Oh, Lisa. Who was that?" He didn't want to tell her that the call was from a fan of *Canoe*. She didn't like those people and never had, and if he downplayed the call she would get upset but she would not be able to understand why. So he began to sing. "Who? Who?"

"Stop . . . Peter, stop."

"Who are you? Who are you? Come on, tell me, who are you?"

She started to laugh, finally sitting on the bed next to him, putting her head on his chest, banging her fists on the tops of his thighs.

"It's the oddest thing," he said.

"What?"

"You're not a particularly goofy person and yet here we are being playful all the time. It's a change."

She did not respond.

"Lisa?"

She looked up at him. He wanted to stop. He knew he was being a little mean. But he was losing her and he was angry about it. He had built his adult self around the guarantee of her stability. And now with so much of her gone, sure, he was resentful—in flashes—before returning to this new caretaker role.

When he didn't move, Lisa pulled the flannel sheets back, grasped his shoulder so she was pushing him down with her into the bed. He felt her spittle on his chest and was reminded of thirty-five years ago, just after Belinda was born, when they would go to sleep holding each other and he would wake in the morning with his undershirt drenched from her breast milk.

He said, "Wait. What are you doing?"

"Going to bed. Bedtime."

"No, no," Peter said. "Can't you feel the sun? It's nearly lunchtime."

"Bedtime."

"No." Peter bit back the catch in his voice. "Please don't."

"At least kisses, then."

"Yes to kisses!" Peter quickly took her in his arms and kissed her, her thick braid flopping onto his shoulder.

"Now what?" she asked after half a minute of quiet. He knew she would, by then, have forgotten that she wanted to go to bed. But the phone call would have penetrated somewhere else, into some more emotional place in her mind. In a different voice, she said, "What was the call? More stupid stuff about *Canoe*?"

"No, no," he said. "Nothing for you to even bother thinking about."

He stroked her neck and shoulders and she closed her eyes. His life had always been one way with Lisa and he had never imagined he'd have to relearn her. He had become fairly good at taking care of her, but she had never needed him before and nobody had prepared him for this reversal of roles. There had been no time for her to explain how she managed him. When they were younger they had never bothered to delve deeper into the meaning of their lives together than what could be found in the passages of his book. He watched her now. Had she ever even read it? Really read it? She must have, he had to believe that, but now it was too late to ask.

No one seemed to understand how much he was struggling with the loss of her. They thought he was full of wisdom. After all, he had created *Canoe*, remembered and recounted and celebrated for coming up on forty years in print. Really, it was just a bunch of simple life lessons, none more complex than what was found in greeting cards or country songs. He was the main character. The oracle! The book had meant a hell of a lot to the multitudes. *Marriage Is a Canoe* helps people! Peter Herman, you can't deny it! When he'd tried to deny it, people wouldn't let him, even if they made fun of the book in the next breath. He had come to understand that when people decide a thing you made is part of them, you shouldn't dare try to change it. They'll think you're trying to take it away from them. It was yours once, sure. But now it's theirs. After some years of wrestling, he had given up. His little book belonged far more to its readers than to him.

"Let's go get you some lunch," he said. "We've got the doctor later."

She shook her head no, and her turned-down mouth was a reminder of how she'd been for so many years. She made her way and wasn't pushed around by anyone. Certainly not him.

"Fine, no lunch. Then at least kiss me."

Again, she shook her head.

He pouted his lips and tugged at his big ears and kissed her. This new version of her laughed and forgave him.

And why shouldn't she? He was still tall and handsome, with a wild thatch of gray hair. He had begun to hope that this new levity in her personality had in part come about because she had begun to see him as he had been forty years ago. What was coming true now was a product of the hard work from back then, when he had tried to fool the world into thinking he was kindhearted gentry in his green tweed blazer and pale blue button-down shirt, with a dream backstory of one great book and an endearing inability to outfox anyone, ever. He was distinguished, like Gregory Peck but with softer edges, a small-town Gregory Peck. By the time Reagan was president, Peter fit in as well as anyone in the Hudson Valley. If the fact that he'd written *Canoe* demanded that people see him as a study in contrasts, then they invariably concluded they were not especially sharp contrasts.

"Not going," Lisa said. "I am not going to the doctor today."

"Okay, we won't go. You're stubborn. Do you remember how stubborn you are?" he asked. They'd had forty happy years. Fifty, if smudged, and why not smudge a bit? Smudging the truth had been the smartest thing he had ever learned how to do.

"No, you," she said now. "You're stubborn. Stop petting me down. You . . . Who called you?"

"Someone from Ladder & Rake."

He was testing her. Mentioning Ladder & Rake used to make her glare and flare her nostrils. She would be angry that the royalties weren't right, worried that they might want to take him away for some event or another, reminded again of the world just beyond their little town encroaching. But now she had no reaction. How lost you are, he thought, as he appraised the uneven work he'd done on her braid.

"Come downstairs with me," he said. "There's Triscuits. And cheddar from Pantomime's. We'll try eating that. Then we'll see about the doctor."

She said, "People call you . . . Hubbell Gardner."

He shook his head no and watched her try to find other words. She made noises, looking for a tune to sing. But she was lost. Her voice turned into meaningless low notes that wandered into the corners of their bright bedroom at the top of the house, big as any country person could ever want, bay windows overlooking Lake Okabye, gray-

and-green-striped carpet over oak floors and white plaster walls solid as stone.

He held her hand and stared at her lips, the sheer pink of them. They didn't age. No one besides her had ever called him Hubbell Gardner. A few weeks earlier they had watched a DVD of *The Way We Were* on the downstairs television because she loved Barbra Streisand. He hated the movie when he was young, and had even brought it up in interviews as a kind of antithesis to *Canoe*. Though he knew the reference was a clumsy one that had never quite worked. But his post-publication antics never hurt the book.

"Do you say that because you remember watching *The Way We Were* with me?" he asked. "Are you making a joke?"

"My funny valentine . . ." She tried to sing but lost her words. She smiled down at her hands. He took her in his arms and gently raised her to her feet. She would remember this hug, this same old awkward hug. She fell on him and he loved her for her trust. At the very least, she trusted him, still, as much as she ever had. And they had loved each other. So he had lost the stable love he'd had with Lisa and had it replaced with this lengthy goodbye.

Peter did not enjoy listening to doctors. He wasn't nearly as good as Lisa had once been at absorbing and analyzing the information they shared. But he did understand that, regardless of how he parsed out what he understood of Pick's disease as it related to his wife's brain, new options did not arise. Pick's disease meant that their time left together was limited and everything that was wrong with Lisa was absolutely not going to be right again.

Stella Petrovic, July 2011

"You say this year is the fiftieth anniversary of what?" Helena Magursky's voice was both scratchy and strident. "I'm not sure I heard you."

Stella Petrovic frowned. She watched Helena Magursky, president and CEO of Ladder & Rake Books, lean forward, a half inch per second. They were twenty minutes into their weekly Wednesday morning nine o'clock, or whenever-Helena-wants-to-start-and-she's-always-late-but-you-damn-well-better-not-be meeting, recently retitled "Free Thinking/New Billing."

The living legend that was Helena Magursky was why Stella had left Orange Blackwell and come to the far bigger Ladder & Rake, so called because of its origin as a press for home repair and gardening manuals born in the back of Olitski Brothers Hardware Store in Woburn, Massachusetts, in 1907. And a middling regional press is what LRB would have stayed if Helena hadn't been hired right out of City College as the secretary for the single New York City–based salesperson in 1968. She had then gone on to hold nearly every position in the company, including several she'd made up. Helena had snatched Ladder & Rake from bankruptcy and merger more than once. The reason for this, people said, was because she knew content. She knew content and audience and she wasn't afraid to appropriately charge the audience for content that they liked. Helena was long-divorced and had one daughter, Elizabeth, a pediatrician who lived in Chicago with her husband and daughter. For decades, Helena had been Ladder & Rake's mother. And that was how she was treated, like a mother, a stern mother who everyone wanted to please.

Now, Helena commanded the attention in Ladder & Rake's very best conference room—the Dreiser Room—a long, thin space on the twenty-third floor of 38 East Fifty-Seventh Street, with windows facing uptown and Central Park.

"The book is *Marriage Is a Canoe*," Helena's current assistant, Lucy Brodsky, said.

"Yes, that's what I thought I heard." Helena pushed her lower lip out in a frown. She had allowed her black hair to go gray. Today it was in a high ponytail. She propped her lower lip up with her fingers and looked at Lucy.

"You want us to skip this item?" Lucy asked. Helena quieted her with a thrust of her chin.

"Let the young editor gather her thoughts and finish whatever point she's trying to make," Helena said to Lucy. Lucy had a high ponytail, too, and she wore a slinky J.Crew charcoal suit and a pale gray blouse. Stella thought Lucy should quit publishing and become a junior account executive for an old-school ad agency, J. Walter Thompson or Leo Burnett. She'd fit in better. But Stella knew that Lucy had taken the job as Helena's assistant because she loved books and wanted to stay true to her undergraduate, English-major self. So Lucy put up with an unending parade of days filled with Helena's ever-changing moods, all so maybe, someday, she'd get to switch jobs and become an editorial assistant. Stella smirked. She didn't believe Lucy was going to make it. Stella had done a year in marketing before going into editorial, and though that year had been a nasty grind, she'd learned a lot. And now Stella was an editor. A very young editor, too. That had been her dream and now here she was, living it. Stella's throat and cheeks turned purple whenever she talked about how much she'd loved Alice Munro in high school and then Mary Gaitskill when she'd been in Wisconsin for college. And now she'd just about die if she could discover the next Junot Díaz or Miranda July or Tom Vanderbilt, since she'd learned to be interested in nonfiction, too. You have to nurture your passion, Stella thought. You have to look the corporation right in its eye and be unafraid to make enormous mistakes. Because someday you will be so, so right.

Stella cleared her throat and repeated herself, "Fiftieth anniversary of the events upon which *Marriage Is a Canoe* is based—"

A door opened and Alex Wales, head of National Accounts, came in and whispered to Lucy, who whispered to Helena. Helena held up a hand for silence, and got it.

"Hold there," Helena said.

Stella went still. A few weeks earlier, Stella's direct boss, Melissa Kerrigan, whom she barely ever saw, gave her a copy of LRB's nonfiction backlist catalog and asked her to see if she could figure out how to get any of those old, barely-in-print books to start selling in a real way again.

"I mean, we can't expect you to draw blood from stones, but you can at least find out if any of those stones have a pulse." Melissa had laughed and then disappeared, keeping to the pattern she'd created since hiring Stella.

It was a horrible assignment, but Stella knew she'd never be able to buy any big new books of her own if she didn't first do some shit work for Melissa. And that was how she'd discovered *Canoe*. It was the fifteenth or eighteenth nonfiction book she'd taken home and she was as cynical about it as she was about all the others, many of which she'd left on the seat next to her on the 7 train. But then she'd found herself actually reading it. That was weird. She listened to her new boyfriend, Ivan, and held hands with him, just like the book said to. After the listening and hand-holding worked and they found themselves out past midnight, hungrily making out in the scary parking lot of a low-income high-rise near their apartment, she realized she thought about *Canoe*'s hokey lessons all the time. She figured if she could buy into *Canoe*, she could convince others to do the same. And then, one morning while taking an overlong shower with Ivan still sleeping, she came up with an idea for a contest.

Stella folded her hands in front of her on the table and waited. She had just turned twenty-eight, and she had too-long, honey-colored hair that she wore loose on most days. She had a proclivity for checked fabrics: houndstooth and tweed and nubby wool. Today she wore a dress with a brown-and-white wave pattern on it, very Ray Eames, with a bright red cardigan.

Helena liked a long silence and an overly warm conference room, which was why the young assistants whispered that the Dreiser Room ought to be called the Drowsy Room.

"Mmm." Helena looked around the room and smiled. "Let's hear more from Stella. But first let me finish with Alex, since he flies out to Amazon later this morning. So, all of you relax and let's let Stella get her bearings and I'll be right back with you."

Everyone in the room smiled and took the opportunity to begin to whisper. Because Stella was in mid-pitch, no one talked to her. So Stella looked around and began to count things. Ionic columns framed three evenly spaced entry points.

Fifty-nine people sat in the room, twenty-seven at the table and the rest on hard chairs against the side walls. Twelve windows in three bays. Eighteen bookshelves, and between the bookshelves, in halogen-lit nooks, there were fourteen framed #1 *New York Times* bestsellers, all published since January. Stella stopped counting and began to poke at the little microphone that was set flush into the conference table in front of her. If she poked it, it popped up, like a tiny periscope. She poked it.

"Don't play with that."

Stella looked up and saw Melissa Kerrigan sitting a couple of seats to her right.

"Sorry. Hi, Melissa. I didn't see you there."

"But if you had," Melissa whispered, "you would have mentioned that you were pitching something big this morning, right?"

"Yes." Stella smiled. "In fact, I did mention it, but then the meeting was canceled a few times so maybe you forgot."

Melissa glared and didn't speak. Stella began to poke the microphone in front of her again and it popped up an inch. Poke, poke. Stella looked away from her boss. This was the first Wednesday-morning meeting in over a month. They were always canceled when Helena was out, and she'd been away often lately, first at a Future of the Book conference in Cologne, then for a vacation with her daughter at a spa in Montana, and finally for the sales conference of a trade magazine group that was in a completely separate division of LRB's current parent company, Timmler Products Incorporated. The trade magazine group needed Helena's input and comments because they hadn't seen positive revenue in over two years and were in danger of being shut down. Publishing was simpler than that, Stella thought. You needed hits. Everybody knew about the easy road to oblivion. It was no secret. No hits? Get the fuck out. You took the job. You knew the deal. You invested plenty of hard work and lots of company money in your books and prayed for the best. But then . . . you got no hits? Sooner rather than later, you were done and it was time to go.

Stella hadn't minded waiting for this meeting. The waiting made everything more intense and the intensity turned Stella on. She loved books and she was ambitious and she knew it. Her ambition was why she'd come to Ladder & Rake. It was why she was so fascinated with Helena. Stella thought about BookScan percentage increases week to week, and surprise pop-ups on the *Times* and *USA Today* lists when she was having pre-workday sex with Ivan. When a grapefruit- and sprouted foods–based diet book she'd been shepherding was mentioned on *The View* and they did a rush printing and the cartons began to fast-ship from the warehouse to Ingram and Levy distribution centers, the whole process rebuilt itself in her dreams. She had read that UPS workers had box nightmares. She had box *fantasies;* squat rectangular boxes filled with twelve and twenty-four counts of books, taped shut and then circled once with yellow plastic tape that said STRICT ON SALE/DO NOT OPEN UNTIL. Oh yes, boxes filled with units that would perk right up like fresh daisies on the new release table and then move through the register. So there she sat, silent, focused, and excited. Turning purple and covering her neck and waiting for Helena's attention. Since arriving at LRB, Stella had begun to idolize Helena even more than she'd thought she would. Now she watched as Helena dismissed her salesperson.

"Okay. *Canoe.* I know *Canoe*," Helena said. "I practically invented it—you say it's the fiftieth anniversary of the events? I mean, even that's so odd—the events? This discussion would make me feel old if I indulged in that feeling, which I do not." Helena massaged her breastbone by kneading the thick gold chain she wore every day.

Stella said, "Upon which the lessons are based, yes."

"Well, so?"

Stella said, "I did some research and I think it's something we could exploit—"

"How?" Helena asked.

The room grew quieter. A few of the senior

people seated nearest to Helena began to smirk and shift in their chairs.

Helena went on, "We haven't heard from Peter Herman since dear old Jane Segal drove up to interview him. They sat down on a Saturday for tea and after two utterly innocuous questions he threw her out of the house." Under her breath, but so nearly everyone could still hear, Helena muttered, "Must we go on with this?" The comment and its import rippled down the table via nudges and eye rolls.

But Stella was patient. She had dug deep on *Canoe* and she was sure Helena would listen to her pitch. This was just standard hazing. Since arriving at LRB, Stella had occasionally heard Helena allude to a tougher early life than her official biography revealed. So Stella figured that Helena was entirely self-made and a bit of a street fighter. That was okay with Stella. She was a lot of things, but she was not afraid. She knew that if she didn't make noise and create a hit that got her noticed now, she'd blow her chance to become a go-to editor at LRB. And then she'd lose two or more years of her life as she sat unnoticed before moving on to take another shot at some other house. She was not going to let that happen.

"We hold a contest," Stella went on. "I've done some research. *Canoe* is a very special book."

"Do you remember what Erica Jong called it when we asked her to write one of those new introductions a decade or so ago?" a lieutenant to Helena's right whispered. " 'The Art of Loving for Dummies.' "

"Haw," Helena said. "Good one."

"And Maureen Dowd?" said Sara Byrd, the associate publisher for the women's fiction imprint, Ladder & Rake Romantic. "She called it 'The Art of Loving Dummies'! Because it'll help you learn to love and put up with anyone! Remember she sent Hillary a copy!"

"Which isn't exactly logical since that's not what the book is about." Helena was suddenly serious. "Though that logic stretch is certainly Maureen Dowd's gift. You see, Stella? We know it's a special book since these very smart and important women have made light of it. So we all knew that before you said it. But please, go ahead. Take up more of our time. Elaborate. Indulge. Expand."

Stella breathed deeply. Her palms were dry. The heat at her temples would not transform into perspiration. She had been in rooms like this before. She had won the respect—if not the love—of those rooms.

She said, "As we at this table have just noted, *Canoe* continues to be one of the most widely read self-help books in the country. But all we've got is steady sales, of about eleven thousand copies a year—in the very best years. And the trend is down, not up. But it's because people share those copies! They don't cherish our edition. They pass theirs to a friend and that person passes it on and so on. But with a great marketing plan and a new special edition we could revive *Canoe*. We could make it a phenomenon. So we hold a contest. Let me connect with publicity and do a press release . . ."

And here, Stella took her gamble. She paused. She believed that if she was headed in a bad direction, Helena would cut her off. One beat, two beats. No interruption.

Stella brought her finger to her temple and deferentially wiped away a nonexistent bead of sweat. "On this, the fiftieth anniversary of the events that are the basis for *Marriage Is a Canoe*, the preeminent book of marriage advice of the twentieth and now the twenty-first century, *Canoe*'s author, Peter Herman, invites one couple to his home for a day of home-cooked meals and homespun advice. The day spent with Peter Herman will be cherished by the winning couple for the rest of their happily married lives. This is a 'save your marriage' contest. The contest and the new edition will force the book back to the front of stores and to the top of the digital charts. Everybody has marriage troubles so everybody can relate. Then we put Mr. Herman and the winning couple on morning shows, like *Good Morning America*—"

"Unless the couple won't talk to the press,"

Helena cut in. "And then what happens if the poor devils break up! Forget about Peter—I haven't seen him in New York for more than a few hours since the eighties. We did do a few very successful book tours with him—this was way back when I invented the book tour, which I did for him, for writers like him anyway. Actually, I should call Peter. Lucy?"

Lucy nodded. Stella could see that she had already made a note on her iPad.

"Though the elusive quality of our contest wouldn't hurt a classic," Stella said. She was beginning to feel upbeat. "If there's secrecy, we maintain the mystique. Buy the book to learn what they learned."

Then Stella shut up. She knew she'd flubbed it by talking too much. Her excitement was the same as when she had rambled back in high school and lost debates. But she was determined to learn from her mistakes. Shushhh! Shut up! She drove her fingers into her thighs and frowned. Take big risks, she thought. Risk everything! That's the only way to win.

Everyone in the room watched Helena and held their breath.

"Mmm." Helena nodded. "You'd have to guar-antee pictures of the meeting, at the minimum. The couple on either side of Peter Herman, all of them smiling. Maybe video. You'd need video."

"I can promise all of that," Stella said, quickly.

Helena frowned. Then she arched forward, like a drug addict on a doze, until her overlarge forehead tapped the tabletop and her gold chain clanked against the table's rim. The room had seen this before. This was a great woman doing some serious thinking. The room waited and stared at the part in her steel-gray hair. Eventually, Helena came back up and blinked at them all.

"Fine!" Helena said. "Done. I mean, I largely hate the idea. But do it. Just make absolutely sure not to destabilize the core sales pattern. Tell me details, two weeks. And make it happen for the fall. Rush it! I like an inspirational story. So make it inspirational and we'll all enjoy that. Gives me a nice story to tell the TPI board. Okay, next item?"

"Hang on . . . ," Lucy said.

"For goodness' sake, Lucy! Let's not spend what's left of our miserable lives in this horrible room, am I right? I was feeling good just a moment ago. Now what is the next item?"

"I don't know—it's not here." Lucy glared at her iPad and shook it.

"Then we're in luck," Helena said. "Because our meeting is over."

Stella covered her smile. She didn't want to appear to be laughing at Lucy and have Helena see that. She knew Helena was insanely protective of her assistants, no matter how inept they were, since she had hired them and took responsibility for their growth. So Stella bit her lip, gathered her things, and got the hell out of the room as quickly as she could. Melissa Kerrigan was standing just outside the doorway, talking to Jenny Oh, the woman who handled the Target account. Stella bobbed and nodded, and mouthed a hello to Jenny, who lived somewhere near her and who she knew for a fact regularly ducked her on the subway. Stella made it down the hall. She was at the elevator bank when she heard the voice behind her.

"Oh, Stella?"

She turned around. Should she dare to call her Helena? Their names were kind of similar. Should she mention that? All around them were dimly lit blowups of bestsellers from the past fifty years. There was *Valley of the Dolls* and *Love Story* and then there was Michael Caine's autobiography and a special section dedicated to the memoirs of ex-presidents. Each cover was uglier than the last. But these covers were bestsellers. And they were bestsellers because Helena knew the audience and she knew content. And so many others, incredibly, didn't.

Helena was now a foot away, smelling of dry cleaning and too much foundation.

"Have you ever spoken to Peter Herman?" Helena asked.

"Well, no. His wife died last fall, so I stayed away. Of course we sent flowers and a note and a donation—as a house. But I thought it best to wait until I'd proposed my idea to you before contacting him. I understand he's a very private man—"

"I know what kind of man he is," Helena said. "Since I near invented him."

"Of course," Stella said.

"And I know his wife died. Very sad. But much better if he's a widower, believe me. Everybody loves a man who loved his wife vigilantly until she died. My soul is already making this story feel good. Stop. I mean the opposite."

Stella reared back and fought off a smile. "Right. I mean, yes, me, too. I'll put everything I've got into it."

"Go see him if you have to. Or—he may not want that. But I think your idea has a shot and I want to see it succeed. Your colleagues in the digital group might be able to run with it. Don't ask me how, but I imagine they'd say that. They always do. Have a meeting with them and see if they don't say exactly that. When you do get in touch with Peter, you tell him Helena says hello."

"Yes, yes I will."

"Good," Helena said. She didn't move.

They were, as Helena always was, shadowed by Lucy, who held her iPad in front of her the way a schoolgirl holds her notebook to protect her breasts from boys. A half dozen others also stood nearby, listening.

Stella was not good at letting silence go unfilled. She said, "Did you . . . edit him?"

"You can say that again. Practically made up half the book myself, goddamn it. That, *Small Is Beautiful*, and cheerleading for *Jonathan Livingston Seagull* made my career. And believe me: working with Peter was a lot more fun than dealing with those others. But last time I checked—and given the nonstop nightmare we're living through, I have no choice but to check every day—who gives a shit? We need billing today, not a million years ago, got me?"

"Got you," Stella said.

Helena kept staring at her.

Stella stood still and wished she more closely resembled Helena. If only she were more . . . black-and-white like Helena and Lucy. But no. She was invariably unkempt and slightly hippieish, since she was one of five children brought up by husband-and-wife garden designers who had moved around a lot when she was young, and who now lived on a flower farm outside Charlottesville. Stella was the only one of her siblings who worked in an office. She could never be quite corporate enough, no matter how she tried. She'd even attempted the inversion of being so noncorporate as to actually be extremely corporate, so that she spent some weeks making a point of arriving at work looking like she was going to spend the afternoon drinking on a bench under an umbrella at a beer garden in Williamsburg. That hadn't worked either.

"Good," Helena said. "You tell that lonely old man I say hello, and when it's all locked up, get him here to New York and we'll have a breakfast and talk about the old days when life was simple and books were made out of paper." Helena turned to Lucy. "Where are we going?"

"To see Bob Payne," Lucy said. "New Google litigation update."

"Shit, shoot, goddamn. A bad day gets worse . . ." Helena didn't move. "Stella?" Helena's voice rose higher.

"Yes?" Stella found herself staring down into Helena's dark brown eyes. They were filmy. But Stella saw the beauty there. The beauty of being able to get people to do whatever she wanted.

"When you're up to something as wacky as this, or really when you're doing anything, always ask yourself: Where is the romance? Got me?"

"Got you." Stella smiled and tried not to look overly focused in a way that would reveal she was trying to remember every single word Helena said.

"Come on," Helena said with a laugh. "Say it like you damn well have got to find out where the romance is."

Stella took half a breath. She remembered the way she felt with Joe, who she had been with before Ivan, who had always kept the romance and the sex to a minimum—that asshole.

"Where is the romance?" she asked through bared teeth.

"Yeah," Helena said, and smiled. "Go find it."

Helena walked away. Stella stood at the elevator bank feeling taller, lighter, and more kempt. She knew she ought to be frightened of the attention she'd received, that there were enemies everywhere and she didn't even know who some of them were. But at the same time, wow! Helena was obviously brilliant because she'd seen the potential in Stella's idea—and she'd made a great point. Stella felt vindicated. She had been right to come to LRB and to get close to Helena. And she had a good idea but didn't yet know where the romance was . . . in it. But now Helena was helping her and Stella was definitely feeling inspired. She was going to find it!

From *Marriage Is a Canoe*,
Chapter 1, First Day

On the morning of my first day, before I went fishing with Pop, I helped Bess with the chores. Pop had gone into town to buy groceries and a few things he said he thought we might need for fishing.

Bess and I started in the little bedroom above the kitchen, where she threw a summer quilt in the air. It floated down onto the single bed that my mother had slept in when she was a little girl and that I would use during my stay.

"Did you see that?" Bess asked.

"It's a nice quilt," I said.

"It's not just nice," Bess said. "This is a wonderful patchwork quilt. It is made up of squares of fine and different materials double-stitched together so tightly that not even an angry outdoor cat can claw it apart. It's stronger than it looks. Do you understand?"

"Sure," I said, uncertainly. I didn't yet know whether I wanted to be there or not. I missed my friends. But my grandparents' world was so fresh and new and I didn't yet dare to even act grumpy around them.

"Now we'll open all the windows so that sweet Lake Okabye air can rush through the house."

"Okay." Obediently, I went into the hall and opened the window at the top of the second staircase.

"Light as feathers and strong as iron," she called out to me.

"What is?" I asked. She followed me into the hall and then we went into one of the spare bedrooms and started on the bedding in there.

"Our quilts are," she said. "Will you get us some pillowcases?"

I went and found them in the linen closet. When I got back she said, "Sit with me a moment."

So I sat down with her on the side of the bed in that big spare bedroom that nobody ever used.

"Peter, listen. We know you've witnessed some ugliness between your mother and father." She hugged me before going on. She had blond hair that I'd watched her put in curlers the night before. I thought she smelled like flowers. "If you want to talk about it with us, you can. Now let's make this bed."

I think we both knew I wouldn't be able to really talk to her. I was too embarrassed. I was twelve. She threw another patchwork quilt in the air. I stared, transfixed by the orphaned bits of fabric, now stitched together, spinning in the light.

"Pick up an end and pull," she said.

And I did just what I was told and I couldn't help noticing that it was light as feathers and strong as iron!

"I like this quilt," I said.

"Yes, this is a good one—I made it out of Pop's old shirts and some Italian wool he brought back from the war." She paused. "I think I hear him now."

I pricked up my ears and I could hear him, too.

"Hello!" Pop yelled. Bess smiled. We could hear him lumbering around in the kitchen.

"Ready, Peter?"

"Are we done, Bess?" I asked.

"I'm not but you are. You two see if you can catch some trout."

"Okay," I said, though I'd never touched a live fish before. I followed Pop to the kitchen. He was much, much taller than me. He was a burly, clean-shaven man with a bald head, in a white T-shirt and blue-jean overalls, always with a Lucky Strike cigarette either between his lips or tucked behind his ear.

"Let's gather what we'll need," he said.

I found myself nodding, uncertain about what to do next. But just like his wife, Pop smiled patiently at me.

He said, "We can only bring with us what makes sense to bring. And not more than that. Why do you think we can't bring more?" Pop stared down at me and waited. I understood that he was trying to teach me a lesson, though it looked like it had been a while since he'd done that.

"Because the boat will sink?"

"Yes. And who needs the weight? Not two

people in a canoe. When Bess and I go out, which we've been doing since long before your mom was born, we just bring what we need. You can't bring too much in the canoe because it'll just get in the way. Wait'll you see our canoe! It's strong, and if you care for it through the seasons like we've been doing, it'll support you and it won't break down. But it's just built for two adults and maybe a few children, at the most. Try to make it hold more than that and it's just no good at all. But we do need our icebox for sandwiches and the bait bucket and a towel for you in case you want to swim."

"Sure thing," I said.

Pop wrapped the sandwiches and I put them in the icebox. It was so quiet in that house that we could hear Bess humming Hank Williams's "Crazy Heart" on the floor above us.

We gathered the rest of what we needed and went out to the great lawn behind the back porch. And, because I'd come in after dark the evening before, that was the first time I saw the canoe. It was old and the outside was painted a milky green and the inside had mahogany ribs that glowed in the sunlight.

"This is sure something!" I cried out. And I didn't stop myself the way I would have in the city, where I was learning to play it cool and not show too much enthusiasm for anything.

"As I said, Bess and I have done a nice job of taking care of it," Pop said. "You know how to paddle?"

I felt some heat on my cheeks, and I frowned and shook my head, looked down at the shiny grass beneath my sneakers.

"Never paddled a canoe?"

"No, sir."

"Don't call me sir! I'm your Pop. All right, what about fishing?"

I could only shake my head.

Pop laughed a big belly laugh and he smacked the back of my neck and I stumbled forward. I glared up at him when he did that, because I felt ashamed for not holding my ground.

"That's fine! First we'll learn how to handle this canoe. You'll see what it can hold and what it can handle and what it can't. Then we'll learn to paddle it, together, just like me and Bess did when we first met, so that someday you'll know how to take a moonlit canoe ride with your sweetie. And then we'll show you how to fish!"

"Okay," I said, and then lower, "thanks."

"Don't thank me. You're going to work this summer. You'll do your share. And we'll have you paddling and catching fish soon enough!"

Good love is a quilt—
light as feathers and strong as iron.

A good marriage is a canoe—
it needs care and isn't meant to hold too much—
no more than two adults and a few kids.

Peter Herman, August 2011

Peter Herman leaned into the white picket fence that surrounded the front garden of the Lake Okabye Inn. He wore moccasins and had one foot up on a horizontal board, his forearms snug in the fence's interstices. He set his chin on his knuckles and looked out at the traffic. Still as a bird on a wire, there in a pose that he hadn't much changed since he'd gotten involved with the inn nearly forty years earlier.

He raised his big head and smiled at a former cook, driving by the inn with her children in her pickup. When children looked at him now, he imagined they saw an old man with eyes that were placed far apart, like a fish. His ears had grown large and they were covered in white fuzz. When he was unhappy with himself, as he was now, he thought the world saw him as a sort of aged cartoon version of the handsome man he once was. He sighed and breathed in deeply. Thirty years ago, in the same spot, he would have been able to smell chickens baking in the kitchen off the restaurant. But they'd quadrupled the size of that kitchen, added a bakery, and moved it to the back of the property in the expansion of '86. Now all he smelled was the newly blacktopped road and the end of the morning dew. He tilted his head back and listened to a screen door squeak open. That would be Henry. His old friend's footfalls ended with a couple of squishes in the grass.

"Actually, they don't like a widower hanging around the place so much anymore! Those days are gone, windbag!"

"Morning, Henry." Peter didn't turn his head, only reached out and clapped Henry Talkington on the back. "What'd Maddie say?"

"You mean your girlfriend? 'Oh, hell,' " Henry said. He leaned the other way on the fence, so he could look into the breakfast-room windows. Henry was short and round. He was puffy in the places where age had pruned and etched at Peter.

"Now that doesn't sound right. I've never heard her curse. Not once."

"With me, she curses. You're asking about before she left for California? She's back this week, I believe. She stopped by for lunch with me before she left. But you'd know that."

Peter rubbed his chin with his thumb. "I didn't feel like making the trip," he said.

Henry nodded and said, "I know it."

Peter waited for Henry to say more. Lisa had been gone for nearly ten months and he was now involved with Maddie Narayan. She wanted him to leave Millerton and begin a new life with her in San Francisco so she could be near her daughter, Anjulee. He was not so sure he wanted that. He'd recently discovered that he wasn't even quite ready for a weeklong visit.

"Maddie's trying to get a handle on what you two have, is all," Henry said. "She can't gauge it and you're not helping. But she does know she's loving the Bay Area."

Peter only turned to Henry and smiled. When they'd first met, Peter was the talkative one and Henry was the hired man who listened and took care of details. But since Lisa died, Henry had become the talker. People like Henry, who had known Peter for most of their lives, filled in the new silences Peter created, and didn't appear to notice the difference.

"Also she doesn't like to feel that she's being made to chase you," Henry said. "She loves you. She respects what you had with Lisa. Now she feels like you're a prize that she can't quite seem to win. I know better. But not her. And I can't explain to her why you don't give in, since I think you ought to."

"Maddie's too good for me. I should visit Belinda at Vassar. She must know some old professor ladies who are single."

"Your daughter's coworkers? Now they'd be too good for you, too!"

"Thanks, Henry. What'd Manuel put on the menu for the lunch special?"

Henry sighed and stared at his feet. The bright sun shined through the sugar maple trees and down on the top of his bald head. The wind wasn't much and the two men were still. Peter realized that yet again his old friend Henry had cornered him to try to make him see his point, which was that it was time for Peter to let the inn go, sell his house so he could pay his bills, and move on to a new life with Maddie.

"Catfish sandwiches," Henry said. "Lightly fried. With a celery root rémoulade. And French fries, not that I'd allow either of us to have any."

"Any good?"

"Pretty good. I've seen him do it before. It's not catfish, exactly, but close."

"Whitebait?" Peter squinched his lips, as if he tasted something rotten.

"Or something. It's fresh fish, I believe. From the fellow who comes over from Orient on the ferry."

"Maddie say when she'll go back to California? I don't like to ask her too many questions. So that's why I'm asking you."

"She'll be going back and forth fairly often. She's also thinking about selling her place. Apparently she's waiting on you more than she could ever have imagined. So she says."

Peter shook his head and said, "Why anyone would ever bother waiting on me—now that is the real mystery."

"I agree. She's fifty-two," Henry said. "And she's a beautiful woman. She might want to get remarried. You should figure out if you're capable of that before stealing any more of her time."

"Thanks, Henry. Thanks for the light talk."

"Anytime, anytime. Now get off the damn fence!"

Lisa had just turned sixty-two when the disease showed itself, though later, Peter understood it had been growing for some time. A growth of tau proteins that had forced her brain cells to shrink, pressed them down and impacted her ability to be herself, the self that was nice to him and took care of both of them. He had assumed the newly constant surliness in her character represented some kind of reconfiguring that came with age. He also felt partly to blame. She made unprecedented mistakes and got upset about the bills, and she worried over relinquishing these tasks to Peter since he had always been the one who was clumsy with money. He felt bad and believed he had overburdened her.

What was Peter left with after Lisa died? A jolly shell of a self he'd been avoiding but now had no choice but to get to know. Forty years earlier, he had returned to Millerton within a year of publication of *Canoe* because working in Manhattan for McCann Erickson as a copywriter was sapping his ability to write a second book. He had a few thousand dollars and the arrogance that accompanied a very young man's success. And he went and found the girl he'd kissed when he was twelve—only then she'd been called Honey, and she'd been the innkeeper's daughter.

"Peter Herman! We've been reading about you in the newspaper," she'd said.

"Had a laugh at my expense?"

"Oh, now," said Lisa with a frown. "I wouldn't put it quite that way. I'm sure your book is very sweet. I plan to read it."

It was the summer of 1972. He had paced Main Street until he found her coming out of the post office. She wore Levi's overalls and her hair was up in a messy bun. It didn't seem to him that she was in a rush to find a man, and that was refreshing after all the fast and free love he'd seen in Manhattan.

"The fact of the matter is that I've come for your hand," he'd said, and meant it.

She was twenty-four and he was twenty-three. They were married in the fall at the inn, a storybook wedding that worked as the opening chapter to a sweet fable of a life.

The *Times* covered it: "*Marriage Is a Canoe* Author Marries Woman from His Book." Peter Herman and his childhood sweetheart step into their own canoe. Suddenly they were managers of the inn, with a child of their own, Belinda. The second book? Well, no.

Lisa, who had always planned to help out with her parents' inn, discovered that she had an accountant's love of business. Within a few years, she was able to ensure that the inn saw positive cash flow at the end of each month. The waitresses who joked with Peter during their shifts wouldn't look at Lisa because they knew that if they stole even a few dollars, she would catch them. Peter found that both his wife and their employees depended on him to be the center of good times. Everyone needed his levity to cover up for the never-ending war between the petty thievery that eats away at a business like an inn and his wife's vigilant desire to keep the place both honest and profitable.

"We're a team," she said in 1978, when Belinda was three. By then Lisa's parents had moved down to Key West, to retire and keep an eye on a couple of B&Bs where they'd invested their savings. Lisa left Peter each day to run the inn in Millerton from a suite of offices behind the kitchen.

Nineteen seventy-nine was the last year he stayed home to write in the office that had once been his grandfather's study. He mostly sat at the desk and doodled. Or he'd eat a bagel with plenty of cream cheese and tomato and that would lull him into a nap. He knew he did not have a block. He understood there was nothing else he needed to say. In the afternoons, he drove down to see Lisa and help out. Some days they had lunch with Henry, who was an assistant manager at that time.

"Did you write well today?" she would ask.

When he could no longer bear to answer that question, he came up with the idea of building a new inn in nearby Hudson. He wasn't a good businessman and they both knew it. But she loved him and she let him try to make a go of the Hudson Inn for many, many years.

At home in the evenings, he'd frown and try to understand why he was so unable to make the Hudson Inn turn a profit, when the Lake Okabye Inn had no problems at all.

"Don't brood," she liked to say. "You know I don't like it."

And then she'd put away her papers and get up and sing, there on the back porch, bits and pieces of Pete Seeger's "Where Have All the Flowers Gone?"

"Don't forget I'm a hippie at heart," she would call out. Though the truth was that at heart, she was patient, uncomplaining, and a fine innkeeper. She was playful when she could see that was what he needed to keep going. He would whistle and stomp his feet. Lisa had a strong alto voice. Singing had gotten them through more than a few ugly impasses. Weeks when town gossip about his drinking and his jokey intimacy with the maids made every room in both inns feel sour. Those weeks became just over a decade that covered the eighties. But Peter and Lisa stayed together. And Peter still didn't write. He knew not to even try.

Then came 1993, the year when there was very little singing and Lisa had to focus all her energy on shutting down the Hudson Inn and selling shares of the Lake Okabye Inn to Lockport Savings Bank, where she'd known the bank manager since grade school. Lisa had to work hard to keep them from losing both places. It was Henry who eventually took all his savings and bought the shares back from Lockport Savings. That move made Henry a partner. Lisa never blamed Peter.

Lisa loved singing and numbers. They grew older and she kept the business solvent and the vendors paid and feeling just a little bitter, which is how she thought it ought to be. After the long stumble that Peter had created with the Hudson Inn, Lisa had to work to tame the numbers day in and day out. And she did it. She saved them from bankruptcy. When she got sick Peter wondered if so many years of keeping their finances under control was the problem. When the numbers saw the weakness in her mind, they reared up and took their vengeance.

Peter had felt immobilized and was unable to stop the loss of their savings. He knew that sooner rather than later he would have to sell his stake in the inn to Henry. Lockport Savings had become First Niagara and he understood that there wasn't much point bothering with anybody there anymore. All his relationships with banks had grown pretty stiff. This was because, at the end of her life, before they had fully embraced the diagnosis and implications of Pick's disease, Lisa had played with their savings on Poker Junkie and PartyPoker and Full Tilt Poker and the rest of the Internet casino sites with a brain she could no longer control. He imagined that the tau proteins in her brain did it to set her free, because her soul resented having to save him, and their money, so many times over nearly forty years. If that were true, he couldn't blame her. When he'd discovered that he had nothing more to write after *Canoe*, he'd gone to work and built something that did nothing but bleed their money away. If life was only about money, Lisa had spent most of hers repairing the damage Peter had done. If life was about more than that, they had done well together. They had a smart and beautiful child. Lisa had laughed longer and harder with Peter than she would have without him. If Peter were being honest about the choices he'd made, he could admit that by coming up to Millerton and staying with Lisa he had snuck away from the grand stage *Canoe* might have afforded him. But Peter didn't think that way too often—not about money or choices or any of it. Not until he was forced to.

Now, his income paid for heat and gas and insurance and not much else. And because he'd leased a new Subaru before discovering that Lisa had lingering medical bills, he had come to owe more than he had. What he had was his home and a fifth of the inn. Millerton was a little town and people knew his situation. They knew his finances needed fixing and they wanted to help. They wanted to have him back, voluble and kind and with enough money and not much need. And if Peter couldn't be made to be that way, they wouldn't want him around. They would feel that moving away with Maddie Narayan was a darned good idea. Because if he was seen as dragging Millerton down, they would want him to leave.

A few weeks before Lisa entered the hospital for the last time, they had spent an evening on the back porch with mugs of hot tea.

They could hear Jim Foxton out on the lake, paddling around in his canoe. Jim often asked Peter to join him. But Peter had once overheard Jim bragging at the Sally Forth bar about canoeing with the world's most famous paddler and he hadn't said yes to Jim since. That had been more than twenty years ago.

"When I go, I want you surrounded by women," Lisa said. "That will make me happy. I'm cold. Let's go in and eat."

Peter didn't stir.

"I want that for you because I'm dying too early." She was crying, but not loudly.

In a few minutes, he would heat up pea soup, thinned with water. He would put bread in the oven, a nice garlic bread she had taught him to make when they were first married, that he still made, thick white bread with butter and sliced bits of garlic. She would only eat soup and bread.

"Hot, sexy women," she said. "That's what I want for you."

"Don't be ridiculous."

"I want you to be open to what comes. Compliant." He watched her mouth lose its shape around the big word. She said, "No, that's not it. Just agreeable. That's all I want from you. Just be agreeable with this change in your life. In our lives. I want happiness for you. I know I never let you figure out what kind of man to become."

He tugged at his ears and made an O with his mouth. After she died, he regretted that in that moment, and in many others, he had chosen to pretend not to understand her, or at the least, absolve her of guilt. His aimless life was certainly not entirely her fault.

"Don't just be with Maddie Narayan." Lisa had grinned and stuck out her tongue. "I know you have a thing with her."

Peter was surprised. He did not have a thing with Maddie. But Lisa wasn't wrong. He did have things. Over the years he had indulged in a long and indecent hug or a hard kiss with a waitress or a maid after closing time at the Sally Forth. Maybe a little more than that. He didn't like to think about it. Once he and Lisa had gotten past the first few years of marriage, and he'd found his footing, he had never again dared to launch into a full-fledged dalliance. Well, here and there he had. But never in the sort of stupid-making way that would push him to wonder if he ought to leave his wife's side.

He said, "What the hell are you talking about?"

"I'm on to you. I'll be watching." And then she lost her language and made a nonsense sound.

He was looking at her beautiful hair. She dyed it auburn and had done so for years, but then stopped once they'd found out, and now suddenly there was an inch and a half of dense gray at the roots. He liked the gray better than the auburn, but couldn't figure out how to tell her. He was afraid she thought of it as her dying hair. And he wanted so badly for her to live and stopped abruptly at the beginning of any conversation that seemed to be about her death. But then, that was all they seemed to talk about. He felt stupid and confused and again, baffled at who exactly he was supposed to be. Worse, what was he supposed to become?

He'd overheard her once, talking to Henry in the office, when he was stopping by the inn to pick up a cake the chefs had made for Belinda's big college send-off dinner. He'd been walking, preoccupied, and he'd jerked his head up when he heard his name.

"I tell Peter whatever he wants to know," Henry said.

"Not about our finances," Lisa said. "We can't let him get involved. Never again. I'm too old to fix everything another time."

Henry whistled. He said, "Okay, we'll do just as you like."

Peter came around the corner and watched Lisa draw away from Henry. If he hadn't overheard, he would have wondered if they were having some kind of affair.

"Hi, honey," Lisa said. "I was just telling Henry that we'll gather at the house at six for the picnic."

"I'm picking up the cake right now."

"Sounds good." Lisa made Henry nod alongside her.

"Can you believe it? Eighteen years and she's just about to disappear." She'd looked away from both of them. "Why don't you two drive over to the house together? There's just a little more I want to take care of here."

Peter had accepted the white lie. He understood his role. He was good with people, bad with money, and something of a town fixture—well-loved and respected and expected to be as he'd always been. And he'd always been a charmer. Taking care of their daughter. Not too tethered to any one job. Cared for by a good wife who wasn't afraid to bend the truth if that was what was necessary to keep them together, solvent and happy.

• • •

The worst was when Lisa had been in Lambert Hospital for three straight days. She was given drugs that allowed her to reclaim some of her distant memories and she'd immediately tried to tell him every secret she'd kept. A man at a financial seminar she'd attended in South Carolina one summer. Another in Sonoma County, where she had gone once in the late seventies for a week with her roommates from the University of Buffalo, where she'd been secretary of her sorority. An unexpected royalty windfall that she had lost and never recovered when she had optimistically invested in a friend's Christmas tree business, back when they were very young. In fact, between the money she had encouraged him to spend on the inn in Hudson and the poor investments she had made, they had wasted nearly all of his royalty money. The unexplained losses and the hidden infidelities were coming out now.

"How lucky I am to have spent my life with you," she whispered. "I should keep my secrets, shouldn't I? You don't want them."

He didn't. He said, "You know, you're right. How lucky you were to have married a man who truly understands what makes a marriage happy." They laughed about it together.

Her body became increasingly stiff. The doctor began to worry less about the progressive debilitation of the healthy cells in her brain and more about the common infections she was no longer able to fight. She got pneumonia and the doctor said there wasn't much hope. He said the pneumonia was stronger than she was, that it was massive and sprouting like a common cold in a punch bowl at a holiday party. She was given painkillers. She floated. While her beloved watched her from his chair.

Peter dried his tears with a handkerchief she had brought back from a walking trip in the Scottish highlands she had taken with her sister Gwen, who lived down in Florida and who had died just two years before.

"You had moments with other women, didn't you?" she asked.

He only shrugged. She was always and inter-mittently able to find her voice. At the very end, with shame, he found himself wishing she would stop being able to access these harsh, appraising parts of herself. The buzz of the hospital's lights was cut by the clipped voices of the nurses in the hall.

"You wouldn't remember Erich Fromm," an old nurse said to a young one, now within Peter's range of hearing, which was still as good as it was when he was a boy—and he'd been quite an eavesdropper then, too.

"No, but I know my Mitch Albom. *Tuesdays with Morrie* for couples! Imagine the money! Imagine having that to guide my marriage. I bet he could've saved it. That man in there could have saved my marriage. I feel sure of it."

"I'll bring you my copy."

"Too late."

"You could still use it—for next time. Here, I'm programming a reminder into my phone."

He listened to the nurses' sneakers as they wandered down the hall. Years earlier, someone had given Peter *Tuesdays* and he thought it was pretty bad—maybe even a bit derivative of his own work. He was fonder of Dr. Phil because they'd corresponded at one point and Dr. Phil had mentioned *Canoe* on his show. He liked Dr. Phil.

Peter never claimed to be brilliant. Of course he had made up parts of the stories, embellished where necessary, toyed with the through-lines of the days spent with his grandparents until the anecdotes were taut, self-effacing, and sometimes gorgeous in their accept-the-dusk-but-welcome-the-dawn sentiment. But *Canoe* was no cynical exercise. Over and over, the book conveyed simple truths. It was not his fault the world loved the idea of a book full of answers to unanswerable questions.

The cover of the book's newest edition was a photograph of a couple's hands intertwined. The sunlight behind them was red and gold and white, their glossy wedding bands glinting. What crap. He had never worn one.

From *Marriage Is a Canoe*,
Chapter 2, On Desire

The end of our first true day of fishing found us
without a single trout in our green bucket. I felt
guilty about it, as if that sad empty bucket was all
my fault.

Pop said, "First thing tomorrow, we go out
again."

His voice was steady as we came off the lake.
There was deep golden late-afternoon light all
around us, settling like a promise that that
evening, that sweet mid-July evening, would be a
pleasant one.

Pop showed me how to hop out of the canoe and
drag it up onshore, flip it over, and prop it up on
the wooden beams attached to the tiny dock.

I remember I was thinking of a cigarette I'd
smoked with a friend some weeks earlier, on Third
Avenue, in front of a candy store. My brain had
been so addled that I'd nearly walked into traffic,
thinking, No wonder adults smoke all the time. I
wanted a cigarette right then, after our day of
fishing.

"Did you hear me?" Pop asked.

I shook my head no.

"You dreaming of something?"

"I guess I kind of miss being at home."

"Are you boys coming in?" Bess called from the porch. I looked up. I saw she was smiling and I worried over whether she could read my mind.

"Yes, we are," Pop said. "Didn't catch a thing, though."

"That's all right. I baked a chicken."

"Now that is truly a fine woman!" Pop yelled out. "What is it I always say?"

"Don't tell the boy things like that." Bess shook her head.

"If I don't, who will?" Pop asked. He looked at me and pointed at her. He said, "I'm her servant as sure as I'm alive. Whatever she wants, whatever she desires—be it milk or fresh air or hand-holding—that is my desire, too."

"He's laying it on pretty thick," Bess said. "But that's my good man—not afraid to keep life sweet as syrup. You two come on up here and we'll have some dinner."

"Desire?" I asked, thinking, I know what desire is. It's me wanting to get a hold of a Winston and smoke it out on the road where they couldn't see.

Pop turned to me then as if he were thinking of something so great that it was not meant for me alone, as if his words were not only for me, but for you and me both.

"Desire, young man, is what your heart wants when it's not fettered by your brains."

And at that moment, all I knew was that the desire he was talking about had nothing to do with cigarettes.

Desire for your loved one gives you the strength to paddle on.

Emily Babson, August 2011

"Wait, I see someone I know," Emily said. "Sherry, let me call you back. Hi!"

Emily ended the call with her sister and dropped her phone in her bag. She was alone in the self-help section of a bookstore on Smith Street, a few blocks from her apartment. Lately she was quick to jump off the phone before Sherry tried to get into what was going on with Emily and Eli, because talking about it was going to make the problem real—fast. Emily did not want it to grow into a bigger deal. And if and when it did, then it would in large part be Sherry's fault.

Emily pulled a paperback copy of *Marriage Is a Canoe* from the shelf. Sherry had sent an old edition of the book to Emily in a care package from L.A. when she was there during pilot season a few years ago. She had sent it with a Post-it note on it that said, "Remember this?" Because before their parents were divorced—when Emily turned thirteen and Sherry was ten—their mother had kept a copy sitting on top of the toilet tank in the bathroom off the master bedroom in Milton, where Emily and Sherry had grown up.

Emily held the book in her hands and closed her eyes. She stood in the quiet bookstore and tried to explain to herself—yet again—that Eli, her husband of almost three years, had experienced some kind of epiphany a few weeks earlier on a business trip to L.A. and was going to do something nonprofit-related with his company. He had barely told her a thing about it. She had begun to suspect that he was figuring out the new business with Jenny Alexandretti, who was now helping with everything related to Roman Street Bicycles. Eli rarely asked Emily questions about his business anymore. Ever since Jenny had moved to New York from L.A. a year ago and started working at Roman Street, Eli had been a little evasive. Something was wrong. Emily was sure about that.

The most interesting thing that Emily had learned about Jenny Alexandretti was that her father was a famous photographer who had taken nude pictures of her at twelve, pictures that were still kicking around the Internet. She knew that Jenny no longer spoke to her father. Eli had told her that, back when Jenny still came up in conversation. She knew from Sherry that since Jenny had started at Roman Street, she had tattooed several bike parts on her body. First a fork, Sherry had told her. Then a sprocket. Sherry couldn't recall the name of the latest part and where it was on Jenny's body, but she had assured Emily that this had nothing to do with Eli. It was just that Jenny was the sort of person who got really obsessed with scenes. Thus, the tattoos. Because she's kind of lost, Emily had said. Right, Sherry said. Nothing to worry about. Just a lost soul who, thanks to Sherry and Eli, had found her calling. But now Emily suspected that Eli and Jenny had had a kiss. Which meant there was something to worry about.

Emily put *Canoe* back and went over to the magazine section. She looked for the bike magazine where Roman Street placed its ads. Eli had been featured on the cover back in May. She had blocked the magazine's name, just remembered that it was stupid and she didn't like it. If Eli had consulted her, she would have steered him toward smaller ads in bigger magazines like *Sports Illustrated*. When they first began dating seriously, Eli had checked in with Emily about everything related to marketing Roman Street. At first, he'd been shy about it. But she knew he was aware that having her help steer his business had been one of the keys to its success. Eli never denied that.

She had met Eli five years earlier, when he was a guest lecturer at a night course Emily was taking on industrial design at the New School, where he'd been an undergraduate. Emily had always loved lectures. She tried, whenever possible, to visit the New School or Parsons or FIT and catch lectures on design. Her job at Yes was to explain industrial design to people, to market great design and its relationship to technology. And she was good at it. Every few months she would visit OXO's headquarters on Twenty-Sixth Street, where they'd created the Good Grips line. She would be brought back to a conference room where a designer would be sitting with a new kitchen gadget. She'd say, I see you've got something there. Want to tell me about it? And they would try, and fail. She would coax out the best name for the thing, the best description. She could create a whole way of thinking about a new object, so that people wanted it and believed they needed it. And then she was on to the next company, and the next thing.

She had discovered this talent after college, when she'd first come to New York. Back then she worked nights at a law firm copyediting legal briefs and spent her days as a freelance assistant at a big design firm that mostly worked on branding for film and music festivals. She imagined she'd go to grad school for art history, or go further in design management, or at worst, go to law school and hate it but have money in her future and something to talk about with her father during their infrequent dinners that occurred when he was working on a case out of his firm's New York office. And then she went to a lecture on a third date with Gordon Dubrow, who was a grad student in computer science and wave theory at NYU. They had met during a day trip she'd taken one Saturday with a girlfriend around New York Harbor on an old sailboat. Gordon had been on the boat alone. She had observed him for half an hour while he obsessively watched the waves and every so often stuck out his hand and tried to follow their pattern, looking like he was doing a dance step from the eighties. She sat down next to him and they had ended up talking about boats. At that lecture, she sat holding hands with Gordon and listening to a professor from New Zealand talk about what wave theory could mean for ship design. It was then, when she found she was better at explaining to Gordon how big ships ought to look in order to perform well on the high seas than he was to her, that she realized she didn't want to build things. She wanted to explain them. And she had discovered a career. She then fell in love with Gordon and they'd spent six foggy years together.

During her twenties, whenever she was at a loss or just had a free evening, she went to lectures on math or science. But she also went to anthropology lectures at the Museum of Natural History or lectures on art history at the Met or MoMA. She went to screenings of documentaries and stayed for the Q&As. She sought out lectures on urban planning at the Museum of the City of New York and lectures on textiles at the Cooper-Hewitt. Her most recent obsession was Gary Hustwit, the man who had made the documentaries *Helvetica* and *Objectified*. She loved his tweets even more than his films. He knew how to explain the world. She thought he shared her gift. He made his subjects sound better and clearer and, when he was at his best, more charming. Emily could do that, too.

She often felt like her profession was dorky and, if she was feeling really down on herself, boyish. She felt guilty that she didn't see more friends and go to more parties. She hated that she could be so bold in a meeting and yet so quick to cross the street or hide behind a car when she saw an acquaintance. Over the years, the best way she'd found to unite these parts of herself had grown out of becoming part of an e-mail Listserv that kept its exclusive group of never more than 111 members updated on industrial design events in New York and general global ID trends. She raised eyebrows at the other members of the Listserv at events and followed them on Twitter, though she never tweeted. Showing up at events and silently acknowledging others wasn't quite work life and it wasn't precisely social life, and that made her feel okay. Not so shy. Though she hated that word. She understood that she had consciously chosen to inhabit a small world full of awkward people who freely admitted they'd rather work with objects than humans. She felt happy and even a little proud to have found her place in this group. When she occasionally contributed a thought or passed along an article to the Listserv and received positive responses, she got so excited she had to stop looking at all personal e-mails for a few days, until she flattened out and felt like herself again.

Eli had been a guest lecturer, back when Emily was getting over Gordon Dubrow, who had left New York for a good teaching job at Oregon State University. The final year with Gordon had begun with the offer for the OSU job. The job offer engendered an intense, two-day discussion that constantly verged on a fight, that revolved around how Gordon's work would always be theoretical and how he would probably never build a sailboat of his own. At the end of it, Emily realized she'd been attacking him. They had spent much of that year realizing that though they loved each other, she wasn't leaving New York. And when he volunteered to stay, she said no to that, too. There was an imbalance. Though she loved him, he loved her more. She understood this but dared not articulate it, for fear of hurting him as badly as she had when they fought about the sailboat he would never build. She would miss him. But she wanted to be in New York with its unending supply of lectures, its promise to keep her busy and engaged, no matter how shy she became. She also suspected that she wanted someone cooler, someone just a little outside the world she'd made for herself. Though if Gordon had grabbed her by the shoulders and demanded that she move to the

West Coast, she probably would have gone. But he hadn't grabbed her.

Eli had started his lecture by talking about his first career as a graphic designer and how he'd enjoyed that. But he'd had a growing fascination with bicycle design. He'd already built one bike and was thinking that it might be more than a hobby. And so, on a trip to Italy, he came up with the idea for his company, Roman Street Bicycles. The longer he stood in front of the class, the less he talked. Instead, he showed pictures on PowerPoint. He began with a silver-colored, steel frame, single-speed bicycle. He showed the class how he stenciled "Roman Street" or "RSB" on each part in ghostly white paint. He showed pictures of himself shaking hands with the lanky owners of independent bike shops in Williamsburg and Fort Greene and on Third Avenue in Gowanus. There were photographs of his bikes in their windows. He showed how the city was newly lined with bicycle lanes, so many lanes everywhere that they looked like some vast interlay of green threads. Within eighteen months, he was importing steel tubing from China and manufacturing completely new bikes in a factory in the South Bronx where the laborers were mostly illegal but were paid as if they weren't. He showed pictures of the factories in China and his dozen workers in the Bronx. His lecture trailed off completely as he showed pictures of his inspirations, ancient Bianchi bicycles, photographs of working women bicycling in Rome in the fifties, Greg LeMond, the Italian national cycling team, and rain-soaked commuters biking up hills in Seattle.

Afterward, instead of bowing her head and sneaking out during the applause, Emily fought past the constraints she had allowed to define her and went to the front of the room to talk to him. She wanted to know how much of what he did was fashion and how much was building custom bikes. How much was really for the riders? He stood up straight and she was afraid that he might not like her questions or how tall she was. He asked her to come for a drink at Café Loup.

He had such dark eyes. He spoke with his thick hands. He shaped bicycles in front of her, showed her discarded logos on napkins, eventually took her hands and held them in his while he explained how it felt to build a bicycle and then use it to take you anywhere you wanted to go. She did not tell him about Gordon and the theoretical waves and the unbuilt sailboat. She didn't tell him how in love she'd been, and how recently. To compensate for these omissions, she didn't ask many questions about his past.

"I know I'm having a hard time finding the words to explain all this," Eli said.

"That's okay," she said with a smile. "I understand everything you're saying."

She stared at his hands. She found out he was five years older than her. The elusive thing that had not happened with Gordon in six years happened with Eli in only a few hours. She could imagine being married to him.

Now Emily imagined Eli stenciling "Roman Street" between the pair of sweet dimples she'd seen above Jenny's ass. In Emily's mind, Jenny had started to look like Megan Fox, but smarter and with those incredible lazy ringlets of hair. Emily fantasized about finding Jenny mistakenly riding her Roman Street bicycle onto the Brooklyn–Queens Expressway and running her down with a big car. Cool-ass Jenny. Easy going, L.A. Jenny. There was something Emily hadn't given Eli and he had found it in Jenny. Where Emily liked things that were explainable, Jenny had accessed the part of Eli that was inexplicable. And now Emily was miserable and frightened and confused.

Emily shook her head and reminded herself that Eli was an excellent husband. He had an autographed Thurman Munson baseball in his sock drawer and that was the only odd thing in there. She had never found a fetish-porn magazine, a suspicious USB cartridge, unexplained lipstick-stained boxers, or a duct-taped manila envelope stuffed with photos of a girl from high school or college. There was never anything like that. He was obsessed with his work and thought about little else, and she had always loved guys like that, since she was a teenager. There had been nothing to worry about for years and years until there was Jenny.

She pulled out her phone to call Sherry back and then just stared at it.

Fucking phones. She had picked up Eli's phone on a morning two weeks earlier to find a text from Jenny that said, *Can't wait to see you at work today.* After that, Emily had scrolled through her own texts back and forth with her husband and there weren't a whole lot of *can't wait*s. They were both guilty of a ton of *I'll be late*s, so many back and forth, informing the other not to be disappointed about this latest reduction in the time they would spend together. There was also a whole lot of discussion of food and when to eat it. The texts he exchanged with Jenny were not dirty. They were solicitous and kind. They were kinder than coworker kind. *You were great today! I just got the name of an investor who I think you'll really like. Call me later? Want to connect with you before bedtime.* And then when he'd returned from L.A., a text from Eli to Jenny that said, *Thanks for the hug, work wife.* A hug from a work wife. Emily had intended to be his wife for work and for home. But that was over. Still, she had hope. She had to figure out how to push them through this thing, past Jenny. If only she had any idea how to do that.

Her home screen was a picture of Eli winking. She thought of his muscular legs and the way she loved him as she stared at his face. She leaned against a bookshelf. She was in big trouble.

Emily put her phone away and left the self-help section. She picked up the August *Vogue* and *Me on You*, a second novel by Ida Abarra, an Ethiopian-American woman who had been at Sarah Lawrence when she was there, someone she had never been that close to but had really admired. She'd always had funny conversations with Ida at the extremely drunken dinner parties that they'd both gone to right after college in too-small apartments in the Lower East Side and Greenpoint, before everyone paired off and moved to the softer terrain of brownstone Brooklyn.

I'll be supportive and buy Ida's novel, she thought.

Her phone vibrated.

"Are you finished with whoever you ran into?" Sherry asked. "I only have a few more minutes to talk before I go onstage."

"No, still catching up," Emily whispered. "Sorry." She hung up again.

She loved her younger sister but didn't want to hear about the date she had with a movie producer after she finished her show. She knew she was being awful, but she couldn't help it.

It was warm in the bookstore, this rather alien

outpost of a new minichain that had sprouted up six months earlier, a brightly lit place with plenty of bleached wood tables and some oversize canvas-covered armchairs where high school kids were surreptitiously touching one another's thighs.

She walked toward the front of the store. She and Eli were going to make dinner together. She needed to buy fish because it was Monday and they were often virtuous early in the week, before succumbing on Wednesday or Thursday evening to takeout Thai or just cereal or reheated spaghetti, eaten standing up in the kitchen with beer.

And then, before she got on line to pay, she circled back and scooped up the version of *Marriage Is a Canoe* she'd come in to look at. Admittedly, she already had the book at home. But this was a different edition that appeared to have a shortened version of the original exercises in it. She had always loved the book. She had read and reread the copy that lived in her parents' bathroom when she was growing up. When she was twelve, she had fantasized about being the girl called Honey who Peter Herman had kissed and later married. She realized, suddenly, that that was twenty-one years ago. And ever since, she had kept a copy of *Canoe* with her wherever she lived.

She hated people who made fun of *Canoe*. She loved the elegance of it, the simplicity of its lessons and the fact that they were undeniably right and true. The book kept the dream of the ideal marriage alive. *Canoe* had helped her look away from her parents' marriage, which was cold and New Englandy and had lasted fourteen brittle years. She and Sherry always joked that it had gone on about a dozen years too long. By the time Emily was in seventh grade and Sherry was in fourth, her mother had refused to celebrate Christmas and her father wouldn't celebrate Chanukah, so the winter holiday arrived heavy and silent in the house. Emily and Sherry mutely understood that their home life was stagnant and wouldn't last, so Sherry forced herself on their friends and Emily spent much of her time alone, reading. This marital outcome was precisely unlike the ones described in *Canoe*, except for much of chapter eleven, a chapter Emily always skipped when she reread. Emily loved *Canoe*. Though, ever since college, she kept the book on a high shelf where friends wouldn't see it and tease her about it.

She paid and smiled at the cashier and thought about how she ought to share more about herself with people, to not be so tight-lipped and interior. But she only really knew how to talk about objects—she didn't see a way to explain herself. And maybe that was beginning to crop up as a problem with Eli, too.

She called Sherry from the street.

"Emily, what the hell are you up to?"

"Nothing!"

"Have you talked to Mom this week?"

After her divorce, their mother had left the house in Milton where she'd brought up her daughters and cooked healthy dinners for her lawyer husband, and she'd reclaimed her existence as Rebecca Bauman. Now she taught English composition at Bates, had the sense of humor of a mid-career Joan Baez, and talked to her daughters nearly exclusively about their relationships and her academic career. She revealed almost nothing about her personal life. It was possible that she was gay, and embarrassed about it. Though both things felt wildly improbable, Sherry and Emily hoped that was the explanation. That or something like it. They both preferred to imagine that their mother hid a life better and richer than the one she shared with them.

"Yeah." Emily nodded. "She suspects the worst so she wants to rip Eli's head off. I'm not sure how that's supposed to help. Then I had to hear about all her problems with the Henry James book. She says she's close. I know she's lying to herself."

"What?" Sherry asked. Emily could hear Nancy, the other woman in the play, also talking on the phone in their shared dressing room. Sherry was always tense before a performance, and her teeth were chattering. Emily listened to her sister's clicking teeth and remembered her mother yanking open the door to the master bathroom where Emily had thought she'd locked herself in. Her mother had found her reading *Canoe* and she started laughing hysterically. "Great, Emily! Keep reading! Keep dreaming! That fucking stupid book—memorize it! And pretend you can't hear another word of this!" And then her mother ran out of the bathroom and back down to the living room to continue fighting with her husband. Emily didn't much care for her mother's full sentences or her sarcasm. But Emily also wasn't forthright enough, even as a child, to tell her mother that was exactly what she had been doing.

"Emily? I've really got to go. It's true Mom will never finish that thing. Call me later, or tomorrow morning. Look, it's probably not as bad as Mom thinks, and please stop hanging up on me! It's just a work-wife thing which is exactly what they're both saying. That's all it is."

"*Hugs with a work wife.* I hate it. I hate how that stupid line is imprinted on my brain. Be ready, because I am going to call you later," Emily said.

"Can you hear my teeth chattering? I hate previews," Sherry said, and hung up.

Emily began to rush down the not-too-hot August street. She saw the fish store closing for the night. Part of her wanted to talk her way past the guy fiddling with the pull-down gate to grab up the last piece of tuna. By channeling the saleswoman in her, she could be quite good at that sort of convincing. But no, no. Too late. Move on. Her timing was just horrible lately. Driving Sherry crazy right before she had to go onstage, choosing odd ways home, obsessively attending inarguably dull lectures on subjects like the design of Byzantine coins, and avoiding her husband.

Her handbag dragged at her shoulder. Her life felt too up in the air and here she was, buying books she already owned to weigh her down. There was something frozen that they could heat up and eat, she was sure of it. That would be fine. Some ribs that Eli had cooked for friends two weeks earlier. No. Defrosted ribs were gross. He could have them sometime when she was out. She was sure there was pasta. Probably there were some frozen beans, too.

Her husband was really just a driven and occasionally distracted guy who had said, "You make me better," when he'd asked her to marry him at Café Loup after they'd been together a little over a year. He told her all the time how much he loved what she had made of their lives. Still, now, knowing he was a good guy wasn't helping. She had to believe he wasn't up to anything with Jenny. They were just in a mental I-would-so-do-you type of affair because they were both good-looking in a similar dark-and-sexy way, and also because Roman Street had been unstoppable lately, transitioning from a cool brand with serious supply problems to talk of growth plans and distribution partnerships and a feature on Forbes.com. And what was a hug, anyway? A hug was not a kiss. And Eli was such a poor writer that she doubted he was capable of a euphemism. He wasn't traveling anytime soon and she would just be more vigilant. She would kill whatever was growing. Somehow, they'd get past it. She would figure out a way to get them past it.

Emily was now basically counting the minutes until Sherry's play was over so she could call her and learn more about Jenny and try to figure out what to do. Since Sherry had gone to Amherst with Jenny, she knew the woman's awful history and Sherry owed Emily the truth about whatever she'd left out when she had first introduced Jenny to Eli at that pie contest, over a year ago. So what if Eli had won the contest and, as a gesture of celebration, hired Jenny on the spot. It had all been funny and festive at the time and even Emily had gotten drunk enough to stay up singing "We Are the Champions" over and over with Jenny and her sister and Eli.

Jenny had started working for Eli a few weeks later and he had been less stressed ever since. Eli needed an awful lot of people around him to keep his business going. And Jenny, the hot little work wife, she was a blessing. Until everything that had made Emily act supportive when she first met Jenny began to feel very wrong. So yes, Sherry had no right to be angry at Emily for constantly hanging up on her, considering how badly Sherry had fucked up Emily's life. Well. If not exactly fucked it up directly, then Sherry had certainly set the goddamned bike wheels in motion.

Peter Herman, early September 2011

Maddie Narayan drove up Peter Herman's driveway in her brand-new, black Mercedes station wagon. She got out and wrapped a purple shawl around her shoulders. Though it was early September and still warm at dusk, it would grow cool within the hour. Peter watched her.

"You're always so well prepared," he called out.

"That is my welcome?"

"Sorry. Good trip?" Peter came down to meet her.

His front porch faced a small field of mown grass. Beyond that, behind Maddie's car, there was the longish driveway, lined on both sides with sugar maples. His blue painted-steel mailbox was just visible at the point where the driveway met Lakeview Road.

She met him on the brick path to the house and he reached out to kiss her. She smelled mostly of lemon and her hair was shiny and black, cut above her shoulders so it bounced as she walked. She smiled and jutted her sharp chin up at him.

"It was a good trip. Anjulee is so beautiful and glowing that I could not keep myself from crying. When the baby comes it will be very healthy."

"I'm glad. I would love to meet her someday. And your house is okay?"

She raised an eyebrow at him. She had come from her house outside Hudson, thirty-five minutes away.

"Yes, of course. Why would it not be?"

"It's just—a neglected house . . ."

"Peter. Please."

He wrapped his arms around her. She was soft in the belly and shorter than him, but her black hair was splayed out, and when she stared up at him he did find that he loved looking into her familiar black eyes.

"I'm ready," he said. "Why don't you tell me about the wonders of the city of San Francisco?"

"Now that really is a terrific place," she said. She held his shoulders and continued to look up at him without blinking.

He loved how sharp she was, this proper, middle-aged woman who never contracted a word. So sharp and proper! He knew that wasn't right, though. To love how a person was, rather than to just love the person. He'd written an essay and lectured on it a few times a quarter century ago. But he quickly discovered that people didn't like the idea, because it was too honest and therefore, too brutal. So he stopped talking about it. When he was questioned about the essay, he admitted the underlying truth within the concept eluded him. Then he'd wait a beat and say, "Put another way: I know I wrote it, but I'm not so sure I understood what I meant when I was done." That always got a laugh.

"Wait," he said now. On a chair on the porch were a bunch of poppies and cornflowers he'd bought from Jo at Country Gardeners Florist in town. He held them up to her.

"See?" he asked, and kissed her again.

She said, "My favorites."

"I hope they'll brighten your neglected house. Let's go on the back porch."

She followed him through the front rooms but then stopped in his kitchen. He looked back at her. It was bad, this thing he did where he was appraising and cold and distanced himself from people. And Maddie could make him happy. She was always smart in conversation and she liked to rub up against him. She could be funny, too. She was even able to be self-effacing about her proper ways.

"I will make tea," she said. "It will take a few minutes."

He went out to the back porch, turned on the sconces on either side of the kitchen door and leaned on the porch rail. He looked in at Maddie. They were near enough to speak, but they didn't. She hadn't known Lisa well, though they had met when Lisa got sick, when they needed an adviser. Maddie had been a financial administrator who worked for different museums in

New York. But she had moved up to her country house when she split with her husband, James, who was North American CFO of an India-based steel company, the sort of hard-nosed man Peter sometimes saw on television, in the first-row seats at Yankees games. He had left her for a very young woman, a McKinsey consultant. Maddie had taken money and their Hudson Valley country house. He remained in their apartment on Riverside Drive. Their divorce was nearly final.

"Will you sit with me?" Maddie asked, after she'd come out with a tray.

She settled herself in a wicker chair and put the tray on a low table between them. She sat back. She had a habit of drawing her arms inside her shawl if she wasn't using her hands. Peter liked that—its economy charmed him.

"I am only back here for a day but it feels like a week," she said.

"But if you truly settled here the days wouldn't feel so long."

"That is nonsense. Savor the freezing weather that will come? I do not think so."

"I would love to build you fires." He tried not to sound tentative.

"I do not want to stay here, Peter. I want to go. We could build fires in San Francisco."

Peter didn't speak. He took a mug of tea and sipped at it. He would have liked some scotch, but

Maddie frowned when he drank. Everyone seemed to. He looked out at the dark lake. Maddie made a noise in her throat. She said, "Why will you not admit that you are tired of having people ask you to go for a paddle with them in the lake? I would hate it."

"That never really happens."

"It happens all the time. I have been with you twice when it happened! Remember at Gilmor glassworks? That was awful."

"They were just tourists. And it's not my fault that Jessie Gilmor still likes to poke fun at me. It's good for her business."

"It was not funny. Having our picture taken with tourists was not funny."

"And at Pantomime's." He smiled.

"Yes, there, too! You think Arthur is your friend but look at what he does each time we are in the store! That is not protecting and caring for a neighbor."

"No," Peter said. "I suppose it isn't. But there's not much business up here. We do what we can to take care of each other."

"Take care of each other? You think they want you around. But you are wrong. Henry wants to make improvements at the inn. He wants to be free to try again to expand to Hudson. Maybe even down to Rhinebeck."

"So that's what you two talk about at your lunches?" Peter frowned and stood up again. "It's impossible to make it in Hudson. The gossip from the antique-store people kills you before you can even open your doors. Henry should know that by now."

"Henry is friendly with those people. Why should he not try? And what do you think we talk about if not our plans? You sound paranoid and not very supportive of your friend."

"Please, Maddie. I don't know why you can't take it easy on me."

"I am trying!" She shook her head and looked away from him. "I am sorry. It is because life was so nice and new on the West Coast and here everything is the same."

Peter took her hand and said, "Do you want to eat? I could make us some soup and toast?"

"Soup from a can? I have good food in the car. I returned home and before I knew what was happening I found myself cooking for you." She smiled up at him. She said, "I will bring it in."

But Peter kept her hand. He kissed the tips of her fingers. He ran his other hand up the length of her arm and around to her breast. He heard her breath change.

She said, "I do not like pushing you. But when I leave here and see the whole world I cannot help but return and want to take you along with me back into it! I am going to sell my house this fall for sure. Then I will go to San Francisco and all I can do is dream of what fun we could have there.

You could write! You could, you know. It is being here that paralyzes you."

"Can't you leave that alone?" Peter pulled away and waved his hands in front of him. "Really, we should have fun together. Not argue all the time."

"I do not believe you want me to leave anything alone."

He said, "I'm happy just being here."

"I do not believe that. I cannot be here with you, watching you growing old and doing nothing. I do not enjoy being so harsh but the situation demands it."

"We should eat," he said. It was finally dark.

"I will go and get the hamper from the car," she said. "Tomorrow morning we can drive to my house and swim in the pool. I want to use it before I lose it."

The phone rang inside the house and Peter made no move to answer it.

"Shall I?" Maddie smiled and went into the house.

"Couldn't hurt," Peter called after her. Though he knew that if the caller was his daughter, Belinda, it could. He needed to bring Belinda and Maddie together for a dinner. He was being slow about it and Belinda was growing impatient. He knew his daughter would be happier and worry less about him once she met his girlfriend. Again, his inactivity made him seem thoughtless.

"No," Maddie said, a moment later. "I will not

bring him to the phone unless you tell me what you are calling about." She was quiet, listening. Then he heard her say, "Hold, please."

She returned to the porch and said, "It is a woman from your publishing house, called Stella Petrovic. She says she is sorry to call in the evening but she has had trouble getting you to answer during the day and did not want to leave a message. Do you want to talk to her?"

"Wow." Peter hunched over, so he could feel the lower half of his belly surge against his belt buckle. "I haven't had a call from LRB in forever."

"So? Do you want to talk to her? She is waiting."

"No, I won't talk to her just now." He turned away and hid his smile. He didn't want Maddie to hear the simpering tone he tended to use with anyone connected to LRB. He said, "Take the number, won't you? I will talk with her but not now. I can't speak with her this evening is all."

They had sex after dinner in the big four-poster bed that he'd used for nearly his entire adult life. Maddie was slow with sex, slow and good. She was entirely different than she was in conversation. She was never cool with him or detached, the way Lisa had been. Peter meant no disrespect to Lisa, but he was a little crazy for Maddie when they were in bed. She held him tightly before falling asleep first, as she did on most nights when they were together. Then she turned away and curled in on herself. Peter listened to her even breathing. The bedroom was quiet, though light spilled in from the moon reflecting on the lake.

He knew he was supposed to do his homework and begin to try to imagine leaving Millerton and moving to San Francisco. He knew he was supposed to ask Maddie to help him structure the sale of his interest in the inn to Henry for an appropriate sum, pay off the lingering debts that haunted him when he drove around Millerton, sell or rent his house, and start the next portion of his life.

Instead, he thought about a different kind of night. A hospital dusk. Almost nine o'clock and still there was light, last July.

Lisa was lying on her side, staring at him, as he sat in his chair. She said, "You remember. I was poor when I met you."

At that point, when Lisa talked, he didn't know whether he was listening to the drugs, the evil tau proteins that were the heart of Pick's, or the woman he knew. He no longer tried to divine the difference.

"Yes, I remember." Though she had never been poor. He rearranged the carnations he'd brought. Stupid flowers that made them both happy but couldn't do anything to fight the hospital odor.

"Something I need to tell you," Lisa said.

"Another secret?" Peter covered his head with

his hands. He couldn't stand more revelations. "Let's wait. There's no rush."

"It's okay. I know how much you loved me. It's okay. I forgive you."

"Forgive me?"

"For giving me less than all of you."

"Lisa, please."

"Is Belinda on her way?" she asked, turning so she looked up at the yellow ceiling.

"You saw her this morning. But yes, she's on her way."

"You weren't ever really, truly in love with me."

"Lisa. That's not fair. I always was." He wondered at how, as he lost sight of her, he also lost his ability to be honest with himself. But it couldn't matter. Not now.

"Sometimes. Not always."

"Sometimes?" he asked. "Isn't sometimes good enough?"

She allowed him to hold her hands and they were both still. He was sickened by her eagerness to destroy the story of their lives.

"Be honest for us both, now. We were happy. Is enough." She stopped speaking and fell asleep.

Now he touched Maddie's warm back and thought of when he'd brought his zither and played George Harrison songs for Lisa at dusk. What was a college affectation had become a hobby he wasn't too bad at.

They shut the door to her room and he played disconnected notes for her, for nearly an hour, until a nurse came in and gently asked him to stop.

Afterward, he sat in the hospital armchair with its fake red leather–covered arms attaching and detaching from his skin, the zither still in his lap. He plucked a string and listened. There were thirty-eight strings, and he plucked one and then another so a note sounded lonely and clean before it died and he plucked the next. He put the instrument down, fearing the nurse.

"Oh, Lisa. What can I do? What can I do for you?"

He had already dappled her thin lips with water, settled her pillows, and straightened the pale blue sheet over her bloated legs.

While waiting to have his hair cut once, in the late nineties, Peter read an article in *People* magazine about George Hamilton and discovered that he was just like him. He had started out as a bit of a fake and now was celebrated for the persona he'd created, not the person he was. Lisa had known this. He had not given her the deep, transformative love she deserved, and in return she had lost the money he made from his book. But still, they loved each other. At their beginning he'd been a little cool when he should've been hot. Now he was broke and a little nervous. Now he lived ruefully with the consequences of his life with Lisa.

At seven the next morning, Maddie drove them over the dewy back roads that crossed and recrossed the Taconic, on their way to her house for a swim.

He ran his hand through her hair. They'd had sex again at dawn, and were both acting a little smug about doing it so much in so short a time. Although his doctor had mentioned Viagra when Peter told him about Maddie, Peter had discovered he didn't need it. He was proud of that and wanted to boast about it, but there was no one to tell. He couldn't imagine saying that sort of thing to Henry. Perhaps in San Francisco men were more open to such a conversation?

"Was any of the book true?" Maddie asked.

He glanced at Maddie and suddenly felt how little they knew each other, which transformed instantly to anger, and with that anger, some of his false befuddlement fell away. "Don't you know me well enough by now to understand how little that matters?"

"Come here," she said. She was going to hold his hand and drive with just one. He could see it. He reached out and they held hands. They turned into her long driveway. Her house was high up on a mountain and made of stones. They drove up her gravel road in silence and she came to a stop. Turned off her engine.

"We are not getting along very well," she said. "And now you would like me to apologize for asking such a question?"

He shook his head no and gripped her hand, hard, for support as if he were going to fall. He glared out the windows. He could see the morning mist burning off the tops of her trees. He liked Maddie so much. The sex they were having was better than anything he could have imagined for himself at this stage of life. But the truth was that the cool quality at the center of her made him feel so alone. Still, what else did he have? He had nothing else.

He said, "There was a chapter I added to the second edition, about how Bess fell asleep at the wheel of their Buick Skylark and drove herself and my Pop off Spook Rock Road, right where it crosses that little river, and they got caught in a current and were dragged to the river bottom. But it wasn't so deep that they couldn't be seen." He stopped and looked north. He said, "Not five miles away from here. They drowned in sight of the road before anyone could get close enough to wrench them free. When they finally pulled them out, their bodies were tangled up in a frantic hug, so every bit of them was touching. That was true. I wrote it prettier than how it really was."

"I cried when I read that," Maddie said.

"I cried when I wrote it." Though, had he? It

was a stock response to anyone's claim that they wept when they read *Canoe*, as rote as the flick of a horse's tail when the midday flies won't stop buzzing. At this rate, he wouldn't have an end like that to his life.

"There are two kinds of people," Maddie said. "Those who see the wisdom in your book and respect it. And then there are those who make fun of it because they are cynical."

"No, there are three kinds of people. The two you just mentioned and then there's a third kind, the kind who undulate constantly between their cynicism and the romance of engagement."

"Now it feels like we are talking about all the kinds of people." She turned and smiled at him. "I cannot wait to swim." They got out of the car and he followed her toward her house. He watched the outline of her backside through her skirt. Wait. He ought to let her lead him through the rest of his life. Anything else was nonsense.

He called out, "Wait."

"What?"

"Have I never promised you that I will go with you when you go to California?"

"Peter, do not play with me."

"I am promising now."

"Really?" She stopped in front of her silent house and cocked her head to one side, examining him.

"I promise you, Maddie. I will move with you.

It's time. We make each other feel really good. I like us."

"Peter! Do you know how happy you are making me?"

He smiled and went in to hug her, pushed himself against her.

Emily Babson, early September 2011

"You must be Emily!"

"Yup, that's me." Emily gripped her bag with both hands. She looked past the girl and into the crowded room. She had hoped to arrive just before the midpoint of the party but it appeared that she had miscalculated. She was late. The party was roaring and hot, the room she looked in on filled with bodies.

"Eli talks about you all the time. It must be so fun being married to him! Emily and Eli—that's so cool! Let me take your coat." Emily handed it over to the girl, a pretty twenty-two-year-old in a black Roman Street Bicycles T-shirt. She'd never seen it before. It was just a week past Labor Day and still quite warm out. Emily had no idea why she'd worn an overcoat.

"We're so excited for this party!" the girl called out as she walked away.

"Me, too." Emily heard people come up the brownstone steps behind her and so she had no choice but to move into the crowd. It was a Roman Street cocktail party hosted by Eli's new lawyers, a couple called Rick and Steven who worked out of their town house in Fort Greene. Eli was brilliant at convincing people to throw parties for him. He loved to preside over parties. He rocked them.

This party was meant to kick off Eli's new venture. He wanted to create a bicycle advocacy nonprofit and spin it off from Roman Street, using the same lists and assets and people. Eli had realized that he spent a lot of time advocating for bikers' rights and that it didn't always fit with selling bicycles. He wanted a more politically motivated nonprofit structure for this new company, which was meant to address the "next wave" in urban biking, finally bringing big American cities in line with places like Amsterdam and Stockholm. But the mission was awfully broad and ambitious and simply wasn't related to his core business. Emily had helped him work through the idea on weekend walks. Though they hadn't talked about it in the few busy weeks leading up to this party, and now she had lost track of the new company's final form. She did not even know what he'd decided to call it.

The whole of the town house's parlor floor was open and people streamed around her. Emily thought they were rushing to the bar but immediately realized she was wrong. They were rushing to talk to one another. Still, she was able to look across the room and catch Eli's eye. She could see that he felt her presence. He turned and smiled and left the conversation he was in to come to her.

"Hi, sweet thing," he said, and kissed her. "You always look so graceful when you enter a room. I'm, like, proud to be with you." He reeked of beer and workday sweat, but on him it smelled good.

"I'm sorry I'm late. I hope I didn't miss anything."

"Don't worry about it. It's been crazy. Before everybody arrived we were on a funding call with these West Coast donors and I got tense." Eli nodded and smiled at people as he talked to her. "But Jenny made some jokes about the price of fuel next summer and we came out with real promises. Don't forget to say hello to Rick and Steven, okay? They always ask after you. Don't get shy now, okay? I want to be right next to you but you know I can't pull it off since I'm hosting."

"Is Jenny here?" It had been three weeks and Emily still had not confronted him. She hadn't gotten further than telling herself they were both too busy, no matter how much her mother and sister pushed her to at least talk to him. The situation with the hug seemed static. She had come to hate the word *hug* and intended never to think the word again. She'd been training herself to use only the word *embrace*. Except when it applied to them. Eli and Jenny. Their hug.

"Is Jenny here?" Eli repeated. She watched him grit his jaw. He said, "Sure, of course she is. She's around somewhere. It'd be great if you two could connect. Look at how many supporters we've got.

This is really great for Roman Street and the new thing, UBA!"

"UBA?"

"Urban Bicycle Advocacy! What do you think, word lady? I wanted to surprise you." Eli smiled. He had bright white teeth. She smiled back and tried as hard as she could to stop him from bringing up Jenny again without actually saying it. She was determined to get through the party without speaking to her. She had been sisterly and supportive once. That would not happen again.

"Word lady," she said. "Don't call me that."

"Sorry. I meant word person," he said with a smile. "But what do you think?"

"Another acronym."

"Yeah, but this one is different. It sounds primal. Jenny figured out the name. She's probably with Rick or Steven—we've been working here all day."

"Wow, you and her . . . really keyed into something." Emily bit her lip. She couldn't find it in herself to smile.

"Come on, Emily. How about not losing your patience in a heartbeat? Tonight is important."

"I wasn't," she said. Then, "I didn't." She tugged on his plaid shirt. "Can't I be a little jealous? What's wrong with noticing when somebody has a crush on you?"

"A crush?" He laughed. "This is all about UBA."

She hated the name UBA and could have come up with a better one in half an hour if she'd been asked. But she hadn't been—and that made her almost as angry as their hug. She had helped enormously in giving direction to his messy business. And now it was out of her control. Jenny had thought up the name. Fucking idiot. She wanted to fire Jenny. She caught Eli looking at her, shaking his head at her frown. Then he gave her his tight-lipped smile and faded into the crowd, like an old Jules Feiffer cartoon found in one of the books her parents had had when she was a child—he just grew thin-lipped and crinkled his sweet eyes and faded away.

She was suddenly alone, standing a foot from the bar, which was manned by a handsome kid, probably an undergraduate from Pratt. She grabbed a glass of white wine and didn't move. She touched the tablecloth and looked at the rows of glasses and the huge wedge of Parmesan that people had begun to hack into chunks. There were bowls of fat purple kalamata olives, too. It was going to be a thirsty party. Emily loved the olives and began to eat them one at a time, carefully, so the skin didn't get caught in her teeth. She began to berate herself for not being able to glow from all the warmth in the room. She tried to work up to glowing, or at the least work down from feeling too tall and pale and damp. Did anybody even know who she was? She doubted it. Roman Street was blowing up so fast and it was all about Eli. She watched Eli embrace people. It looked almost like people were waiting in line to get some of his affection. His hair was getting longer. He looked a little bit like Che Guevara. No wonder he'd gotten into the idea of a nonprofit. She turned away and decided she was about ready for her second glass of what was turning out to be some pretty good pinot . . . Then she looked up and couldn't find Eli anywhere. She didn't want to search for him. But she had no choice. She knew nobody. And she was afraid to run into Jenny. Jenny was short. She would keep her eyes aimed high.

She glanced around the corner into the kitchen and saw him, talking to the husband of an actress whose name she couldn't recall but who Sherry had kissed once in a play four or five years back. She eavesdropped. They were talking about banjo playing. Eli was a proficient banjo player and an excellent banjo conversationalist. She frowned. This was such a networky event and she was so not a networky person. Eli wasn't supposed to be either. He was supposed to be charming and awkward. A savant industrial designer slash bike lover slash grease monkey genius. But now she saw, as she glanced around, that if that had ever been true, it wasn't anymore.

"Emily?" Someone was calling her name from behind her. She felt a spike of relief. Someone wanted her! Unless it was Jenny? What would she say? You stay away from my husband! How could she say that? She couldn't.

She turned fast and bumped into the woman who had called out to her.

"Ida!" It was Ida Abarra—the novelist whose book she'd bought back in August. Phew.

They hugged and kissed hello. Ida had a glass of white wine in her hand. She said, "I haven't seen you in a thousand years. Then I did see you on the street a couple of weeks ago but you were strutting alone and obviously thinking hard about something. I didn't want to break into your head space."

"That's embarrassing. I hope I didn't look too crazy," Emily said. She must be looking like that every night lately, when she was walking home. She smiled at Ida, raised her shoulders and then dropped them.

"No, just thoughtful," Ida said. "How are you? Wait. I think I read about your job." Ida had big eyes—you could see white all the way around her black pupils, and Emily remembered how that made talking to her feel intense no matter what you talked about.

Ida said, "You're the person who is going to dream up the name for whatever we all carry around in the future. I read the piece on you in the alumni magazine."

"Yeah, that creepy guy from the year below us is running it—Jeremiah Bazelton, bald with Philip

Johnson glasses? He won't stop sending me e-mails. But wait—congratulations on your novel! I bought it."

"Have you read it?"

"Not yet." Emily looked straight down at the floor.

"I'm glad. Don't read it. It's not that good." Ida sighed and smiled at Emily. "I've made my peace with it."

"I'm sure that's not true. You were the best writer in college." More than anything, Emily hoped that Ida wouldn't walk away. Ida held a goblet of white wine that was bigger than everyone else's glass. She also had a bit of dark hair on her upper lip. And she didn't seem to give a shit about it and that was really cool.

Ida said, "Yeah, so what's your deal? What else do you do when you're not forecasting the future?"

"Oh, god. I don't know. And that's not really what I do. I'm just a consultant. It's stupid."

"Don't tell anybody, but the truth is I hate innovative people. Not you, but, like, inventors."

Emily laughed and looked down. Ida was wearing a pleated green skirt and high black boots covered with a sea of maroon beads—she'd seen those beads on a pair of Miu Miu pumps last spring and wished boots could be beaded that way. And here they were: her dream boots, existing in reality, on Ida's feet where they looked even more perfect with just a few beads carelessly knocked off.

"I love your boots," Emily said.

"These? I got them at Century. Thanks. Anyway, what are you doing here? I know Steven and Rick. They did a film option for me with this Uruguayan filmmaker. So now I show up at their stuff. They don't make me donate."

"Actually I'm here because—" But Emily let Ida cut her off.

"You know I got married?" Ida nodded and Emily could tell that Ida was still trying to get comfortable with the words. "Yeah, about two years ago."

"Is your husband here?"

"Lord, no. Billy hates this stuff. He's a trader and on the side he writes a newsletter about the World Bank. He wants us to move to D.C. but it's not happening. I hate that town. In Brooklyn, I'm a face in the crowd. Every time I go down to D.C. somebody tries to pin a medal on me."

"That sounds cool." Emily imagined Ida and her genius husband at balls at the Watergate Hotel and parties in the bowling alley at the White House with powerful speechwriters and lobbyists for international trade organizations. She was sure they stayed up late in bed afterward and laughed and gossiped together. Eli sucked at gossip.

"It's not cool," Ida said. "It's boring. But whatever, it's my fault. I love him. I married him. So he's home and I'm at this random thing. I see your ring. Who'd you marry?"

"Um," Emily said, and then she just shook her head and closed her eyes. "Eli," Emily said with a shrug. "Eli Corelli."

"What?" Ida asked. "You're married to Eli? I am so, so sorry I didn't make the connection!"

"How could you," Emily said. "I'm standing here and I don't even know where he is." Emily worried that she was hovering over Ida so she gave her some space. But Ida moved closer. They both leaned against the doorframe to the kitchen, with just inches between them. Everybody else had to maneuver around them. Emily could see that Ida so did not care.

"Wow, everybody loves your guy."

"True," Emily said. "Wait, who's he with now?"

Eli was in the living room with the actress and her husband. The three of them were huddled in front of an enormous black marble fireplace. Eli had someone else's banjo in his hands.

"Looks like Trent Norman and Genevieve Winslow-Homer."

"That's her name," Emily said. "I kept forgetting it."

"You forget it because she stole it from a famous artist and if you're anything like me that disgusts you. Her actual name is Jennifer Puddle or something. I see her at yoga. She has flexible hips."

"Where do you go?"

"Kula."

"I never see you there," Emily said. "I've been doing a lot of yoga lately."

"I do yoga in binges," Ida said. "Sometimes constantly. Sometimes not at all."

"He didn't tell me he was going to perform," Emily said.

Genevieve had long blond hair, tiny lips, and normal eyes. Nothing special there. Still, she was beautiful. So was her husband.

"Maybe the camera finds something in her that I can't see," Emily said.

"You're too kind."

The actress stood between Eli and her husband and began nodding her head. Trent snapped his fingers. He and Eli looked like bandmates, with their plaid shirts and jeans and longish unkempt hair. Trent had a child's bongo cradled in the crook of his arm.

"Everybody get ready!" Trent called out.

"Are you okay?" Ida asked. "You look a little trembly."

"I'm fine. I bet they're going to announce his new nonprofit now."

"Everybody ready?" Eli yelled. The room nodded back at him.

"Wait, Jenny, come in front," Genevieve called out.

Emily felt a stab of something cold between her

ribs, as if someone had slipped a piece of ice down her shirt. While Emily and Ida watched, Jenny Alexandretti appeared out of nowhere and made it a foursome. Her dark ringlets were longer than Emily remembered and she had no bra on under her purple dress so she was bouncing all around. Her breasts seemed bigger, too. Everything about her looked bigger than when Emily had first seen her and thought of her as a wet mouse who needed care.

"Anybody seen my wife?" Eli said.

"Emily Babson?" Jenny called out. "Are you out there?"

"You should go to them," Ida said.

"He's just doing that for show. He knows I'd rather die than stand in front of all these people." Emily held her glass with both hands and took a deep breath.

"Hang on," Eli yelled. He parted the crowd and came straight for Emily. "Please?" he asked, when he got to her. "I need you."

"I'll hold your glass," Ida said, and took it away from Emily.

"Don't move, please," said Emily, looking at Ida. "I need to come back to you."

Emily arrived at the front of the room. She had her back to the crowd and she was staring at Trent, tiny-faced Genevieve, and Jenny.

"Honey, turn around. Stand here next to me," Eli said.

"The work wife makes way for the real wife," Jenny whispered loudly. She added a laugh, a *huh-huh* noise that felt very pointed and sexy to Emily. Very *I prefer men to women.*

"Let's get started," Eli said. "We're here to announce a new pro bono company."

"What's that company called?" Genevieve Winslow-Homer sang out.

The little group drew closer together. Jenny wrapped her arm around Emily.

Jenny said, "I haven't seen you in forever. How are you?"

"I'm good," Emily said as her ribs contracted and she fought her urge to see if the tips of Jenny's fingers were touching Eli's back. But how could she know? They were all pressed up so close to one another.

"Urban Bicycle Advocacy!" Eli yelled.

"Yeah, UBA," Jenny sang. "And what are we going to do?"

"Bike to the future!" The crowd called back. There might have been seventy people watching, all of them clapping hands and smiling.

Eli stepped forward and waved at the crowd. He said, "And I want to introduce you to the president of Urban Bicycle Advocacy, Jenny Alexandretti!"

And that was when Jenny bumped her. Jenny stepped forward and got her little ass around Emily. Then she bumped Emily so Emily was in the background, with her shoulder blades up against the mantel. It was a subtle move, a barely there knock on Emily's thigh. Emily felt herself disappear, though she was still onstage. She decided she was imagining that she'd been pushed. But no. She could feel Jenny's ass pressing against her, holding her back.

People began to clap. Jenny grabbed Eli's arm and took a quick bow. Emily looked left and right but saw no way to escape.

"Thank you all. And may I thank the founder of UBA for my title?" Jenny called. There was more clapping.

"Oh, shit." Emily had spoken out loud without meaning to. She covered her mouth. She looked at the back of the room and saw Ida gesture at her, *take it easy*.

"Can I hear you sing Urban Bicycle Advocacy," Genevieve sang. The four of them stood as one in front of Emily, surging forward away from her to connect with the crowd.

Everyone tried to sing "Urban Bicycle Advocacy . . ." to the tune of Bob Marley's "Get Up, Stand Up." But it didn't work at all and came out as more of a chant. Trent frowned and tried to find a rhythm on the bongo. A few people turned back toward the bar.

Emily watched Jenny grab Eli's hand and squeeze it. She began to whisper, "UBA, UBA." She used her other hand to bang on her hip. Emily shrank back from another kneading from Jenny's ass.

Jenny wailed, "Oo-bah, Oo-bah . . ."

That got the crowd's attention. Soon everybody jumped in, whispering, "UBA, UBA."

Emily saw two guys who must have been Rick and Steven race down the stairs from the floor above with their arms full of maracas that Emily imagined they had collected over many trips to different parts of South America. They tossed them into the outstretched arms of the crowd.

Jenny caught a maraca and began shaking it. Genevieve did, too. Eli began manically playing the banjo and Trent was clapping and singing.

"Oo-bah, Oo-bah . . ."

Eli sang, "Clap your hands and stomp your feet!"

"Oo-bah, Oo-bah," Emily mouthed. But she made no sound.

"Yeah, let's all bike everywhere and put those cars to shame!"

"Faster!"

"Roman Street, Roman Street!"

Emily locked eyes with Ida and mouthed *stay there*.

Eli yelled, "Between all of you and Roman Street we can raise awareness for UBA and then we can all . . ."

"Bike to the future!" Genevieve and Jenny jumped in the air.

The cheers were loud and everyone tried to dance in place without scuffing the rugs.

"Yay!" Jenny hopped on one foot. Then the four of them turned in to one another and did a high five that turned into a group hug while the crowd roared and then turned away, ready for more drinks and food. Emily was still stuck to the mantel.

"Join us," Jenny said and flailed a hand at Emily, who shook her head no and motioned at the back of the room, as if to say, it's okay, I've got somewhere over there where I have to be. Emily told herself she wasn't running back to Ida, but she also felt like it couldn't be helped if it looked that way. She walked quickly across the room and arrived at the doorway she'd been sharing with Ida.

"Thanks for sticking around."

"It didn't look so bad," Ida said with a smile. And Emily was shocked because she'd imagined it hadn't looked any way at all, and now she knew it must have looked awful. She closed her eyes and swayed and then felt Ida wrap an arm around her back.

"I'm okay," Emily whispered. "Look, I don't want to monopolize you. You must have other friends here." If Ida left her she would find a bathroom and lock herself in and cry. Her paperback copy of *Canoe* was in her purse. She would lock herself up with it for five sweet minutes and read the square dancing chapter and cry and then she would either feel better or slip out to the street without anyone noticing and cry some more.

"Emily. Hey, Emily?" Emily opened her eyes, and looked at Ida. She loved that Ida's huge eyes were glittering. "I'm filling in the blanks. He made her president without telling you? Is that what it is?"

"No, worse. He has a thing with that woman, Jenny. I'm sure of it."

"Hang on," Ida said. She reached around the doorway and came back with a sweating bottle of white wine. She had the cork out in a moment and was refilling their glasses. "It can't have gone that far if they pulled you in like that. They must want you to, like, interrupt it. I've been there. Me and Billy. We're a good team. It took a long time to get there, though. Other people flirt with you and you flirt back. You get in a fight over something stupid and you don't have sex for two straight weeks. It happens. But your husband—I can see that he wants you. He's just a little overexcited, with all the focus that's on him."

"He always gets attention. And we never had problems before but now you're saying even if . . ."

"Yes, even if," Ida said. "I think he's looking for you right now."

Emily turned her back to the room. She said, "I can't believe I just found out what's happening with my husband's business in a sing-along. Did you see her bump me?"

"She is a frisky little thing. He's coming this way," Ida said.

"You don't want to be here for this," Emily said. She tried but couldn't keep her cheeks and mouth from tugging down.

"Wasn't that amazing?" Eli called out.

Emily gulped and clamped a hand over the bottom of her face before turning toward her husband.

"What'd you think? I know. Goofy, right?" Eli looked at their full glasses. "Can I get you two some food? Cheese? I was talking to the caterers earlier and they've got some great little things coming out now, on platters."

"Yeah, Eli. Really great." Emily fought to keep her voice flat. "I'm just talking to Ida here. She's a friend from college."

Eli pushed his hair back and then shook hands with Ida. He said, "Ida, really nice to meet you."

"Congratulations on Roman Street and the new thing," Ida said. Eli nodded.

"We wanted you to be involved," Eli said to Emily. "I'm happy you got up there with us."

"And I'm surprised you're so far along with this new company. UBA? And Jenny is the president?"

"Yeah. I told you that. Didn't I tell you that?"

"You didn't." She gave up and let the anger show on her face. "I think we need to go somewhere and talk," Emily said.

Someone called Eli's name but he kept staring at his wife.

"Well, I've been trying to tell you about it. The final structure is barely three weeks old. And we just came up with a title for Jenny this afternoon, as, like, a thank-you. You know, 'cause we can't pay a lot because it's nonprofit but we can hand over this big title." Eli tried a laugh. "Don't you think that's smart?"

"There's a garden." Ida touched Emily's shoulder. "You go straight out that way, through the kitchen." Ida's eyes were impossibly wide and she looked straight at Emily. "It was good to see you. Let's get drinks soon and we can talk more."

"I would love that," Emily said. "I'll e-mail you."

"I have to go back to the party now," Eli said.

"Wait," Emily said to Eli. She gripped his arm. "We need to talk more." She hugged Ida goodbye without letting go of Eli. "The garden. Let's go there now."

"Why?" Eli asked. "Why now?"

Emily pulled at Eli's hand and whispered, "Give me five minutes."

"Okay, okay."

They walked quickly through the kitchen, past the waiters who were laying out trays of chicken satay and topping triangles of toast with beef or cheese and an asparagus tip, and down the iron-railed steps into the dark garden. Emily shivered

132

in the sudden cool of the empty garden and wished she hadn't given away her coat. The garden was long and rectangular and made up of two blue slate paths and wooden benches and little trees. She could hear cars rushing by on Greene Avenue. Emily found her footing and faced her husband.

She said, "You didn't tell me you were going to have her run UBA."

"I thought I just explained this?" Eli looked over her head at the bright kitchen windows and the noise of the party.

Emily felt electricity in her lips. She said, "You did something with her in L.A. I know you did."

"What are you talking about?"

"I know you did something. When you went there last month. I can feel it. I saw the text."

"You don't understand. That was, like, that was like a hug."

"A hug? Why are you using that word?"

Eli sighed. "We had a thing."

"A thing? Would you care to be one iota more specific?"

"I want to. Listen, I do. But at the same time, let's not get into specifics," Eli said. "It was basically less than what you think it was." Eli put his hands on her forearms. She shook him away. "Look, Emily, it would've been selfish to tell you. It would have made it bigger than it was."

"So you hid it?"

She watched him take a long breath. And in that breath she imagined that she could see how he had been in this position before, if not with other wives, then other girlfriends. He said, "You're right. You're right about everything and I am totally sorry and that is the worst thing I ever did and I am sorry."

"Hiding it didn't work so now you're admitting it?"

"This thing that happened when me and her were drunk? That was like a hug? A hug. Yeah. I mean, this is not the place to talk about it. I feel awful. But Emily, it happened because things were going well for the business. It was stupid, like a high five. I'm embarrassed to even be talking about it."

"A high five? Really, Eli? And now all you do is see her and plan things with her, and you lie to me and hide from me! Shit! Something's been wrong all summer!"

"All summer? That is not true! Please. I feel terrible about what happened and you are right and I'm sorry! I am sorry. But the two things are not related. UBA is hers. She found the investors and I'm just helping out. Look, don't make this bigger than it is."

"Make it bigger? Are you kidding me?"

"I said I'm sorry! You want to decide what's okay and what isn't. And then it doesn't matter in the end because nothing is okay according to you." He pushed his eyebrows together and shook his head. "I kind of hate that, that you do that."

"What? Now you hate how I am?"

"No. Forget it. Let's not ruin tonight, please?" She watched him try out a pleading smile. He said, "We can spend however long talking about what happened and I can swear I'll never do it again. I fucked up and I know that. I don't know what you saw in a text but nothing bad happened. Just let's not talk about it tonight, okay?"

"Eli?" A man looked down at them from the open kitchen door.

"Rick, I hear you, man," Eli said. "I know I need to be up there."

"We have to do another toast. The Neubergers came after all with some other people and so another quick toast is really important. Hi, Emily."

"Okay, okay," Eli said.

"Please give us a minute," Emily said.

"This toast is important," Rick said before closing his kitchen door.

Eli paced away from Emily, toward the back of the garden. She could see him touch the vines growing up the fence. It was darker back there than she thought the city should ever be.

"I can't believe this is happening," Emily said. "You don't see the emergency. You don't even know how big of a deal this is. Your mind can't even compute it."

"I do see! And I will. But look, if you really love me, give me some time right now, okay? Give me the time to do right by this party and then I am all about you. I owe you everything. I know that. And I love you."

"Owe me?" She dropped her head to one side. "What do you mean? We're married. It's not about owing me. Please—" She walked to the back of the garden and felt her way along the fence and found him. She reached out and touched his frowning face. His breath was hot and she could feel the sweat on his cheek and neck.

"How did we get here?" he asked. "I don't want this to be happening and neither do you. But right now? Give me the time I need now. And then we'll fix this thing, I promise."

"What happened is a big deal, Eli. I'm really hurt. Really fucking hurt."

"Look, I know. I want to focus on you. But I need to go back to the party now. Just for another hour, okay?"

He reached forward and kissed her on the lips before she could move. Then he turned and took several long steps through the garden. She thought he looked like a deer leaping across streams. No, not a deer. He was a satyr. No, he was the devil himself. He grabbed the stair rail and launched himself up the steps and was at the kitchen door. Once he was up there, safely far away from her, he turned. She couldn't see his expression. She was sure he hadn't said anything. He slipped into the house and left the door swinging open behind him. Emily listened to a burst of clapping.

She looked up at the light shining from the tall kitchen windows and heard a surge of noise from the party. She turned and threaded her fingers through the fencing and the vines. There was only the one way out of the garden and that was up the stairs, through the door, and back through the kitchen. She would have to walk through those crowded rooms.

"Eli?" she whispered to herself. "You went back to the party?"

The garden was quiet. There was only the sound of idling engines in the street. She covered her mouth with her hand and wrapped her other arm around her chest. She stared up at the bright dancing light that streamed through the windows of the house.

From *Marriage Is a Canoe*,
Chapter 3, Marriage and Intimacy

Out on the porch at about five o'clock one afternoon, after we'd been on the lake for hours without a catch, I sat with my legs swinging and whittled a stick. Pop had given me a three-inch pocket knife with a pearl handle and I'd taken to whittling little sticks with an eye toward eventually assembling a miniature raft.

I could hear Pop and Bess moving about behind me in the kitchen. I didn't know what they were doing. I was bored the way boys are bored when they say they are bored but they mean something deeper: confused, adrift. Though at least I had it in me to whittle.

"What are we up to?" I asked. I had been there about ten days and I was beginning to think of the three of us as a group. Not a true family, but three people living together.

"Your Pop and I are going for a walk."

"Around the lake? Which way?" I jumped up. I much preferred lake walks that took us toward town, because if we ended up there, I might buy a pack of baseball cards and check the Yankees scores.

"We are going round the long way, and then up to the ridge."

"Okay." I pushed myself up so I was standing.

"You might go into town on your own," Bess said.

"Alone?" I raised an eyebrow and dared to glare at her. I did not like what I was hearing.

"Go ahead." Bess moved closer to me. "Take some time for yourself and we'll do the same. We love you. You know that. But we want a little time to be together." She kissed my forehead and left me there, on the porch.

I had a piece of chamois cloth and I began to wrap up my stick and knife in it. I heard Pop and Bess talking in the house but I didn't listen. Instead, I went down the steps and stood out on the grass. I kicked at the grass and pulled out the knife and threw it down into the dirt, hard, so it stuck in the soft earth.

"Hey, there," Pop said. He'd come up behind me. When he wanted to he could move very quietly for such a big man. "Listen up, now. Don't get yourself in a snit. We take a little time each day to be alone together—just me and my Bess. You understand." He gave me a mock salute and went back inside the house.

I got my knife and wiped it on my shorts and then wrapped it and the stick in that chamois. I ran and put the bundle safely away in my room and changed into my jeans. Off I went, hurt, and never looking back.

In that day's dusk, I walked down to Main Street

and that's where I saw Honey for the first time, walking with her parents. So I knew for sure something more than good comes of giving those close to you time for themselves. What happened after I saw Honey, you ask? That's another chapter.

Find time to be together every day—
just the two of you—
in your canoe.

Peter, September 2011

"I'll come down and fire him myself," Peter said. He banged open the hall closet and grabbed his coat. "I'll be there in twenty minutes."

"Peter, I'm not asking you to intervene," Henry said. "I'll handle it."

"Let me get it straight," Peter said, and turned back to his kitchen, where he grabbed up his cup of coffee and took a sip. "A cook's been there three weeks. He closes down the kitchen for the night, drinks a couple of bottles of our wine, beds down on the rice sacks, ends up setting fire to a wall with a cigarette, and you're going to have a talk with him? He's gone!"

"No. First I have to bring in the insurance people and file a report and all that. I know how to handle this," Henry said.

"This is crazy. He's finished. I'm coming down there."

"Stop. Do I have to spell it out for you?"

"What?"

"You can't fire him. He's new. He doesn't even know who you are. I was trying to get across what a pain in the ass running this business is. That's all."

Peter sat down at his kitchen table, nodded at the trees outside his window. "I get it."

"Can you believe this asshole? We'll take care of it. What about coming in for some lunch? We're auditioning an eggplant dish."

"I'll be in later this week. I can't stand eggplant. I used to like it. But not anymore."

"Got some mail here for you."

"Yeah. It can wait. I'm sorry I misunderstood you. I'll talk to you later."

Peter ended the call and stood up. He put his coffee mug in the sink, ran cold water over it, and placed it on the wooden rack. He licked at his dry lips and tasted the bad old-man smell that seeped out of the widening spaces between his teeth.

He heaved himself out of the kitchen and went to the hutch in the front foyer. He was afraid to call Maddie now that he'd told her he would move to the West Coast with her. Surely someone else needed him. Surely . . . yes. He found the phone number for the young woman from Ladder & Rake. Stella. Sexy name.

He had worked with quite a few young women during his many years with LRB. His favorites had been flirtatious; a few had been strangely inept, some had been curt, and one or two had been entrepreneurial. These smart ones got around Lisa and tried hard to draw him out. They were handling editors but they were also ever-so-carefully interested in a new book from him. A new book meant big money. But they all lived with the fear that he might not return their calls and Helena would find out they lost him.

He dialed the number. Voice mail. He apologized for the few days he had taken to return her call and said he was free to talk.

And then he went for a walk around the lake. He felt the cold on his face and wrapped an old wool scarf of Lisa's around his neck. Kept going. He hadn't thought about LRB in so long. The one-million-copies party they'd had for him at the end of the seventies. And then the party for twenty-five years in print at the Grill Room at the Four Seasons. Helena had presided over both events. Could she still be there? Most likely she'd retired to the little house he had heard she'd bought in the village of Sag Harbor, where she could spend her days gardening and her evenings at intimate dinner parties with Ed Doctorow and his wife and Louis Begley and the rest of her old publishing friends. Or maybe she'd left that snobby scene. Maybe she had a new husband—he believed she'd broken with the old one. A new husband would mean getting used to a new life. Perhaps there were stepchildren in addition to her daughter, Elizabeth. He was sure she was still close to Elizabeth. The one bit of gossip he'd heard was that Helena had been heartbroken when her daughter had gone to Stanford and had never gotten over the new distance between them.

He found the big black rock he'd always liked

and settled on it until he felt the shock of cold through his lined khakis. The clouds were hanging low. But maybe a cold tailbone and brisk weather were good things. He kneaded his hands against his knees. Lisa had been seated next to Helena at a few dinners in the early years, when he and Lisa still ventured down to New York for publicity and marketing meetings. Helena had been the key to the book's success, so Lisa had tolerated her as best she could.

Okay. Enough of this indulging. He was freezing his butt off. He whistled the opening sequence to *A Fistful of Dollars* to himself as he made his way back home. He'd watched the movie the previous evening once he was sure Maddie wasn't going to visit him. He was surprised at how much he still loved the movies he'd watched when he was young. If Maddie didn't come around again tonight, he planned to find *Duck, You Sucker* on Netflix and watch it on Lisa's computer screen if he had to. Belinda had given him a couple of CDs of Ennio Morricone's film scores when she'd caught him watching *The Good, the Bad and the Ugly* late one night, the year before, when Lisa was dying and she had stayed over. She'd discovered him huddled on the couch, crying into his shirt sleeve. The only thing he'd found to say in the moment was, "I just love this music." The CDs were probably in a downstairs closet and he would find them. He might put a speaker up to one of the windows that opened onto the back porch and listen while he looked out at the lake. Sure. He ought to do something like that at least once before moving out to live in a high-rise condominium in San Francisco.

The phone was ringing as he came through the back door.

"Hello? No, now's a good time to talk," he said, once he'd settled himself with the cordless on the hard chair by the hutch in the front hall. He tried to cross his legs. Nope, couldn't do it.

Stella went on for a while, introducing herself. And then he heard her say, "Really, we want you just as you are."

"Want me just as I am? I don't understand." He laughed but refrained from the easy joke, from saying, You mean finished? Packing up? Getting out of town?

"You've helped so many people. Now we want to bring you and your book to an even larger audience. And that's why we came up with a contest."

"A contest?"

"We want to send a winning couple to visit you later this fall. You just sit and chat with them. They're the winners."

"Chat? You mean about marriage?"

"Yes. I know it sounds weird, but we think it will really strike the right chord with the public. Don't you agree?"

He breathed in loud enough so she could hear. He didn't imagine he had actually helped any of the couples he'd talked with over the years. He mostly managed to weasel out of any sort of in-depth conversation. There was that period in the late seventies when evenings found him at the Sally Forth bar, drinking good scotch for free and talking to just about anybody. But then that scene had gone bad and they had to shut down the bar. He didn't remember that period so well. Of course, *Canoe* did affect some people deeply. He knew that. But hanging around with him didn't enhance the reading experience, that was for sure. Then again, he was usually pretty good at making people feel like they were glad they checked in with him. People found him emotionally intuitive. He kind of was.

"Well, I wrote the book on it, didn't I?" he asked, partly to reassure himself and partly to see what she'd say.

"Yes, yes of course you did. It's funny that you put it that way because that's just how I like to say it around the office."

"And I'd need to stay where I am for a little while, wouldn't I?"

"Do you mean stay in Millerton? Why, yes," Stella said. "To welcome the winners."

"I don't know."

"We can offer you . . . forty thousand dollars against future advances for your participation.

And another forty thousand in six months if sales substantially increase, let's say by two hundred percent beyond where they are now. There's paperwork on this that I can send you."

"My wife used to negotiate for me," he said. "At first I didn't have an agent. And then my wife was my agent. We were never sure if we had a good deal. But we always remembered to ask for the best that could be offered."

"I've been empowered to offer you the best possible amendment to your contract. I can assure you of that."

"You know, the more I talk with you, the better I like your idea. Let's do it."

"Wonderful," Stella said. "And I hope you won't find me too forward when I say that I'm surprised we're seeing so eye to eye on this contest! After so many years of you . . . keeping to yourself."

"Was I doing that? I don't think so. I've just been minding my own business." There was something else he wanted to ask. He wanted to know whether Helena had retired. "Tell me, is Helena Magursky still working at LRB?"

"Yes, she's our president. She asked after you. Do you have a message you want me to pass on to her?"

"No, no. I'm just curious. She was my first editor. It's been a lot of years . . ."

"I've been here just less than one year," Stella

said. "But I can't tell you how excited I am to work with you now!"

"Yes, I'm looking forward to it, too."

"Will you want to see our marketing materials before we release them? I can't exactly give you approval—but I can at least involve you in the process."

"No, no. Do what you like. I'm sure you know how to do your job. I trust you. I just want to meet the nice young couple. Let's make them young, please. And solid. They ought to be solid, handsome people. That will make things smoother."

"Of course. We'll send you a few essays and you can select your favorite. And we'll check their backgrounds as best we can."

"That's smart. I'm glad to talk with you, Stella. It's better to call in the mornings. I'm most—I'm at my best then."

After the call was over, he was surprised to discover that he did want to drive to town and catch up with Henry and look over the damage from the fire. But Henry was right. He would observe but he wouldn't interfere with the life of the inn. Who needed the trouble? He only wanted to have lunch with an old friend. But he'd be damned if Henry would get him to try the eggplant.

Press release for the
"Win a Day with Peter Herman Contest,"
sponsored by Ladder & Rake Books,
a division of Timmler Products, Inc.

AN ANNIVERSARY AND CONTEST
FOR *MARRIAGE IS A CANOE*

Peter Herman's *Marriage Is a Canoe*, continuously in print since it was first published by Ladder & Rake in 1971, is the preeminent self-help book of our time on love and marriage.

Marriage Is a Canoe is the spellbinding true story of Peter Herman's thirteenth summer, which he spent with his grandparents on Lake Okabye, near Millerton, New York, in 1961. During that summer, Peter absorbed lessons about life and marriage from his grandparents, largely while trout fishing with his grandfather.

Mr. Herman wrote his book directly after graduating from Columbia University, where he received a degree in English. He wrote in the mornings and at lunch while working as an advertising copywriter for McCann Erickson in New York City. The first edition was published in October 1971, when Mr. Herman was twenty-three. It is his only published work.

This sensational book began its life as a gift edition–size hardcover emblazoned with a painting of two figures paddling a canoe on a lake at sunset—a timeless American image meant to appear nostalgic. *Canoe* sold 5,900 copies in that first edition, copies that are now rare and worth thousands. Since then, *Marriage Is a Canoe* has been in print as a paperback Ladder & Rake Evergreen edition, with three distinct revisions, five new forewords, and several afterwords, addendums, and notes to new and old readers. There are over two million copies of *Marriage Is a Canoe* in print, and thirty-eight foreign editions.

The book has never appeared on *The New York Times* or *USA Today* bestseller lists because expert publishing analysts have called it the most shared self-help volume in the world. At the same time, its consistent sales over so many years must be attributed to the undeniable universal wisdom that every reader discovers in the book's anecdotes.

Two thousand eleven marks the fiftieth anniversary of the events upon which the book is based. In celebration of this anniversary, beginning on October 1st and ending on November 1st, Ladder & Rake will hold a contest. The winners of that contest—one lucky married couple, a couple with normal everyday problems—will visit with Peter Herman.

All contest entries must be no longer than two hundred words. The most compelling dozen entries will be read by Peter Herman, who will select our winning couple. Then, on a Saturday in November, toward the end of leaf season, he will meet them for a stroll around Lake Okabye followed by afternoon tea and supper at his home in upstate New York.

Our winning couple will also enjoy a complimentary weekend at the Lake Okabye Inn, in Millerton, New York. They will receive the entire back catalog of important self-help books from Ladder & Rake, and a signed first edition of *Marriage Is a Canoe*.

One hundred second-prize winners will receive signed copies of the new, fiftieth anniversary edition of *Marriage Is a Canoe*, to be released with selected new commentaries in a handsome collectible hardcover edition, priced at $40.00 and available to all for purchase in late December 2011.

Emily, September 2011

"I'm serious," Eli said. "Please hold my hand."

Emily and Eli were walking on the Brooklyn Bridge, toward Manhattan. Eli had on sunglasses so Emily couldn't quite see his eyes. His hair was standing up in places and he had on a furry white pullover Patagonia sweater that made him look like a sheep, a handsome, dark-headed sheep.

She took his hand, but didn't speak. He pulled off his sunglasses and gave her the same pleading look he'd been using constantly since the UBA party. They had been through several bad days, arguing over what had happened and what it meant for them. Eli would not stop apologizing. Emily couldn't figure out what to do. She had told herself they were married and she couldn't imagine that what had happened would destroy their marriage. She had tried to stress to herself how tiny and meaningless the infraction had been. She had talked to her mother, who agreed with her. But she felt she had lost all control of their situation, and frustratingly, she no longer possessed a clear vision of their future. She was now back in a place she thought she would never have to visit again, where she had to be patient and wait and see where her life was headed.

Canoe had never suggested that marriage ought to contain this sense of loneliness and loss.

They arrived at the spot where the wooden slats ended and the walkway turned to concrete. Emily immediately missed the slats. They were scary because a crazy person could come and saw through them and then everyone would fall into the East River, but at the same time, on the slats you were suspended and buoyant—there was rushing air all around you. The concrete meant you were coming down from that suspension. Her footfalls were harder and she turned back to look at the wooden part of the bridge.

"Watch out for the bikers," Eli said.

"I am. I always do." She glared at him.

They were planning to see Sherry in *Flight*, her new play at the Minetta Lane Theatre. But they had a few hours and they weren't hungry. It was windy out. Emily suddenly yanked her hand away from Eli and wrapped her coat tightly around her. She'd been so proud, just a few hours ago—of being able to fight through this funk for long enough to wriggle into her pale gray skirt and charcoal tights, her brown suede flats. In the mirror she'd had a moment of fantasy of looking like Gwyneth Paltrow, at her absolute gloomiest, with darker brown hair. Then Eli had come in to the bedroom and told her how beautiful she looked and the furtiveness in his eyes pushed her right back into that awful over-landscaped garden in Fort Greene. She flashed back to the minutes that she'd stood alone in the garden before Eli came back down the stairs, after the toast, and begged again for her to forgive him. She'd carefully gone back into the house with him, found her coat on a steel rack in the hall, and left. Eli hadn't stopped her. That was on the list now of things she was not sure she would be able to figure out how to forget. That had been four days ago. She was keeping a list in her head of the moments when Eli had incontrovertibly failed her.

Eli kept opening his mouth and then stopping, swallowing his words. Finally, he said, "This play—Sherry has a good supporting role?"

"It's an ensemble."

"I thought this was the one about the photographer who is just back from Iraq?"

"That was the last one."

"I went to the last one," Eli said, carefully. "The one about the family that was all women in lead roles, the Chekhov one."

"That was the one before last." Emily wiped from her eyes the tears that always came with the wind.

"Tell me the plot of this one."

"No."

"No?"

"No, I don't want to tell you the plot of Sherry's play right now."

Eli took a deep breath. He said, "What do you

154

want me to do? I know it was awful! I am awful! I am furious with myself. But I love you. And I can wait—I'll wait for however long it takes for you to forgive me."

"Let's not talk about it."

"Then tell me about the play. So we don't have to talk about it. Please."

"Fine," she said. "Ready? Sherry talked so much about it that I know the story by heart."

"I have an idea," Eli said. "I know we're headed toward Bleecker and Sixth but let's veer far west, into Tribeca, on the way there. It's calmer and there's not so many tourists. If we're late we can take a cab."

"That sounds fine."

"Okay, the play. Ready."

She said, "A winged man crashes through the ceiling of a penthouse where a dinner party is going on, in an unnamed city. The dinner is for a young couple who are going to announce their engagement to the bride's parents, who don't want them to be married. They don't trust the fiancé because of a financial deal that has nearly bankrupted all of them."

"He's an angel," Eli said.

"Maybe he is. Anyway, he crashes into this apartment, the winged man, right when they're eating oysters. Sherry had to learn how to open oysters without cutting herself. They throw the shells at him. He's like a seagull or some seabird."

"Is that a metaphor?"

"Yeah, he's vermin, like a rat. Then he starts talking to them. They reveal all their problems to him and he says he finds their problems really fascinating. He says they are problems of the ground and not the air."

Eli nodded, looking forward. He said, "I get that."

"You do?" she asked. "I didn't. I thought it was, like, the worst line I've ever heard." She arched an eyebrow at him. "Come on. You should be laughing at this."

"No, I'm really listening. He's an angel, right? Angels talk like that."

"I think I already said that I don't think that's clarified."

"Sherry is the bride?"

"Yes. She didn't tell me the end. She wants me to be surprised. She might go off with the winged man. I know someone goes off with the winged man."

"Through the roof?"

"Let's hope."

Eli pursed his lips. He adjusted his sunglasses and then quickly took them off. His brown-and-violet eyes were bright and she thought it seemed like the sunset was reflected in them.

They slowed down in the human traffic of City Hall Park. A teenage girl checked Eli out. She had on tight blue jeans and a puffy jacket and she was pushing a baby carriage with her boyfriend. A pair of female security guards on a bench outside a back entrance to Tweed Courthouse watched Eli through their cigarette smoke. They were definitely gay and they gave him a good slow appraisal anyway. Emily used to think it was funny, that he was so good-looking. Because it didn't matter. He belonged to her. And yet again, in a way that felt like a fresh hurt every time it hit her, he just didn't feel like hers anymore. She began to cry.

He turned to her, fast. He said, "Fine. Let's talk about it again. Let's begin with me apologizing like it's the first time I've done that. It was the second worst thing I ever did, what I did with you in that garden. And the first thing was with Jenny and that was just idiocy. I fooled around with her and it went too far and I am sorry. I will always be sorry. I just want this problem to go away and for things to be like they were before."

"Fooled around?"

"It was just that. Sex. It was nothing."

"You left me out there in the garden. Now you're telling me this?"

"Yes. Sex. Okay, I said it. I hate myself for it. Jenny and I had a meeting yesterday. She's going to move back to Los Angeles. You are never going to see her again. I probably never will either. I wasn't going to tell you till it's official, but let's call it official right now."

"Moving back across the country is kind of a big reaction to something you keep trying to diminish." Emily walked faster.

"It is and it isn't. She wants to go back to L.A. She's upset about it, too. It never should have happened."

They walked along Church Street, past the strip of tiny fast-food restaurants. Emily had consulted on the logo and mission statement for 5 Napkin Burger. The place was empty. Then they passed a couple of bars where they'd been very drunk once, years ago when they were dating. She drank whisky sours and was so hungover the next day she almost couldn't see. She remembered vomiting in the bathroom of his old apartment on Mott Street while he was in the kitchen making blueberry pancakes and she felt the beginning of being in love with him. They weren't big drinkers. They had just been out of control and they were falling in love. They passed Babezta, a store that sold children's clothes. She fixated on a tiny red-and-green plaid shirt that was achingly cute and then quickly looked away.

"You can hold my hand," she said.

"You're sure? Even though we're fighting?"

"You don't want to?" she asked. "All I'm asking is for you to hold my hand."

They held hands and turned and began to head uptown. She didn't know which street they were on. Then she saw that it was Hudson, a lovely windblown street that was utterly wasted on what had become a terrible late Saturday afternoon.

She breathed with her mouth open and fought back her anger. Sex. At least it had a concrete name now. Sex was clearer than hug. She held his hand as tight as she could. She sucked in her lower lip and bit at it, feeling pain and what she imagined might be blood on her tongue.

"I mean it about her moving," Eli said. "I know it's irrelevant to what's going on with us, but it's still true. She cares about this business. I understood that and I was—I did—set her up to go away. She can take UBA anywhere. The idea is she takes it to L.A., where it makes sense. We don't actually need more bicycle advocacy in New York. And she's got a boyfriend out there."

"I don't want to talk about her."

"You'll never have to." Eli kept nodding his head. "Never again."

"You can't make her move. And that doesn't solve it. You shouldn't think it will."

"She wants to. The boyfriend is serious, I think. She was trying to get away from him when she moved here. But she's realized she loves him."

"She cheated, too?"

"Stop it. It wasn't like that. Stop saying that."

"I'm sorry," she said. But she didn't mean she was sorry—her mind had drifted for a moment, past this impasse, to where they might be better. He did seem contrite. Likely, it had happened more than once. She discovered that she could admit this to herself. There were worse things. A million worse things. She had arrived at the entirely logical conclusion that it was worse than what either of them was saying aloud, because he was taking it so seriously. And yet, even her mother had begun to say it was a fixable thing. Still, though. Sex was a betrayal. She walked for a few steps, staring forward and not realizing that she'd dropped Eli's hand. Then, when she couldn't feel him next to her, she turned around and looked back.

He was down on his knees in the middle of the sidewalk, facing her. He wasn't smiling or laughing. He was just staring at her.

"What are you doing?"

"Please come back to me, Emily."

"What?"

"I am on my knees."

She looked around, embarrassed, and saw that they were at the little triangle of park at Hudson and Duane, Duane Park. People passed the two of them. They glanced back at Eli, who only looked up at her.

"Why are you doing that? You look like a monk." She walked a few steps back, toward him.

"I promise you I will never, never do that again. Not any of it. You mean everything to me. These last few weeks are like a watershed. I fucked up. I will never fuck up again. I swear."

She kept staring. His voice was different—solemn and without any levity. He did belong to her. They could make it that way again. She liked that.

"Are you getting a marriage proposal?"

Emily looked up at the person talking. It was not a crazy person, just an older woman walking a tiny curly-haired dog. The woman looked charmed. The dog yipped at its owner. It wanted to keep walking.

"Am I?" Emily asked, and then covered her mouth.

"That's so sweet!" The woman picked up the dog and whispered, "Say yes—he's so serious. It's beautiful. I won't get in your moment, but say yes."

Eli smiled his brilliant smile. "Don't you think she should say yes?"

Two women came around the corner of the park. One of them said, "She looks ready to cry. Get her to say yes before she does!"

And then a few other people saw the situation and jumped in, calling, "Say yes, say yes." A man in a truck yelled it and a few teenagers hanging out at the fountain in the middle of the little park called out at them. At the same time, there were others who walked by and ignored the scene. But even the people who ignored them were smiling.

Emily frowned. She pulled in mouthfuls of cool

air and then called out "Yes!" as loud as she could. Just to get everyone to leave them alone. To make it stop.

There was scattered clapping and Eli jumped up and hugged her.

"Wasn't that amazing?" he asked. "I love this quiet park. And wasn't that great, with everybody helping us? You know I planned this whole thing."

She didn't want to say that she still felt unsure. She leaned in and let him kiss her hard, her mouth going soft against his, the long kiss if not truly erasing than at least glossing, sexing over everything that had gone wrong.

They held hands as they continued up Hudson Street.

"I want everything to be okay," she said to him. "I hate what happened, though. I want you to know that. I hate it and I am not going to forget it."

"Do you accept my apology?"

"Is she really moving away?"

"Yes. I promise she will. But that isn't important. What's important is that I'm devoted to you."

"I want her to go away. I want it to be like this didn't happen." Emily set her jaw. She was vanquishing Jenny Alexandretti. Making her leave their lives and forcing Eli to be truly humbled and contrite and even more hers. Or, hers again.

"It's done. I love you so much. This is done.

162

She'll go live with her boyfriend in L.A. and you and I can go back to how we were."

"Not how we were," she said. "Not with you feeling free to do what you did."

"No, better. Of course I'll never do it again. I'll be better."

Emily didn't say anything about better. She didn't trust better. She wanted them to be different than the way they were before. And she wanted never to have another moment like the one in that garden. Eli would have to get rid of a part of himself that she hadn't known was there. The part of him that could have an affair. She wasn't sure it could be done. But she would have to let him try.

"You promise?" She looked up at him. He had his arm wrapped around her and she let herself be tightly pulled into him, his furry sweater against her cheek.

"I promise," he said. "We'll never have a bad moment like that again."

"You didn't even get on your knees when you proposed."

"This is like—it's like we're really married now."

She didn't respond. She felt a little bit better. But she didn't feel good enough to admit that to Eli, not just yet.

Stella Petrovic, October 2011

Dear Peter Herman,

My wife is leaving me. We did what you said and it didn't work. I know we don't get money back from her purchase of your stupid book.

But can I have something back? You don't have anything in there about exterior problems. Let's call them that, okay? I don't have lots of money and she doesn't either. So we don't. Both our sets of parents undercut us emotionally sometimes—pretty often, actually, now that I think about it. We both work too hard at jobs we don't love. You don't get into what to do about those circumstances. You say support support support. In the canoe. We never go in the canoe.

Why'd we blow it when you make it sound so easy. I'm angry. I want to die.

The only thing we have to thank you for is for not writing another stupid book.

I would like to win the contest so my wife and I can come to your home and talk these things out with you.

Likamy Sobstory, from Fukyu, MA!

At least it had levels to it, and humor. For some reason Stella had begun to receive entries via regular mail, dozens each day, though she'd said that e-mail was fine. She had a couple of assistants from marketing reading the e-mail entries but she couldn't stop opening the envelopes. She took her knife and slit open another. A whiff of ashtray hit her nostrils. She shrank back and groaned. With one arm thrown over her nose and mouth she read:

Dear Peter,

Please keep this confidential because, in the event that we win the contest, I may choose not to reveal what I am writing to you about now. I make love with a man who is not my husband.

My husband is a nice person and he helps me with upkeep on our house and he makes sure the two kids have their lunches and he loves me and even does a good job with our bills. But he does not satisfy me with his lovemaking. No, that is something I like to do with a man from work and sometimes with another man who is his friend. We do it in parking lots in the back of his van. Sometimes there are others. Otherwise we are normal. Am I a sex addict?

Can you help me and my husband? I know he knows because sometimes I hear him in the bathroom crying in the night. And I get so angry and yell at him about it—about what I do without saying what it is that I do. I know we can be fixed. If I can learn to get my husband to satisfy me? Can you teach us how to do this? We are very open sexually. Or at least I am. And you can watch us try to do it and tell us what is the matter. Because I want to get out of doing it in the van with near-strangers and back to sex inside my home with my hubby!

Matilda Gutierrez, Houston, TX

Dear Peter Herman:

I need help with my wife. She threatens to leave me. It is because of money. How can I be held responsible for the miserable state of the economy in this country? I need you to help explain this to her.

Thank you for considering.

Alan Chowski, Philadelphia, PA

Dear Peter Herman,

My husband's name is David and he yells at me when I am sick. He has some problem with sickness so if I cough he locks me in the basement until I say I won't cough more. How can we make him stop???

Other times he is nice to me and we live in a nice house and I know it is abusive. He makes the money for us in his job as a school superintendent and when I say let's go into counseling he says that would only make it worse if I found out how much is the matter with me. Maybe he is right. I don't know, but if we win the contest he would be shamed into going with me to see you and together we could keep David from making me wash all my clothes every day to keep away the germs from him. And burn my underwear at the end of my monthly.

It is getting crazy and I want to run away but maybe your contest is the answer.

I hope we win and then we can visit you and talk.

Anne-Marie Wilkinson, Sherman Oaks, CA

Stella had developed a form letter for these, much like her form rejection letter for unsolicited manuscripts. It listed national hotlines, websites, and organizations that offered counseling. She doubted this was corporately aboveboard, but that didn't stress her out much—she figured she was on moral high ground.

She took a form letter from the top of a stack and wrote, "Your problems sound serious. Please get the help you need immediately," across the top and sent it to Anne-Marie Wilkinson. Then she tossed the rest of the letters in the cardboard box she kept in the credenza, behind her desk.

There were now a few hundred of them, each

one hopeless and upsetting in shocking combinations. She had not imagined there could be so many awful marriages and she was worried that all the human tragedy would rub off on her. What if she brought other people's problems into bed with her and Ivan? She suspected that was already happening.

She hadn't yet found an entrant whose marriage seemed fixable. There was certainly no top ten. And she had planned since the beginning to find a letter from a couple who were easily promotable, who weren't in danger of not staying together. But apparently, once you bothered to enter such a contest, your chance of staying together was long gone. She should have known that. Stella kicked at the cardboard box. She stared up at the quotes from *Canoe* that she had printed out in twenty-eight-point type on white paper and stuck on her bulletin board.

> *Love infinitely and without question,*
> *as if the long days of summer will never end.*
> —Chapter 14, On Doubt

> *Remember that when a man breaks his promise*
> *in love, he breaks a promise to himself, too.*
> —Chapter 3, Marriage and Intimacy

She found her phone and texted Ivan.
Where are you later?

She felt too bummed about the contest to sound any cuter. If she didn't make the thing work, Helena Magursky was going to have her ID card snipped in half. Or, no. If she didn't make the contest work, she'd just evaporate, like the slick of coffee she left at the bottom of her ceramic LRB cup at the end of each day. Invited to no more meetings. Lord knew she'd heard of it happening before. Good editors suddenly isolated, left off e-mail chains about their own books and ignored in the big meetings until they were seen marching down the hall with one of the young women from HR, handbag in hand, sometimes crying. Stop! Stella knew she was being ridiculous. She was smart and everything would be fine. She prayed for just one good letter.

Ivan texted back. They would meet in a few hours at Randy's Shake-It-Up, a new bar near her apartment with awesome deviled eggs. It would be crowded. Or they could just go back to her place and watch a movie on her computer and eat the Thai vegetables and tofu she had leftover from the weekend. Maybe Ivan would be up for that and then later they could have sex. Or maybe not. God, lately she could so take it or leave it and she blamed her depressing job for this since it felt like it was taking over everything. But wasn't this all her idea? Yeah, better to go for some deviled eggs later, some bubbly drinks made with whiskey, and then passionate sex. Throw away the leftovers.

She was still young and deserved to have a good time.

She looked down at a new text from Ivan:

Tonight we splish-splash, tomorrow we figure out how to right this sinking canoe.

Ha. She exhaled as loudly as she could and opened yet another entry.

Dear Peter,

If you ask me, and my husband does all the time, I don't know how to love. Can you teach me how? But I don't want to come to you with my husband, I want to come to you alone, naked and vulnerable . . .

Stella crumpled the letter, tossed it in the air, and slumped back in her seat.

From *Marriage Is a Canoe*,
Chapter 4, What Is Marriage?

We were out on the lake most mornings by eight o'clock. Of course Pop and Bess woke up earlier than me each day. When I heard them moving about, I struggled to wake, and man I wanted to get up. I wanted to catch a fish. I loved the rhythm of our days.

It was just eleven in the morning, on a Friday, at the end of our second week together. We hadn't caught anything and it was hot. We could hear Roger Miller singing "In the Summertime You Don't Want My Love" on a workman's radio, far across the lake. I had on my Yankees hat. I remember taking it off and using it to wipe the sweat from my brow.

"Want to eat now, Peter? It's early but I can see you're hungry."

"You bet I am."

Pop unpacked the wax paper–wrapped sand-wiches Bess made for us. There was olive loaf and Muenster cheese cut thick, which Pop bought from his friend Jake Duncan who ran the deli counter at the A&P in town. There were bright green leaves of Bibb lettuce pulled from the garden the previous evening, and dense slices of sourdough bread that Bess baked herself every few days, all smeared with the tomato jam that Pop and Bess had made together in the kitchen on the morning of the Fourth of July before we all went into town to buy sparklers.

He said, "We had your mother on the telephone last night. Did you hear us?"

"Nope," I said. "I must've been reading *King Arthur*. Or I was already sleeping. How's she doing?"

"She'll be okay." He frowned and looked down the length of the lake, toward that tinny music.

"Pop?"

"Yes, Peter?"

"What do you think happened between my mom and dad?"

Pop wiped his mouth with a blue cotton bandana he kept in his hip pocket. He rocked his head left and right on his shoulders, to the point where I worried he was hurting himself.

"This'll be tough to hear. But your parents, well, they just about shat all over their marriage is what they did."

I tried not to gasp. I'd never heard him curse before and that word, *shat,* so formal and yet a curse word nonetheless, slithered up and slapped me harder than any person ever had.

"All that arguing? And none of the tenderness and loving that marriage needs. Bess and I could see it from up here. It burns me, I'll tell you."

"Why?"

"We brought up your mother as best we could and I'm goddamned if she paid attention for a single moment because—" I watched him stop himself.

"Because what?"

"Because none of this would have happened if she had just listened!"

"That's not fair!" I yelled. I drew my knees to my forehead and brought my arms around my head so I could see nothing but the dark bottom of that canoe and my sneakers, so I couldn't feel the shaking that came from my crying, or the words ringing in my ears.

"Okay, now. You're right. That wasn't fair. I apologize. Don't tell Bess I spoke that way. She wouldn't like it."

We stayed quiet. The lake surrounded us and it was as if it were whispering, Quiet, be quiet. It'll take a while to heal.

"Why didn't my mom listen?"

"Because she was drunk a lot of the time and the rest of the time she was ashamed of it. At least she recognized that you might be a bit of a storyteller and in this way you're like Bess and me. I'll shut my big mouth now."

I raised my head. I said, "Come on, Pop. What's one thing you wanted her to know?"

"It's just a simple thing."

"All right. Tell me and I'll remember it."

"No you won't."

"C'mon. Please, Pop?"

He raised his eyebrows and held one finger up to that hot blue-and-white sky and said, "In locus marriage. When we are together, be with me. Know that even when it isn't perfect, it is sacred. Never let the locus of the marriage erode. It is a sacred ground and you must always celebrate it and be grateful that you may live your life upon it. Be tough about this! Adhere to it."

"But she's not tough, Pop."

"I know. It's not her fault. They went bad together. It hurts, but it's not anybody's fault. But you can remember what I said, can't you? Save it inside for one day when you grow up and get married. You're a city boy and you're tough."

"Yes," I said. I understood that he was desperate, that my Pop needed to believe that in my life I would do what his daughter could not in hers. "I'll remember."

Your marriage is sacred.
When you are together, be with each other.

Emily, October 2011

"I didn't say I agreed with Mom," Sherry said.

"You sure are saying that! You're acting like it."

"Well . . ." Sherry frowned. They were in Emily's living room. It was Monday evening. Sherry was curled up on a red suede club chair that Eli had gotten from a furniture maker in Bushwick in a trade for a bicycle, partly to surprise Emily, he'd said. She didn't like it as much as he did.

"You look good in that chair, Sherry. You look sexy," Emily said.

"I told you I'd take it off your hands if you can get someone to deliver it," Sherry said. "It's kind of unusual that Mom would say this is a fixable problem, you know? I guess I do agree with her."

"I was surprised at how clear she was about it," Emily said.

"When's he coming home?"

"Probably in an hour." Emily stretched farther out on the couch, put her hands behind her head, looked at the ceiling.

The lights were low and they were listening to a new National record, because Emily had dated the lead singer before he got married and she still got their albums early. Most National songs and much

of the rest of the music Sherry liked sounded the
same to Emily, but she never admitted it. They
were drinking red wine. A few minutes earlier
they'd finished picking over steak taco salads
they'd had delivered from Oaxaca on Smith
Street.

Eli was up in the Bronx, helping pack a dozen
bikes bound for a shop in Austin.

"Mom was great, actually. She told me a story
about when Dad started giving this hot paralegal
rides home from work and she said this has to
stop, and it did. I mean, Dad stopped messing with
the paralegal. It was the same thing. A little tiny
affair early in their marriage and they made it go
away."

"Really?" Sherry asked. She dragged out the
word.

"Yeah, this was before Dad quit drinking. It's
amazing he never smashed up a car."

"He had plenty of accidents."

"I don't know why they got married. They are so
completely different. But the point is, Mom said
she believes in me and Eli. She never told me that
before."

"She wants you to have kids." Sherry tilted her
head to one side. "*I* want you to have kids."

"And I'm with you both on that. Now is
supposed to be the time for us to start. I'm thirty-
three."

"True," Sherry said. "Mom never told me that

story. I thought we heard every one of the ugly ones nine times at least."

"If you're lucky, she'll never have to tell it to you."

"It's not like I don't want to get married. I do," Sherry said. "And now? You go back to normal?"

Emily appraised her younger sister. Sherry's hair was swept back. She had on red lipstick and a dark red vintage Mayle dress that they'd bought together at a sample sale. Soon, Sherry had to go meet her producer friend at Black Light Basement, a new lounge across the street from where Don Hill's used to be, on the far west side of Manhattan. She was in no rush to get married.

"We try to fix it," Emily said. She reached out for more wine. "We keep being sweet and romantic and we rebuild trust. Maybe we should come with you later," she said. "Like a double date."

"It's not that kind of date," Sherry said with a laugh.

"You believe Eli can change? You think he'll never do it again?"

"Mom and Dad didn't break up because he cheated that one time. Wasn't that Mom's point?"

"I don't think she'd say I should stay with him just so she can have grandkids."

"Do you still feel sexy with him?"

"Are we still having sex? Yes, totally. I touched his shoulder this morning and then we got into this intense sex. We're doing it constantly."

"And it's good?"

"It's makeup sex. But yes." Emily drank some wine. "I know you said you agree with her, but do you think Mom is actually wrong and I'm being crazy?" she asked.

"Not at all! I definitely hate seeing you be sad. You want so much, Emily. I think that's good. But it makes it hard to, like, live up to what you want. Not that I'm taking his side."

"I want too much? Wait, what do you mean? Are you defending him?"

"Absolutely not. But you can be a little controlling. At the same time you deserve everything you want. You know that's what I mean." Sherry stood up and looked at herself in the mirror over the mantel. "It's just that maybe he was warning you—to give him a little room, you know?"

"Sherry, you sound repulsive right now."

"I know. But he's a big guy. He needs a big world to play in. What comes with being shy is that you're a little interior. You can be rather unto yourself, if that makes sense." Sherry continued to stare at herself in the mirror. She said, "I talked to Mom about this part. We touched on that idea. You control stuff better than either of us does. But Eli is hard to control."

"So you and Mom talked and totally psycho-analyzed the whole thing and that's where you got to, that I'm controlling. I'm the victim but you two think I'm controlling." Emily sat up.

"It's not like that and you know it." Sherry rolled her eyes.

Emily looked up at her bookshelf and saw *Canoe*. She went over and pulled it out and said, "Remember this book?"

Sherry turned around and looked at the book in Emily's hands. "What about it?"

"*Marriage Is a Canoe*. This is the copy you sent me from L.A., a few years back."

"You've been reading it?"

"It's like chicken soup."

"I heard something just recently about that book . . . I don't remember what. Anyway, don't be ridiculous, Emily. Couples therapy, maybe. But not some stupid book. I sent it as a joke. Because I remembered how into it you were when I was, like, nine." Sherry looked at herself again in the mirror above the mantel. She said, "If I knew you valued the presents I gave you that much, I'd give you more of them."

"How about you give me the present of understanding for one second how serious this is."

"Then why are you bringing up a bullshit self-help book?"

"Because the book is actually thoughtful about relationships. Mom isn't. I mean, that's nice that you talked to her, but Mom is an emotional coward and you know it. Let's pray neither of us ends up like her. If I stay with Eli, it'll be because I actually went in and dealt with our problem. Like she didn't do, ultimately, with Dad."

"Emily, I love you. I hear you," Sherry said. She had her phone in her hand.

"And now you're leaving." Emily sat down, hard, on the couch. "I think the truthful thing that you're not saying is that you'd walk out on Eli if this happened to you."

"But that's not necessarily the right thing to do. We're different. Don't be mad at me," Sherry said, after she called a cab.

Eli came home twenty minutes after Sherry left. He rang the buzzer because he'd forgotten his keys and so she had to get the door for him. In the doorway, he hugged her and stared into her eyes the way he did every night now. She'd begun to notice that when he did this, when he aggressively focused on her, she felt less lonely than usual. She had learned not to mind feeling lonely. Her work forced her to be alone, writing, much of the time. But now that Eli paid so much attention to her when they were together, she had begun to realize what a welcome change it was from all that solitude.

Eli said, "Before I say anything else, I have to let you know that we're going to go even further than what we originally planned. I conferenced with Rick and Steven and the best thing for the two businesses is for UBA to spin off entirely. It just makes sense. I don't want to be in the nonprofit business. UBA will be entirely L.A.-based."

Emily nodded. Eli had learned not to say Jenny's name. He dropped his bag by the front door and said, "What've you been up to?"

"Sherry was here."

"She leave to go somewhere fun?"

"Exactly." Emily began to laugh. Eli came closer. He smelled of clean sweat and she felt herself cave in to him. And then he went off to shower and she stayed where she was, by their kitchen island. She leaned up against the island's lip, because sometimes her back hurt and she found that the leaning made her feel better. Within minutes he returned in boxer shorts and a blue T-shirt that had the Roman Street logo.

"What about that trip to Mexico City?" he asked.

They had planned to go sometime late in the winter or in early spring. Mexico City was a good idea because there was a lot of demand for his bicycles there. And Emily could walk and learn the city. She knew she would love it there.

"Come and kiss me," Emily said.

"We can plan that trip?"

"You come here. I'm helping my back right now."

Eli reached out and pressed her breastbone with the flat of his palm. "We'll fix you."

"It's my back that hurts. You're free to massage it."

"Sorry!" He laughed and turned her around and began to massage her back.

She said, "You should only keep doing that if you want to."

"I do," Eli said.

She let her head roll back, suddenly impressed with her insight. She was not so directional, was she? No, she didn't think she was. Maybe she was growing more emotionally intelligent, which would be a consolation, especially if they came out of this and ended up happier than they had been before he had strayed. She had begun to imagine that was possible.

"Hey, hey Emily," Eli said. "Are you reading my mind?"

"No. But that feels good."

She wanted him to want her but she did not want to give in to him so easily. She knew she smelled good to him, that he loved to nuzzle her neck and slip his hands inside her lacy wireless bra. And now he did that. She closed her eyes and then opened them again, just to peek at him, to see what he was really up to, since she didn't 1,000 percent trust him, not yet. His eyes were closed and he was kissing her neck and chest and shoulders.

She found herself thinking back to when she'd met him, to those first few months. She began to insert a moment into way back then, a memory of thinking, When we're married, girls might throw themselves at him and if I'm going to keep him I'm going to have to put up with him cheating. It might happen one or two times. Can I take that?

She looked back at the self that had fallen in love with him and said, Okay, okay, if he can make me this happy, I can forgive him. I admit that I am happy he is mine. But we've got to get control of this thing. We are going to have to do the thing where we really work on our marriage.

Peter, October 2011

"Given that Belinda is a lesbian who has shared no desire to raise children with you, wanting to live near her in order to visit children she does not yet have is not a concern I feel I should address," Maddie said as she and Peter walked into the Sally Forth dining room. "Though I do not understand why you keep us apart. She sounds very smart and kind."

"I only said she might have kids," Peter said.

"Yes. She might. But Anjulee is having a child now. And so moving closer to her before the end of the year is necessary, at least for me."

"And I promised I would do just that."

"Yes." Maddie seemed to be speaking to herself. "You did."

Henry was seated at the table nearest to the fireplace. He waved to them. It was just after three on a Wednesday afternoon.

"Hello, you two," Henry called out. "Maddie, you look incredible, as usual."

Peter glanced at Maddie and she did look good, in form-fitting khakis and driving moccasins, purple shawl thrown over her shoulders, on top of a dark sweater.

"Back in a moment." Peter went off to the men's

room. His prostate was becoming an issue. But he wasn't eager for a visit to his doctor. Part of what had gone wrong with Lisa was one too many visits to the doctor.

At least, thank goodness, Wally Wood's dirty Sally Forth comic strips were still the wallpaper in the men's room. The inn had changed so much over the past few years, but Peter looked around and silently thanked Henry for having the good sense to leave the hundreds of images of a wonderfully big-breasted Sally Forth. Back in the early eighties, Peter had made the decorating decisions for both inns after Lisa's parents retired. He'd had the brilliant idea of wallpapering the men's room in both places with the Sally Forth comics he'd bought from a Vietnam vet at a garage sale in 1975 and hidden in the basement. Lisa never went into the men's room, so she never found out. It pleased Peter that they were still there. Though they were old and yellowed, they were still damned good fun to look at.

And then, as he reexamined the hot little drawings of Sally Forth before leaving the bathroom, he realized that of course Lisa knew about the wallpaper. She knew about everything. He'd written his book, entered her life, and then everything afterward had been scribed by her. And he had been okay with that. He had gotten up the courage to come to her in Millerton. She hadn't expected too much from him after that. And of course he'd been great with Belinda. They both had.

"Bathroom looks great," Peter said as he sat down.

"We ought to rip those dirty comics down and paint," Henry said. "But I can't bring myself to do it."

"Glad to hear it."

"What is in there?" Maddie asked. She sipped from a cup of tea that Peter imagined Henry must have prepared for her before their arrival.

"You'll never know." Peter touched her back, and she smiled at him. "Any chance of an afternoon scotch?"

"During the day we run more of an espresso bar," Henry said.

"Well, that's about the stupidest thing I ever heard," Peter said. "Is it a bar or isn't it? I see a bottle of Johnnie Walker right there! So let me have a glass of the stuff with an ice cube in it. Please!"

"All right, all right," Henry said. "You can make your own drink."

Peter stood up again. He found his way behind the bar. But when he got there, he remembered that Maddie didn't like to see him drink hard liquor, and he found himself with his hands outstretched a few feet from the bottle, waving at it. He hoped they weren't looking and quickly turned around to face them, placing his hands on the bar as if he were the bartender. "Before we get started on your big proposition," he called out, "I have one of my own."

"What's that?" Henry asked.

"There's a contest." Peter went on and told them about it. He felt like he did when he was a boy, excitedly telling a girl about a baseball game he'd played in, and the game was a lie but her disinterest was not. Though now it was the opposite, he realized as he went on—he was watching their faces, watching them lose interest. The more he thought about it, the more important the contest became to him. Why didn't they care? But no. All they cared about was friendship and money and their carefully tended futures and families. To them the contest was as remote as any media, and maybe a little irrelevant and stupid. He closed his mouth. He saw Maddie smile at him. No matter how stupid he sounded, she looked at him like she loved him. It was troubling.

Finally, Henry said, "I'm not even sure we want that sort of publicity."

"What? How could it be bad?" Peter came back and sat down at the table. He let his hands hang loosely at his sides and he breathed in so his stomach ballooned.

"A save-your-marriage contest? The winner gets a two-night stay here at the inn? And advice from you? It doesn't exactly make the place a dream honeymoon location, now does it?"

"When was it ever that?" Peter asked.

"We have honeymooners!" Henry said.

"Oh, please. From Albany, once or twice a year. Welcome to the present, Henry. People live their lives in public now. I've been talking to my publisher, and believe me, this is totally normal."

"You think I'm not familiar with how the culture has given up on privacy?" Henry asked.

"I think you're a cultural bumpkin!" Peter clapped his palms flat on the table.

"Stop right there," Maddie said. She reached out and took Henry's hand. She said, "But of course the winning couple will stay here. Let us set Peter's contest aside. Henry, you have a proposal for Peter."

"That's right," Henry said. He took a few deep breaths before going on. "We have created value, here at the inn. And at the same time, we have taken on more debt . . ."

Henry went on. Peter stared at his old friend. He felt heat in his chest and forehead. Half a minute passed. Peter finally said, "Say that again."

"I'm sorry, Peter. But that's the price this bumpkin has to offer you."

"That's his price?" Peter asked Maddie. Maddie didn't speak. And Peter hadn't actually heard the price. He tried to smile. He said, "Is this a conspiracy?"

Henry could make his eyes twinkle behind his

glasses, and while Peter watched, he went ahead and did it. Peter wanted to call him a shithead but held back.

"I created more of the value than I contributed to the debt," Peter said, carefully. He was outside his range of financial comprehension and all three of them knew it.

"Sure," Henry spoke quickly. "Sure it's worth more than I'm offering. But I'm buying debt, Peter, not value. I'm buying the opportunity to pay down your debt to nothing."

"Yes, for twenty cents on the dollar. I mean— did I hear you right?"

"I could refuse to buy it!" Henry sputtered, and Peter felt his old friend's saliva hit his cheek. Henry said, "This wasn't my idea. It's Maddie who came to me."

"But you set the price. Make it twenty-five cents," Peter said.

Henry shook his head and said, "You've got to trust me. You know I'd never do anything to hurt you."

Maddie stared down at the table. She said, "Peter, you made me no promises in relation to your business. I am being meddlesome and we are wasting our dear friend Henry's time."

"That's right. And I won't do it! I'm not giving in! We'll find some other way." Peter stood up. He said, "I didn't live all this life to spend my last however many years in a fucking cowardly retreat! I own my house free and clear. I'll mortgage it before I give up the inn."

"Your house isn't worth enough to solve the problem. We were more than halfway to setting you free." Maddie seemed to be speaking to herself. She placed one hand on top of the other on the table. She was incredibly still.

"No," Peter said. "No to all of this."

He turned away from them and walked out to the parking lot where he found a maid who was headed home after her shift. It was nothing to convince her to give him a lift back to his house.

Half an hour later he was on the phone with Stella Petrovic. He sat in the kitchen with a cold glass of water in front of him. He found he couldn't stop drumming his fingers while they talked.

"If you don't like the entries you're getting, why don't you soften your sales pitch. It's not about a couple in trouble. It's about a couple who are coming in for a checkup, you see? The save-our-marriage part bugs people. It's more of a healthy talk, is all."

"Go on," Stella said. "I'm typing."

"It's about a couple with a few years of marriage who come to me and—there's nothing to be ashamed of—they sit and we talk about marriage and what it means. We just want a good solid couple. We want to save somebody, but we don't want to die trying."

"I wish I could be a fly on the wall of the session," Stella said.

"Session?"

"Your time together—the afternoon and evening we're talking about."

"Think of it as more of a visit. There's a sweetness to this thing. Believe me, sharing wisdom and fixing problems are not the same thing. It's the wisdom angle that's missing from . . ."

"Yes?" She did sound eager. He smiled. Who didn't like talking with an eager young woman in New York who had been instructed to treat you with respect? He almost laughed aloud. An hour ago he felt awfully old. But now he was better. Dealing with people who didn't quite understand what he was—that made him feel good.

He said, "It's a nostalgic project. Like a catalog I used to get in the mail from Restoration Hardware, of reconstructed products that we used in the fifties and sixties. Nostalgia sells. We know that."

"Of course you're right, Peter. We just haven't seen the right entry. I don't want you to sit down with a couple that is any different from what you're describing. No one wants a couple who would ruin the nostalgic feel of what has become a lifelong project for you."

"Very well said. I appreciate the care you're taking."

"We more than appreciate that you said yes!"

He got up and began to pace the house, trying to

imagine how it would be when the winners visited him. Where would they sit?

He said, "You'll find them. They're out there."

"I'm sure we will. I convinced marketing to spend more money on ads, both in magazines and on websites, but of course the additional money raises the stakes and the pressure . . ."

"Uh-huh." He nodded, half-listening. He looked out at the front driveway and saw Maddie pull up in her silent Mercedes.

Stella said, "I wouldn't do any of this if the stories in your book didn't mean so much to so many people. I mean, I only discovered *Canoe* a few months ago but now that I know about it, your words pop up everywhere for me. I asked my parents about it and even they'd heard of it. My mom gave it to a friend who was going through a hard time once. It's like part of our American fabric is what I'm getting at . . ."

Maddie gently stepped out of her car. She caught his eye and frowned at him. She reached back into the car and tugged out a shawl. He thought, I'll pull that off her. Pull her silky camisole down and tug the straps of her bra from her shoulders, cup her big breasts in my hands. He was proud of himself for thinking sexy. But from the look on her face, it didn't seem as if Maddie was in that sort of mood. Though over their months together she had surprised him with heady afternoon sex more than once.

Stella was still talking but he cut her off, saying, "I look forward to meeting you someday, Stella. Keep me updated."

"I will. We'll find our winner."

"Of course we will."

He got off the phone and went to open the door for Maddie. There was a little pain in his backside, perhaps from crouching in the window seat at the wrong angle.

She came in and searched his face with her dark eyes. "Peter," she said, dropping her bucket bag on the hutch by the front door. She walked through the house to the kitchen and he followed her.

"Want to walk the lake?" he asked. But he could see she didn't.

"Walk? You walked out of the inn and left me there. Was it so awful, Peter?"

"I didn't like where the conversation was going."

He moved in what he hoped looked like slow motion, fooling around, arching his neck back, groaning, trying to act as if he'd been punched on the chin, and then shot in the chest. He staggered back against the butcher block section of the kitchen counter, felt its warm contour in his hands, and steadied himself.

He said, "You have to sell your house, too. We can wait until the spring to go."

"You are sixty-two. You have plenty of time to start something new. Why dawdle?"

"Dawdle? I don't think I'm making enough of

this contest. It's important to me. It's become part of my legacy."

"Your legacy? I am not sure I would agree that a marketing-based contest burnishes a legacy, even if I am willing to be forced to agree that a single book makes a legacy."

"It still sells. It's—at least I know it's still in print." He stopped. Then he said, "Why are you dragging me along? It can't be fun for you."

"You are right." She bowed her head. "I was trying to explain that to Henry."

"Explain what?"

"How my faith in others always gets me into trouble."

He looked away and sucked air through his teeth.

"Shall we walk?" he asked.

"No." She kept shaking her head. He wanted to kiss her shoulder and then he crossed the cold kitchen and did just that, pulling at the neck of her sweater. She pushed him away.

He said, "What can I do, Maddie?"

"I am sorry, Peter. I did all the things my husband wanted to do and I regret that now. My daughter needs my help. You made me a promise and now you are having trouble keeping that promise. I understand that."

He smiled. Had he promised? He knew he could be slippery with promises.

Maddie said, "Earlier you wanted a drink. I will

drink with you even if you are not to be trusted. What about white wine? Do you have any?"

"I'm sure there's a bottle around here somewhere."

He went out of the kitchen and into the pantry, knowing there was no wine there, stalling her, looking for a few minutes to straighten himself out so that he wouldn't reveal with more surety what she had already discovered about him.

"Won't you sing an old song with me?" he whispered to himself, on his knees now, pawing through old bottles of apple vinegar and jars of strawberry preserves. There was wine in the kitchen. He was afraid she would find it and discover yet another lie, on top of the fact that he was afraid to leave Millerton with her, even though, apparently, he'd promised.

She called out, "You know what? Forget it. We will leave each other alone this evening."

He heard her open the front door. "Wait!" Peter struggled to his feet. "Don't go!" He followed her, stepped onto the front porch and spread his hands over the railing.

"Maddie, stop!"

She turned and stood halfway down the path between him and her car.

He said, "I'm going to throw myself into a new life with you. I'm—I get that I'm hedging just a bit. Like you say. But there's this contest." He realized how loud he was—nearly yelling—and that he needed to stop yelling, but he couldn't, so he kept going. "I'm sorry about this afternoon. Let me just make good on my commitment to this contest and then I'll leave with you. Doesn't that sound fair?"

"Since when," Maddie asked, "does fair have anything to do with romance? I think you ought to read your—what do you call it? Your goddamn book."

Emily, October 2011

Instead of meeting Ida Abarra alone for a drink, Emily called her from work on the morning they were supposed to get together and asked if she and Eli could go to dinner with her and Billy.

"Of course," Ida said. "I never invite Billy anywhere. He'll glow. But I should tell you that as of a week ago I'm not drinking."

"That's fantastic, Ida! Congratulations."

"Of course we're not talking about it or telling anybody and we're nervous as hell but I feel like it's the right thing to do. I'm thirty-four, so may as well. How old are you?"

"Thirty-three," Emily said with a nod. Her small office was open plan but she was determined not to edit herself too much in front of others. Nobody at work messed with her. She was one of the few people at Yes who could explain what the company actually did and that made most of the rest of the staff tiptoe around her.

"You've got time," Ida said.

"Eli turned thirty-nine a couple of months ago. He's definitely ready."

"Did you work out the thing from when I last saw you?"

"Sort of. He's really sorry. We're treating it like a watershed."

"Listen, I saw every moment of it and I meditated on it and you two are going to be okay. I promise. Do you want to meet us at Frankie's, at . . . seven thirty? We can have a drink while we wait? I mean, I can't but the three of you can. You'll need more than one if Billy gets going on what Christine Lagarde ought to do with the IMF, which will definitely happen. You've been warned."

"I guess trading on the international markets means you can work at any time. Must be stressful," Emily said to Billy, at the bar at Frankie's.

"We call it trading an international book," Billy said, without looking at her.

Emily nodded and said, "Yes, I know that." Ida had gone to the bathroom. They were lucky to have gotten spots at the bar since it was crowded. Emily was closer to Billy than she would have liked. But he didn't seem to notice. He also ignored the fact that she understood what he did for a living. Emily sighed. She had a glass of wine but Billy had ordered bourbon that he'd asked for by saying, "Do you have . . ." and then a name she'd never heard of, and then when the bartender said no he would try again. So he was grimacing through his fourth-choice bourbon and the bartender clearly hated him. He was pretentious and Emily saw why he'd gone for Ida. She was a prize.

"In fact, I've heard of your husband," Billy said. "Everybody loves someone who can manufacture a simple technology like a bicycle with their hands. He's quite the entrepreneur."

"Don't use big words like that with him," she said. "I'm joking—but you'll see. He's smart but he's smart the way a brilliant designer is smart. By which I mean he is less than well-spoken. I mean, I'm kidding. You see how I'm kidding?"

Billy nodded and didn't smile, which made Emily feel bad for talking so much. Billy was tall with a curly brown mane of what Emily thought of as trader hair, and he wore an expensive button-down shirt and really nice glasses. Ida came back from the bathroom and she and Billy raised an eyebrow at each other. Next to Billy's fussiness, Ida looked even more beautiful than she did on her own.

"My point is that I like that your husband actually makes things," Billy said.

"Billy loves that idea," Ida said. "I make things, too, but he says it's not the same."

"Words are not things."

Ida sucked in her cheeks. She said, "I make books."

"It's true books are things, but things made of words . . ." Billy rolled his eyes and smiled at Emily, who didn't know how to react.

"Thanks a lot, honey," Ida said. "Emily works with words, too."

"No, she explains things to people. She was just telling me."

"Her work is important," Ida said. "She is involved with the practical world in a way that I am not."

"Exactly what I was thinking!" Billy laughed.

"Don't start." Ida shook her head and stared at her husband.

"Yeah? Don't egg me on."

Emily said, "Eli will be here soon, I promise. There was a problem . . ." It was something about meeting a deadline for a bicycle he was building on his own for a billionaire who lived out west somewhere. Was the rich man going on a bike trip with Robert Redford? It was something like that, but she couldn't quite remember. She looked down at her shoes. Or maybe he was lying to her and he was just late like he always was and he was talking on the phone to Jenny. She knew they still talked. She had to accept this contact with Jenny. Accept it short-term, anyway.

Eli came running in and slipped his arm around Emily's waist. He kissed her and nuzzled her neck while he held out a hand to Ida and then Billy and said, "I'm sorry I'm late! It's so good to meet both of you."

"Take notes," Ida said to Billy. "I want the same treatment later."

"So do I," Billy said. "But any good statistician will tell you we can't all have our wishes come true on the same night—otherwise the world would explode."

"Shut up now, Billy." Ida winked at Emily. "Eli, can we get you a drink? Can I order you two? I'm pregnant but we're not talking about it, so I'll just smell mine and then you can drink it."

They were seated in a dark corner of the restaurant, next to windows facing the back garden. Emily sat down and looked at the ovens across the room and breathed in the smell of roasting vegetables. She bit into some warm focaccia and thought everything felt oily and wooden and a little louche in a good way and she immediately wished her whole life was made up of dinners like this—and then she fought back against her interiority in order to enjoy the evening she was actually in. She smiled at Ida and Ida began to talk. Within minutes, Billy and Eli were both leaning far back in their chairs, entirely facing each other, deep in a conversation about funding. Billy knew venture capitalists and he was sure they would love what Eli was up to. But how to inject loads of money without losing that artisanal feel? Roman Street was such a modern post-boom business. It was so physical and green and everyone wanted to get in on it, but there were only so many slices to go around. Emily couldn't stop staring at Eli. She wanted him to take her hand while he talked. And then, when she most wanted it, he did reach out and take her hand, not just for a second, but he held her hand across the table, as if he could do it forever.

"See?" Ida whispered.

"What?"

"You two are okay." And then Ida went back to her story. She said, "So I'm having lunch with this magazine person today and she's pitching me stuff and I'm like, no, no way am I going to the supposed bra master for an article—if I am nothing else I am sure as hell past that. Then I pitch her pieces where I actually get to think and she's like, no—not *think* pieces. I'm talking about bras. Think about bras. It's like we were in a bad Funny or Die skit, I swear."

"What about bras?"

"She wants me to write about getting sized and buying proper-fitting bras and how they feel on me. Because I'm a writer so I can describe tit-feel in fabric better than anybody else. I wanted to throw up."

"Who finds you these people?"

"My publicist. Which means at some point, she totally had a conversation with this magazine editor about my tits."

Through her laughter, Emily surreptitiously looked at Ida's perfect breasts and thought the publicist was damned good at her job.

"It doesn't stop there," Ida said. "Then I called

my publicist and complained about the lunch and she told me that I should enter this idiotic contest she'd heard about that's based on some self-help book. About a boy in a canoe? *Canoe*? *The Love Canoe*?"

"*Marriage Is a Canoe*?" Emily leaned in closer and tried through gesture to get Ida to do the same. Ida did.

Ida said, "You win and the author sees you at his house and listens to you and he tells you his old stories. Then when it gets boring you take a walk and look at fall foliage. Like that's interesting. So for me and Billy to win would be a stunt. I was like, why don't you just ram me with a canoe and I'll write about that."

"What?"

"Uh." Ida looked confused. "Which part didn't you get?"

"*Marriage Is a Canoe*? You're sure?" Emily had her hands on her knees. Ida gestured at and then ate some of Emily's pumpkin ravioli.

"Mmm. Yeah. That's it. That's the one. She thinks I can win it because she's seen me with this asshole." Ida jutted her chin at her husband. "She knows we're not going to break up but we drive each other insane. So my career always boils down to some stupid stunt. Though the stunt is mostly about blackness at the end of the day." Ida looked away. "At least she didn't pitch me my blackness."

"I bet she thinks your awesome breasts are about your blackness," Emily said quickly.

Ida laughed and said, "True."

"This contest—it's going on now?"

"Yeah, just started."

Emily said, "I love that book," and immediately felt embarrassed about it.

Ida leaned forward and whispered, "You should enter!"

"I wouldn't. Too shy. But I love that book. My mom had it in our bathroom when I was growing up."

"Totally you should enter. Get on the other side of your watershed. Or at least just entering would be cathartic, you know. Forget winning. That's stupid."

"Maybe, maybe you're right. I should." Emily grabbed Ida's hand and squeezed it.

"What are you two talking about?" Eli smiled at them and sipped at his beer.

"We're going to start a company to rival yours," Ida spoke quickly. "We'll revive seventies roller skates."

"I would invest in that one, for sure," Billy said. "I've got a fantasy involving a couple of women on roller skates."

Ida reached forward and pushed two fingers into her husband's rib cage. She said, "Shut up, Billy." They were all suddenly quiet because of the force of her voice. In the stiffness that followed, the waitress came and took away their pasta plates.

"Sorry." Ida smiled. "It's just that some jokes, I don't want to hear them anymore, you know? Maybe it's hormones." She relaxed her hand and patted her husband's stomach.

Emily stared at them. She watched Billy frown at his wife. He adjusted the collar of her sweater and Ida started glaring all over again.

Afterward, on the street, the four of them stood and said how much they'd enjoyed meeting one another. Ida and Emily watched Billy and Eli exchange cards.

"I've still got plenty of months before we hole up. Call me," Ida said as she hugged Emily. "And enter that contest."

"I'll call you soon," Emily said. "Congratulations again on the . . . um . . . everything."

Emily walked down the street with Eli. He threw an arm around her shoulder and held her close, as he always did now.

"What'd you think of them?" she asked.

"He was really smart. She was, too. I wish I understood half of what he said about analyzing developing countries. That's an awesome way to perceive the world."

"Yes, but, as a couple, what'd you think?"

"As a couple?"

"I mean, they didn't get along. You saw that, right?"

"Did I?" Eli pointed to his chest. He laughed.

"Yes, I guess I saw that. They had that timing thing with their stories that was funny. The no-you-tell-it thing. They're not a disaster, though. He loves her. She's way out of his league."

"That's so nice of you to say!" Emily felt herself brightening. She looked up, and the street lamp that had been broken forever on their corner seemed to have been fixed. She was too embarrassed to tell Eli that she'd called 311 about it, so she kept her happiness to herself. She loved calling 311.

"Nice of me?" Eli asked. He unlocked their door and they went inside.

"I mean, we could both see it. They'll be okay— they're just emotionally tender right now because having a kid is freaking them out. They're cool."

"Cool," Eli said. "I'm not sure that's a word I'd use to describe them. Arch?"

"Sure! Arch is the right word," Emily said. "Nicely done." She kissed him. He smiled at her and looked confused, like a dog, she thought, who was not sure why he was being praised. Now they both stood just inside the door, still in their coats. Their house smelled of them, she thought, of olives and radiator heat and wool coats and bicycle inner tubes. Eli checked his phone and Emily began to open their bills. Soon after they'd married, she had discovered that Eli never dealt with his own bills, and so she'd taken on the financial-management aspect of their marriage.

She opened a letter from the Fresh Air Fund and thought again of children. She was beginning to feel their lack.

"We should give a bicycle to a Fresh Air Fund kid," Emily said, to herself.

Eli looked up from his phone. He said, "Emily, I'm actually not that optimistic about Billy and Ida. Compared to us? Aren't we kind of . . . better than they are? Even though I gave us this awful bump. I mean, I'm not forgetting that. But aren't you sort of thinking that we're more in sync than they are?"

Was she thinking that? She hadn't been. But she loved that he was musing about them versus another couple. She was suddenly angry with herself for being pragmatic, thinking about their mail when her husband was dwelling on their marriage, on the value of their bond.

"Yes," she said. "I love that you're chewing over the night. I get what you mean about them, too."

"I'm exhausted but I'm glad you took us out," Eli said. He dropped his coat on the floor and wandered toward the back of the dark apartment.

Eli was always quick to fall asleep. And so Emily slipped out of bed as soon as she heard his even breathing. She had to see the contest on the Internet. It was real. She couldn't quite believe it, and read through the copy several times. It had been going on for two full weeks. She was amazed she'd missed it. She never paid enough attention to pop culture. It wasn't that she didn't care. No, she thought. That was a lie. She didn't care. She read tech columns and the business section of the *Times*. She looked at arts coverage rarely, always dutifully, and only because she was scanning for new documentary films or design symposiums, which she usually knew about anyway. And because of that, she'd almost missed the contest.

Could she enter? She would. In the morning. Just as a funny thing, another cathartic moment that spoke to the ongoing fix for her marriage. She found her bag by the front door and got out the edition she'd bought at the end of summer when the trouble started. The one she'd talked about with her sister was still on their coffee table. And there was another copy in the bedroom. Given how incredibly nonobservant Eli was of things around the house, she wondered when he would ever notice. Really, did she have to throw the book at him? She curled up with a blanket in the red suede chair.

This edition began with "Stolen Bases."

"Stolen Bases," from *Marriage Is a Canoe*,
a new foreword to the third edition,
first published in serialized version for six
consecutive Sundays in July and August 1982
in *Parade* magazine

Another inspiration for this book came from a game of stolen bases that we played on a late afternoon in mid-August of that summer.

My Pop and I had taken over the baseball field in Robertson's private park, in town.

Pop was teaching me and a few other children to steal bases. He had made a game of it, with scoring. We weren't any good and there was loads of bunting and it was hard work, staying or running like mad and always having to pay attention. The afternoon turned to dusk and it was evening before we really noticed. And then it was nearly eight and one of the kids who lived nearby was called home by his mother. The five or six other kids we'd gathered thanked us and ran off to their own houses, where they'd apologize for being so late and then enjoy their franks-and-beans suppers.

I rounded up the heavy bases, made of sand encased in thick rubber and canvas, and dragged them to the supply shed at the side of the field.

Pop swept the dirt in the running paths back into place. And then we heard a call, and when we looked up, we saw there was a boy still out there in center field, a small boy called Johnny who had helped Pop field balls because he was too shy to run bases.

"We're all tucked away here for the night," Pop said. "Thanks for your help, young man. We're all set!"

"It's Johnny." The boy came closer to us.

"Yes, Johnny. I know." Pop slapped his hands clean on the sides of his khakis. He had a gift of giving the person he was talking to time to settle themselves so they might say what they cared to say without being rushed. But this boy, Johnny, he just stared at me and Pop.

"You're standing there like you've got something to tell us, Johnny. Like there's a thing and you want to say it and you're looking for your cue. Well, here's your cue."

Johnny did just what I'd have done—what any of us would do. He kicked a rock.

"Want us to walk you home, Johnny? Evening shadows bother you?"

"No, sir. It's not that. I don't want to go home."

"We can walk you home."

"It's my parents. I don't want to see them."

"Yes. That happens sometimes and it's okay. We've all got to work together to make our homes a good place."

"I don't like being there . . ." Johnny wandered off and stood on the foul-ball line, a couple of yards past third base.

"We're going to help out a bit," Pop whispered to me. And then, louder, he said, "Let's all walk over to your place together and see about it, Johnny."

Johnny walked toward us like he was in a trance.

He lived just four blocks from the field, on a wide-lane street that trucks used to come into town called Thayer Avenue. His house was a green Cape Anne with more than one broken shutter and a garden that could have benefited from two or three hours of weed picking.

We hadn't talked the whole way there and we didn't when we arrived. Instead, Pop gestured for Johnny and me to stay on the curb and he walked up the steps to the porch and knocked on the door.

"Yes?" It was a woman's voice, a little tremulous.

"It's Hank Latham. I'm here with your boy Johnny and my grandson, Peter."

The screen door swung open and Johnny's mom came out. Johnny's father was behind her. They were not beautiful people, though the woman had streaked blond hair. The man had a clean white shirt on. The woman was small and the man was large in stature, but the woman somehow took up more space in my head. It may have had to do with how her hair made her hazel-colored eyes shine bright, like brass buttons on a camel-hair coat.

My Pop said, "First things first. I've got no right to come to your house, no right to intrude, so if you ask me to leave, I'll leave straightaway."

"That's awfully grave," Johnny's father said. "What's the trouble?"

"I'll come in for a moment," Pop said. "My boy Peter will stay outside with Johnny. They'll play catch there in the street, by the streetlight. There's not much traffic and they'll be safe."

He turned and nodded at us and went inside. The screen door banged shut behind him.

Johnny and I stood together. All of a sudden it was dark out, dark as if it were after midnight and I was waking only to go pee before drifting back to bed.

"I'm going to eavesdrop," I said.

"Okay," Johnny said. "But how are we going to make the sound of catch?"

I looked at him. He was hunched over and he reminded me of a character from *The Little Rascals*, in his tin-colored T-shirt and dirty jeans. I'd gained some weight since I'd arrived in June and I'd begun to stand up straighter. I said, "They won't be listening for us."

That was something I'd learned for sure in my own home, during the hard spring that came before that wonderful summer.

We dropped to all fours and crept up the stairs to take positions on either side of Johnny's front door. The porch was cool and quiet in that dark night, though I could see some chairs scattered about behind Johnny, knocked up against one another and pointing every which way. You could tell no one had sat out there for some time.

"Thank you," my Pop said. I imagine he'd been asked to take a seat. Then there were a full five seconds of quiet. And I could only hear Johnny's breathing. I saw where he'd placed his glove under his knee, a move I found more delicate than I expected from him.

"Sir—"

"Call me Hank."

I looked at Johnny and he had his eyes closed and was humming.

"Nothing? How about a glass of water?"

"All right," Pop said. "You've got a boy who doesn't want to come home at night. I'm sorry to be forward about it. But something is the matter."

"What's that to you?" the father asked.

"I'll leave if that's what you'd like me to do."

"Johnny came to you about our problems?" It was the wife talking now.

"He did."

"That's bad," the wife said.

"He ought to know better," the father said, roughly.

But the wife must have cut him off. She said,

"Maybe we should thank him. Here's a chance to talk and I'm going to take it. We ought to have it out. I will tell you what's the matter. My husband here, he tells me everything I do is wrong. Not just one thing or another, either. Every single god-damned thing! How I cook peas to the way I make beds to the style I like for my hair, to—the way I sneeze! Can you imagine? Can you imagine the life I'm having to live here with this man? And now you—you come in my home, uninvited, and you say—well—what have you got to say about it?"

There was a silence. I dared not look at Johnny.

"Is that fair, what Annie said?" my Pop asked. "May I call you Annie? And you're John Senior, aren't you?" We heard the sound of Johnny's father quietly shifting, twisting around.

"Yes. It's fair. I'm not happy."

There was a stirring across from me and I looked up to watch Johnny do just what I would have done, what I had done only weeks earlier in my bedroom back home in Manhattan, which was to shove his glove into his mouth and bite down hard on the leather, taste the oil and salt and dirt. I knew he would chew and rip at the catgut twine that held everything together, just like I had. The taste of a baseball glove was like yesterday's roast beef or three-day-old brisket. But you couldn't eat it. You could only bite down and taste the oil seeping out.

"How serious is it?" Pop asked. "Is he violent with you?"

"It gets close. John, you're not happy. Are you going to stay?" Annie asked.

"Yes," John Senior said. "I don't want to leave."

"You threaten to leave all the time. You threaten me."

"It's words. I'm ashamed of them."

"You can't take all the blame," Annie said, and I could hear the shudder in her voice.

"That's all right if he does," my Pop said. "It sounds like he knows he's in the wrong. He can shoulder it for tonight, maybe for the summer. For as long as it takes. He looks able to do that."

"Hank is right. I can. Annie, when I'm critical of you, when I tell you you ought to do things different, well, you can just send me right out of the house."

"Easy for you two to say! But in the moment it's not so easy."

"At least it's on the table," Pop said.

"There is that," Annie said.

"You two love your boy. I know there's a girl upstairs sleeping. And I can see you've got another on the way."

Johnny's dad made an *ahem* noise.

"Listen, you know where me and my wife, Bess, live. How about if you all come to our house on Sunday after lunch. We've got an extra canoe and you and your children can go out for a paddle and we'll take our grandson in the other canoe. In the evening, we'll have fried chicken. We can set up a table for the children and one for us adults. And we four can talk and you can maybe bring a little lightness and gaiety into the lives of a couple of old folks."

"You're not old," Annie said.

"We don't mind being old. You won't either, but that's not a concern for a long time to come."

We could hear a shifting, of the three of them getting up from their chairs. Without saying a word, both of us scrambled up and raced to the edge of their front yard and somehow we knew to lie there in the grass, our gloves thrown down at our sides, as if we'd gotten tired of playing catch and had decided to stare at the stars. Though the night sky was cloudy and there were none to see.

"Come on now, Peter," Pop said. "Let's go home. And you, Johnny, I believe we'll be seeing you at our house this Sunday."

"Yes, sir."

Johnny ran up and into his house without saying goodbye to me. We made our way down the street.

"Doesn't look like there's much of a moon tonight. Bess will be waiting. Maybe with some cobbler if we're lucky. Sometimes, you know, you get to have what you want and you get to be what you want to be."

"Always?" I asked.

Pop grew quiet as he pondered the question. We

were walking along a town road, as opposed to the country road we lived on, which was farther out and down the hill from where we were. Those houses by the water were our world and we were away from there.

"I said sometimes. Not always."

Bang went his hand on my head and then he gripped my shoulder and then down, roughly grabbing up my hand and holding it in his own cool, callused one as we crossed the road and made our way home, just ten minutes farther along. We walked carefully, since those massive steel Pontiacs and Fords kept on rumbling by us in ones and twos on that moonless night.

"You listened to us talking?"

"Well . . . yes."

"Sometimes people need a little help. There's nothing wrong with that. Bess? Bess!" He called out to his wife from fifty yards away. Darn the neighbors!

"Yes, yes, hurry before the storms come."

My Pop chuckled and gripped my hand tighter. This was a joke between them. The still night held no hint of a storm.

It was nearly nine. Late for us. We ate a dinner of turkey slices with gravy, green wax beans, and homemade sourdough bread. For dessert there really was cobbler, two kinds, peach and rhubarb, with vanilla and strawberry ice cream.

I went into the living room to read *Tales of King*

Arthur and His Knights of the Round Table while Pop told Bess all that had happened at Johnny's house.

I heard her say, "You're tired. Go out and have a smoke on the porch while I clean up these dishes."

"Bess, you're the best . . . ," he said.

I watched him go outside to smoke the peat and green tobacco that he mixed himself and then tamped down in a cobalt-colored scrimshaw pipe. He liked to sit on the back porch on a hard chair, leaning against the side of the house, the front legs two inches off the floor. I remember he'd told me that he loved to smoke and listen to the bullfrogs croaking at the edges of the lake.

There's nothing wrong with
asking for help with your marriage.

Emily, October 21, 2011

Emily sent her contest entry in via e-mail before departing for work on Friday morning.

From: Emily Babson <Emily.babablackbird@gmail.com> wrote:
Date: Friday, Oct 21, 2011 at 8:48 EDT
To: Marriage Contest <Marriageisacontest@ Ladderandrakebooks.com>
Subject: Could this be the winning entry?

Dear Peter Herman,

I learned about *Marriage Is a Canoe* when I was eleven years old. Your book lived in the bathroom off my parents' bedroom, on top of the water tank, between copies of *The Bonfire of the Vanities* and *The Closing of the American Mind*. Most kids my age were reading either Judy Blume or *Anne of Green Gables*, but I'd discovered my parents' bathroom collection. There were too many weekends when I read in that bathroom with the door locked while my parents fought, before they came to their senses and divorced. Your book was my favorite and I read it over and over again like only an eleven-year-old can.

During what would now be called my tween years, I went to sleep each night with my hands balled up in fists, determined to ignore the misery in my house and to grow up and have a happy life like your grandparents had. I imagined marrying a boy who liked to kiss and walk in fields and think about the world he lived in, a boy just like you were in that book, because you embodied a joyful and thoughtful way to live that was beyond my parents' grasp.

I was a quiet and judgmental child, and I regret that now. But I wasn't wrong. I tried to turn my back on my parents' failed marriage and to make *Canoe* become part of me. I believed that if I read it enough times, I could join its club, like the Christian kids I knew who were jealous of bar mitzvahs and went to every single one in our town. I know I'm not alone. I am sure there are many people my age who read *Canoe* surreptitiously, alongside *Our Bodies, Ourselves* and *The Joy of Sex*. We feel like we know how to be happily married not because of what we saw when we were children but because of what we read in your book. But I have no interest in making a generational declaration. This is my contest entry, and I want to win. I loved your book then and I used it to guide myself into the life I live now. If it weren't for your book I'm not sure I would have gotten married. I would not have taken the chance, after seeing what I saw at home. So, instead of the lives I've seen, your book has become the bedrock of my faith in marriage.

Sure, writing to you is a long shot. This letter is silly and so am I. But it's so silly that it's liberating. I don't feel bashful or ashamed. I am grateful to be able to write to the man who made me believe that married life can be fantastic. And a little part of me hopes he can help fix my married life, which started out as pure bliss and has now descended into an anxious state, an imperiled state that lacks trust.

My husband, Eli, and I have been married for almost three years and you could say we have hit a rough patch. Eli cheated on me. He became entangled in a romance with a woman who works at the company he owns. He tells me it's over. I want to believe him. Despite this recent transgression, I am in love with Eli and I think he has it in him to be a good husband. He is also charming and attractive, to the point where these parts of him could be called a disability. Women used to throw themselves at him when we were dating. And I understood women would continue to do so after we married. I am not naive. But I also knew Eli was good for me. I am a habitually shy person and Eli is gregarious. He has friends who call him out of the blue, who just want to see him. I don't. If it weren't for Eli, I would spend all my time either at work or thinking about work at home. He makes me feel like a whole person. Without him, I would be lost and forever fretful, like the new kid at school.

Up to now I've been very good at not overanalyzing my personal life. But I have come to suspect that I have been lazy about love. Now I'm paying for it. So I am ready for an enlightening conversation about what we may and may not ask of love and marriage. I never imagined that I might meet the man who wrote the book that saved me when I was a girl. And now I feel that nothing could be more important than to sit for a few hours with you and my husband and talk things over.

Sincerely, and with many thanks for your kind consideration,

Emily Babson

PS: I just reread this and apologize for the gravity. I'm not usually so grim.
PPS: I trust you won't share this e-mail with anybody without my consent.

Stella, November 2011

Stella was in a cover meeting with the art department that was not going well at all. They were in Horatio Alger—one of the better conference rooms because it had windows. And Stella had enjoyed good results there before. But somehow this time she could get nothing from the art people, from Angela and Bobby and their director, Julie, who was invariably in a shitty mood because of a divorce that had been dragging on for more than a year. The haggling over the settlement was forcing Julie to be very careful with money, so she had to stay home in Tarrytown with her kids most nights and this made it near-impossible to date. Stella knew all this about Julie because she commiserated with her in the halls and the bathroom. And though Stella wished that listening to Julie would translate to an easier working relationship, it seemed to have the opposite effect. Poor Angela and Bobby weren't even allowed to show their comps.

They were supposed to be discussing the cover for a nonfiction book about the new slow-growth happiness model for life by a *Toronto Sun* reporter that Stella had bought in a little auction six months earlier.

"It needs to feel light," Stella said. "But at the same time very smart."

"The whole book does?" Julie asked.

"Well, yes." Stella smiled and raised her eyebrows, thinking, I am the sun and I bestow brightness and light. "The whole package, you know."

Julie massaged the jade bracelets on her right wrist and stared out the window. Angela and Bobby had images turned facedown on the table. Stella yearned to turn the color printouts over but she was afraid of Julie, who was well past forty and secure enough at Ladder & Rake to feel free to yell at Stella if she dared get between her and her direct reports.

Julie took a deep breath and said, "Stella, we hear you and we do have some ideas, but first you really need to be more—"

The door to the conference room opened and Lucy Brodsky stepped in. Everybody went stiff and then just as quickly pretended not to.

"We were just—" Julie paused and waved her hands in the air. "Does Helena want me?"

Nobody wanted a walk and elevator ride with Lucy Brodsky to see Helena. Nobody. Even if the meeting went great, it was still bad news, because a good meeting led to another meeting. And nobody had two good meetings in a row.

"No, not you, Julie. Don't worry," Lucy said. "Stella? Can I check in with you about one quick thing? Group, I'll have Stella back with you all in a moment."

"Of course," Stella said to nobody as she followed Lucy out of the room. Stella turned and blinked hard at Julie, who continued to frantically wave her braceleted arms in the air, pawing at the space where Stella had been standing as if she could pull her back to safety.

"We're in Melissa's office," Lucy called over her shoulder. "I thought I'd check in with her first, you know, about *Canoe.*"

"Sure, that makes sense." Stella rolled her eyes back in her head and pretended to scream as she followed Lucy down the carpeted hall. She hadn't had a conversation with her boss in days. She stared at Lucy from behind. Lucy was so clean, with her black hair and white blouse and black patent leather pumps. Stella bit her lips and looked down at her scuffed Camper Mary Janes. She'd been promising herself forever that she would throw them away. But instead she'd gotten into the habit of only wearing them on quiet days, when she didn't expect to see anybody important. Boy, did that never work out.

"Just in here," Lucy said, as if Stella didn't know where her boss's office was.

"Hi!" Melissa said, and frowned. "We were talking about *Canoe*, me and Lucy were. And we thought we'd better reach right out to you."

"Okay," Stella said. "Great."

Melissa was standing, wearing jeans and a suit jacket over a flower-print blouse with a floppy collar.

"You were in with Julie?" Melissa asked. "She giving you what you need?"

"I'll get something good out of her eventually," Stella said.

"Wonderful," Melissa said. "Let's sit down."

A small blond conference table squatted between Melissa's desk and the door. The three of them huddled around it. Melissa slouched back, folded her arms over her chest.

"So, Stella. I was checking in with Melissa about Peter Herman. Where are we with him?" Lucy asked. Stella stared at Lucy. She wanted to say, What's it to you? But she didn't figure Melissa would back her up. She glanced at Melissa's desk. There was a wrinkled manuscript spread out across it. The poor woman must've actually been editing one of her self-help/memoir titles and been interrupted for this meeting. Melissa was one of those editors who actually liked to edit.

"Well?" Lucy smiled. "Come on. Help me out here."

"The contest," Stella said, "is going absolutely great. We have thousands of entries and sure enough, sales are inching up. I mean I'm not talking huge, but definitely up like nine or eleven percent this week. Plus, I think we found our winner. I just need to get Peter Herman's approval. That could happen today!"

"Let's focus on Peter. What is going on with him?" Lucy had a stylus poised over her screen.

Stella didn't have an answer. Behind Melissa's desk, on the windowsill, were photographs in silver frames of Melissa and her arts-administration husband, their two girls, and Florence, their dog. They stood in their skinny backyard in Riverdale. And here was Melissa, happily editing in the office. No wonder Melissa didn't speak to her. She had no ambition and was jealous of Stella's youth and unpredictability. Yeah, that's what it was.

"Stella?"

"Sorry. He's great." Stella pitched forward in her chair. "He is really onboard and it's—well, it's exciting to be working with him."

"I see," Lucy said. She tapped the screen on her iPad. "Okay, here's the thing. It's nice that we're seeing sales growth on *Canoe*. That's good, sure. But Peter Herman is a highly valued author. And Helena." Lucy paused. Stella and Melissa stared at her. Lucy bent in toward them. "Helena does not want anything to go wrong with Peter Herman. You understand? So come back to me soon with a happy report from Peter Herman that I can give to Helena. Like an e-mail or something that you could forward? Otherwise, Helena will be unhappy. You see?"

"Yes," Stella said. "I see. But I am saying that he's happy." Stella caught Melissa shooting her a shut-the-fuck-up-and-let's-end-this-meeting glare. But Stella was proud of her project and wanted to talk about it.

"That's the message you want me to convey?" Lucy asked. Her smile turned thin. Stella thought she could give someone a paper cut with her lips. You wish you could be me, Stella thought, suddenly. You wish you could get free of Helena and come up with some wild schemes. Stella looked at Lucy and Melissa and thought, Actually, you both do. Great editors created great ideas. They didn't sit at their desks and try to fix manuscripts. Stella stiffened. Why should she be cowed by the day-to-day vicissitudes of the workplace? Someday, if she was lucky, Lucy would be working for her! And Melissa would edit her castoffs.

"Look, I'm excited," Stella said. "We should all be. This crazy thing is going to work."

"Fine. Let's call this an update." Lucy tapped her iPad and Stella listened to the whooshing sound of a sent e-mail. "Keep us posted will you, Melissa?"

Melissa nodded. "I will. Stella has been updating me regularly so that's no problem."

Lucy leaned in and said, "Between us, I can't imagine why Helena cares about any of this. I mean there's profitable backlist and then there's what you discovered. But let's keep her happy. Goodness knows that will make all our lives easier, right?"

"I promise it will work," Stella said. "At the end of the day, *Canoe* is going to be huge all over again."

"It's just marketing," Lucy said, and shrugged. "I'm sorry you all have to do so much of it when it's not really your job. You wouldn't believe the nasty things Helena says about the marketing people. Hey, do you need a second reader on that?" Lucy jutted her chin at the pile of paper on Melissa's desk. "I prefer fiction but I'm dying to read anything."

"Not this." Melissa stood up and went behind her desk. "I think my author wrote it in German and then sent it through Google Translate."

"Okay, maybe not that," Lucy said.

"I have a couple of novels I can e-mail you," Stella said.

"Would you?" Lucy smiled. "I promise I'll write great reports. Because if I don't get out of executive and into editorial soon I swear I am going to off myself. Bye, you two!" And Lucy clicked down the hall.

Melissa sat down behind her desk and kept smiling for a full five seconds after Lucy left.

Stella figured, What the hell, common enemy—I'll take a shot. "She's too clean for editorial," she said to Melissa.

"Editorial? Is that what you think you're doing?" Melissa smiled at Stella. And suddenly Stella felt that she'd lost her read on the situation.

She stood up and said, "I'm sorry she bothered you."

"You're sorry?" Melissa stared at Stella and licked her lips. "Listen, I have no idea what the fuck that was all about. And I don't want to know. But I do want to tell you that I've been here eight years without one problem and it's all because I know enough to stay the hell away from Helena. That's the only politics I play. Get it? So clean this *Canoe* problem up, Stella, 'kay? Because I do not want to be on Helena's radar."

"I can—"

"Don't you have Julie waiting for you in Alger? I believe Alger's where that lapdog dug you up."

"Right," Stella said, suddenly remembering. "Sorry. I'll clean it up right quick."

"Clean what up?" Melissa said. "You don't get it, do you? You are blowing up a balloon and you think you'll be able to hang on to it and it'll sail you over all our heads, but what if you don't have enough gas?"

"Um. I understand that metaphor but I don't exactly follow the sentiment," Stella said, and wished that Melissa would just come out and tell her she didn't like her instead of being so subtle about it.

"Now's a good time to figure it out. Because

they're watching you. Next time it won't be the foot soldier coming at you. You get me?"

"I promise I'll make us look good."

"Us?" Melissa rolled her eyes and pulled a plastic container of apple slices out of her handbag. "Sure you will. Now go back to your meeting. I don't need to have issues with Julie, too."

Emily, October 2011

"What is this?" Eli asked Emily. He'd just come out of their bedroom, where he'd been getting dressed. He held the book out to her. She gasped—speechless in front of this longed-for image of him with his hands on a copy of *Canoe*.

She'd learned that he never looked at what was on the coffee table, or at the books and things on their nightstands. So she had placed a copy of *Canoe* on top of the *Sports Illustrated* and *Bicycling* and *Fixie* magazines that lay in a steel crate next to the toilet. And then when he didn't pick it up there either, she'd jammed the book into his laptop case.

She said, "It's that *Canoe* book. I want you to have a look at it."

"Why?"

"Because I have a surprise for you."

It was mid-morning on a Saturday and they had planned to part soon. Before he had gone to get dressed, Eli had peeled and eaten a grapefruit, and now the rind lay in a perfect swirl on his plate on the kitchen island, where he'd left it. His rinds were so beautiful. She used to dry them because she'd always imagined that she would make something out of them, but she could never figure out just what. She had one on her bulletin board at work.

He began to page around in *Canoe*. He appeared to note the new afterword and foreword and index and exercises. Then he turned his face up to her, silent and wide-eyed, looking for an explanation.

"It's a good surprise," Emily said. "I like watching you read it."

"This book." Eli held it up between them. "It's like a cautionary measure."

"What's bad about that?"

"I guess nothing." Eli stared at her and nodded. "I understand. Of course it's okay."

"I love that you're so open. Anyway, that edition starts out with a kind of sports story. I want you to read it. You can read while I go to yoga."

Eli stroked his chin. She saw him read a few lines. He winced but caught her watching and pretended as if he hadn't. He said, "You know about the different editions of the same marriage advice book?"

"I do. We're in a good place now, right? But you understand that I'm still not totally happy. I'm still healing."

"Yes," Eli answered quickly.

"Then I want to reveal more about myself. Isn't that part of what you're asking for? For me to be more open?"

"Yes, definitely. Open. So I can love you. And so we can repair. Like we said."

"This is part of how we're doing that. I still get angry when I think about it. Really angry. But this is helping. When I get back I can tell you the surprise and maybe we can . . . spend the day together."

"Why don't we go for a ride and that'll be us spending the day together?"

"Maybe. But right now I really want to do a class. Then we can be together, and if we end up on bikes, that's fine."

She grabbed her bag and her mat and practically ran out of the house. Totally calculated and a bit dishonest, she thought. But Eli liked surprises. He liked to think about situations and then be surprised at how they turned out. She'd learned this about him at their beginning. It was true when they cooked together. It was especially true when he worked. So she had created a way for him to discover what she had done that was sympathetic to how she believed he actually was.

She ran to Yogasana. It was her third-favorite studio but it was the one nearest their apartment. She was late but they let her in. In the last row, too close to the clanking radiators, she went through the poses, trying desperately to engage. And she was amazed to discover that by the time they arrived at headstands she was there, not thinking of Eli or the contest she'd won, but instead entirely able to relax and let the energy out through her toes, which were still and pointed toward the dark ceiling.

"Really nice, Emily," the instructor said as she touched Emily's calf. "Now picture your arms as big strong cables and plug them into their sockets. There you go. Beautiful."

In the super-calm that came at the end, while she relaxed in corpse pose, she felt happy and was immediately angry at herself for slipping so easily into happiness. Maybe it was because she was a winner now? That was ridiculous and she hoped that might be the answer. But she'd also felt like she was going to win the moment she'd e-mailed her entry. It was nice to win something. She was proud of herself. And she was giddy at the idea of meeting Peter Herman. This wasn't fate. It was even better. It was her, taking control of her destiny—in much the same way she had met Eli. And she believed that was when she was her best self, when she tried her hardest.

When she returned to their apartment, she found Eli in a chair he had dragged to the front bay windows. His head jerked around in a way that made her suspect he had been dozing. But he still had the book near him. That was enough.

"I'm enjoying this," he said.

"You are?" She sounded surprised.

"You want me to care about it. I like that."

She kneeled in front of him. He reached forward and kissed her forehead and then her lips.

"I have a surprise."

"I'm hungry. Is it a food surprise?"

"There was a contest related to this book. I entered it."

"A contest? This is the thing you were talking about with Ida at that dinner? I knew I overheard something weird."

He kept shaking his head while she told him about it.

"I can't believe this is where we are," he said. "I can't believe this is happening."

"I know," she said. "I can't either. We've been through something bad but now we're winners. You have to see it that way."

"I do?" he asked.

She went to the kitchen for water and she looked at the grapefruit peel, still on its plate. He hadn't cleaned up. She'd once explained that peel stuck to her bulletin board to a woman at work, and the woman had given her a funny look and said, "Wow, you must really love your husband."

And Emily had said, "Yeah, I guess I really do."

Now Eli called out, "I feel like this isn't a surprise exactly . . . This is more like being pushed into doing something without totally being asked. I mean, marriage counseling? That's essentially what this is."

"Because we need it!" Images of Jenny Alexandretti came rising up in Emily. She fought against saying her name and tried to fake a laugh. She said, "Don't erase my yoga glow by questioning this."

"No, no." Eli shook his head like he'd sworn already, to himself, not to do just that. "I get it. I was just—you're pushing me a little. But I'll do it. I'll do whatever you want. I owe you."

He came into the kitchen.

"Thank you," she whispered. "Peter Herman, the guy who wrote the book—I'm sure he's really old now but I used to dream about him as a kid. I almost know that book by heart."

"Yeah?" Eli wrapped his arms around her. She had a sports bra on and he worked his fingers beneath it.

"I promise it'll be fun. And I'll tell you more about the book and what it meant to me. And about when I was a kid. This is me, like you asked. Me revealing myself to you."

"Good," Eli said.

"And don't forget that we're winners."

"Sure. You . . . planned to win. You're such a good writer."

"No, I'm not. Don't say that."

"The moment you entered, I bet you knew you'd win."

"Maybe I did. Thank you for being cool about this."

"It's more than that. I want to do whatever you want. You know what I think about? I want to get back to where we were last summer when we were seeing your sister a lot."

"Before . . ."

"Yes," Eli said. "And now it's more than a year later and let's go in the bedroom."

"Not out here?"

"No, in there where it's not so bright," Eli said. "I want to smell you in the dark."

"That's stupid."

"Humor me." Eli pulled at her arms. "Like I'm humoring you."

"Did you get the idea of what he's saying about the canoe? The safety of it?" Once they were in the bedroom she was surprised at how much she wanted him. She pulled off her yoga pants.

"It's you and me in a canoe." Eli threw himself down and looked up at her. "This bed. This bed is our canoe."

She looked down at him. They were having sex more and more often now. And she would be lying to herself if she didn't admit that she was happy. Happy, in some ways, that the bad thing had happened so they could get over it and get further toward the real love they were having now. And back, soon, to being ready to have children.

"You're amazing," Eli said. "I'm lucky to be with a woman who surprises me. A marriage counseling contest? Only you, Emily. Only you could win that."

"Stop," Emily said. "I'm lucky, too."

"You promise that you feel that way? Come here. I want to touch you."

"Let me stand here for one more second," she said.

Stella, November 2011

Now that she had a winner, Stella was on to phase two. Which was short-lead publicity. After they'd agreed on Emily Babson and Eli Corelli as the winners, Stella was hesitant to get in touch with Peter Herman again until she had some real media hits. He had been so easy to deal with and she was afraid to waste his time. But her winners were motivated and her publishing house was curious and Peter was happy. So she was in a rush. She spent a few days trying to get on the phone with her ex-friend Elspeth Simon, who worked at *The New Yorker*. Elspeth had just been promoted to Talk of the Town from the website and was getting a big head about it.

Elspeth Simon had been her roommate during sophomore year, when they were nineteen. And just two years ago and a full seven years after something similar happened when they were roommates, she had stolen Stella's boyfriend, Joe, an acoustic guitar player who opened for Will Oldham from time to time. Joe was the guy before Ivan, and it had taken her some time and a few casual hookups before she got over him. There had actually been three, but Ivan was the one who stayed. And that had been a nice result. Still, she sometimes missed Joe, even though he'd been so incredibly withholding. He was a sweet and gentle guy with eyes the color of raw almonds.

At the time, Stella had let Elspeth take Joe without a fight. The new couple was humbled by Stella's generosity. They had been caught by mutual friends at the seventh anniversary of a "Let's Be Naked" party, and someone more insecure than Stella might have been a real jerk about it. About how cliché it was and also about the fact that the context implied bodies were major factors in the hookup. Like, oh, check this out! Look at all that's still working here at twenty-six! Let's use these hot bodies for some serious pleasure-fucking! Really, it was both depressing and repulsive in equal measure. Also a bit of a turn-on, Stella thought.

To this day, she berated herself for having gone to a lamb tasting that evening to celebrate a new April Bloomfield cookbook. She had eaten too much and found herself, at ten, feeling far too fat to meet Joe at a party where she would have to be naked. So her ambition had already lost her one boyfriend. Still, things had worked out in the end. She loved Ivan, maybe, and wouldn't have hooked up with him if Elspeth hadn't yanked Joe into a bathroom or wherever at that party while Stella lay at home, watching her stomach rise and fall. Or maybe Joe and Elspeth got into it out in the open? Ugh!

"You owe me one big naked-ass favor, to say the least," Stella said once she got Elspeth on the phone.

"I totally agree," Elspeth said.

"It's about this weird self-help book, *Marriage Is a Canoe*." Stella went on to describe what she needed. "I already messengered a copy over to you."

"So that's why it's on my desk," Elspeth said. "It'll be a Herculean effort, but I think I can make it happen."

"It'd help me out a lot," Stella said. "I also think it would help us both, karmically."

"I feel you. I'm on it."

From *Marriage Is a Canoe*,
Chapter 5, On Beginnings

My summer wasn't spent entirely with the older folks. There was little Johnny, who became a good companion, if not a close friend. And then there were kids who lived in houses up and down the lake. I didn't play with them too often, but enough so I was invited to a square-dancing birthday party in the Lindermans' barn, which was up on a hill about a mile from my grandparents' house. The birthday girl had honey-colored hair and she said I could call her Honey. Everyone did. Honey Linderman. Thirteen years old and she rode a fourteen-hand mare, one I'd heard had come all the way from a stable in Wyoming.

"I've been looking for you," Honey said, when she saw me. "Come on!"

I had to chase her to the middle of the barn where the picnic tables were. I knew my grandparents thought she was spoiled. But she was so happy, it seemed right to spoil her. She did curse. It was damn this and the hell with that. And she always cursed and I always wondered why her parents let her.

There were twenty or twenty-five of us kids at that barn dance. First we had an icebox cake with vanilla frosting and strawberry ice cream and we sang "Happy Birthday" to Honey, all of us in a circle. We presented our presents, which most of us had bought at Casey's store in town. There was a kaleidoscope and a white patent leather pencil case from her best friend at school. One boy gave her a copy of the new Dion record and I saw her mother thank him and then hide it out of sight.

"Goddamn it, Mom," she said, so only us kids could hear.

The adults began to arrive when the square dancing got started. But first it was a children's dance, with a violinist who we recognized as the druggist from town, and a caller, a tall man with a mustache and a pinstripe suit who no one knew at all. There was a lady singer, too, who got up and sang with her hands clasped in front of her. We danced and sang and I knew I was perspiring and that I probably smelled. I stared at Honey all through the songs and she stared back at me. When we were partnered, I felt sure we were holding our hands together more tightly than anyone else.

The caller let us know that he was going to take a break. He disappeared behind the barn with the lady singer and the druggist. We all knew for sure they were going to smoke and drink whiskey. But we said nothing. Instead, we played and chased and ran. And then Honey came behind me and covered my eyes.

"Come with me," she said. "But don't follow too close. Hurry up."

A moment later, she was gone. I was sure she was going down the path to the stables, just a few hundred yards from the barn. There was moonlight, thank goodness. And I followed her, but not too close, just like she'd said.

"You found me!" she said, too loud, when I came in after her. There were just a few lights hanging from the rafters, swaying up there, and we could hear her family's three horses asleep in their stalls, snuffling through their dreams.

I remember staring at her beautiful face, her tawny hair and sunburned summer skin and bright green eyes. Maybe she wasn't beautiful. Maybe her eyebrows were a little thick. Her voice was husky and that didn't fit either, because though she had a mouth on her, I would later discover that in the really big moments, she was shy.

That first kiss in the stables was more than everything. It was a perfect thing. All around us was the smell of wet hay and strawberry ice cream on our fingers from the party.

We kissed twice and embraced, our long arms encircling each other's backs. We were unsure of what else we might do.

"Don't tell anybody," she said. "Don't tell anybody about this."

"I really like you," I said, not caring if she told anyone or not and aware that in that thought was my first movement toward some maturity. Useless as it was just then, but there.

"Shhh!" She was giddy. "Shut the hell up!"

We ran back to the party, breathless, maybe twenty seconds apart, sure that we'd fooled everyone, though of course anyone who cared knew just where we'd been and what we'd done.

Bess and Pop had arrived and they were drinking with the other grown-ups. I came over and got between them. "What are you drinking?" I asked.

"Take a tiny sip," Pop said. And I did. It was lemonade laced with whiskey that Lisa's parents had made. I have loved that strange too-sweet taste ever since.

"Are you making sure to act like nothing less than a proper gentleman?" Pop asked, with his hand gripping the brown scruff of hair on the back of my neck.

"Yes," I said, and ran back to find Honey and dance some more.

Later, as we made our way home on the moonlit road, I ran in circles around my grandparents, like a much younger boy, thinking of when I would see Honey again.

In his third revision, Peter added the following:

Less than a decade later, I would come back to Millerton as alone as when I was a child, to bury my grandparents and to find Lisa again.

I married her in our Millerton town hall and we had the party in that very barn, her family's barn in Millerton. She was still the same—headstrong and charming and clear about love.

I'm not suggesting that we all should marry the first girl we kiss. But then again, why not? Once you're in love, if you follow the path that love provides for you, why not stay in love? With that one person—even if they've got a bit of a foul mouth!

Most likely, true love is nearby.

From *The New Yorker*'s November 14, 2011, Talk of the Town section

TROUBLED WATERS

We don't know about you, but come mid-November, we look forward to indoor parties with fondue and Scrabble-and-scotch sessions with friends. But a few days ago, we decided to shake up our routine with a brisk canoe ride. The desire for such a trip was stirred by news from Ladder & Rake Books that it plans to reinvigorate *Marriage Is a Canoe*, the book of marriage advice by Peter Herman. LRB has created a contest that's meant to celebrate the fiftieth anniversary of the events upon which the advice book is based, which had to do with a summer Herman spent as a boy with his grandparents on Lake Okabye in upstate New York.

One lucky couple has already been selected to spend a Saturday with Herman, who has maintained a Pynchonesque quiet for the last decade (everyone knows where he lives, no one will give you directions). We were in no mood to chase down a sage. Better to leave the task of intimate talk about marriage with Herman to the contest winners. Our desire was simply to take a paddle on a lake in Herman's inarguably sylvan part of New York State.

Further investigation led to Fred Benton, who has run Hudson Valley Canoe Tours since 1985. Benton is married to Annika Benton, who teaches kindergarten in Poughkeepsie. The couple have two children, Roderick, nine, and Annaliesa, fifteen. Benton agreed to take us on a morning trip around Silver Lake, one of his favorite spots, which probably wouldn't be too windy.

And so, on a gray Thursday morning, we found Benton at his preferred meeting spot, in the parking lot of the Village Diner in Red Hook. The "historic" Village Diner is clad in steel and shiny, not unlike the canoes used at camps all up and down the East Coast. Benton waved us over. He is a thin man in his fifties with gray eyes and a horseshoe of stubble around his otherwise bald head. The Michael Stipe of East Coast canoeing?

"In the summers I give tours to families and I'll run expert paddling seminars out of Jay's Camping Outlet on Mamaroneck highway on the weekends if enough people sign up," Benton said as he drove us to the lake in his hunter-green Ford F-150 pickup truck. There were several canoes tied up in a steel canopy built in the truck bed and they jostled one another in the wind as we rode. "But once fall hits it's the off-season. So today, it's just us."

We parked and watched Benton nimbly untie a canoe and bring it to the water. He had chosen his favorite, a bright red Old Town Guide 147, made of three layers of polyurethane.

"It's a cheap and basic model but I swear by it," Benton said. "Can't hurt it even with a baseball bat, practically. The wooden ones are museum pieces if we're being honest."

Fred handed over a Carlisle Scout paddle to this paddler. He got us out on the water and we felt the welcome of the great outdoors, safely bundled as we were in bright orange Extrasport Volksvest safety vests. Fred himself didn't wear one. He used a beat-up black plastic paddle.

"Bad habits," Fred said, alluding to his lack of vest and junky paddle. "Can't break 'em."

We paddled and gazed at the turning leaves. Fred explained that Silver Lake was about a hundred and eighty feet deep and was typical of the lakes in the Hudson Valley region. It was his favorite lake because of the Silver linden trees that lined the banks. They averaged only about forty years of age and were still buoyant and held their leaves longer than most.

Did Benton know Peter Herman?

"I believe I've met him once or twice over the years," he said, once the shore felt to this city paddler to be several midtown blocks away. "I'm not much for social life. Ask my wife about him if you like." Benton called Annika on his cellular phone. Once he explained the nature of the query, he handed the phone down the length of the canoe.

"Yes, of course I know Peter Herman," Annika said. "Fred and I have eaten dinner at his inn. He's a wonderful man. You say you're out on Silver Lake? Aren't you cold?"

Did she think that the lessons from *Marriage Is a Canoe* actually worked? Did she consider herself lucky to be married to a man who spent his days paddling in a canoe?

"I can't say I ever thought of it that way," she said, and apologized for not being able to talk longer. She had to return to her classroom to supervise morning snack (apples and string cheese).

This paddler wondered aloud about what sort of questions the winning couple might ask Peter Herman, and what canoeing had in common with love.

"There's no secret to a good canoe trip," Fred said. "Keep a steady stroke. Don't jam the paddle into the water. Dip it in. Nice and easy." We gleaned that he might be worried this paddler would splash him with cold lake water and so we evened our strokes.

Did Benton take trips in the canoe with his wife and children? Did he fill the canoe with just enough supplies for a happy day on the water?

"Not since the girl became a teenager," he said, and left it at that.

This paddler went ahead and reeled off a few of the other lessons found in *Canoe*. What about: *Find time to be together every day—just the two of you—in your canoe?*

"Good luck with that." Benton's paddling had slowed. He said, "I'll allow that I agree it's a good principle. So sure, Herman may have something going. If I were him I might add a bit about sticking with your old model canoe rather than trading for a new one—you know, to get across that folks ought to stay married to one person. And something else about not needing an expensive canoe to have a good time." Benton smiled. "Once you get started, this stuff is pretty easy! No wonder he wrote it. What's the one about infidelity?"

We wondered at Benton, who seemed to know a bit more than he was letting on.

You will look at others with lust, and this will challenge the strength of your marriage. But if you're going to have a happy journey through this life, stay in your own canoe.

"That's the one." Benton wouldn't say more. He spat into the lake and raised an eyebrow. He said, "Let's get out of this cold water."

Fred drove us back to the Village Diner and took us inside for sandwiches and tomato soup. Would the homilies found in *Canoe* apply to his own marriage? Would Fred share an example? Fred ate half his grilled cheese and bacon on white. He

252

chewed for a while and then said, "Not being a metaphorical thinker myself, it hadn't come to me before today. But now that we've focused in on it, I agree that the lessons apply. I paddle around all the day long. Thinking about marriage as a canoe definitely couldn't hurt. I'm more patient because I understand the water. I know when the wind will help us along and when we need to really work together to keep going in the right direction." He winked and dunked the other half of his sandwich into his soup. "See? It's easy. Marriage is a canoe. Makes a lot of sense. Can't say the same for kayaking. Kayakers are often loons and loners."

Outside the diner the sky threatened rain and we waved goodbye to Fred Benton, who was checking the bungee cords that held down his canoes. Fred let us know that next month he'd turn to his winter work, tuning up rental ski and snowboard mounts and bindings at Hunter Mountain ski resort.

"I like the summers better," Benton said. "But the winters are quiet and that's good with me, too. You tell those contest winners congratulations from me! Annika and I wish them the best of luck. They ought to come back this way in the spring for a tour with me, and if they do, it's half off!"

—*Elspeth Simon*

Peter, November 2011

Peter drove into Millerton to do some shopping at Pantomime's Grocery. He liked to visit with Pantomime's owner, Arthur Levin. Arthur had built a theater in the grocery's enormous backyard and run it successfully from the early seventies all the way into the early eighties. But as Arthur grew older, the theater and its demands had proved difficult to handle. Now Arthur was a Millerton old-timer who ran a good grocery store with an illogical name that was equally popular with tourists and locals.

Peter moved up and down the store's two aisles. Enormous posters lined the walls above the shelves, of *The Threepenny Opera* and *Oklahoma!* and *Macbeth*, posters that Peter imagined were ignored by the men and women who came in after shifts at Gilmor glassworks and the tire-repair places along Old Country Road to buy dark- and light-colored beer, respectively. Or was it now the opposite? Peter stood in front of the beer cases, meditating on this, while Arthur belted out gossip from his perch behind the counter at the front of the store.

"I hear you're leaving town," Arthur yelled. He stood on a plywood platform, so his round stomach pressed against the counter and was framed on the sides by a pair of thin black suspenders from his mime days. He was five and a half feet tall and had a thick brown beard, just like the one most men in Millerton wore in the winter. He was dressed in his uniform of jeans, dirty white turtleneck, and red hunting cap, flaps up.

"Am I?"

"If I heard it, it's got to be the truth." Arthur smiled.

The place smelled of the briny pickles that Arthur made himself, and the oily wool scarves and misshapen hats made by Arthur's new wife, Vanessa, who had moved up from New York after a weekend stay at the inn with some girlfriends. She'd come in alone on a Saturday afternoon for tuna, sharp cheddar, and sprouts on a pita, and had left with an old man's admiration and a chance at a new life that would leave behind the city that had let her down in the love department.

"Do the glassblowers like dark beer or light beer?" Peter asked.

"You're talking beer fashion? Hell if I know," Arthur said. "Ask my beer guy. Or better, ask Henry. He knows that stuff."

Peter nodded and dropped his basket on the counter. He set out shoelaces, dried cranberries, Cadbury chocolate, Grape-Nuts, a bag of baby carrots, and a quart of low-fat milk.

"And how are you?" Peter asked.

"Me? Who cares?" Arthur said. "I read about your contest in *The New Yorker*." Arthur gestured at the laptop computer that sat between the credit card swipe machine and a red tin bucket filled with maple syrup candy. "Good piece."

"What piece?"

"The save-your-marriage thingy?" Arthur made a ball with his hands and mimed laying it in a hoop. "Neat idea. That's probably the most Fred Benton's talked to a stranger in ten years. She must've been a hot young thing, that reporter. If I were still married to Françoise, I'd have entered your contest with a little entry essay that'd knock your socks straight into Connecticut. But with Vanessa, there're no problems." Arthur's voice went up and he sounded just a little giddy. "Look at you!" he said. "Between your imminent departure and your contest, you're the busiest old boy in the 'burg."

"Back up," Peter said. "Fred Benton talked to a reporter about me?"

"He said he didn't know you. As I recall you and he had words back at the Sally Forth years ago, when you couldn't keep your hands to yourself and he and Annika hadn't yet made it legal. But Fred's not one for speaking ill of his enemies."

"Because he's not one for talking, as you noted." Peter frowned and grabbed up *The New York Times* and a *Poughkeepsie Journal* from the wire rack. Then he took a *Millerton Gazette*, which was free.

"Anyway, it's true," Peter said. "I did promise Maddie I'd move to California with her."

"And I admire you for it," Arthur said. "She reminds me of that young girl on *The Office*—Mindy Kaling. Steady gaze, hot, modern—maybe Maddie doesn't have as much of a sense of humor but the rest of it makes sense. On your charge?"

"Yes."

"So you've got these winners coming to meet with you. Why not bring them down to Pantomime's and we can put on a show. We can talk folksy about marriage and they'll see how human you are. I'll make out to be real impressed by you and then I'll tell them about me and Vanessa. We can give them some apple cider donuts. We take pictures and I'll get some press that'll help me with the tourist trade. What do you say?"

"God. I don't know, Arthur."

"Couldn't hurt."

"No, I suppose it couldn't. And I'm moving away soon afterward, aren't I? Since you only hear the truth."

"Indeed." Arthur leaned forward. "Look, Peter. A woman wants you—go with her."

Peter dragged his paper bag off the counter. He cradled it in his arms. The bag felt heavy and alive. He hadn't managed to get comfortable with shopping for one and it still felt wrong. Did he buy too much? Too little? He could never tell.

"You've had a good run here," Arthur said. "Now you've got a woman who cares about you and you're getting out. Believe me, that is okay."

"I'm glad everybody's got an opinion about where I ought to lay my head."

"What the hell else are we supposed to talk about?"

The door opened and a young couple came in, stretching from what appeared to be a long spell of driving—most likely from the city to visit someone for the weekend.

"Where's your coffee?" the man asked. Arthur smiled and held up a hand in a just-a-moment gesture. Peter moved toward the door.

"Don't stick around for no reason!" Arthur called out. "I'll never forget when Peter Schumann walked in that door and asked me to join up with him and his Bread and Puppet theater operation up there in Vermont and I said no because I wanted to make my own way here. A bunch of fucking geniuses about to make history and I said no!" Arthur made two fists and pumped his arms at his ceiling, which was decorated with bits of colored paper from piñatas and Cinco de Mayo celebrations. "Peter Schumann saw a kindred spirit in me and I said no. He makes history and I make coffee. Somebody asks for your hand, you give it to them, you get me?"

"Yeah. I'll see you soon," Peter said.

"And remember to bring your winners here! I'll put together some fresh quinoa salad and some other stuff. It'll be a party." Arthur turned to the couple. "Now, you young people, what kind of coffee would you like? Because I am going to make it fresh for you. And while I do, I am going to tell you the story of that man who is right now walking out the door."

Back at home, Peter got Lisa's computer going and read the *New Yorker* piece.

Well, he thought, if the winners are as awkward as old Fred was with that reporter, it will be a hell of an awful long Saturday.

He glanced at the framed black-and-white photograph on the wall above the light switch, of his Pop coming in for the day with a few fish in a bucket, wearing a green vest and a blue T-shirt, blue jeans, a Lucky Strike hanging off his lip, nearly perpendicular to the grassy waterfront. Not even sixty in the picture and looking about as Peter did now, save that he was smaller and had more of a paunch. Just an occasionally kind and generally affable old man who could bear the weight of Peter's aphorisms in death. Not a drunk, thank god. Just a retired salesman with a pension from the army and a little bit of money on top of that from his wife. A wife who, in turn, was much as he was. A daughter who had started out well enough and then moved to New York City for no good reason. An easily confused woman who became Peter's mother and who was dead of alcoholism before her son finished college.

Peter went and found the cordless phone in its cradle in his study, picked it up, and weighed it in his palm.

He got Stella on the phone and said, "I am sorry to be slow about returning your calls."

"Oh, no," Stella said. He could hear her getting up to close a door. "Not at all. We are doing this on your schedule. Though we have scheduled the weekend for our winners and we do need to confirm all that with you."

"I read the *New Yorker* piece. A little smug."

"That's the right word! They are so smug. They just do whatever they want. I'm so sorry if any of it offended you. I can call someone over there and complain?"

"No, no. I'm sure they're impossible to control. And Fred could've been a whole lot worse," he said. "There's a backstory there."

"I'm sure there is." She laughed. "Do you want to tell me about it?"

Peter considered. What good was there in telling her? Young people didn't need to know about decades-old misunderstandings. Well, offenses, really. He'd taken it too far with Annika one night when they thought Fred had passed out. They'd been wrong and Fred had popped one eye open and reached across the booth there at the Sally

Forth, grabbing Peter by the throat and swearing never to forget. An unfortunate evening.

"Better not," Peter said. "What a pretty laugh you have."

"Thank you."

"Yes, it's high and sweet. Delicate as a balsawood canoe."

"That's so, Peter—that's so well said . . . I mean, my voice is nothing. But your words . . ."

"Let me go into the other room, to hear you better," he said. He'd figured out that the older he acted, the better Stella liked him. People always walked around while on the phone, without telling the person on the other end of the line where they were going. And so did he, old ham that he was.

"Listen," he said. "You are saving my life. I'm old enough to be truthful. You were decent and you waited for me to mourn and then you approached, brilliantly, and now here we are. Those people at LRB ought to give you a medal, or at least promote you."

"That's kind, but I'm very happy. I love this job." She was breathless.

He was in the front living room looking at himself in the ancient mirror, at his beardy-white jowls and peppery gray hair mushed over his head, his too-tall body stooped to fit into his khakis and itchy red Bean sweater.

"I can't wait to meet you," Stella said. "You're a legend around here, you know. It's everyone's dream to write one book that backlists forever. Not that a new book wouldn't be . . ."

"Maybe after all this contest business I will come and spend some time in New York. It has been a while."

"That would be absolutely great! If you're not too busy, we can go for lunch or drinks. I'm sure there are plenty of people here at Ladder & Rake who want to see you. But for now, for right now in advance of then, shall I continue to firm up plans for you to meet with our winners?"

"You're free to make all the plans. I loved that young woman's essay. What was her name? Emily Babson? Solid name. Well done."

"Thank you, Peter. Your trust is inspiring! I'm sure you'll love our photographer. Would you like me to e-mail you a link to her website?"

"Photographer? No, no. There can't be any pictures. That will make us all uncomfortable. No to that."

"I see." He heard her disappointment. He decided to ignore it.

He began to root around in the coat closet, looking for a blazer he might wear in Manhattan. But, wait. Maddie could help him pick a jacket. She could choose something for him, no problem. Why didn't he think of her more? They were a couple, weren't they?

He said, "We ought to talk about a new project when it's all over, too."

"Ohhh, Peter! We would love that . . ."

"Something about how as we age, we need to welcome the future, even as it changes."

"Yes, yes, absolutely! You're sure about the photographer? Because pictures are key—"

"Out of the question."

"All right then," Stella said.

"But a new project is not."

"A fair exchange," Stella said. And he could hear that she hadn't meant to say that aloud. A new book? He shook his head. A new book was a trick he'd used before with handling editors. Still worked, apparently. No, nothing he did could hurt anyone too badly. Except sometimes. Except of course he had hurt one or two people, way back when. But a bit of carrot on a stick never hurt anyone, did it? Carrot . . . He jerked his head up and realized he'd left his sack of groceries on the front passenger seat of his car.

Stella, November 2011

Every third Tuesday, if Helena was in the office, she took the morning to do a surprise set of "management by walking around" visits. Most employees had figured this out and set their Outlook calendars accordingly, but Stella had never been able to get the hang of the schedule. Of course up to now it hadn't mattered, since she didn't rank high enough to get on Helena's stop-by list. However, because of the new multigroup focus on her *Canoe* activities, Stella was on alert. And sure enough, Lucy Brodsky shot Stella an early morning e-mail titled "Watch out!"

Stella didn't fool herself into thinking she'd been warned because Lucy liked her. She knew Lucy had done it because if Stella really screwed up, Helena would be in a nasty mood all day and Lucy would suffer.

Stella just had time to snag a flower from someone in Ad/Promo's engagement bouquet and put it in a coffee cup on her desk. She printed a fresh copy of Emily Babson's essay. She hadn't spoken to Emily personally, not just yet, on the off-chance that Helena wanted to weigh in on the winner and reject Stella's first choice. Stella wasn't afraid of the messy sequencing—she believed she could spin with the best of them. Nobody knew who the winner was, so they could just pick another. And in-house counsel could deal with Emily Babson if she caused a fuss. The only real problem was that Stella didn't have a runner-up, since all the other entrants appeared to be so irreparably damaged that to put them through the weekend and then reveal them to the public would be an act so immoral Stella would not even consider it. Not because of the act's immorality, but because it would be a professional disaster.

Stella bustled around her office one last time, clearing her head and rolling her shoulders in her blue-and-silver paisley shirt. The shirt was intentional. She would be electric today. Helena would absorb her energy and then want to be around her more. She adjusted the *Canoe* quotes on her bulletin board, moving aside rejected covers and pulling down a few photographs of her out at night with coworkers, women whom she wasn't actually friendly with at all, though they all had their cheeks together and were blowing air kisses in the pictures.

"Knock, knock!" Lucy Brodsky called out, musically, from somewhere down the hall.

"Who's— Hello!" Stella moved backward as Helena and Lucy stepped into her tiny office.

Lucy made bug eyes at Stella and then went to stand and listen in the doorway, as was required of her, while she punched in updates on her iPad, which listed Helena's next stops. Although it subverted the surprise, Lucy alerted the targets with an ETA that was plus or minus one minute so everybody was in their office and off the phone and prepared and no time was wasted—or at least, Helena's time was not wasted.

"Hello, hello," Helena said as she stepped inside and dropped into the single chair across from Stella's desk.

Helena wore a purple turtleneck and she had her hand on the ever-present gold chain. She smelled of something flowery and light that Stella imagined was custom-mixed in a tiny boutique just off Madison Avenue. Her eyes were that same filmy dark brown. Stella found herself staring into them. Helena's eyes, Stella realized, tricked you. They were warm and loving. But the things Helena said were not often that way.

"So," Helena said. "I'm told you have a winner."

"We do," Stella said. "And our contest even made it into *The New Yorker*! I have friends over there. Would you like to read the letter?"

Helena shook her head no. She said, "Peter Herman read it and liked it?"

"He did. He's been a sweetheart. He—"

Helena held up her hand. She said, "Enough about Peter." She lifted her gold chain and then let it go so it thudded against her breastbone. Stella held her breath and waited. "What else do you need to tell me?" Helena asked.

"Plenty!" Stella smiled. "We'll schedule the visit this week. Then we've, well I've, been setting up some parameters around the visit—what should be expected, what both parties will say to any early press requests."

"Photos or video?"

"Um, photos. We'll do a photo session with the couple. On the famous porch."

"You should also do video. Do you have pictures now?"

"Of the couple? Yes, I found them on Facebook."

"Together?"

"Yes, I think there's one of them together."

"Show me."

Stella tapped quickly at her keyboard. She found the image while snapping closed pages of personal stuff: her tiny Greenpoint Savings bank account, currently in overdraft; a blue-and-white wave-patterned pillow she wanted to buy on Etsy; an e-mail she'd been writing to one of her older sisters explaining why she wasn't going to make it home for Thanksgiving—all the while knowing that Helena probably didn't give a damn. The image struggled to load. One second, two seconds . . . Maybe she should show Helena the pillow?

"What are you excited about lately?" Stella said, in what she prayed was an offhand attempt to break the silence and maybe learn something about what mattered to Helena.

"Right now, I'm excited about seeing this goddamned photograph." Helena's voice was toneless. Stella felt a familiar hate directed at her—a schoolteacher's hate for a pretty student.

"Well! That's exciting for me!" Stella said while simultaneously remembering that Helena did not like cute in women. She bit her lip.

"Here it is!" Stella twisted her monitor around.

The picture showed Emily Babson and Eli Corelli at a Save Prospect Park benefit. Eli and Emily stood on a grassy hill with the white conservatory building behind. It was twilight. Eli was in a blue blazer, blue jeans, white shirt, and no tie. Emily wore a light summer dress. They were not fat or thin, but solid-looking, confident. They looked, Stella thought, as she watched Helena stare at the photo, like an actor couple, a pair of hardworking actors from a show like *Weeds* or *Mad Men* or something on HBO. Solid, friendly people who smart people liked.

"If you squint, the husband looks like a South American polo player," Stella said. "Like that guy Nacho who models for Ralph Lauren . . . you know who I'm talking about?"

"A model named Nacho? Like a nacho chip?"

"Um, forget it. They've been married about three years. In their thirties. No kids yet. They feel familiar, you know? Emily could be a friend of mine's older sister. I'm absolutely sure they are not going to break up."

"And that's what we're going for."

Stella couldn't figure out if Helena was asking a question. She said, "Yes?"

"They're the prettiest couple so I guess they won't do," Helena said. "Stop. I mean the opposite. They are fine. The man is handsome. The woman is quite attractive. She's our letter writer?"

"Yes, I—" But then Stella knew to clamp her mouth closed and let Helena talk.

Helena said, "Oddest little contest I've ever been involved with, that's for sure. If nothing else it's generating some industry chatter. Gives me something to talk about at lunch tomorrow with that snooty bitch who runs Funk and Whooten Press. Lucy, who is next? Get in here."

Lucy pivoted into the room and fake-smiled at Stella, who stared back at her wide-eyed, the warning of a week earlier suddenly stark in her head. Helena yawned and kicked at Stella's desk.

"Nice flower," Helena said. "I like lavender."

"Thank you."

"I mean the color. I'm not crazy about the smell in here."

Stella tried a smile.

"We're off to see Richard Glickstein," Lucy said.

Helena did not appear to have heard Lucy. She stared at Stella.

"The thing is," Helena said. "The most crucial

thing is to keep Peter happy. We have a long-standing relationship. You know what I mean?"

"Yes," Stella said. She glanced at Lucy who gave her a quick *right answer* nod.

Helena reached forward and smelled Stella's flower. Then she said, "You smell it," and gestured to Lucy, who immediately leaned forward and smelled the flower. "See?" Helena said. "Smells musty."

"You're right," Lucy said. "It so does."

"And can I take it?" Helena asked.

"The flower?" Lucy and Stella said, in unison.

Helena raised an eyebrow at Stella. "No. You. This contest. If you uptick sales by thirty, forty-five percent, maybe even change the distribution pattern so we get some mass merch going, get into Kroger or the airports or Costco—I mean, that's great. We should've been there all along so that's fine. But if Peter stops speaking to us, if he disconnects further from LRB—that's a problem. I would not like that."

Lucy made a noise in her throat. Helena didn't turn back to look at her.

"Who?" Helena asked.

"Glickstein."

"Right. Fuck. Motherfuck me." Helena stood up and continued to stare at Stella, who was transfixed by the sweetness in Helena's eyes. "Hard. In the ass. If he mentions the novel he's writing, pull me out of there."

"Will do," Lucy said.

Helena didn't move. She would not stop staring at Stella. Helena said, "More pretty flowers, that's what we all need. But not old ones from someone else's bouquet. More fresh flowers and more romance."

"Right," Stella said.

"Goodbye, you," Helena said. "Let me know next steps when you've got them."

"I'll keep you updated." Stella took a deep breath. "In fact, I'm even hoping that Peter may be writing again. We've touched on a new book in our conversations. Wouldn't that be wonderful?"

"Well now." Helena smiled. "He says that to all the girls. Don't get taken in. Though of course a girl can dream."

"Then I'll dream," Stella said. She thought, This goddamn thing might just work! The photos were kind of a huge problem, sure, but she'd figure that out.

"I'm sure you will, dear. And remember what we talked about a few months back."

"What was that?" Stella asked, and instantly wished she hadn't.

Helena only smiled and toggled her chain before walking out of the room. Stella followed her into the hall. And then Helena and Lucy turned right and disappeared. Stella found she was still waving goodbye.

From *Marriage Is a Canoe*,
Chapter 6, Speaking of Togetherness

One evening in the kitchen, just a few nights before the end of my stay, I watched Pop throw his arm around Bess and hug her tight. She squealed and rubbed her forehead on his chest. I looked out the window. I could smell a roast in the oven and I kept my eyes on the lusty pink of the sun's final rays as they pierced through the clouds. My grandparents' affection for each other didn't look like anything I had seen at home with my mother and father.

Later that night, I had plans to meet Honey under an oak tree at the edge of her property. I was hoping for moonlight and I'd memorized the path to that tree. I kept running the path through my head so I wouldn't think about anything else. But right then, with my grandparents, I couldn't help but feel a weird anger overcome me. I know now that I was angry because I felt that they were flaunting their love, that they were trying to stuff their love into me, all because my parents had none to show or share and my grandparents were trying to make up for that. And I felt the indignance of the boy who realizes that the gambler isn't teaching him how to gamble, he's trying to teach math. When I finally looked back at them, they were still in each other's arms.

So I said what I was feeling aloud before I could think it through: "Could you two not kiss and show off so much in front of me?"

"Why, Peter!" Bess sang out. "You should be happy to see us happy."

I glared at her. Because I didn't think she should take being happy for granted that way. Happy, I thought, is not so easy.

A few hours later, my Pop took me over to the far end of the porch and said, "Peter, you upset Bess earlier, with what you said."

"I'm sorry." I shrugged his hand off my shoulder.

"And I'm sorry your mother and father aren't treating each other well. But that doesn't mean me and Bess are showing off for you! What you see is how we actually are. Believe it or don't. Now in your life, you'll be shooting for our kind of happiness, won't you?"

"Yes. I will," I said. We'd just had banana splits and my stomach rumbled with the nuts and ice cream and hot chocolate pleasure of them.

"You going to go see Honey now?"

"Yes, if it's all right."

"Sure. Sure, it is. You be kind to that girl just the way I'm kind to our Bess." He wandered off to find his pipe.

• • •

It took me a long time to come to believing that true love between a man and a woman who are married is the one and only thing that gets people through life's storm, safe and in one piece. But now I want that belief in marriage to be true forever, for as long as I'm alive and as long as this book survives me, should that come to pass, and forever after that through your lives and your children's lives, too.

The rest of life is fine. The hard work that makes up each day and the family relationships and playing games and hobbies and friendships and all the other things that make us who we are. Sure. That stuff is good. But the marriage between Bess and Pop? That happy thoughtless incidental love in the kitchen? That's the one true thing we've got to celebrate. Every day. Reader, won't you agree?

Honor your love and
know that it is the one true thing.
Sing out in celebration of your love!
Call out hallelujah from your canoe!

Stella, November 2011

"You promised Helena photos and you can't deliver?" Sara Byrd asked.

"Because stupid Peter Herman won't let me!" Stella hammered at her desk with her little fist. "He called this morning and gave me a bunch more restrictions. No pictures, no recordings. Nothing. I'm afraid to ruffle him, because of Helena. I thought I could figure it out but it's been several days and apparently no, I can't figure it out."

Sara Byrd had taken to Stella because of a pair of two-toned sunglasses she'd seen Stella wearing once, on line at the we-toss-it salad place off the lobby. They had ended up talking about the Sol Moscot shop on Delancey Street and how fun it was to try on funky frames there.

"And the event is happening this weekend?"

"Yeah." Stella took a deep breath. It was happening and she'd created it and she had shockingly little control over it.

"Boy, have you got an unenviable set of problems," Sara said.

"I know." Stella folded her arms over her chest and frowned. "If you got caught being me for half an hour, what would you do?"

"Yikes. Let me think for a moment."

Stella stared jealously at Sara. Sara wore a charcoal dress under a charcoal cardigan. She looked sexy and smart, less like someone in editorial and more like the head of a sales group that was beating its numbers. It was just after lunch and Stella had run into Sara in the elevator and asked her to stop in. Stella had heard that Sara was one of the few people who really understood how LRB worked. And on top of that were the glasses, which she'd given to Sara in a padded envelope via interoffice mail eight months ago. She knew the gesture had been totally over the top but what the hell? Back when she'd started, Stella had wanted to be known for grand gestures. She'd quickly discovered she couldn't afford to sustain the habit.

"I like that pen you've got there." Sara smiled.

"This?" Stella held up a black mother-of-pearl pen she had bought in Chinatown when she'd arrived in New York after college. She'd promised herself that she'd use it to write one smart thing. Just one intelligent thing that she would never regret. It hadn't happened yet. Sara snatched the pen from Stella and swished it through the air.

"Maybe she'll forget," Sara said.

"No. Lucy is there whenever I talk to Helena."

"Ah, the trusty little iPad girl who's always trying to read for me. Well, maybe you can

Photoshop something together. Do you have favors logged in with the art department?"

"Yes. Stop. I mean the opposite," Stella said, remembering her last crappy meeting with Julie and her team.

"You don't know the history there, do you?" Sara squinted and tapped the pen against her cheek.

"History where?" Stella asked. "With Julie and the art department? I don't mess with her."

"Helena and Peter. They've got a history, those two."

"I'm not following."

"Imagine her younger than you. She liked to wrap her arms and legs and her whole body around a problem. You know? Granted she can be icy now, but imagine how hot that iciness was forty years ago." Sara tapped Stella's pen against her lips. Then she bit it.

"Oh, no." Stella felt miserable but tried to sound glib. "Kill me. Use the pen. Stab me. She told me and I didn't listen. I'm a dead person."

"Look, the only things more fragile and carefully protected than the current state of publishing are the oldest relationships in publishing. Helena discovered Peter Herman. Peter is a large part of how Helen came to be Helena. I mean, she's really just a poor Jewish girl from the darkest wilds of Brooklyn, out where only Chowhounds dare to go. And sometimes an editor has to create a writer in order to become a bigger editor. See? I do believe Peter is entirely hers. Plus in those days, people worked intimately. Way more than now. Get me?"

Stella rubbed her face with her hands to keep the blood flowing. "She spoon-fed that info and I missed it. I'm playing with an old flame."

"And old flames never die. But it's stronger than that. Once you make someone famous it sticks with you. It's kind of annoying, actually, to make other people famous. That plus whatever happened on the personal side? It's a volatile combo. So be careful—"

"Not to get burned. I get it. God you're good." Stella jolted forward in her chair and knocked Sofia Coppola's *Memories of Youth* to the floor with her elbow.

"You're young enough so your awkwardness is still charming," Sara said. "But that won't last much longer. So swallow this: If this contest works, she thought of it." Sara smiled again. "I really admire all the media you got for this thing. Stephen King making fun of the contest in *EW*? I should dream! Though admittedly you've got marketing throwing around too much money. A banner ad on the *USA Today* books page isn't cheap, and trust me, it'll beat the stuffing out of your P&L. When the marketing people get nervous, they spend arbitrarily and that can end up looking very uncool."

Stella stood up. She kind of wished Sara would leave, if she was just going to be insulting. At the same time, she desperately needed help. Stella said, "I pitched the contest in front of a room full of people. They'll all remember it was mine. How can I change that?"

"Are you stupid? You can't. But if it works, they'll remember it was hers—and you should pray for that outcome."

"Wait. You're saying I blew it up too big before I was sure it'd work? Melissa said the same thing. Except she used an awful metaphor."

"Melissa's no dummy. You see anyone telling her what to do? She's brilliant." Sara smiled. "Anyway, we're all saying the same thing."

"So what do I do?"

"What would you imagine Helena would say to you?"

"DFU. Don't fuck this up."

"Sure, that. What else?"

"Find the romance. Wow." Stella's voice was tentative. "The romance. That's what she told me to do and I forgot . . ."

Stella listened while Sara ticked off several more things she would need to learn about LRB so she could find real success at the company, until Stella felt that Sara sounded smug. And in a moment that coincided with that, Sara got up to go, reinforcing her incredible prescience.

"Remember, if you bet wrong and the whole

thing is a bust, you must never speak of it," Sara sang out. She turned to go and then stopped. "Oh—your pen."

"It's yours. Take it."

"Why, thanks, Stella. You have such a generous spirit. I admire that about you. I'll see you at the summer-power-titles-three-sixty-sales-review meeting at four in the Gilman Room!"

Stella dialed her boyfriend before returning to work.

"I was just thinking about you," Ivan said.

"You were?" Stella felt confused. Did people really say things like that? Her other boyfriends never did. In her experience they were usually thinking about something else.

"I loved watching you asleep this morning, watching you breathe. Your chest going up and down. Remember how I woke you?"

"I do," Stella whispered. He wasn't teasing. Stella squeezed her eyes shut. What was he up to? She said, "You said you loved me."

"That's what I said." He didn't add anything to that. He was waiting for her to say it back. And she was almost there. She *was* there. She was just too frightened to say it.

"Ivan, can I call you later? Somebody's at the door. I can't stop thinking about you, too." She got off the phone. Ivan was pretty great. But sometimes he was kind of a Russian poet who didn't care about the real world and that made her nervous. He had no comprehension of the pressure she was under.

Stella sat there and stared at her *Canoe* quotes and a mock-up of the new edition of the book they were rushing out. She liked the old edition better. The crappy one with the two hands intertwined and the wedding bands and the sunlight. This new one seemed false. It was a hardcover bound in pink imitation moleskin. Who had approved pink? She surely hadn't said yes to pink. And the jacket was just the title, big and super-embossed in metallic foil, Michelin-man puffy, just that massive stupid title with *Peter Herman* in script underneath it and the new tagline below, which she'd come up with in the cold middle of yet another sleepless night:

The definitive edition of the book that already saved your marriage!

A line she'd written with her Chinatown pen, based on studies that said people bought and rebought self-help books about problems they were enmeshed in and couldn't hope to fix. Like dating books for the eternally single. And diet books for the perpetually fat. Duh. No kidding. Writing that awful line had bummed her out a ton because it was such a cynical piece of marketing, and wasn't she an editor, at her core? Fuck! She'd once spent a whole Christmas afternoon at her parents' house rearranging her memory chest, removing pictures of boys and ex-friends and haircuts she wanted to forget so she'd be happier when she opened it the next time she visited.

She held the new *Canoe* edition in her hands and tried to figure out how she was feeling. Maybe just a little disturbed with her role was all. And she wished she wasn't so self-referencing and self-analytic. She read through Emily Babson's letter again. At least she didn't have that woman's problems. She'd figured out that Emily was at least five years older than she was and married to a handsome guy who had totally cheated. Emily was clearly miserable. But Peter would fix that, right? And then Emily and her husband would want to celebrate the weekend and everything would be okay. There would have to be photographs. If not in Millerton, then in New York. Why did she just give in to stupid old Peter Herman? He wasn't so tough. All he did was pause and sigh and go quiet on the phone and then hang up on her, and she gave right in to him. But she had to keep him happy. Did other people do this? Did other people set things in motion only to lose control of them? Or was she unique in her habit of rushing forward without calculating the consequences of her actions? But it was too late. The winners would be on their way to Millerton the next day. And she had to make the contest a success.

Otherwise, Helena would kick her in the teeth with her Joan & David boot. That was the whole point Sara was trying to make. Stupid, stupid, stupid. She'd promised plenty of photographs in the very first meeting. They had to come out happy. All three of them would have to come out happy and they would have to meet with Helena and everybody else in New York. Maybe at a luncheon. But that would mean a whole lot of people listening to her and doing exactly what she asked. And that sure didn't seem to happen very much lately, if it ever had. Stella punched herself in the arm. And then, because it hurt, she did it again.

Emily, Winners' Weekend, November 2011

"I'm only saying that when I think of the story of my life, of my journey and what people think about when they think about me—that we won a marriage counseling contest, that's not on the list," Eli said. "It's not something I could imagine wanting." He had both hands on the steering wheel and he beat out a rhythm with his thumbs while he talked. "And the older I get, the more I dislike driving."

"I said I would be happy to drive."

"You're better with directions. And I love you for it. I suck at directions."

They were nearly in Millerton, in their old white Saab, which had first belonged to Eli's cousin who designed high-end speakers and lived in a suburb outside Denver. They had Emily's iPod plugged into the car's amazing stereo and they were listening to *Exile on Main Street*. Emily always wanted to listen to Feist and Eli preferred Dinosaur Jr. Listening to the Rolling Stones and Caetano Veloso was how they compromised, leaving them, Emily knew all too well, both somewhat satisfied and also wanting something else.

"You see, we're already into the good part of the

weekend." Emily reached out and touched his thigh. "I didn't even know you think about the story of your life."

"I guess that's good. It's like I'm rewriting who I am right now, before we even get there. Like I'm becoming more modern and public and shared."

"Sharing your personality, as opposed to the you that makes things."

Eli nodded. "Right. I never think about me or us that way, but it makes sense. We're being more about . . . us. It's not you controlling me. It's me, changing. We exit at twenty-two—that's the exit, right?"

"It is," Emily said. "Go left. Just another quarter mile."

They stopped at a red light on Main Street. Harris Harvey Real Estate Agency was on their right. Emily looked through the agency's window at photographs of white salt-box houses and converted barns.

"Can you imagine having a country house out here?" she asked.

"Remember, only one of us comes from that world, and it isn't me," Eli said. "And that's more than half a million dollars we don't have."

"My dad might want to help out. If we had a baby. We're close to Boston. It could be a place for all of us. Sherry, too." She reached out and touched his cheek. She said, "Don't act like you grew up underprivileged."

Eli turned and kissed her finger. He said, "Okay. A country house . . . that could be really sweet with a kid. For apple picking. There are cool people up here. I'm surprised we don't know more of them."

"Apple picking?" She snuggled closer to him and said, "I love cider. We're here."

Eli pulled into the inn, which was set back from the road at what appeared to be a quiet intersection toward the end of Millerton's main street.

"Maybe Peter Herman knows of a house out here to buy," Eli said. "I'll bet he does."

"Wouldn't that be amazing?" she cried out. "And this town is just as pretty as that woman at Ladder & Rake promised it would be. What was her name? Stella. Cool name."

"It is. We're sort of like her . . ." Eli pawed the air for the word.

"Guinea pigs," Emily said. "I know. I love that you're allowing yourself to get so into it. It means a lot to me."

"It's because I'm into you." Eli reached out and nuzzled her neck and kissed her. She shivered when his cold nose touched her skin.

"Look at me," she said. They were sitting in the dark, in the car.

"What?"

"You can be negative about this. If you're feeling annoyed about it. You don't have to be sweet every second if that's not how you feel."

"It's okay," Eli said. "We're on a path together. I get that. I mean, we're staying at an inn in the country. I'm not going to be distant or ironic about it. I'm not that way."

"You're using a lot of words you don't normally use."

"Am I?" Eli shouldered their bags inside where they were greeted by a woman who had on a name-tag that identified her as Jenny, Assistant Manager.

"Come in, come in! Shake hands. Let's meet," Jenny said. "We're so proud and happy to have you with us." This Jenny was heavy, in a long black velvet dress, with her hair in a bun that Emily was sure must unravel past her butt. She wore bright red glasses that accentuated her black-rimmed eyes. Emily glanced back at the nearly full parking lot. She looked at Jenny and thought of Jenny Alexandretti. They hadn't talked about whether she'd already gone to L.A. But Emily doubted it. There would be so much to organize.

This Jenny said, "Most of our rooms are occupied by guests who are here for a local wedding. Two weddings, in fact. But don't worry; they're all off at their rehearsal dinners. May I show you to your room?"

"Thank you," Eli said. "I can carry the bags."

"You'll have the Okabye master suite."

They followed Jenny down a corridor and up a flight of gold-carpeted stairs.

"This is wild," Eli whispered. "I forgot places like this still existed."

The dark red walls and staircases were dotted with shelves full of wooden decoy ducks and reproductions of antiques from the Revolutionary War. There were silver kettles that imitated designs by Paul Revere. Hand-stitched coverlets and bits of ancient quilts were nailed to the walls in between framed Hogarth prints and oil paintings of the Hudson River.

"And later, when you're settled," Jenny went on, "we have dinner waiting for you in the main dining room. We have such a long history here at the inn with the Herman family and we're so proud and happy to be involved with this weekend."

"Do you know Peter well?" Emily asked.

"Know him? Of course! I've known him since I was a little girl."

"Is he . . ." Emily wanted to ask a question she was not sure Jenny could answer.

But Jenny went on, as if she understood. "He's sweet—and very gregarious. Admittedly, after his wife passed he did step away a bit from the inn."

"Do you feel like he's easy to talk to?"

"Yes. I would say he prides himself on being just that way." Jenny laughed to herself. "Here we are." She opened the door to the Okabye suite, which was full of furniture made of white painted wood. There were armoires on either side of the bed and another stood between the small windows that looked out at a close-cropped meadow and beyond that, a running path. The parking lot was just visible to the right.

"You have my favorite room in the whole inn," Jenny said.

"It's lovely," Emily said.

"If you need anything at all, I'm at the front desk. Ask for me by name." She pointed at her name-tag and said, "Jenny."

When she was gone, Emily turned to Eli. He was sitting in one of the twig chairs, staring at her.

"She was funny," Emily said.

"I liked her," Eli said. "She loves her job. People like that are cool."

Emily found a sweater in her bag and put it on against the drafty room. She went over to him, to kiss him. "She was all facade. I wonder what she really thinks of all this. But I love that you like her."

"Come sit in my lap," he said, and propped his sneakered foot on another chair, a white wicker armchair below a window.

"We'll break the chair."

"Then let me take you to bed."

"You're not tired from the drive?"

He shook his head. She thought he looked like a rock star who had been on a tour bus for too long, curly hair and dark circles under his eyes and brooding brow.

"He's going to see that we're so in love," Eli said. "It's going to make this whole thing hard for him. You know, like, he won't have anything to say."

"There's going to be a ton to talk about. And I am going to share what went wrong. I have to. You understand that?"

"Maybe I'll be the one to share it." Eli nodded and set his jaw so he looked serious. "That's the scenario I've been imagining."

"That would be amazing."

"Responsibility is sexy?"

"Sure. With you it is."

She had her hands in his shirt and then she was tugging at his jeans.

"I bet Jenny is listening right outside the door," Eli said.

Emily unbuckled his belt. "Then maybe she's got her eye at the keyhole, too. And she should see this. Would you like that? Would you like it if someone watched me do this to you?"

"Emily . . ."

"Would you?"

"Yeah. Yeah, I like that. Not the other part. It's just you and me. Nobody has to see."

Hours later, after they'd had sex and showered and gone down and had dinner, they lay in bed.

Dinner had been good. They had been seated at the round table in front of the fireplace. There were candles between them and the menu was fixed; they were only asked if there was anything they wouldn't eat. Everyone who worked at the inn knew who they were, so they treated them in a manner that was more than friendly. It was as if people were especially solicitous with them. Far beyond professionally caring, Emily felt, and all the way to tender.

There was course after course, with beef tenderloin somewhere in the middle and scallops in a dark sauce. They drank a bottle of burgundy that they were told was specially selected by Henry Talkington, the inn's current owner and a personal friend of Peter Herman's. After complicated fruit tarts were served with sorbet, there were small glasses of cognac and curly shavings of intensely dark chocolate.

It was warm at their table. Eli kept talking about how her skin was glowing. Emily became flushed and even a little dizzy. Knowing she only had to walk up a flight of stairs to go to bed helped her think of nothing but how in love she felt.

They made love again. Afterward, she watched Eli begin to fall asleep.

"I could get pregnant," she said. "I think the timing is right."

"Nothing could be more perfect," Eli whispered. "That would be amazing."

He was being so careful and kind with her, as sweet as she'd ever seen him. She had begun to feel that they were now reclaiming the great thing they had lost. She wanted their marriage to turn real again and to feel truly scribed, etched into stability and goodness.

She lay on her side next to her husband and felt his body begin to rise and fall. She stroked the slack muscles in his back. He slept fitfully, with one hand flung behind him that reached to her stomach, his fingers curled in a loose fist, his knuckles pushing into her flesh.

Peter, Winners' Weekend, November 2011

Maddie came over on Saturday morning and Peter came out to greet her.

"Looks like you've got a boatload of cookies there," Peter said.

She walked past him, so he could only look up at the sky. The weather was going to be perfect, cool and dry, all day long. *Crisp,* Peter thought. There was no better word than *crisp.*

"I'm so grateful to you," Peter said, as he trailed after her into the kitchen. "I was just looking for something to set out for them. I was going to call the inn but they're already handling dinner. I felt guilty."

"It is nothing," she said.

"Four different kinds of cookies?"

She smiled up at him. She had made hazelnut, cardamom, sesame seed, and chocolate chip cookies. She arranged them to look like fallen dominoes, on a plate with crab apples in the middle.

He said, "Maddie, you are a wonder." He stood watching her, his hands bunched up in the pockets of his khakis. She laid out napkins and silverware and other things for tea on a tray.

"I can do that," he said.

"I had a meeting with Jim Stevenson yesterday, to talk over how he might go about selling my house."

"How did that go?"

"I think it is fair to say that in regard to my real estate, I will do well, regardless of the current market."

"Of course you will." Peter took a sesame seed cookie and ate it. It was impossibly light, as if her recipe involved meringue.

"Unfortunately Jim Stevenson cannot help me with the more challenging logistical problem that is you." She smiled at him.

"Don't push, my love. I am with you." Peter gently sat down at the kitchen table. Maddie sat across from him, her back erect, her elbows on the table and her forearms and palms spread out and up.

"Do you know what you will say to them?" she asked.

"I don't have a speech. I reread her letter. There was some adultery. We may touch on it. We may not. Up to them."

"Adultery." Maddie shrugged. "Of course. But what will you do if, on top of that problem, the husband grows scared during their time with you and acts mean?"

"You're putting me through a rehearsal?"

"Not at all," she said, smiling. "I only meant that I am old enough to forgive adultery, but not meanness. So I am curious about your stance."

"If he is being mean I will suggest how sweet life can be if he resolves not to be mean."

Maddie raised her eyebrows. She said, "That is not much."

"It can be enough. You may think that's stupid. But sometimes keeping things simple can really help," he said. "If things are simple then even very intelligent people like you cannot help but understand them."

She widened her eyes in response and looked away. He hadn't meant to be abrupt or dismissive with her and he felt ashamed of himself. She was only trying to be kind. But at the same time, he felt as if he had walked into some kind of trap. Talking to Stella Petrovic about the contest on the phone was fun. But actually confronting an unhappy couple—that could be real work. And he knew just what Maddie meant. Unhappy people could be very mean.

"I'm sorry," he said. "It's just that I have a style. And I know the woman already likes my style so I will stick to it."

"A style?"

"Sure. Throw another scenario at me."

"What if you can see that they are not in love?" She was almost whispering. "What if you can see that they married for the wrong reasons and you know they should not have?"

"I suppose," he said, "that anyone can look at a

couple and think they can see that. But no one can know how a couple behaves in private."

"I know that. But what if one of them reveals it through words?"

He didn't answer. He touched his newly shaven cheek with his hand.

"If they are very unhappy, it will be a serious visit. Don't worry, I always come up with the right thing to say."

"I would like to hear what you come up with." Maddie swept some crumbs off the table and into her palm. She said, "My marriage failed. But we did not look for solutions to our problems in a book. My husband left me and that was all. He did not offer me an opportunity to save our marriage."

"And maybe that's just as well. I won't defend my book. It's not magic. Look, as soon as today is over, I will tell you everything that happened."

"I would hope so! My friend Carol and her husband, Dan, saw them at dinner last night at the inn. Carol said they were attractive people. They were smiling and laughing."

"That's good news. Maybe they are the sort of people who just like to win things? And the real win here is only to have a visit that gets added to the history of a happy marriage."

"Maybe." She looked down and shook her head. "I wish you would say all the right things to me sometimes. You are welcome to use some of your trademark style with me."

Peter watched her. He liked her so much. But he could not pretend that he loved her. That would be cruel. Peter said, "What else did your friend say about them?"

"She said the woman talked about you, about your book and how it informed her life when she was growing up. But then Carol felt bad about eavesdropping, so she stopped. They ate nearly everything on their plates. They held hands when they left the dining room. Carol felt sure they were going to make love. Either that or they were just showing off for the room. And so we can deduct that they may show off their love for you."

"Sounds like they don't need me at all!"

"Perhaps not. You could talk with them about the food at the inn, how good it is."

"They might as well spend the afternoon with Henry."

She stood up and took her bag from the kitchen table, sniffed the air. "Maybe they would like that."

"I could do that—take them around to old men, to Henry and to Arthur at Pantomime's."

"No, Peter. Stay here with them and talk." She reached out and grabbed his hand. "I believe you will take this seriously. But I want you to promise you will. Promise me. Even though everyone involved seems to feel that this is just a stunt, they are married and they are coming to see you. It is real. Be nice."

After she was gone he meant to tidy the house

but he quickly found there was little to do. He walked from room to room, opening and then shutting windows against the wind. Be nice, he told himself. Be nice! Take them in your arms and love them. He got out a pen and paper and began to make a list of the simple things he must not forget to tell them.

> If she gets sick, take care of her without
> question until she says she feels well.
> If he loses his job, be patient with him
> while he works through his funk.
> If your child is ill, do not take that stress as
> a license to treat each other badly.

He stared down at the words on the paper and then crumpled the sheet and threw it into the trash. He found himself opening the front door, doing little but watching the driveway, supporting himself with his arms stretched up so he could grip the lintel and sway. Certainly he could listen and then find something to tell them that would be unique to their situation and that thus would be good and rare and, at the very least, equal to their expectations. He had played this part successfully before. Master of the obvious! He waited for them and prepared to play his part, reminding himself over and over that he must give himself entirely to the role because that would help him hide away the unattractive parts of himself they mustn't see.

Emily, Winners' Weekend, November 2011

"It's only because I thought flowers were an odd gift for a man," Emily said. "Do you think I made a mistake?" It was just past one in the afternoon and they were in their car, driving to Peter Herman's house.

"You did the right thing," Eli said, as he drove.

"You're sure? It is kind of a dinner party. Or later it will be." There were two bottles of pinot noir in a bag tied with a red ribbon on the backseat, which Emily had bought at a boutique wine store near her office a few days earlier.

"We're sure he didn't want us for lunch?" Eli asked.

"Yes. We spend the afternoon and return for dinner. Don't be nervous. Be open to what happens. It means so much to me that you're here."

"I will be open," Eli said. "I promise you."

They had been stiff and shy with each other during the morning. Eli had started out on a run but quickly returned to their room, saying it was too windy, that he'd try again before dinner. They had ended up staying in bed and drinking coffee, watching most of *Say Anything . . .* on Starz. Emily had cried through the middle of the movie and Eli had held her. Toward the end, when John

Cusack held up his boom box and played "In Your Eyes," Emily completely fell apart because how could one not? And it was then that Eli got up and went to take a shower and spent what she felt was an awfully long time in the bathroom.

Emily said, "I couldn't have us show up with nothing."

"Even though we're the winners."

"Even though."

Emily stared at the directions written on a slip of paper she held tightly in her lap. The other Jenny's curly script made the directions look like something out of folklore, so Emily felt as if they'd left the inn and turned into characters from one of Grimms' fairy tales.

Go up the main road, right at its end; follow the lake road, left at the sign that says "Herman" ☺*!* Well, Grimms' for Dummies.

"There's not a photographer, right?" Eli asked.

"I don't think so. Why? Are you feeling shy?"

"Come on, Emily. Shy is the least of it. Let's not pretend that this is anything but totally nerve-racking."

Emily waved her hands in front of her and said, "I don't know if there will be a photographer. I hope not. There's going to be publicity, but I can spin it for both of us, I promise. I have to admit that I'm impressed at how many media hits Ladder & Rake has managed to get. It almost feels like media people are sympathetic to books.

Which makes sense, doesn't it? Because media people grow up liking books and sometimes they even write them and now they want to be supportive and they feel bad because it constantly seems like their dorky-little-brother industry is dying . . ."

She looked at Eli, there in the driver's seat. He wasn't listening to her. He had his tongue out, tasting his lip, taking in the pretty road. And then he nearly came to a stop at the top of Peter Herman's driveway. He was absorbing the house and the glimpses of the lake beyond it. He was so much more of the moment than she was—look at him, with his bicycling! Did you need a book to survive in this world? No. But given all the tension over energy, you were probably going to need a bicycle. They could all talk about that, she thought, if discussion of their marriage became too much.

"We're here." Eli slowed the car down to a creep and said, "I love you, no matter what happens."

"What's that supposed to mean?"

Eli parked a couple of car-lengths back from the Subaru that was already in the driveway.

"Ready?" He turned and smiled at her, bent in to kiss her. "It means I'm scared."

"You shouldn't be. I'm serious. Thank you for doing this." She kissed him back and they bumped noses.

He turned off the engine and they sat in the car

for a moment, listening to the chirping birds. She suddenly wished she was dumber and not so desperate to fix things. Then she was ashamed and angry at herself for wishing she was dumber. It was their marriage that was at stake. They should do everything to save it. Maybe she was a fool, and this was a fool's errand? Trying to fix his cheating. Probably. Reaching out to strangers for help with explanations for incontrovertible problems? Yup, childlike and dumb.

"Eli, am I dumb for doing this, for making us do this? Do you think I am a dumb person?"

"You're definitely not a dumb—"

But she had already seen Peter Herman. She opened the car door and that brought a blast of air so sweet she felt like she was going to lose her mind.

"Hi! I brought wine," she said to no one, and then left it in the car and drifted toward Peter. She had meant to be calm and inquisitive, to approach the way she would approach Gary Hustwit after a lecture. But instead, she forgot all the layers of self she'd grown since she was a girl and just walked toward Peter.

"Hello, you two!" Peter Herman made his way down his brick steps to them. She could hear each of his footfalls and the country noise around them, the wind coming from the lake and the caw and honk of birds.

"Hello," she whispered.

"Hello!" Peter said. And then with less certainty, "You are Eli Corelli and Emily Babson?"

"That's us," Eli called out.

"I had a feeling." Peter smiled and twinkled his eyes at them.

She felt too shy to meet his eyes and instead gazed at his khakis and blue ragg-wool sweater, his brown cordovan loafers that were nearly as old as she was. He bent toward her to shake hands.

"I'm a fan," she whispered.

She loved him intensely and immediately and felt, for only the second or third time in her life, an overwhelming fated happiness. She thought to herself, Here he is in front of me and I have walked in his words since I was a little girl. Walked in his words! She felt amazed that she was so in touch with her sentimentality. So what if his book was a little hokey? It had helped form her! The man had explained how to love. He had helped to form her idea of what marriage should be. Her forehead felt hot. She took a step back and braced herself with a hand on the car.

"It's good to meet you," Eli said. "My wife is a huge admirer of yours and we've both enjoyed reading your work." Eli bumped Emily's shoulder to create more space. He shook hands with Peter.

"Huge admirer?" Emily took a deep breath and smiled at Peter. "It's more than that. I love your book. Since I was little I've loved it."

"That's enough—don't embarrass me," Peter

303

said. "Your essay was charming. And it was honest. Now here we are. Well, what do you know?"

Emily tried to watch Peter without getting caught. But he seemed to know what she was up to. He turned and took her hand. "I mean what I say," he said. "It was funny and sad."

Eli walked ahead of them but then he slowed and turned around. He kept his distance, though. He understood that this first part, the part about getting to know Peter, needed to belong to her.

"Let's go around the house," Peter called out. Eli nodded and found the path that went down to the lake.

Emily said, "I never write about myself. So it wasn't easy."

"I imagine not. Writing never is."

"I mean, I didn't think anyone would actually read it. It was more of an exercise, you know? And now to be here with you, it's so strange."

"Don't worry." Peter let Emily's hand go but when she stayed close, he put an arm around her. "I can already feel that we have a lot to talk about."

"This is a beautiful spot," Eli called out.

"Let's go down to the water," Peter said. "It doesn't get a whole lot more picturesque than it is today." They could see their breath in front of them and it was pretty, a pretty feeling, knowing that they were cold and crisp now but soon they would be inside and warm. They arrived at the water's edge.

"There it is," Emily said, when she saw Peter's Old Town canoe, resting on sawhorses, just up from the little dock.

"The very one," Peter said. "The same one I used with my grandfather."

"The green really does glow," Emily said. The canoe's dark green canvas walls looked fossilized.

Eli walked onto the dock, which was thirty feet long, made of beautifully weathered wood, with cattail fronds sticking up around the supporting columns. They could see other houses peeking out at them across the lake, from behind trees covered with leaves that had turned flame orange and red and deep brown and plum.

"Any chance we could go for a ride?" Eli asked.

Peter looked at Emily and raised an eyebrow.

"Yes," she whispered. "Let's send him out, just for a little while."

"Sure thing," Peter said. "Let me help you bring it to the water. There's a paddle tucked inside—there it is."

"There's room for the three of us?" Eli asked.

"How about you go alone," Peter said. "More fun for you that way."

Eli nodded and Emily could see that sounded good to him. He had his hands on the canoe. "Look at this thing," he said. "Here's a design that hasn't changed for well over a century. Wow, look at those ribs. Just beautiful . . . okay. I'll take it for a spin and be back in ten minutes."

"Take your time," Peter said. He helped Eli slide the canoe into the water. Eli jumped in and paddled away.

Emily shivered as they watched him go. She said, "It took him a little while to wrap his head around coming here. He's being great about it now, though."

"He seems like a nice fellow."

Eli waved from the canoe. He yelled, "So smooth!" And paddled directly away from them, toward the middle of the lake. They turned and went back to the porch. They sat down on the straight-back chairs on either side of the door and watched Eli paddle.

"It's good to give him this break," Emily said. "I'm sure he's happy, paddling."

"He's fast," Peter said. "I can see that he's never spent time in a canoe before and he's teaching himself."

"I like that about him. He's adaptable. When I told him this was important to me, to visit you even though winning was so weird, he said yes and never looked back. I have to tell you something. I really did read your book when I was eleven and twelve, when my parents used to fight before they split up. I used to lock myself in the bathroom off their bedroom and read and imagine

I was Honey and my parents weren't about to get a divorce."

"My book wasn't meant for little girls. That must have been a rough time for you."

Emily nodded. She said, "I wonder how much reading your book had to do with the work I do now. I explain things for a living. And so do you. Except I explain how stuff works. And you explain love."

"Love?" Peter laughed uneasily and turned to Emily. "Now remember, I only try to explain marriage."

She only stared at him and she hoped he was able to understand her expression, that she was trying to say there's no reason to be light with me. What you do is important and I know it and so do you.

"But what you say about when you were a child reminds me that the same was true for me," Peter said. "I wrote because of my parents. I created this world up here with my grandparents and wrote about it because of them, because of all the fighting and the anger I had to put up with at home."

"Really? I always wondered about that. You shaped the stories to fit what you imagined marriage to be like."

"Some of it was real," Peter said. "Anyway, when I wrote, that kind of shaping was okay. I understand that's not true anymore." Peter sighed.

She watched him stare straight ahead at the lawn. She looked out but Eli was so far away now. She waved at him but he didn't see. "Right there, my grandfather did tell me he was sorry about my mother and how things were. He hugged me. It helped. I don't deny it. But that's not what matters today. What matters is you and your husband and your future. You two want to be happy. It isn't complicated."

"I wish it weren't. When I met him I meant for it all to be simple. But it hasn't been. The way he and I are, I can't find a way to speak clearly about it. I try to get control of it and it just spins away. Or, he does. But he's trying not to anymore. That's why we're here."

"Looks to me like he wants the same things you want. And you're right. He's not running away." Peter nodded at Eli, who was making his way back toward the dock.

Emily shielded her eyes with her hands. She said, "I hope you're right."

"Today we'll shape something new, a new way for you two to live. It won't be perfect. But we'll construct something safe and good for you. Just like you and I did for ourselves when we were kids."

"I'm so happy we won." Emily stood up. "I would love that. But even if it doesn't work, don't worry. I will always be grateful to you for your book, no matter what."

"You're kind," Peter said. "You and I, in a way we've already given one another more than a happy afternoon. Now let's get started on the hard part."

"What a great place," Eli called out, as he bumped the canoe's nose on the dock. "Is it very expensive to live out here?"

"It's about all I can afford!" Peter laughed. He turned to Emily and said, "Let me help him out and then we'll go inside. We won't sit for longer on the porch, not today."

After they'd set the canoe back in its place, Eli obediently trooped toward the house. Emily watched him pivot for a moment and then resist his urge to go back and play at the water's edge, skip stones or just look about for fish or birds or whatever else.

The three of them went up the back steps and in through the kitchen. The house was perfectly clean. Peter didn't stop them there, so Emily could only glance at the knotty-pine cabinets and dark wood floor, at a pair of scissors with blue plastic handles on the butcher-block counter next to the apron sink and some flower stems lying in a puddle of water next to them.

They went into the living room and stopped near a green couch in front of picture windows that looked out on the driveway and the front lawn.

"I do want to talk broadly with you," Emily said.

"About the way you show love in a story. I want to talk about your gift."

"One thing at a time." Peter looked back at her. "Let's begin with you and Eli. Later we'll have dinner together and you can ask me anything you want. I'll be getting some help with that so you needn't worry about my cooking! I don't have a gift for it."

"Sweetness?" Eli reached out and touched Emily's shoulder. "Isn't this a great house like we were talking about in the car yesterday? Do you want to ask about that?"

But Emily didn't look at Eli. She sat down next to him on the couch, but didn't respond to his touch. Emily could only look at Peter. Maybe they really could get back on the path toward the life she'd once dreamed would be hers. And here was Peter Herman, ready to help them try. His marriage and his life were everything she had imagined for herself, the marriage she would have, the happiness at holidays, all of it. Everything that Eli had nearly wasted was here, in Peter.

"You helped explain me to myself," she whispered. Neither man heard her. She turned and felt a flash of pure hope as she looked at Eli.

"Let's begin," she said. "Please forgive how awkward we are. It's just that I don't want to waste a single moment."

"I should start by saying that I don't have a philosophy," Peter said. "Everyone thinks I do, but I don't. Still, I believe I can be helpful to you."

No one spoke. Eli rolled his head back and cracked his neck.

"What about the line 'Marriage is a canoe'?" Emily asked. "That's metaphorical philosophy."

"Is it?" Peter smiled. "I think it's just an aphorism. I only mean that the anecdotes in the book don't add up to a philosophy. For today, perhaps we could call them more of a point of view, like we discussed out on the porch. Do you see? How really it's all about being kind?"

"Please." Emily waved her hands over her eyes. "Can we just call it a philosophy?" She looked at Peter and gestured at her husband as if to say let's keep this simple for his sake.

"You're very smart," Peter said. "All right. It's a philosophy. Would you like a cookie? They were baked by a friend of mine just this morning. Try the cardamom."

"But you just said you don't have a philosophy," Eli said. "I'm confused."

Emily saw Eli squint. He was a businessman, after all. He could be a little tough when someone was indecisive. And she also knew that for her sake, he wanted what happened at Peter's house to be valuable. He did not want her to feel cheated.

"Look," Emily said. "We've been through something bad. We're not afraid to hear real advice."

"I understand," Peter said. "Forgive me. I'm a little rusty."

"Of course we'll be silent and unable to talk now." Emily tried to laugh. "It's my fault. We started in too fast." She uncrossed her legs, spread her knees apart and then brought them together again. She was wearing corduroys and felt the fabric on her thighs. She could see Eli to her left, crouched over, looking at the palms of his hands.

"I hope there's not going to be a photographer?" she asked.

"Let's leave all that aside and you start," Eli said to Emily. "We both know you want to."

"Fine," she said. "I will. I'm going to try again to jump right in even though this is completely awkward. I am going to trust you both."

"Go ahead." Peter spoke through a mouthful of cookie. "You can trust me to listen and to keep your secrets."

But she didn't speak. She could not choose what to say first. She looked at both men. The room was perfect and quiet. She didn't mind how constructed the moment was. She understood that. It was something else. It would be easier without Eli here, she thought. She glanced at him.

"I can't wait anymore. I need to talk," Eli said. "I am feeling the trust here and so I need to say this. I almost blew up our marriage." Eli put his hands out in front of him, palms up, like a man trying to find his way in a dark room. "I got too deeply involved with my business and there was this woman—"

"Jenny," Emily said. "Who you hired a year and a half ago."

"Jenny." Eli nodded.

"Wait," Peter said. "Before you get into that territory. Can you tell me about how you two are together?"

"Like why we love each other?" Emily asked.

"Sure. Yes."

"You go," Eli said. "Emily can explain anything to anybody."

Emily saw that now Eli was red-faced and looking at his sneakers, possibly angry about having risen to the moment too fast and then been rebuffed just as quickly. Emily wasn't sure why Peter had shut Eli down. Unless Peter just liked Emily better. And why not? Emily wondered. Peter should like her better. She was the winner and the number one fan.

"If she can explain anything," Peter said, "then why don't you begin, Eli, with what's good about the two of you. We can talk about what almost went wrong later."

Eli brushed his dark hair back and looked up at both of them. His chest was inches from his knees.

"I can try," he said. He drew his arms into the little space between his legs and chest so he was constricted and half his normal size.

"In my life I'm like a workman, head down, a blacksmith working at a bench. I never look up. I just work and make things and try to . . . celebrate the making of them. And that's how Emily found me. At the moment in my life when I was building something with my head down. And she, she . . . showed me the rest of myself. I made her happy, too. I made her laugh and she can be kind of serious a lot of the time so that's a good thing. So we fell in love because we fit together in a way that's complementary. That's how we're good together."

Eli looked at Peter when he was done speaking, instead of Emily. And Emily looked at Peter, too. She was afraid that Peter would accuse Eli of being hopelessly vague and maybe even dull.

When no one else spoke, Eli slowly allowed his head to hang low, so low Emily thought it must be hurting him. She reached out and touched the back of his head and felt his greasy hair.

"That was nice," Emily said. "You're still my rock star."

"I don't know how to fix it." Eli didn't move. "I know what I did wrong. I know I hurt you, Emily."

"Soon we'll want to talk about the problem," Emily said. "I'm sure of that. But Eli is right. We fell in love for a thousand reasons, but for sure we complement each other and we're obsessed with each other and he's the guy for me, you know?

314

But I didn't know he would put me through such a test."

"Eli?" Peter asked.

"I love Emily. I want us to have children together and grow old together. I don't want to lose her to some stupid thing."

"I have to be so strong." Emily looked at both of them. She said, "I think I meant that as a question."

Peter raised his eyebrows at her. She shook her head as if to say, No, please don't make me explain myself.

"Both of you have to be." Peter brought his hand to his lips, his pointer finger grazing the space above his upper lip. She watched him sweep his hand over his mouth to show he was intentionally being quiet, to show he was listening. She thought the gesture felt fake.

"You must be parched. And I've offered you nothing." Peter stood up and went into the kitchen and came back with a carafe of water and some glasses on a plastic tray.

There was a grandfather clock in the hall and Emily could just hear it. She could also hear what she imagined were honking geese out on the lake. She closed her eyes and breathed in. Eli took her hand and she was confused for a moment. She'd forgotten he was next to her.

"Sorry," she said. "I was just enjoying being here."

"I love you," he said.

"I love you, too."

"I feel bad about how I've been. I want to take it back."

Emily shook her head no. But she thought, Yes, I want to keep you. She said, "You can't. But I feel really good about how this is going."

Once Peter had sat back down, Emily said, "This is helping." She smelled the dusty house. She poured herself half a glass of water and choked it down. "We are healing."

"Is there something else?" Peter asked.

"Is that what you want to ask right now?" Emily asked.

Peter shrugged. She was surprised. Maybe he had no idea what he was doing! Maybe he didn't even remember writing the book. She suspected that all he had was the dim memory of a hug from his Pop in the backyard. She wanted to go away right now. Take her infinitely apologetic husband with her. She sat as far forward on the couch as she could. It was past four. When could they go?

Peter went on, "Okay, let's leave the other woman out for a while longer. Sounds like she's in the past. Eli, we've touched on the thing, the bad thing. What about you?"

"What about me what?"

"Are you happy?" Peter stopped there. She watched his face and saw that he was comfortable with the silence. She changed her mind again.

Peter Herman was subtle. He was in control. He was brilliant although at the same time horribly awkward! This was likely part of his brilliance. There was more silence. Emily fought her impulse to talk. Peter could do something she couldn't do. He could help people discover themselves.

She smiled at Eli. Likely, he had some problems with her that kept him from always being happy in their marriage. She was certainly aggravated with herself on a regular basis. So it would be good to find out about the parts of her that they could agree they didn't like. The idea of saying this stuff in front of Peter was even kind of sexy in a way. Maybe they could fetishize her bad habits and at least have that weirdness as something new? The way she could be controlling. They could talk about that.

"And let's be honest," Peter said. "I appreciate how you've both been honest so far."

"Honest." Eli rubbed at the knees of his jeans. "No, things are good with Emily. She doesn't do things I don't like. I love Emily. But I lied to her. I have been a liar. I did sleep with Jenny. We had some times together. It meant nothing and I'm ashamed of myself. We got drunk and it happened. It was meaningless in just the way they say, too. We were at a meeting to get some funding in L.A. and it went really well. We got overexcited and we were staying at the Mondrian and, for some reason, we ended up in bed together. It had been coming for some time—this animal thing. Just a stupid thing. But we got control of ourselves. We stopped. After that, me and Emily grew so formal. I know there's no excuse. It's just with Jenny, I—"

"Why do you keep coming back to her?" Emily asked. "Why can't you stop doing that?"

Eli's mouth was wide open. He said, "I want to flush it out."

"Okay," Emily said. "But can't you focus on us?"

Eli stood up and then sat down again. Then he turned to Emily, so Peter couldn't see him. And he glared at her. The sky had grown dark. It was nearly five in the afternoon. "I want to be forgiven for real. Before anything else happens."

"Let's slow down," Peter said. "A lot has just been said. Forgiveness is a big deal."

Eli kept staring at Emily. She watched his glare fade to pleading. She wondered if, by returning his gaze, she had forced him to hide his secrets. Like a little boy, she thought. But I chose him. I knew he was like that.

"May I use your bathroom?" Eli asked.

"Yes, of course. It's around the corner, in the nook under the stairs."

Eli nodded and went out. Peter reached across the table and took Emily's hands.

"Can you forgive him?" Peter asked.

"Yes," Emily said. "I think so. I love him. In some part of me, I knew this would happen.

People find him attractive. They want to take care of him. I knew that when I met him. I can live with it. I was just thinking that. By which I mean, I am saying exactly what I am thinking."

Peter nodded. "Your heart is beating loud enough to feel."

"Please help. I don't want to give up."

"Of course not. You're strong, like you said. And you won't. That's very apparent in you." Emily didn't speak. She watched Peter flush and begin a rush of speech. "And you don't have to. You don't have to create all that pain of ending. You can rebuild what you have and it'll be stronger. That's what we're doing here, you know. I did that with my wife several times before she died. We . . . renovated the house once and knew we were actually repairing our marriage."

"I like that." Emily smiled. "I love simple similes and metaphors. I don't use them enough. But you do. I admire that. How you're not afraid of a cliché."

Peter raised his eyebrows at her. "Clichés?"

Emily said, "In my business we're allergic to them. We spend half our time trying to subvert them so we can be sure we say something new. No one sees their value. But you do."

"I see." Peter took a long drink from his glass of water.

The bathroom door clicked open and Eli strode back into the living room.

"I forgive you," Emily said, quickly. She looked up at him. His mouth was an O.

"You do?" Eli was still standing.

"I want to work through this with you. I know I've said it before, or maybe I haven't, properly. But I'm saying it here. We can consecrate it."

"It sounds ridiculous to say it out loud like that," he whispered. "But it's exactly what I want."

Emily turned to Peter. She was still on the couch. Eli sat down next to her. She said, "Thank you, Peter."

"It's a good beginning," Peter said. "We have so much more to talk about, though. There's uncharted territory ahead. Free of cliché." He winked at Emily.

"Uncharted territory," Eli said, suddenly. "I like that. I feel safe here."

"You never say that," Emily said. "That feels good."

They heard a car pull into the driveway and seconds later there was a hard knock on the door. Peter stood up quickly and turned on some lights. Emily realized that they'd all been barely able to see one another in the afternoon darkness.

"Hold on." Peter stood and went to the front hall. "Hello, Jenny. You can put it all here."

"No, no. Send me straight to the kitchen. I'm going to help Mike. I'm his sous-chef!"

"Oh, I see . . ."

"Jenny Alexandretti," Emily said aloud as she stood up. She clutched at the neck of her blouse.

"We'll get past it," Eli said, automatically.

Jenny from the inn strode past, carrying trays covered in tinfoil. She smiled at them but said nothing. She was humming. Emily thought, She has our dinner and it's sweet that she's humming! She is not Jenny Alexandretti.

Emily said, "I think we ought to return to the inn so we can have a rest. We've been here for a while already. Peter, we don't want to overwhelm you. That wouldn't be right."

"And then we'll see you for dinner in a couple of hours?" Peter asked. "I can promise that the meal will be outstanding . . ."

"Thank you, Peter." Eli reached out and shook Peter's hand and patted his back. "We'll see you later. Seriously, thank you."

Eli went out ahead of Emily. He walked doggedly toward the car.

"I can't wait to come back to you this evening," Emily said to Peter. She was still standing next to him, holding his arm, on the porch. "It's like you said. We're not done. And I am already so grateful to you. I know I'm not showing my best self. I'm—" She felt herself stammer.

"It's okay, Emily. It's a lot to take in. All this brazen emotion can be confusing. Really, I'm so glad this is going well." Peter's voice was mild and he wasn't looking at Emily. "You ought to watch out for Jenny's Toyota. See it there? That young woman never did learn how to park a car."

She let go of his arm and walked away from him, thinking that it was presumptuous to want to get all of him in just a day. He would share a little bit. That was enough. She was already incredibly lucky to have received as much from him as she had.

"Ready?" she asked once she was in the car.

Eli was quiet. And Emily stayed inside herself, too, thinking, We're fixing it. We are going to be okay.

Eli started the car. He turned to Emily and said, "That was good. Emily, you are the most incredible woman in the world. I feel different. I really do."

Peter, Winners' Weekend, November 2011

The phone rang half an hour after they'd left. Peter had two fingers on his temples and was staring out Lisa's study window, trying to assemble more of the right things to say to Eli and Emily when they returned for dinner. They were struggling. He believed they might find some happiness together, someday, perhaps with the arrival of a baby. He liked Emily. The firmness in her character reminded him of Lisa. The phone kept ringing.

"Hello?"

"Peter, hi, it's Stella. How are you?"

"Stella. What can I do for you?" He took on his warm flirtatious tone. Lisa used to make fun of him for it. Maybe he ought to talk to Emily and Eli about what he had with Lisa. How they always knew to quickly plaster over the cracks in the facade that naturally occurred with the changing seasons.

"I'm calling to see how it's going. You're in the break before dinner?"

"We are indeed. You've given a lonely old man a very pleasant Saturday. I can tell you that."

"Oh?"

She was good. To say only "Oh?" That was

smart. He thought he'd like to meet her someday. Stella Petrovic. Not afraid of him like so many of the others. Not afraid of silence, either. And why had he called himself a lonely old man? He wasn't. A liar, yes. Lonely, no.

He said, "This woman, Emily Babson . . . such life spirit! She is a wonder. That helps, I imagine, when you've got to take on a challenge."

He leaned back in Lisa's desk chair and waved "no thanks" to Jenny, who had gotten into his line of vision and seemed to be offering him a drink. He pointed at his glass of water and she frowned a we-can-do-better-than-that frown. But he shook his head so she disappeared. Sweet, dimpled Jenny. Years ago when he was really drinking, he'd hugged her good night a little too long and even let his hands wander under her clothes a few times during the summers she worked at the inn before dropping out of college and signing on full time. They'd had some afternoons of good-natured wrestling in the Okabye suite. She didn't seem to bear a grudge. But then who knew, really, whether she did or not.

"What?" he called into the phone.

"I said what kind of challenge?"

"They're just resting at the inn now, is all that's happening."

"So it's going according to plan?"

"Yes. Certainly."

"That's good news!"

He lapsed into silence. Did Lisa know he'd kissed more than one of the maids? She must have. Did she even care? He looked at the blue-and-white needlepoint rug that covered most of Lisa's floor. She was a wonderful woman. But wonderful didn't mean she had a lot of love in her.

"What else should I be telling you, Stella?"

"All I want to hear is that they're happy."

"They are. Or, they will be."

"You know . . . We were asked to video and photograph and record everything that happened and I fended all that off," Stella said. "I'm just reminding you that I agreed with you when you said that was inappropriate. I mean I know you said no to all that but the point is I agree with you. You wouldn't believe how pushy Helena can be about these things. So if there's going to be none of that then I'll need . . . you. And I need them, too. Maybe essays from both of you? Or something recorded? Although photographs would be so much better."

"Helena?" he asked. "She's watching over all this?"

"Helena watches over everything. She really badgered me for pictures. So much of corporate life is show-and-tell, you wouldn't believe it. That's why I'm hoping you can share what's happening. So I can . . . share with Helena and the rest of the team here. Because I can't show anything. Of course I can call back tomorrow if you'd rather talk then. But maybe you could take pictures with your phone?"

Peter laughed. He said, "Helena. Helen. I knew her when she was just discovering how to be that way. We meant a lot to each other."

"Then you can imagine what this is like for me. Please let me tell her we can get some pictures, perhaps here in New York."

"Yes, go ahead and tell her that. Tell her whatever you want and consider me on board."

"Oh," Stella sighed, and he could hear that she did not quite believe him. "Terrific. That's terrific."

He said, "I promise posed photos with our winners. They will be fine. Though, long-term, who can say with such young people? I should go and prepare for their return."

"So dinner will just be a kind of a toast to the day?"

"Sure, if you say so. I mean yes. Let's call it that."

She responded with silence. She doubted him and she was angry! He could hear it and he realized she had a right to be. She wanted more than she was getting from him. And she deserved more. She said, "Can you also create a good shared anecdote for me that I can feed to publicity? You can make sure to tell them to take care of each other, as you say in your book."

"I'm glad you called to remind me of that. You're right, of course. I will do that."

"I'm glad, too, I'm glad because . . ." She began to rush her speech. But he had stopped listening. He muttered a goodbye and clicked the phone off.

Was his love with Lisa a great love? He kept returning to that question, even though he knew the answer. They'd had Belinda. Belinda was a kind of love. They had tried to have other children and failed. They loved Belinda and raising her was a wonder. He missed Lisa now . . . and Belinda, whom he wanted to see. They had talked a few days ago but now he wanted to call her again, and would, tomorrow. And why didn't Helena call, if she was such a badgerer? Too busy, probably. Always had been that way, since the beginning. She badgered, but didn't call. When all this was over, he would call her. And what about Maddie? Would he call Helena from an apartment in San Francisco? What if Maddie overheard? He couldn't do that to Maddie. He would have to go into the street to call, use a cell phone . . . He pressed at his teeth with the tips of his fingers.

"Peter?" a voice called out.

"Yes?" Peter struggled to his feet and left the dark study and went into the brightly lit hall.

"Mike and I are going to go. We didn't want to bother you but felt we ought to say goodbye."

"Jenny! Goodbye now." He put a hand on her shoulder and squeezed. He didn't like her smile, how she seemed to think he was old now, and harmless.

She twisted free of him and said, "You know how to heat everything up? Want to see what we have in store for you?"

Peter followed Jenny into his kitchen, which now smelled and felt like the kitchen at the inn.

"Hello, Mike. Henry treating you good?"

"Better than you ever did, big fella!"

The three of them talked for a few minutes and then he saw them out, after he'd been instructed on how to plate the lamb shanks and when to warm up and serve the other dishes, the brussels sprouts with bacon, the crispy polenta rounds, and the chestnut soup.

"Of course I know how to handle all this. I'm going to clean these dishes before your pick-up tomorrow better than you can imagine! Now, go! And you have my eternal thanks . . ."

After they left, he stood in the kitchen doorway with his hands stuck deep in his pockets. What were the things he used to tell couples when they cornered him, every so often, at restaurants in town? What did he say on book tours, and during his few lectures on marriage?

He went over his old prescriptions and swore to himself he'd give a better performance than he had this afternoon. He'd mention all his old favorites. He would try his very hardest to help them plaster over the husband's infidelity. He owed everyone that.

Don't renovate a home together in the first five years of marriage.

Only live with your in-laws as a last resort.

Don't spend too much time with any one single other couple.

Eat at home and together as often as you can. Make each other breakfast on each other's big days—the day of the big presentation at work. The day of the test your spouse has to take to go to the next level.

Don't leave clothes lying on the bedroom floor.

Let each other flirt with others at parties.

Those and dozens of others like them. His army of strident little comments. He was proud, not of any one of them in particular, but of them as a whole. He would pick out the ones that applied and press them on the winners. He would even go through the exercises with them if they wanted. He was bumping on something. What was it?

And then he realized what bothered him was that Eli seemed proud of his cheating. Wasn't he a bit exultant about it? Yes, that was what felt wrong. He was exultant and maybe a little rebellious. That was the thing he was glad he'd kept from Stella. Though, he thought, smiling, why should Stella care? In the short term, the contest could only be a success. And no one should be bothered that the woman, Emily, had married an arrogant bastard. That was no one's fault but hers. She wasn't stupid. She'd conveyed that this afternoon, that she'd chosen this life for herself. He liked Emily and he understood her. She loved her man. Just the way Lisa had loved him.

He decided to make sure that during the evening he would stick to his little aphorisms, rather than rush into any more of the intimacy that prompted all this terrifying honesty. He went and found a bottle of Johnnie Walker Black Label that he kept in the cupboard in the dining room, next to the good wineglasses. On the other hand, he might tell a few stories about how he and Lisa had been together. Though it felt risky, it also felt as if some of what he had been through with Lisa paralleled the situation with Eli and Emily. He took a sip of scotch from a water glass. Yes. Some of his real life did seem to apply.

Emily, Winners' Weekend, November 2011

"Where are you going?" Emily asked.

Emily lay in bed with the covers pulled up. They had made love again. So much sex. It did feel as if, in addition to all his awkward and new honesty, Eli was trying to prove his love through sex. In order to stop thinking about that, she had closed her eyes. She'd been dozing when she heard him moving around.

"I want to go for a quick run. I saw a path back there and they told me it goes north for a few miles."

"Okay." Emily sat up. "I'm not going to nap."

"It's fine if you do. We have time."

"I won't," she said. She looked around. Their clothes were everywhere. They'd made a mess of the pretty white room. This kind of chaos wasn't like them, she thought.

Eli had on shorts and an Oberlin sweatshirt. He found his sneakers and laced them up. "It'll be cold," he said. "But I'll go crazy if I don't exercise. I wish I'd brought a bike."

"You're taking your phone?"

"In case I get lost."

She said, "Kiss me." She knew she sounded plaintive, as if everything depended on the kiss.

His kiss was good but fast and after he left she listened to him bound down the creaky wooden stairs. She threw herself back on the pillows. Not hungry or thirsty or wanting, really, to talk more. But in twenty minutes she knew she would be all those things. No television. Not right now. And yet, still, it was dark and cold out and a weird time for a run and where the fuck was he really going. She took a deep breath and stopped. He needed to exercise. That was true and she believed it. Everything was good.

She called Sherry, who answered on the first ring.

"So what's he like? Is he everything you dreamed of?"

"You're actually curious or are you making fun of me?"

"Emily, you think I didn't read the book? I know I teased you about it but that book was just as much a part of my growing up as it was yours."

"Yes, yes, you're right," Emily said, happy to find her sister both caring and defensive.

"So what's he like?"

"He's cautious. He's been playing the part for so long and I don't think he likes to break out of it. And I am asking an awful lot of him. We are. I'm not saying I don't love the fact that I've finally met him. I totally do. This was so worth it."

"He's a widower, right? Is he cute?"

"Please. He's the same age as Dad. Also, he

doesn't think that what he wrote is clichéd! Can you believe that?"

"He takes it all seriously?"

"Completely. I mean, I love every bit of it but I know it's kind of kitschy. But he . . . he thinks his stuff is still super-relevant. And when he talks to us it's like he's right there, in our marriage with us. I mean he jumped right in. Which is maybe what we needed. I forgave Eli for what he did. In front of Peter."

"I thought you already did that?"

"Before it was kind of like improv. Now we're making it real. We're beginning to be happy in a real way." Emily gathered the quilt around her and went over to the window. Outside there was nothing but darkness in all directions. She couldn't even see the parking lot. How could he be running out there, she wondered. He would run into a tree.

"The thing is you sound kind of skeptical?" Sherry asked.

"I know, I'm happy but at the same time skeptical. I'm nervous. We've been having sex like crazy."

"Where is Eli?"

"He went for a run."

"What? Oh, okay. A run. Let's have dinner Monday night, and you can tell me all about it."

"Sherry?" Emily took a deep breath. She knew she shouldn't ask so much of her sister. She understood that having to reach out to her right now was not a good indicator of how things were going.

"What?"

"Do you like me? Do you think I'm a fun person?"

"What? Of course I do. What are you talking about?"

"Sometimes I think he's dutiful about being married to me. I don't want him to feel that way, like it's homework."

"Um, I think marriage *is* homework. That's why I'm nowhere near it."

"Don't say that. It's true but don't say it."

"He loves you. You'll be fine. I'm glad you did this crazy thing."

"It's dorky and maybe a little dangerous."

"No. It's cathartic. You realized a dream. I'm jealous. And Emily?"

"What?"

"It's actually kind of glamorous, when you think about it."

Emily said, "I get that I'm leaning too much on you if you feel like you've got to say that."

"Well, at least it sounds like you're doing something that's good for you. If not glamorous, then good. It's like a cleanse, only really special and unique to you."

"Stop. I'll call you tomorrow when we get home. Dinner Monday night, for sure."

Emily went into the bathroom and turned on the shower.

The bathroom was big. There were pink roses painted on the white tiles. Eli still wasn't back. For some reason, she locked the bathroom door. She wanted to get back to a time with Eli, to some moment even before last summer, when they'd had sex where they did new things and laughed together and were awkward in the mornings when they'd brushed their teeth. How to get back there?

The water felt good and she took a hotter shower than she knew was good for her. Not how to get back there. How to go forward to combine that pleasure with the trust they'd developed . . . earlier today. Maybe that was a little ambitious. But that was what she'd ask Peter. How to do that. In just a little while, in an hour or so. She loved her husband. If he was capable of today, he would work with her to get to the place she could describe to him.

Peter, Winners' Dinner, November 2011

"It's so nice to sit here in this beautiful dining room in the candlelight with the two of you," Emily said. "You are my two favorite men in the world."

She smiled carefully. Both men looked pensive, their heads hunched forward and their faces heavy so they supported them with their hands. But where Eli was immobile, Peter kept trying to rise out of the somber state they'd found him in.

"I'm glad I found candles," Peter said. "Usually I can never find the darn things." He was at the head of his table. Emily and Eli were on either side of him, facing each other. He had given them some scotch when they arrived because he'd had a glass in hand when he opened the door. They had skipped the soup because Peter had forgotten to heat it up and it looked lumpy and a bit suspect. They had laughed about Peter's forgetfulness and moved right to the lamb shank, which they had all discovered was cool in the center. Peter had gotten confused about the heating time for the polenta, too, so the disks were hard and shiny, like wheels pulled from a toy truck.

"Have more brussels sprouts," Peter said. "I didn't mess with them." Peter had his scotch glass

336

with him at the table. Emily and Eli had switched to wine. "If the meat's undercooked, I can put it back in the oven," Peter said.

"No, no, it's terrific. Really old-fashioned and homey tasting," Emily said.

"You're too kind," Peter said. "I'll bet the wine they left us is really nice. They brought several bottles so don't be shy about asking for more. My friend Henry down at the inn selected them. He took a course a few years back, at the Culinary Institute at Hyde Park, in the evenings. With a— what did he call it? An oenophile . . . They ended up becoming friends."

"We forgot the wine we brought you! I think it's still in the car." Emily stood up. "I'll get it."

"Please don't," Peter said. "It's cold out there. And remember your status. You're winners. Relax, sit down."

And so she did. He liked how formal she was. She was wearing a gray wool dress and a pale blue cardigan. Eli was slumped in his chair in a red sweater and jeans. They were in the country, after all. But then Peter realized that Emily was probably always more formal than her husband.

"You go for a lot of walks around the lake?" Eli asked. "You ever take pictures of the birds?"

"I used to walk with my wife, Lisa. We didn't take pictures since the birds were so much a part of our daily life. Who needed pictures? But we always held hands." Peter touched his fingertips

337

together. "I hope you two are in the habit of holding hands?"

"We are." Eli helped himself to some more lamb although there was already plenty of food on his plate. "Lately we do that more and more. Which is funny, since most couples do it less and less as they get older."

"You were married for a long time, weren't you?" Emily asked Peter. "Forty years?"

"Almost that many." Peter nodded. His mouth was full and he knew that made him look as if he was frowning.

"I'm sorry," Emily said. "It must be hard to talk about."

"Don't be sorry. I'm glad we're mentioning Lisa. I want to talk about her. We weren't always happy." Peter looked around the dining room. He hadn't had people sit down to a dinner in this room in years. Lisa had used it as a kind of second office. The bottom drawers of the cupboard were full of papers that needed to be addressed and then moved into her study. Or thrown away, more likely. "Then again, no one is always happy. But that's not my point. Do you want to hear this?" he asked.

"Of course we do," Emily said.

"She and I—I came up here to marry her and I did that in a way that was intentionally dramatic and so that act, I think it was meant to become part of the life of my book. I know how I'm feeling my way here, with my words, but hear me out—she seemed like the right life for me. And so we both worked hard to fit into each other's worlds. Like you two are doing. We wanted more children but in the end, we only had one. Belinda. There's a painting we had done of her." Peter pointed at an oil painting of an eight-year-old Belinda kneeling at the edge of Lake Okabye. She had a round face and Peter's big eyes and ears. Emily and Eli nodded and smiled at the picture. "Do you two want children? I should have asked earlier."

"We are talking about it. It could happen for us soon," Emily said. She bit her lip and didn't look at Eli. Peter finished what was left of his scotch and pushed the glass away.

"Once you have children it's different," Peter said. He lowered his head and smiled at Emily. "Another cliché. But we understood the pressures a child creates and we gave each other room to grow. The eighties were hard for us. My transition to my forties—this was in the late eighties . . . I drank too much then. I did a few things wrong. Like you did, Eli."

"I actually don't drink that much," Eli said.

"I meant the other thing that came up this afternoon."

"Oh," Eli said. "That." Peter watched Eli frown and struggle to find his way back to feeling bad about his cheating. Peter thought, Let him be. I'll keep talking and that'll be a way of letting this poor lost man be.

"My wife. She knew what I was up to. There were a few years where our silences had a mean tinge to them. But by then we had Belinda, like I said, and we had built a life together. I never meant to hurt Lisa." Peter went quiet. Emily wasn't looking at him, or Eli. Was he being too vague? Too honest? Both? "I'll stop," he said. "You didn't come here for this."

"How'd you get past all that?" Eli asked. "Now that you've brought it up, we may as well take it on. It certainly seems relevant." Eli pushed his plate forward and took more brussels sprouts off the serving dish with his fork.

"We let each other make big mistakes," Peter said. "She suffered through quite a few nights when I was drinking at a bar called the Sally Forth, at our inn in Hudson. This was a long time ago. And that place didn't work out for us. We wasted a lot of money and we fought over those losses. And I suffered some coldness from her. She needed a good measure of control and that turned into a silent tug-of-war for us. But we never thought of leaving each other. We soldiered on. That doesn't seem so bad, does it? To give in to each other? My Pop and his Bess didn't do that, I don't think. I recall that they had quite a bit of fun together. And I wrote about that as best I could. But in my life, I suppose I chose to soldier on. You two could do it." Peter stopped again. He reached for his scotch glass but he didn't see the bottle on the table and he willed himself to keep from going to look for it. He said, "You two have plenty of promise in you. You don't need to hear all this personal stuff. It's not what you came for. We'll stick to what I put in the book."

"No, this broadening is okay. The parts of marriage you just mentioned, we are getting better at that, too," Emily said. "Giving in. Soldiering on. I like that Eli is asking so many questions. He never does that." Emily smiled at her husband. "I have questions, too. How do you make a marriage a safe space where you can have fun, like your Pop and Bess had? How does a life like theirs really work? Not in the big moments. I want to know what happens in the little ones."

"You mean the interstices." Peter smiled. "You want what I left out."

"Doesn't everybody?" Emily said with a laugh.

"Our marriage is a safe space, isn't it?" Eli asked. "We have fun, don't we?"

"We did. Now we're rebuilding," Emily said.

"Oh." Eli tilted back in his chair. "I stand corrected." Eli made a noise in his throat. Peter watched Eli. He hadn't seen him behave this way before. Emily and Eli were watching each other, both of them with their eyes too wide, circling each other without moving. Like cats, Peter thought. Peter suddenly found that he was struggling for the right thing to say. He thought he ought to lecture them on how to get along. Even if he bored them, that would be all right—it would draw their event to a proper close. He could feel that they wanted to be honest with each other and he blamed himself for bringing that on, all because he'd stupidly veered from his original plan and indulged in talking about Lisa. Nobody needed to hear about the life he had with Lisa.

"In my book—" Peter said, but Emily cut him off.

"Peter, I'm sorry. Just a second. Eli's mad at me. Aren't you, Eli? Are you upset that I did that?" Emily breathed through her mouth and looked at Eli. "That I corrected you?"

"Why do you ask me so many questions?" Eli asked. "Can't you trust me? I'm not passive. If I'm upset, I'll say so."

"That's good, Eli," Peter spoke quickly. "This afternoon was quite an undertaking. I can imagine that you have some comments that you still want to make. I would. So yes, say them. I recall that so much of the time, my grandparents didn't hesitate to speak their minds. But they were never hurtful or mean. Never."

"What about me?" Emily asked. "Can I let some things out?"

"Yes, you can." Peter smiled. "A few minutes of it can't hurt. So long as you're both kind and solicitous. Just as Pop and Bess always were."

Eli frowned and stared at his full plate.

Peter watched Emily breathe in and out. He found that he had balled up his hands under the table, that he was hoping that the worst of it was over and at the same time, he knew it wasn't. He hadn't meant to steer them into this territory. He went ahead and poured wine into his scotch glass. Or had he?

Emily said, "As we all know, Eli, you did something and then you tried to hide it from me, so I don't totally believe what you just said about trust. Not yet."

"This stuff," said Peter, gesturing at the polenta. "I can try to reheat it, maybe it'll soften. Food gets better as leftovers. Even in the same meal. Over the years I found that to be true, I can swear to it."

"Leftovers?" Emily asked. "I'm sorry. Of course that's true. We feel that way about food, too."

"That's good," Peter said. "You want your safe space question addressed? I'm no fan of complete honesty. In some ways, constant kindness precludes it. You see? And, further, I like leaving the mystery in a marriage. Forget what I said about Lisa. The pain of losing her is still a little too fresh for me. That said, a baseline of honesty is key. Do you see the beauty in that undulation? But you two, you're well on your way there. You shouldn't worry about these things."

"Yes, we are on our way," Emily said. "Thanks in part to you, Peter, and what we talked about this afternoon." She looked at Eli. For a long time he hadn't touched the cold meat or the polenta. But now she saw that when she hadn't been looking, he had quickly and thoughtlessly eaten all the food on his plate. Still, his cheeks were hollow and his eyes were wide. He was staring at the painting of Belinda, or at least looking in its direction. It wasn't such a bad painting, she thought. It had a little Wyeth in it. Eli wasn't moving.

"Eli, let's get on the same page here," Peter said. "Let's get back to where we were this afternoon, when we parted."

"I can't."

"Why not?" Emily asked.

"Because we're not on the same page or on our way there." Eli placed his hands flat on the table. "We're just not."

"What do you mean?" Emily asked. "Can you explain? Or are you simply noting that we are working on it and I'm being presumptuous because, really, we should be cautious, like we've been saying? That would make sense, if you were saying that."

"Emily, maybe now is a good time for Eli to find his own words," Peter said, and then immediately wished he hadn't. He said, "Wait. Let me get in here for a moment—"

"Can you stop clearing up everything I say?" Eli asked. "I want to get safe like we keep talking about so we can get back to building some sexy mystery between us. Don't get me wrong. I love that we're doing this. I'm, like, more into this than either of you, I think. And I am really accessing some stuff. First, about Jenny. And I know, Emily, that you want me to shut up about Jenny. But I don't want to. There was something there. Something real. And I killed it because I am married to you and I love you."

"Eli?" Emily shook her head. "Do you understand what you're saying? Because if you do, do you see how that shatters me? Do you mean what you're saying?"

"I think I do."

Peter watched Emily. She quaked a little, her shoulders and head swaying. And then she went still.

"This territory is all wrong," Peter said. "You two are twisting everything around." He reached out for their hands but stopped short of actually touching them. They had both moved farther down from him and away from the table. His hands were out in front of him though, and he felt his ribs touch the table's edge. He tried to show that he meant to be in this position, crouched forward, toward them. But it didn't matter because they were not looking at him.

"Maybe you think you're being kind by sounding so harsh. You work hard at this marriage, right?" Emily asked Eli. "Do you think you work too hard? Are you tired from the long day? Is that what's the matter right now?"

"I want to save it," Eli mumbled.

"Are we in that dire a situation? I forgave you. I don't know how I did it but I did. Now I am steering us back. I mean, we are. If we're twisting things around then let's untwist them. Right now."

"Sure." Eli looked at Peter, at the way he'd positioned himself, and imitated him. He raised his hands, palms up, so they were on either side of his face. He pushed his plate away and crouched over the table. "Let's do that. But—fuck it. Look. I've been with some women."

"Now Eli." Peter raised his voice. "You've already said something that hurt Emily, more than you know, I think. Let's not share more of what's meant to be hidden."

"Why not?" Eli asked. "What do you mean, meant to be hidden?"

"In your life?" Emily asked. She was very still. "Sure. You had a whole life before me. Women love you."

"I don't know why they do. But I can't resist. I say yes. You know that, don't you?"

"What are you asking me? I know what?" Emily asked. She was increasingly upright, in her chair. Eli's body was still crouched and low.

Peter gritted his teeth and said, "I think you two should stop. Let's reel this in. I think we did just what we were supposed to this afternoon and we ought to leave it there, if you want to know what I think."

"It's not just Jenny," Eli said.

"Not just Jenny," Emily repeated.

"I've been with others. I want us to stay married. Jenny says—"

"Jenny says? You're talking to Jenny about all this?"

"Excuse me." Peter stood up. "Let's take a break. I am going to bring the dishes in and you, Emily, you can help me."

"No." Emily went to him fast and grabbed his hand. "Stay, please. I'll help you clean up later. Please stay."

Eli reached across the table. He said, "Hold hands with me. Not him."

"No," Emily said.

Peter sat back down. He said, "You two need to back off each other. You are like fighters in a ring. I can tell you there's no place in marriage for how you're behaving right now. I can say that for sure."

Emily glared at Eli. "Say what you want to say and we'll see if what we're doing is fighting."

"So now it's a test."

"Fucking talk, Eli! Not just Jenny? What are you talking about? How is this healing? This is bloodletting. You are so stupid!"

"Thanks," Eli said with a nod. "Thank you for reminding me that you feel that way about me."

"I'm sorry. I apologize," Emily said.

"That didn't feel much like an apology. And Peter." Eli jutted his chin at Peter. "Here's Peter, with his book, which I read, and his okay marriage that we just heard about. He believes you can save anything. So save me. I cheat. We've been together over five years and I have slept with other women. It's something I do. Women like me! I want to stop. I want to settle down with you. I think that's what I want."

"You think that's what you want." Emily's voice was very low. "I am going to sit very still and I will continue to hold Peter's hand now. I hope that's okay with you."

"I can hold hands," Peter said. "But I am not at all happy with how this is going."

"Fine," Eli said. "You do what you need to do. I love you but it's like I can't access you! You just want this ideal thing, this bullshit he keeps talking about. And it's not real to me. It never has been. But I see how other people are and I want to please you so I say yes to you, but at the same time—"

"You found an outlet elsewhere. Several."

"Yeah, that's what I did. Jenny, she doesn't care about this marriage stuff, this conventional stuff."

"And it's because I'm controlling. I control everything. You don't like that, do you?"

"Yeah. I don't."

"You don't like it. You don't even like me! Why

should I forgive you for that? You don't like me! Why should I forgive you?"

"You don't have to. This is impossible. I don't even know why I'm here. I should go."

"So you're leaving," Emily said.

"He's not going anywhere," Peter said. "That won't be necessary." Peter looked fully at Eli. Eli would not stop staring at his wife. Peter could entirely imagine Eli angrily driving back to New York. Eli was setting himself up for that outcome. Peter could see it. The worst thing that could happen! The very worst.

"Let's slow down," Peter said. Emily still clutched his hand and he moved it, gently. But Emily wouldn't let him go. He said, "Can you both please find a memory of a happy time you had together? Let's talk about that. And then if I can, I will match your memories to a chapter from my book."

"You called Jenny from your run, didn't you?"

Eli shook his head. He said, "You sought me out. You came after me. You fit me into your story. I hate that, how you explain us to ourselves. But I want this to work. I am saying I want this to work."

"How can you say that? You're not even making any sense! And what you're saying I did isn't even bad. If you loved me, you would be happy with how I am. I don't forgive you, not for Jenny and certainly not for any part of what

349

you've said tonight. Other women? How many other women?"

"That's not the point." Eli breathed in deeply. "I won't list them."

"But you've been trying so hard this fall? Which is the truth, Eli? Has today just been too much? Is that what it is? Are you emotionally exhausted?"

"Today would be a challenge to any man," Peter said, quickly.

"No," Eli said. "You are denying what I really am. You want me to fit into something and I don't fit. I want to. I try all the time. Today I was all crumpled up and I was trying to fit. But I don't."

Emily let Peter's hand drop. She said, "I want you to get out!"

Eli stood up. He said, "You're going to stay here?"

"If he'll have me."

They both stared at Peter, there at the head of the table.

Peter said, "This isn't what any of us intended. We can still dial back from this moment. Let's please try."

"Not what we intended?" Eli asked. "Who cares? Life doesn't work that way."

"Please stay," Peter said. "And I will help you navigate toward a better place."

"He shouldn't stay if he doesn't want to," Emily said. "He's a liar. He's been talking to Jenny all through this. I understand that now. He lies to me and he lies to himself."

"No." Eli shook his head. Peter frowned and thought, She's right. Eli lies to her. Because from moment to moment, he does not know what he is.

Emily turned to Peter. She said, "I can just imagine. Everyone saw him on the phone outside the room. Running in circles and talking to another woman. Everyone at the inn saw him do it. I don't want to go back there! This is humiliating!"

"Most of me wants to fix this," Eli said.

"I'd tell you again that you're lying," Emily said. "But I'm beginning to realize that would mean you have some idea inside of you of what the truth is. And you don't."

"How does that make me different than him?" Eli jutted his chin at Peter.

"I didn't say it did. Maybe I'm wrong to love him, too. To love his book. But that mistake doesn't hurt as much. Because he's not threatening to walk out on me. He's not standing up and glaring at me. I married you. You're my husband. Obviously, I don't control you. Leave or stay. Up to you."

"Stay," Peter said. "You both know there's a way out of this."

"Not together there's not," Eli said. "She's right. Half the time I'm fooling myself."

"Then go," Emily said. "I'll get a bus back, or something. I'll find my way back. Please just go."

"Is that what you want?"

"That's what you want, Eli. Run. You want to run."

"Stop telling me what I want!"

"Just please go." Emily stood up and went out of the dining room. Peter listened to her steps, her sudden uncertainty about where to go. Then he imagined she must have seen the bathroom under the stairs so she ran inside and locked the door. Eli didn't move from where he stood. Peter did not get up from his chair.

"I didn't mean for this to happen," Eli said. "I want you to know that I'm sorry. You did good. You created a safe space."

Peter didn't say a word. Slowly, he stood up.

"Why don't you take five minutes to yourself," Peter said. "I believe you two can make up. If you like, I'll go upstairs or into the kitchen while you do it. Then she'll come out and you two can reconnect."

"Can I ask why you think we can fix it?"

"It's like I said. I was with other women, too, during my marriage. My wife suffered because of it. It was the wrong way to be. But we got through it."

Eli nodded. He said, "I'm sorry. Your book is really nice. But your marriage doesn't sound so great. Shake my hand?"

Peter put out his hand. But Eli bent in and quickly hugged him. And Peter felt suddenly suspicious of Eli, suspicious of this meaningless masculine hug. Peter walked with him to the front hallway. Eli went quickly out of the house and down the steps. He started his car and eased it out of the driveway in one smooth, purposeful motion, like a river that's suddenly able to breach its dam.

Peter went back to the dining room. He stared down at the plates but didn't touch them. He blew out the candles. He thought, The jig is up. Should've stuck with talking about nothing but the goddamned book.

He went to wait for Emily in the living room. He found the bottle of scotch there and poured an ounce into a fresh glass thinking, This is just circumstance. The bottle happened to be here. I wasn't looking for it. He sat down and waited for her. He would not go and bother her from the other side of the bathroom door since he knew from experience that that would only make a woman cry harder. Twenty minutes passed before she came out and sat down in the soft chair near his, which Lisa had used.

"I saw him go from the bathroom window," she said. "The only thing I can stand to think right now is what are we going to tell them? We can lie about it to whoever you're reporting all this to. To that awful girl, Stella. I'll lie to her, no problem. The last thing I need is her asking me questions."

"That doesn't matter. We'll figure all that out later."

"Wait, I want to say something. I'm not going to suggest that even though this happened, you still have all the answers," she said. "I understand that you don't. But no matter what, you mean so much to me. You signify something important, you and your book. You can't deny that."

Peter tried to smile at her. He thought, Can a single day go by when I'm not told what I can and can't do? He said, "Let's not worry about me just now, and what I am or am not."

He looked through the window out at the dark of his driveway and was surprised that Emily's husband really wasn't there. He was reminded of when he walked out on Maddie and Henry a few weeks ago at the inn. He shook his head. If a man believes he might be cornered, he will run.

"He's not at the inn," Emily said. "I called there. I'm sorry. I apologize for staying so long in the bathroom. I tried to call my sister, too, but she's working. She's an actor and in this play she's in she has to wear a harness because at the end of the play she floats above the stage, and it takes a while to put it on because it's a safety issue. She should be the one listening to me now."

"What about your parents? Your mother?"

"I'll call her later. She didn't want this. I'm not ready for how she might react."

"Don't move," he said. "I'll bring you your wine." He went to the dining room and found her glass and the bottle, and when he returned to place it on the table next to her, he found that she was curled up in the chair.

"You need a blanket." He went and got the soft blanket that lived on the window seat and put it over her. She reached out with one hand and he took it and kneeled in front of her. She drank from her glass as she stared at him. When he saw she was still and not shaking, he moved away from her and kneeled in front of the fireplace. He lit the kindling under the logs that were already there and then sat down, facing the fire. There were dim lights on all over the first floor of the house.

"I can't believe this is happening to me," she said. "I'm a nice person! You don't understand that because you've only seen me one way. But I'm not an awful controlling person. I'm, like, solid. I do not let people down."

"I know that you are a nice person," he said. The fire caught. He eased himself back into his chair.

"I wanted him to love me the same way I loved him. To be as in love with me as when we were first together. You know, to live out the promise we made to each other. Just like you say. Is that too much to ask?"

"You know it isn't," Peter said. "It's just—if I can be completely honest, then I would say that it sounds like this life you built was one that he couldn't . . . He didn't fit into it."

"But you're not so different than him. How did you manage?"

Peter looked at the floor. "I don't suppose that I always did manage. Look, you know what you want. And he couldn't give it to you. You're a wonderful woman. If he runs, he runs. No one ought to have to chase a man who runs away."

"I can't believe we came to you to learn about how to have true love and a happy marriage and he ran."

"I'm just damned sorry you got hurt," Peter said. "Nobody wanted that. Believe me."

She had begun to stare at him and he wished she would stop. He knew what all that staring meant.

She said, "Do you have a story about true love? Can you tell me one? I need that."

"I told you my book isn't about true love. It's about how to have a good marriage. They're a bit different, don't you think?"

She sighed deeply and he could see the disappointment in her face, see it in her stare. She had been so happy this afternoon. And now he watched her as she listened to him say things that meant nothing.

She said, "Tell me a story anyway, please. Something that isn't in the book."

Peter looked away from her. The room had gotten warmer. He knew he ought to only fill the silence but he could not help himself. He talked about his own past. He said, "Imagine a couple in New York. It's fall. They are falling in love. But the man believes he has obligations elsewhere.

356

They are walking in midtown, holding hands . . ." He went on about a couple who come apart because the man runs. He tried to soften the story's landing, to show that any love is worth something, to blur the sad end so this night would end in a way that was equally blurry. He did hope Emily would somehow fix her marriage. He was not sure that she could, but he hoped so all the same.

"So they just end it?" Emily asked. "But you stayed with your wife. You were married to her forever."

"That's true. I was," Peter said. He went away from her, to the fire, and pushed the logs apart. He was angry at himself, again, for letting her push him beyond the simple message he was supposed to share. Though he couldn't stop now. He said, "Nobody meant tonight to be like this. It was supposed to be . . . good-natured palliatives. Not this."

Emily had her head in her hands. She mumbled, "Well, there you go. What do you know?"

"What do you know."

"We blew up," Emily said. "We were so careful and then we blew up."

"It's late. I'll call you a cab. If your love is real and true he'll come back and you'll fix it together. I can tell you that for sure."

Emily went wide-eyed and searched his face. He wished she'd stop it but he didn't want to say that aloud. He went to call a cab and he could feel her gaze following him.

She called after him, "Peter? But isn't that . . . isn't what you just said kind of obvious? He'll come back or he won't?"

Peter winched his mouth down. "Look, nobody ever said I was a genius. In fact, they mostly said the opposite. Let's go in the front hall, where we can see the driver's headlights."

Once they were standing, he reached out and hugged her. He said, "Your sweater reminds me of one my wife made. Hang on."

He went into the hall closet and found the big sky-blue sweater flecked with white and gray that his wife wore on cool evenings. It was folded neatly and he was glad he hadn't donated it with everything else. He'd meant to give it to Belinda but he kept forgetting. Belinda wouldn't mind. He would tell her the story of what happened with this foolish contest and she would understand.

"Do you want to stay here for the night? In my daughter Belinda's room?" He handed her the sweater. "Actually, I see it's nothing like the one you've got on. But my wife made it herself. Here, take it."

"It's beautiful. I can't stay here. If I stayed here tonight, I would never want to leave."

Her eyes were full now and instead of the disappointed stare, she was crying.

"You're exhausted by all this. And so this is the

one thing I can give you. The rooms at the inn can be drafty. She loved this sweater."

"He's not out there, behind me. Is he?"

"There's just the cab, coming up the driveway."

Peter hugged her again. She quaked into his chest and shoulder.

Emily, Winners' Weekend, November 2011

In the cab on the way back to the inn, she twisted the thick sweater around her neck. She wondered why she had refused to spend the night in Belinda's bedroom. It would be better there than in the room she'd just shared with Eli.

They hadn't gotten to talk about that special summer with his grandparents, and what it was really like. Another regret. She almost told the driver to turn around. But no.

She watched the slump-backed cabdriver fumble with his cell phone. She listened to him call his wife to say he would see her soon. And she felt the first bite of her new state. But no. She was not really alone. Not yet. She felt that if she could find a distance, she could see herself as only the victim of an oddball prank, a misguided marketing attempt. Unfortunately, she had blindsided herself and everyone else by denying how deeply troubled her marriage was.

The inn was quiet when she slipped inside. The young man in a too-big white shirt and floppy red tie who'd handed over her key was on the phone, murmuring to a girlfriend. He didn't look at her. This was madness! Madness crept along with her on her walk up to the empty bedroom at the top of the second flight of stairs.

Once inside the room, she took off her coat but kept the big sweater wrapped around her neck. She sat in one of the big chairs by the window and waited. She hadn't checked the parking lot to see if their car was there. Eli might be . . . what? Sleeping in it? She looked out there. No car. She got up and found her cell phone. Eli had been calling her. She held the phone and didn't move, curled back up in the big chair and closed her eyes and fell asleep. A phone rang and she looked around, confused by the foreign ring of the room phone. She answered.

"I'm sorry," Eli said. "This is all my fault. I love you and I will always regret how I treated you. I'm so sorry. It's entirely my fault. Although I recognize that this is part of my journey, I know there were missteps along the way. Those missteps hurt other people. They hurt you. Even with just hours apart, I can see that. But I want you to know I tried so hard."

"Your journey?" she asked. She thought he sounded as if he were working from a script that someone else had written for him. She silently admitted that there had been something the matter with his language for days now. She had not allowed herself to grow suspicious.

"Okay," she said. "That is all really great to know. Thanks." She hung up. Jenny Alexandretti is one hell of a bad writer, she thought.

Someone else would have left him long ago. Emotionally unavailable. Cheated on her. Didn't love her back. An incredibly attractive and charming man. Legs thick as old tree trunks. But after the first moments of love, moments that she now understood belonged more to her than to them, he had never picked her up and carried her anywhere. Never biked her anywhere. Now he had run away. How dare he be sorry.

This was not her fault. Was it? She certainly was not that controlling. And how could she forgive him for this? She couldn't. And how could she have thought entering a contest would solve anything? How stupid could she have been? And how lost was she now?

Stella, November 2011

Wednesday morning and Stella Petrovic got in the elevator at her office and closed her eyes. Though her workday was starting, she was unwilling to think of anything but what had happened with Ivan before she'd had to run out of the house.

As the doors clanged shut, she remembered staring up at the underside of his chin and the strain in his neck, all of him happily thrusting away. She had come several minutes earlier but just then she was only looking up at him, loving him. Then she turned to her side, saw the alarm clock, freaked out, and said "Hurry!" And, with an attempt at a smile, "If you don't come soon, I'm going to be late for Free Thinking/New Billing!"

Upon hearing that, Ivan had cracked up laughing. She pushed him off and got free. He fell off the bed, dick still hard as a chair leg, and rolled onto the floor. She took the opportunity to jump up and race around him into the bathroom, making sure to stay at least five feet out of his reach.

"Wait!" he called out, while he lay naked on the floor, still hard and laughing.

"No, I've got to go. I don't even have time to shower, goddamn it."

"I'm not done!" he yelled. "And I love you!"

"I love you, too, Ivan. But I don't think Helena Magursky would consider hot sex a good excuse for being later than her."

"How would you know?"

"Good point! I wouldn't. That's how screwed I am."

She struggled into tights and a red plaid skirt, a white sweater with a diamond inlay pattern she had bought at the McCarren Park outdoor market two weeks earlier and kind of hated. She glanced at a pair of blue corduroy overalls she loved but hadn't worn out of the house in two years. She could wear those. She couldn't wear those.

"You look great," Ivan said. He was standing in the bathroom doorway. She turned and smiled up at him and realized that, for the third time in her life, she was in love.

"Wait," she said. "I do love you. This is where the romance is, isn't it?"

"Yes." Ivan seemed confused at her obviousness. He was a subtle person, she got that—and he didn't like to be so on the nose in his language, because of his proclivity for Russian poetry, she supposed. But he also accommodated her. Why? Because he loved her. He really loved her.

"Of course this is where the romance is," he mumbled as he kissed her neck. And then they'd tumbled right back into bed.

Now, in the elevator she reached down to scratch her leg and felt come there, under her tights, that was guaranteed to itch all meeting long. And possibly smell? Definitely, if she sweated. Jesus! And she was on the agenda, right there in the top spot: *Canoe* Update.

So she was in love, for real. And she was in trouble, for real. She had no plan beyond hoping that there'd be an e-mail or some missive from the woman, Emily Babson, or less likely from that awful Peter Herman. But when she checked her e-mail from her phone, there was nothing.

Canoe Update.

She didn't have one. She might say, "It's ongoing!" But no. She was iced and knew it, but to be late and have to make something up? That would make her rude and a liar. She might as well go directly to HR for the COBRA benefits lecture.

She joined the parade of women and the few men making their way into the Dreiser Room. People were still rustling into place and finishing up their gossip as she found a seat.

Helena called out, "Let's begin! Let's begin. I'm sorry if I'm late. But you all are used to it, aren't you. Forty years of it, and so you'd better be. I believe we are post our winners' weekend." She glanced at Lucy who nodded a yes. "So where are we? Have we got a happy pair of marrieds we can introduce to Diane Sawyer? A droll and verbose Peter Herman who can get up there with them and talk about how he fixed whatever was the matter? We're dying to know. Who can fill us in?"

"I guess I can," Stella heard her own voice and tried to catch her brain up to it. If things were going well, a marketing person would've stepped in by now and started taking credit. That had been Stella's plan. But things were not going well. And Stella was looking at a quiet room free of supporters. She felt horribly junior and out-of-body.

"Who's that?"

"Me. Stella."

"Okay, me. Good. Talk."

"My update is actually not quite ready," Stella said.

"I don't understand. The weekend happened, didn't it?"

"Yes, yes it did."

"And yet, no update to share!" Helena laughed deep in her throat. There were titters from her lieutenants, too. A young woman three seats from the head of the table, who Stella didn't recognize, slid a piece of paper down the table until it stopped in front of Helena. Helena glanced down at it and then her whole head drooped so it was at a ninety-degree angle from her neck. Everyone waited. Helena's forehead hit the paper. She banged her forehead against the paper several times, as if she were trying to deny the order of scissors, paper, rock.

"Jesus Christ," Helena muttered as she raised her head. "Can this be right?"

The unidentified woman nodded.

"I've just learned that with the *USA Today* ads, we've spent quite a lot of company money on marketing for this contest. Looks like we got overexcited. Regardless, after we spend *money* to do *things,* with the hope of increasing *sales,* we like an update."

Forty-seven women and nine men nodded their heads.

"I will have a cohesive update that I can present to you next week," Stella said.

"Cohesive, huh? That'll be special. Will you have pictures?"

"Mr. Herman wouldn't allow pictures."

"No pictures? But I thought you—all right. So much for the goddamn twenty-first century. If he doesn't end up on Terry Gross at the very least when all this shit is over I'm going to punch him in the nose. I should really call him. No more pussy-footing around." Helena lowered her voice. Everyone bent in to hear her and she went on, "Lord, nearly a quarter million unchecked dollars on some half-assed contest and we've got less than nothing to show for it. Fuck. Fuck me. Lucy? Let's not forget that phone call."

Lucy nodded and noted that Helena needed to call Peter Herman. Stella wondered at this, as there must have been some communication breakdown in the past few weeks about just this phone call. It kept getting put off. Or perhaps these old people were playing phone tag? She shook her head. Though if Sara Byrd was right, she could see how Helena might have a hard time making the call.

After a moment, Helena went on, saying, "So we'll have to wait a week for you . . . Stella? That feels wrong to me. Instead, let's bring all the players in for a meeting. That'll get us to the bottom of this morass!"

Stella smiled and nodded. The ugliness of the word *morass* hung in the room like flatulence that everyone smelled but no one would acknowledge.

Stella said, "Yes, yes of course."

"Yes! Yes, of course we will! As I have just said we would. And let's not think about bringing in the players. Let's actually do it. No more thinking. Let's do some doing! Now we move on." Helena looked at Lucy, who nodded once at Sara Byrd.

Sara Byrd said, "I've got this proposal in, called 'Swords of the Single Ladies: An Analysis of the Seven Traits That Keep Women Single and Unable to Find Husbands.' The traits are different kinds of swords and the conceit is, like, 'Ladies, put down your swords!' The neat thing is that it's written by a medieval studies professor at Princeton so it has a charming Joan of Arc theme running through it. It's anti-Joan, incredibly. Obviously it's not for me but I thought I'd mention it—"

"Sounds wild," Helena said. "Very what-can-we-learn-from-the-Dark-Ages. Check with me later and anyone who's interested, get to Sara quick. We know there's an audience for marriage advice. Don't we, Stella?"

"What? Yes." Stella spoke quickly. "Right!"

The group smiled and rustled, waited for Helena to move on. Stella made sure to only look down at her hands. The group focused their attention on a hot new novel about a glassblower who falls in love with an ice-skater, and Stella dared to look up. From her spot against the wall, she stared past the table full of senior staff, at the eighteen or so women lined up on the wall opposite her, perhaps sixteen feet away. Though their mouths were closed, they were laughing at her. Another eager editor blows her big shot. Now it would be that much easier for them to get theirs.

She'd been calling Peter since Sunday morning and nobody had answered the phone. Emily Babson wouldn't answer her phone, either. And she'd never once talked to the husband, Eli. She had no pictures. Nothing except the entry essay and those few semi-charming but ultimately very lurchy phone calls with Peter Herman. In every one of them he had promised to update her and now he was unreachable. She sighed and touched her fingernails to her lips but made sure not to bite them. Because she'd need to get them in good shape for her upcoming job interviews. Maybe she'd become an agent? She shuddered at the horrifying prospect. A work life full of pitching jerks like her? Sure enough, the stuff on her leg warmed and began to itch. She dared not touch the spot. She thought of Ivan and grew angry at herself for dwelling on something that made her happy right at the moment when her career was going to shit.

"Who was that woman with the piece of paper," she whispered to the marketing assistant to her right, who was mostly hidden behind a life-size presentation cardboard blowup of Pete Sampras, smiling and holding his new book, *A Surprise or Two, but Mostly Pete.*

"New business manager. Looks after the accounting as the expenses happen. I heard they're calling it Monitoring as Spending Happens. MASH. Stupid, huh? I mean that's what monitoring *means*. They're trying to do a better job of tying costs back to editors."

"Great," Stella said. "Fucking great."

"Shhh." The assistant nudged Stella.

Stella glanced around the room and tried to pick up the conversation.

Everyone was laughing appreciatively at something Helena had said and Stella joined in. The joke seemed to be at Lucy's expense. Stella looked around for Lucy and saw her leaning against a post at the side of the room, pretending to take notes. Lucy looked miserable and she was shivering. Had she lost her seat? It seemed that way.

Stella dared to look at Helena. And then the weirdest thing happened. Helena caught Stella's eye and she smiled right at her. And did she wink? Was that even possible? But the smile was real and Stella felt it for what it was. One last chance.

Peter, November 2011

Where was the goddamn book? Lisa kept a copy on her shelves somewhere. If he couldn't find it, he'd have to go down to the basement and unpack a carton. He had been avoiding the basement. He nosed around in her bookshelves, grazing through her gardening books, her Ovid and Krishnamurti and Galbraith and her investment manuals. For minutes he couldn't find it among all these fine books of philosophy and economics that he had never read.

But then it appeared in front of him, several versions, all in a row. He pulled one out at random—a copy from 1981 that wasn't any uglier than the ones before or after it, and that contained the exercises at the back. The goddamned exercises. He hadn't even asked Emily and Eli if they'd done them. Standing there, he flexed his long legs and flipped around at random in his own book—the book he should have stuck to. He found what he was looking for. He poked a finger at the page and read chapter 8:

On Sin

"The twist I never saw coming was the twist and shout!" Pop loved to say that—it was his rock 'n' roll joke.

I found it funny the first time, and kept laughing after that, just as Bess did.

But eventually I discovered that the joke was also meant as a kind of code for adultery. He never said: Look what happened to your parents because of adultery. But I was beginning to be able to understand him pretty well. On this evening, Bess had gone off to play bridge in the back room at the library and Pop and I were watching the sun go down together out in the canoe. He was drinking Yukon Jack whiskey from a copper flask and I was whittling.

"You will have your head turned by a pretty lady, you can be sure of that. You will twist. You may shout!"

His rough yell across the lake was like a crow's caw. I still hear it when I see a pretty woman in stockings and a tight skirt pass me by in the busy midday street.

"Pretty girls are nice to look at," I said, thinking of my Honey. "I mean, how can a guy keep from wanting to be with lots of girls?"

"You cannot keep from wanting. You will commit adultery. It's a fact of life, like playing sports. You'll keep playing sports as you get older, won't you, Peter?"

"Yes."

"At least football. You must play that in high school, or basketball, so you'll know what it is to be on a team and to trust your teammates and work toward a common goal. But here is what you must remember. Even if you don't take a woman who is not your wife in your arms and love her, you are certain to look at a woman with lust. This is adultery."

"Adultery," I said. And I won't lie—it felt good and illicit to speak such a word aloud.

How little I knew! How innocent I was. But my Pop knew that from the moment I clambered off the bus on Main Street, with my army-green duffel stuffed with white T-shirts and blue jeans. I was blank enough for every sort of imprinting, right or wrong.

But everything I learned that summer was right. Especially this:

You will look at others with lust,
and this will challenge the strength of your
marriage. But if you're going to have a happy
journey through this life, stay in your own canoe.

Peter snapped the book closed and laughed aloud at his own ridiculousness. The hubris he must have had to type such blather! Yet people liked it. And Emily Babson—she really believed this stuff. How could that be? She seemed intelligent. Maybe she was just being kind. And then everything had blown up around her. He had failed her. But what about the exercises? Maybe they were the kernel that held the true value and everything that surrounded them was so much husk. Maybe the exercises would be his excuse to call Emily. He would read them, and then he would call her because he wanted to talk about them. He could say that she and Eli ought to do an exercise. He imagined the two of them in their apartment in Brooklyn. Probably not speaking to each other this week but possibly, just possibly living through each day with the hope of salvaging their marriage.

He had been slow to write the exercises when he was asked in 1977. But Ladder & Rake had been after him to expand the reach of his book then, too. The later seventies were a healthy sales period for the book, because the energy crisis created plenty of marital problems among people who liked the idea of *Canoe* in the first place. The sort of people who were sick to death of hearing about the wild sex the guys in rock bands like Led Zeppelin and all their teenage fans seemed to be having. The people who loved *Love Story* and wished there were more books and movies like it to get them through the tough years, they were Peter's audience. He was okay with that. It was a big audience.

The best he could do was to keep the exercises short. He decided to make each one no more than a dozen or so words. Let readers figure out the rest for themselves. Though he tried to be cool about it, he resented LRB's insistence that he add the exercises. Though he didn't say it aloud, he had begun to think of his book as a koan. He made a few things up and checked them with Lisa. She agreed they were reasonable and harmless. They had tried each of them at one time or another, and hadn't been hurt by them. So, if he dug a bit, he could rationalize adding exercises to a program that was not entirely logical in its underpinnings. Doing these little things was part of his life. They were not lies. Of course, they also weren't really exercises:

1. Erase a trait. If there's something your partner doesn't like about you, change it.
2. Buy each other dinner. And not just at the local diner.
3. French kiss for a minute or more each day.
4. Make out in the parking lot after the movie against your car and then inside in the backseat.
5. Tell your lover all the little things about you that will help them understand you. Why are you holding back? Your lover needs to know.
6. Excuse behaviors you don't like. If your partner can't erase the trait, accept it.
7. Be free with money. You'll be dead soon enough.
8. Go dancing somewhere that's just a little dangerous.

9. Take a trip to a nearby spot you've passed dozens of times and treat it like a five-star vacation.
10. Hold hands in the supermarket.

Everyone wanted more. More advice. Specifics. LRB thought he should give stock market tips. But he didn't understand how to invest money and so he wouldn't answer. He understood that not having money led to the worst periods in married life and often destroyed otherwise stable marriages. Peter ended up going on *Wall $treet Week with Louis Rukeyser* to talk about stability. Helena immediately published a pamphlet based on the exercises that was endorsed by the American Society of Certified Public Accountants.

None of this would help Emily. Peter pulled out another, newer edition.

In the fall of 1993, after Belinda left home to begin her freshman year at Berkeley, he rebuilt the exercises. This happened because he'd been at the ShopRite outside of town buying groceries and was arrested by a six-pack of Charmin toilet paper. He noticed how thick the rolls had become, and how the language on the packaging seemed more terse than he remembered. More emphatic, more conscious and deliberate in its flirtation and subsequent demand that the consumer complete the purchase. It was looking to be a quiet fall, so he set his sights on tightening up the exercises that had always bothered him. Also, he was grateful that he and Lisa had survived their own spell of bad years and were still together, and he wanted to commemorate that.

He sent the changes in to Ladder & Rake, and they were happy to revise the latest edition and send out a press release. They also sold first serial rights to *Woman's Day*.

The new exercises were entirely different and were even less like exercises. Really, they were commandments:

1. Listen to and respect every word your lover says.
2. Accept. Accept the love that's given as a whole. Do not parse it out or solicit more to garland the love that's already been given.
3. Give. Give wholly. Speak fully, share completely, and don't hold back.
4. Make out in the parking lot.

It had been a grave fifteen-year period, during which he'd gone from being a man in his early thirties who laughed easily and lacked a true sense of the world to a man in his middle forties who hadn't entirely lost his sense of humor, but did live with a growing sense that he was often the butt of the joke. The Hudson Inn had ultimately been both a wasteful and painful project. He'd had no idea what the people from New York who came to visit Hudson for the antiques wanted in an inn or its restaurant, and he was hurt a lot more by the discovery of his obliviousness to sophistication than he could ever admit.

Readers wrote to Ladder & Rake and said they preferred the first group of exercises. Could an edition be published with both sets? Ladder & Rake complied, because they were contractually allowed to do so. He checked and discovered they could do whatever they damn well wanted. This bothered Peter quite a lot. It was during the ensuing disagreement that he stopped writing for good and broke off contact with Ladder & Rake and their then-corporate parent, Baron Holdings.

Ladder & Rake tried desperately to reconnect with him for over a year, and then gave up. Baron Holdings' CEO ultimately dispensed with the issue by sending a handwritten note to Peter suggesting that time would heal the wound. Peter did not reply, though he agreed with this sentiment. He was surprised at how much the book and its legacy mattered to him. And he reminded himself of that now—that no matter how much he sneered at his book, it was always there with him. Its lessons were in him and he cared about them and was responsible for them. He was responsible for them even when they failed, as they obviously had for Emily Babson and her husband, Eli Corelli. Or no, he had failed Emily. The book hadn't.

The stupid contest was hubris. If it were remembered at all, it would be known as the icing on his cake, the last nail in his coffin. Suddenly, he was ready to leave Millerton with Maddie. He was ready, but he had a whole laundry list of things to do first. He had to settle up with Henry and close out his interest in the inn. See his daughter a few times. Rent his house to someone he trusted— maybe even to Jenny; she was an excellent caretaker. And also feel better, happier about all that he'd promised Maddie. It was quite a long list of things he needed to handle. Still, even if he left town, he hated to admit his failure with Emily Babson. He had to give her a call. That call belonged before everything else, at the very top of his list.

Emily, November 2011

Emily sat in the back row of Tishman Auditorium at the New School. She was wrapped up in her navy belted raincoat and shivering. She imagined she was about a third of the way through what was turning out to be a really awful lecture by an English artist named Ryan Gander. He'd opened by explaining that what he was doing was actually a "loose association exercise," not a lecture. She'd caught the eye of another 111 member when he started, and they'd twitched their noses at Gander's lazy style.

"A rope bridge," he said. "An arch at the new Yankee stadium, a children's story by Oscar Wilde." A series of pastel drawings of little boys and girls were projected behind him. The boys and girls had large eyes and they looked out at the crowd and remained completely unrelated to what he was saying. The program explained that they were drawings of his friends from childhood. Enlisted, she wondered, to participate in his nonsense shows for perpetuity? Or did it all work? Maybe it did. In her current state, she had lost her ability to discern. She wiped her runny nose and was ducking her head down when her phone vibrated.

It was a text from Eli: *Can you please let me know youre okay*

What was the matter with grammar? Even Ryan Gander, whose Elton John glasses took up all of the space between a seventies porn-star mustache and a bald skull, sounded like he knew where to put an apostrophe.

"Central Park. We love you, you urban forest. The beauty of new bicycles . . ."

She shook her head no and stooped down to grab her bag. Not bicycles. Bicyclists seemed constantly to want to run her over these days. Just before coming here, she'd argued with a man on a bike who had barreled through a stoplight on Sixth Avenue and Thirteenth Street.

Please? Eli texted.

She didn't respond to this, his eighth or tenth message, and felt a curdling in her stomach. She jogged through her thoughts, to their familiar intransigent end. He wasn't coming back. So she did not want to talk to him. She looked again at the phone.

Can you please let me know youre okay

Am I okay? No.

She did not write back.

"The old magic that is Stonehenge. I am an Englishman so I build a new ritual each day with old stones. Now let's look at a new work by Andy Goldsworthy . . ."

She again shook her head no, pushed open the

heavy doors, and slipped into the warm lobby. She thought: I don't need to reassure you that I am okay and I don't know what's the matter with me that I could have ever chosen to be with someone who could dare to ask such a question. A question you're compelled to ask so you won't feel guilty! You left me in Millerton. You ran. You fuck, you ran! That was the question and you answered it. You departed. And before that, you betrayed me. So, no. You don't get to know if I'm okay or not.

It was Thursday evening, and she had lived for four days past her winning weekend. She stood in the lobby and texted Sherry, *Can you meet earlier? My lecture ended early.*

Sherry texted back a no. She was doing a read-through of a friend's new script. Emily shrugged and figured she would go to the restaurant. Go have a glass of wine at the bar, alone. A newish activity that already felt maddeningly familiar. Emily rushed down the street. Daylight savings had come and Eli was still gone. She looked up at the sky and found the darkness profoundly resolute.

She went east on Twelfth Street. She tried desperately to focus her thoughts on a new semi–pro bono project—happily unrelated to her core day-to-day tasks—which centered on rebranding New York City's parks. She'd taken on the job in addition to her regular work since, goodness knew, she now had the time. The person who ran the project with her had contracted with Susan Sarandon and Jay-Z and other celebrities to do thirty-second spots about their favorite parks. Sonic Youth had recorded a song about Tompkins Square Park that was rhythmic and bittersweet. She hummed it as she walked. She wished Susan Sarandon was her friend. Susan Sarandon knew something about heartbreak and how to deal with it. So did Kim Gordon, come to think of it.

The restaurant was called Tony's Hot Spot, on Second Avenue and Eleventh Street. She settled in at the bar, ordered a glass of merlot. The bartender was a woman with unsurprising tattoos who left her alone. But then a man came and sat two stools away and watched her while he waited for his martini. She reached into her bag for something that would serve as a shield to keep the man away and found *Canoe*. She still carried it everywhere she went and couldn't let it go, even after all that had happened. The man sipped his drink and made an *ahhh* sound. She instantly hated him for it.

She held *Canoe* and looked deeper into her bag. There were bills. Eli hadn't been back to their place and she kept fantasizing about putting them all in a big envelope and sending them to him. But that would be small and she knew she would regret it so she hadn't done it. Also, it was much too early for that kind of thing. An AT&T bill was on top. The cell phone bill. It listed the calls made on both their iPhones. Number, time, and duration.

She thought back to the honesty of his underwear drawer as she tore the envelope open and spread the pages flat over the bar. Eli's calls were right there, time-stamped, right up to Monday morning. He wasn't calling his parents while he struggled through their weekend in Millerton. No. What she had long suspected was true. She glanced back through the month. There were dozens of short and long calls to different, strange numbers. Three minutes. Forty-two minutes. She paged up to the Millerton weekend. Timed precisely to when he went for his run was a twenty-six-minute call to a 310 number, which she knew perfectly well was Los Angeles. Jenny's phone. The sheets of calls filled in his absent moments so deftly and undeniably that she almost felt bad for Eli, was nearly sympathetic to his head-spinning inability to figure out what the fuck he was up to. But the pages went on and the calls became regular and revealed that eventually, yes, he had made his choice and figured out what he wanted to do.

The tears that fell as she stared at the phone bill hurt her face, as if they were too salty or were made of acid. She kept wiping them away with bar napkins and then examining the smears for color or texture or smell. What did she expect? Orange and smoky and redolent of kung pao chicken?

Kind of. There was definitely something suspicious about her tears. She mashed the pages of the bill together. She reached into her bag, past an Eckhart Tolle book one of her yoga instructors had given her after she'd cried in class a few days earlier, and got out *Canoe* and paged around. She gulped down wine and read:

On Healing After Disagreements

"Don't you ever fight?"

I was with my Pop, out in the canoe. It was cool out, early morning, mist still on the water that I never stopped confusing with smoke from a fire. We hadn't put bait on our lines yet. We were just sitting out there, listening to the morning.

"Not a pretty word, is it, Peter? Fight? Bite off the last bit of the *t* in order to say it right and it sounds like something ugly."

"Like a cuss."

"Yes, exactly like a cuss. You have your hat?"

I put on my New York Yankees cap. On that day in August I was finally past my sunburn and my nose had gone from pink and freckled to a dark tan. My hair had changed color, too. It was sandy brown instead of the dark mink color it had been when I arrived. And by then I was in love with Honey—if a twelve-year-old boy can feel that kind of love.

"You know what the best part of a fight is?" Pop asked.

"Making up," I said.

"Yes. And what is making up?"

"I don't know."

By then, I'd learned that honesty was prized above all else and so not knowing an answer was better than guessing. My grandparents had no love for ingenuity. The philosophical talk that informed the way they chose to live was like black bread, dense and warm and honest and heavy and ready to absorb any challenge that came.

"Forgiveness is at the heart of making up. Because if you can't forgive, you can't make up."

"What if . . . what if someone really hurts you?"

I was thinking then of another little girl—a green-eyed girl from Manhattan called Irene. A few months earlier in the spring, before I met Honey, I had told Irene I liked her and she said she liked me, too. But then a bigger boy named Charlie Gimmelstop told Irene he liked her, and she thought about it and then let us both know she liked him more than me. I was cast aside.

I realize now that I wasn't asking about hurting. I was asking about betrayal.

"Even if someone really hurts you, you can forgive them. But in serious relationships, like marriage relationships, people try not to hurt each other terribly because, you know, they promised not to when they got married. But sometimes—heck, all the time—there are little things that go wrong, little moments of forgetting or ignoring or a little less caretaking when there should be more caretaking. But if both members of the relationship practice forgiveness, then there's no mounting up of pain, you see? Instead, there is peace. And peace is the best goal."

By then the mist that I thought of as smoke had lifted. The day was growing warm.

"Absolute forgiveness. You can't get there easily, that's for sure. But you can keep on striving for it. You see?"

I was just quiet. No, I didn't see.

"Absolute forgiveness brings peace. Sure as a kind call brings the dog. Sure as seasons follow, as the Yankees play great baseball. Absolute forgiveness is the fastest and best way to peace."

"Okay," I said. I pulled down hard on my cap. It was a big thing to hear. I'm not sure I totally accepted what he said, then. I didn't feel like forgiving that girl, Irene. Not ever.

"Okay? Come on now! It is magnificent! You'll understand that someday. Now let's quit talking and catch a fish for a darn change!"

After an argument, only absolute forgiveness puts your canoe on a smooth path once again.

Emily put the book down and she knew that, though it was not nearly over, it was going to be okay. Someday she would be able to forgive Eli. That didn't make her feel better, but it was true.

After his things were gone and the agreements were signed and the lawyers were paid.

Emily's phone buzzed again. She was amazed that she could feel it through the new Kanye song that was shaking the bar. She didn't recognize the number. But she thought, Openness, forgiveness. Answer it. It's probably a wrong number. That's okay. If it was Eli calling from some strange phone, well, she would just hang right up on him.

"Hello?"

"Hello?" A man's voice.

"Yes?"

"Is this Emily Babson?"

"Yes?"

"It's Peter Herman."

She went blank for a moment. She had locked him up in her mind and didn't imagine that she would ever be in touch with him again.

"Listen, I want to come and see you."

"What?" The music grew louder and she could hardly hear.

"I'm moving to California but before I go I owe you a visit."

"You don't have to do that," she said.

"It's time I came to the city. And I want to see you and Eli. Are you okay?"

She could hear how he had to strain to have a phone conversation and she felt guilty. She looked at her knees. She held them tightly together and pressed them against the bar. They were starting to hurt. She felt a hand on her shoulder and there was Sherry, smiling at her, about to apologize for being late, even though she wasn't late. Emily motioned, *just a moment*.

"Please. I need to know. Are you all right?"

Emily said, "No, I'm not all right. And I will not see you with Eli."

Sherry shook her head, rubbed Emily's back. She picked up Emily's glass and drank from it.

"Then I will see you alone. I'll be there on Tuesday or Wednesday. Can we agree to meet on Wednesday evening?"

"Couldn't you just tell me on the phone what to do? You saw us together. That's the crazy thing. You saw us together and you saw us fall apart. It's over, right? Or is that not true? Did you see something between us that you want to tell me about? Is that it?"

"No, Emily. I just want to talk with you. That's all."

"Wait." She wrapped her free arm around her sister. Peter Herman was on the phone. He wanted to help her. She wanted to say: Tell me what to do right now, this minute. She felt herself stuttering into the phone, grasping to hear him, realizing that even his breath on the phone made her feel some hope.

"Eli isn't sleeping at home. And it's freaking me out, like, really badly. Please." She clenched her eyes shut against a sudden and gritty breeze that came through the bar's open door. "You were there with us. Can you tell me what to do right now?"

Sherry frowned and looked around the bar.

"You know I can't do that. I wish I had some magic to share with you," Peter said. "But we should talk. I'll be in touch soon, as soon as I get there. Tuesday afternoon. Or Wednesday. I'm not sure yet. Goodbye, Emily."

"Who was that?" Sherry asked when Emily set the phone down on the bar. Sherry had one hand on her belly and the other around Emily. She always worried that she was growing a gut when she was between jobs. Emily didn't move. She wanted her sister to hold her.

"Peter Herman."

"Oh, Christ! That sanctimonious bastard! Can't he leave you alone?"

"Sherry! Don't be so theatrical—I'm sorry!" Emily covered her mouth. It was the meanest thing she could say to her sister.

"It's okay. I mean, like I care."

"Listen. I was just looking at my phone bill. Eli's calls are there. Eli was talking to Jenny the entire time we were together in Millerton. I know that for sure."

"He is such a bastard." Sherry sighed. "I shouldn't have said that about Peter Herman. I was being kind of theatrical. Eli is the bastard."

"He was lying to me the whole time. To himself, too, I guess."

"I hate him, Emily. I really do."

"Mom apologized for calling me controlling. She agrees that what he did is unforgivable. He wasn't really with me, you know?"

"I know." Sherry hugged Emily tighter.

"I had to take the morning-after pill. I told you that, right?"

"Yes." Sherry kept holding on to Emily. "Emily, I know."

"I should have married Gordon. I should be in Oregon with two children and Gordon right now, walking on a—on a rocky trail."

"Stop," Sherry said.

Emily looked around the bar, which was all black wood and mirrors. She and Emily would eat in the back at a table with a candle and a red-and-white checkered tablecloth, and they would drink lots more wine and eat things slathered in red sauce. They could be sloppy together. It didn't matter.

Sherry said, "God, sometimes I wish I didn't have to stay in New York when I'm not working. This place seems perfect when I'm happy but right now it feels a little dead."

"It's a good restaurant." Emily took another inch of bar napkins and began to tear them to shreds, caught herself doing it, and stuffed the mess into her bag.

"I know it is. But I don't always want good."

Emily stared at her sister. Her sister would know if Eli was with Jenny now.

"I do. I always want good," Emily said.

"Emily," Sherry said. "I know you do."

Sherry pulled Emily closer and since Emily was still on the barstool she buried her head in Sherry's chest. And Emily began to cry all over again because she knew from Sherry's silence and how she hadn't gotten upset at Emily's comment about her being theatrical, and how the news of the awful phone bill didn't surprise her at all, that Sherry had just confirmed that, yes, Eli was with Jenny, now. And Emily had to accept that her marriage was over, all over again.

Stella, November 2011

"You see, it's a problem," Melissa Kerrigan said, on Monday afternoon. She leaned in Stella's doorway, pink sweater thrown over her shoulders, arms crossed over her chest. Stella was thinking it was Melissa's inability to manage a direct report that was the problem. That was why Stella had come up with the *Canoe* contest and was also why she had gotten so close to Helena. Yeah, because she'd been too free. She wanted to scream, You're the problem, Melissa! You . . . shouldn't manage people. But she knew she'd demanded the freedom. She had wanted to gamble and win big. And so Melissa had left her alone.

So she said, "I know. I agree with you." She looked at Melissa's shoulders, which were broad. Melissa had been captain of her water polo team in college. Why Stella knew this, she had no idea.

"They won't talk to you?" Melissa asked. "Not a word from any of them?"

"Shroud of silence." Stella raised her hand as if she were testifying.

"Everybody is saying she left her husband for him. Is that true?"

Stella shrugged. She had been asked this question several times a day for the last week. If it was true that made her some kind of engineer of disaster. All aboard the disaster train! I'm Stella Petrovic and I'll be your conductor!

Melissa frowned and said, "It's all awfully public, that's all."

"Which was the intention," Stella said. "I mean, I don't want to go on the defensive."

"No. You don't."

"Look, I'll see it through to the end. It might work out." Stella smiled and told herself that Helena probably wouldn't appreciate a manager torturing a potential rising star.

"Yes." Melissa smiled. "That's a good point. Maybe you should make a list of ways in which it might work out."

"Thanks for the tip."

"Seen anything else on the backlist that looks hot?"

"A few things." But she was lying. She'd figured that *Canoe* was her ticket out of the backlist. She had not looked further.

"Good! And new stuff?" Melissa's arms were still folded.

"Um. Yeah. There's a new book on the value of supportive friendships for women that's kind of interesting."

"That's really good. If you see a diet book, we could use one. Don't you have a friend at *People*? Can't you find out who is thin lately and who we can still get for cheap?"

"I'll try."

"You do that. I'm here if you need me." Melissa pivoted off the doorframe and disappeared.

Stella lay her forehead down on her desk and hoped for an idea to pop out or just burp up, like they always did for Helena. She would even settle for spitting one up, right there on her skirt. But of course nothing happened save that she felt weird and a little head rushy.

Her phone rang—an outside line.

"This is Stella."

"Stella, this is Emily Babson."

Stella gasped. She needed Emily to tell her everything and then go on TV otherwise the contest was a failure and Stella wasn't sure she could survive that. She said, "Emily? Hi."

"I'm sorry I haven't returned your calls."

"No, no! That's okay. How are you? How are you and Eli?"

"That's not why I'm calling."

"Okay," Stella said.

"I'm calling because I want to tell you that Peter Herman is coming to visit . . . me."

"Like for a date?" Stella bit down on her lip and shook her head in amazement at herself.

"What? No."

"Sorry, sorry. Kidding. I've been so tense lately. So he'll be here in New York?"

"Yes. Anyway, I'm letting you know."

"So . . . Is there more you'd like to share, about

how helpful Peter has been to you? That would in turn help me a lot, you know?"

"Um. No."

"Please, can you tell me what happened up in Millerton?"

But Stella could only hear Emily breathing into the phone.

"Do you want to get together for a drink?" Stella asked.

"I guess we could. I need to explain my situation to you," Emily said, but she sounded like having a drink with Stella was about the last thing she wanted.

"That'd be great. Let's meet tomorrow night. I had plans but I'll cancel them."

Stella named a bar in Brooklyn and was happy that, just this once, the name came to her in the moment, just when she needed it. She rested for a second with her eyes closed, and felt a smidgen of hope.

And then her phone rang again. Lucy Brodsky. There was nothing to do but answer it.

Lucy said, "I thought you'd want to know that Peter Herman is coming to New York for a few days. We're putting him up on Helena's expenses. He called her office by mistake. I guess he lost your number."

"Okay," Stella said. "In fact, I'm aware of this visit, but thank you for calling me."

"I see. Helena said to tell you that she's pleased.

We'll have a breakfast meeting on Thursday morning at ten. You'll be there along with your contest winners. No reason to have sales and marketing in attendance until we know what's what."

"Of course. Can you e-mail me the meeting details?"

"Oh, definitely."

"Thanks, Lucy." Stella smiled. "This could work out just fine, couldn't it?"

"Um. I can't predict stuff like that."

"Hey, Lucy . . . How are you doing? Everything okay?"

"What are you talking about? I'm still here, aren't I? I'm fine." Lucy hung up on her.

Stella kicked back in her chair, put her heels on her desk, and smiled. Everybody was coming in. The smidgen of hope grew bigger. Big risks! That's what it was all about. One minute you're stuck in your office, being blabbed to death by your bore of a boss, and then a couple of phone calls later and a few good decisions, next thing you know you have to run a very important breakfast meeting and write a press release about a wildly successful contest. Next comes the sit-down with Helena where she reaches out to you with a three-year contract and a big bonus. Come Friday, you're in a black car headed downtown to lunch at Locanda Verde with the handsome new CFO from Sweden who everybody gossips about and his girlfriend, the blond NYU cinema studies grad student. They both want to hear all about that wacky creative stuff you do in editorial. Yeah, let's have a good bottle of wine. Hell, let's have two! Awesome. Stuck in a thankless go-nowhere job? Fuck that! Stella was going to leapfrog right over Melissa Kerrigan, probably by late spring if not sooner. Stuck? I think not.

Peter, November 2011

"So now the answer is yes?" Henry laughed.

"Yes. At the same numbers we talked over a few weeks back," Peter said. They stood outside the door to Henry's tiny office behind the reception area at the inn.

"I get that you're trying to do something. But I love you too much to take your money today. Have a smoothie?" Henry walked around Peter and began to make his way toward the restaurant.

"A what?"

"Oh, please, you know what a smoothie is."

It wasn't quite noon. A little early for lunch. Peter stopped in the central hall and looked around. A couple came through the front doors with tense grins and wedding guest outfits in dry-cleaner bags slung over their shoulders. Peter quickly moved forward and held the door for them. Jenny was training a new girl on the front desk and he watched her observe as the trainee welcomed the couple. Henry had them all wearing name-tags now. Peter thought that was way too corporate looking. People ought to be able to introduce themselves by name and leave it there.

"Come on out to the porch and let these people

do their jobs," Henry said. "We'll get you a club sandwich. It's not good for you but I know it's what you want."

Once they were seated at a quiet table next to the emergency exit, Henry settled in and focused on Peter. He took off his glasses, dropped them into his shirt pocket, and folded his hands.

"So, let's start again," Peter said. "I've thought about it and I want you to buy me out."

"What about Maddie?"

"What about her? We're moving. Ironing out the details now. But she's not relevant to this."

"All right then. But Peter, there's no rush on the deal."

"I thought there was a rush. I thought you wanted my shares so you could build and expand back to Hudson and make good where I failed. Did I get you wrong?"

"You're not wrong, except for the failure part. But I've thought about all this, too. And I realize that old friends shouldn't rush each other."

"Well, then," Peter said. "It's too early for me to eat. Is this alarmed?"

Henry reached out and flicked a switch on the emergency door.

"Nope."

They went outside to walk the grounds of the inn, starting in the parking lot, both of them stooping to pick up cigarette butts and gum wrappers. Then they went through the grass to the big wooden fence and began to walk the perimeter of the property.

"Maddie is packing up her house," Peter said. "Jim Stevenson will handle the sale. He's pretty good."

"He'll make her real country-house money, I'm sure. With his connection to Sotheby's Great Estates, he's got huge reach. He could bring her two million or more. Two and a half. You haven't thought about your place in quite the same way, I imagine."

"Not quite ready for that, am I? No rush, like you say. Plus my place is worth about a third of that. Maybe half on the kind of good day the market hasn't seen for years."

Henry looked away and smiled.

"Need anything in New York?" Peter asked. "I'm going down tomorrow or the next day."

"What could I need from New York?"

They went through a gap in the fence and stopped in an adjoining field that the inn used for tented weddings. The sun slipped behind a cloud and Peter shoved his hands in his pockets and turned away from the wind. Henry motioned that they should head back.

"Let's at least have a cup of coffee. You . . . know much about San Francisco?" Henry asked.

"The food is supposed to be good. Fresh-food movement, I think it's called."

"No, it's slow food that you're talking about,"

Henry said. "I taught the staff a joke about that; seems we've come into fashion. Our kitchen was already pretty slow!"

"Ha," Peter said. "There's a line that'll get you nowhere with the sophisticates in Hudson."

They went back through the parking lot. The sky had begun to turn gray. Peter had been in Millerton for nearly forty years and had never gotten used to the quiet that came with the wind.

"What changed, Henry? You wanted me out of your business and into a new life. What changed?"

Henry scratched his nose.

Peter said, "And I have in fact been reading my goddamned book so don't say that line."

"I suppose—"

"You suppose what?"

"Cool down now." Henry laughed. "Don't yell at your old friend Henry. I suppose that if you're lucky enough, you'll get it figured out for you all over again. You say you're headed west with Maddie. And that's fine. But you better be sure that's what you want."

"It is."

"Well, I'm not your therapist." Henry waved at a driver in a linens delivery truck who was pulling into the inn's back driveway. "And I won't go further with you than we've just gone."

"But what about the deal?"

"I guess we won't make a deal today. That's all. When I find the courage to open in Hudson you'll be among the first dozen people I call." Henry laughed and clapped Peter on the back. But Peter could tell that Henry was holding something back. Henry wasn't a meddlesome person. And Henry loved Peter. Peter knew that.

"No deal today," Peter said. "I don't get it."

"Shoot, Peter. It's been a hard year. We all miss Lisa. She is a part of us."

"We all miss her," Peter said. "Yes we do. Now what is it that you're not telling me?"

"For goodness' sake." Henry opened the emergency door to the dining room and then slammed it shut so they were still outside. Now they were staring at each other.

"You never did curse, did you?" Peter asked.

"Nope, never did. Okay! I can't stand it. I was listening to Maddie, not you. She was telling me what to do. That's why I set up the deal. And it's kind of a stupid deal when you think about it for two minutes. But I was acting on what she wanted. You know I listen to women first."

"You did with Lisa." Peter nodded and finally broke into a smile.

"Especially with her."

Peter looked away, out at the parking lot. He said, "What else?"

"Since I've betrayed Maddie's trust and I feel lousy enough about that, I'll add something of my own. You better be in love with Maddie if you're going to go any further with her. That's what else."

"I think I'm going to go with her," Peter said. "It's what she wants." He motioned for Henry to take them inside. Peter watched his old friend frown as he wrestled with the door.

Henry said, "Well, now I've talked too much after I promised myself I wouldn't. I'll look after your interests here. And if you come back, you come back."

Peter breathed in the good smell of the dining room. He smiled. "Thank you."

"Fine, then." Henry looked away. "You got the truth out of me. Now you'll do me the favor of having an early lunch with me. I keep saying you want a club sandwich. The fact of the matter is that I want a club sandwich. You can order whatever you like. It doesn't matter to me."

"You're going to miss me, aren't you?"

"That's a part of it," Henry said. "That is a part of it."

Stella, November 2011

On Tuesday evening, Stella met Emily at Stanislaw & Daughters, a restaurant that was nowhere near where either of them lived.

Stella came in and immediately recognized Emily, who was the lone woman at the bar. She already had her coat off and a glass of water in front of her. In person, Emily was even more perfect than in the pictures Stella had found. She was actually wearing pearls with a black cardigan and jeans. Her hair was in a ponytail and her face looked soft, if guarded. She really was the right person to win, Stella thought. She could imagine Emily on a stage, perhaps even at a sales conference, in conversation with Peter Herman. That was all Stella needed to do, just convince Emily that she had an obligation to play this thing through with LRB. Maybe Stella could just figure out a way to leave the seemingly absent husband out of it entirely. The brooding husband happily married but disdainful of publicity. There was precedent for that. That'd work. Focus, Stella told herself. This could still work out just fine.

"It's nice to meet you, Stella," Emily said, once she'd settled onto her stool. "And thanks for suggesting this place. I don't spend enough time in Bushwick."

"Did you find it okay?"

"No, but I was grateful for the challenge."

"I'm sorry about that." Stella gave her guiltiest smile. They were at the short end of the L-shaped bar, near the great front windows that looked out on the industrial gray of Moore Street. She chose a stool between Emily and the exit.

"It was the first place I thought of. I should've researched better."

Emily nodded. "That's okay. I always get lost on the letter trains. I've learned to accept that."

"You're lucky. I live on them," Stella said. She watched Emily check her out. And she gave her time to do that. Though checking her out was possibly making Emily dislike her even more. Stella was at least five years younger, in her tiger-print scarf and pointy black boots. She'd found a long black skirt in her closet that was really old and now she was wearing it as often as she thought she could without being accused of wearing the same thing every day. Emily was staring at her so hard that Stella began to wonder if she could see whatever was left of the Virginia hippie underneath the Bonnie and Clyde outfit.

"Shall we let the bartender choose something for us?" Stella asked, with the hope that Emily would let her be bossy from go. Emily shrugged a yes.

They began with a half carafe of a white

recommended by the bartender—a plaid shirt–wearing young man whom Stella dimly recognized from just after college when she had gone to a lot of parties. It tasted kind of bad, and there was an awful lot of it. Stella thought it was a horrifying amount of wine.

Emily raised a hand and got Plaid Shirt's attention.

"This is nice but it's maybe a little sweet for me?" Emily asked. "Do you have anything with a little more acidity? It took me so long to get here and I realize now that red wine was what I was really looking forward to. So, let's make it red and let's keep it simple. Merlot."

"For me, too," Stella said, nodding hard. "I want the same thing as her." She was surprised at the way Emily sounded, how she was both tentative and a little manipulative. But at the same time, Stella realized, Emily sounded just like her letter.

Emily's phone buzzed.

"Excuse me," Emily said. "It's work. I need to respond." She hunched over and began to type.

Stella looked around. The bar was so new that it still smelled clean, like fresh paint and fruit soap. A waft of cooking pig fat came from behind a kitchen door. That made Stella feel better. She thought, The thing that doesn't fit in this picture is Emily. There was a table in the back filling up with what appeared to be German models. The men sitting at the bar were all good-looking carpenter-types. Everyone Stella knew seemed to want to marry guys like that. The kinds of guys who dressed in stiff denim that wore like tin and weren't ironic about it. Stella figured Eli Corelli would fit in at a place like this. Maybe at the end of their drink, once she loosened up, Emily would thank her for discovering it. She'd say that even though it wasn't her kind of place, she'd take her husband here. Yeah, Stella thought, they could eat here once everything was all better. Stella would get LRB to pay.

Stella watched Emily. Focus! Whatever happened in Millerton didn't matter—she had to get Emily to say that Peter had helped her and her husband. She just had to.

Emily looked up. "All set. But let's get our wine first."

Plaid Shirt gave them two different merlots to taste. They chose one and Emily thanked him. He smiled and rushed away from them to help others who had begun to settle in at the bar.

"So you're an editor?" Emily asked. She didn't look at Stella.

"I am. Most of the time."

"But you dabble in marketing?"

"We have to, now."

"You do a lot of self-help, that sort of thing?"

"Yes, it's part of what I do. You do PR?"

"You could call it that if you want to."

"What would you call it?"

Emily said, "I'm a branding consultant." And then she made a pained noise in her throat.

"Right. I mean, I'm familiar with you, you know. I googled you. I know what you do."

"No doubt you did your due diligence." Emily didn't smile. "As best you could."

"Are you upset about something?" Stella asked, and then stopped and put her tongue between her teeth and bit down, hard. She tightened her scarf.

"I'm glad you asked," Emily said. "I feel an obligation to tell you what went wrong."

"Okay, great." Stella sipped some wine and then let her tongue hang between her teeth so she would not interrupt.

"Whose idea was the contest, anyway?" Emily asked.

"That would be me," Stella lisped.

Emily looked at Stella and shook her head. Stella stared back at her. Emily was bigger than Stella. Even her eyes were bigger.

Emily said, "I used to worry that I'd come up with something like this when I was starting out, like having people win something that was likely to fuck them, like a boat that they couldn't possibly afford to maintain or learn to sail. But then I realized that I'd be okay, I would never do anything awful like that."

"Excuse me?"

"I'm saying," said Emily, staring hard at Stella,

"that I know where the lines are. The lines of manipulation. Where not to cross. You don't."

"Can we back up a step?" Stella asked. "You'll forgive me for being really confused right now."

"What happened is that it didn't work." Emily sipped her wine. "I love *Marriage Is a Canoe*. And I like Peter Herman. A lot. He's a good man. But I don't like what you did."

Stella pointed at her chest and widened her eyes. "What I did?"

"The contest. How you made a sucker out of me. How quickly you did that."

"I didn't—"

"You did. My marriage is over."

"Oh, god," Stella said. She covered her mouth.

"Have you ever met Peter Herman?"

"Um," Stella said. "No. Look, I'm so sorry. I had no idea—"

"You don't know me and you don't know him and now you're sorry? Doesn't that strike you as rather disingenuous?"

"Wait, wait. I'm going to trip all over myself. I apologize a thousand times in advance. But we're getting ahead of ourselves. Don't you think there's a chance—I mean, you're married and married people go through an awful lot—that there's a good chance that everything will be fine?"

"No." Emily took two deep breaths. She said,

tactless, the process had taken less than a single glass of wine.

Emily stood three feet back from her stool. She said, "You were just doing your job. I'm leaving now."

"Will you at least tell me when you see Peter? Because maybe I should see him, too? I mean before the Thursday meeting at LRB."

"He's a grown-up. If he wants to see you, he'll let you know."

"You'll come to our meeting?"

"Yes, I think I will. Incredibly." Emily's nostrils flared. Stella had no idea what to do with herself. She sat perfectly still and admired Emily's stature, her elegance, the way she stood and glared. Stella thought she wouldn't mind being her in a few years. Though, if she were being honest she would never have entered the contest she had created.

"I'll go to your big meeting. I'll go there and make sure whoever you report to shuts this contest down."

"I wish you wouldn't do that," Stella said quickly.

"I think I'm through doing what you want, unwittingly or not."

Stella watched Emily walk out. She turned back to the bar, to Plaid Shirt, who stood, arms folded, just four feet away. He uncrossed his arms and smiled.

"She was upset," he said. "Is she all right?"

"No. I think she's breaking up with her husband," Stella said.

"That's awful." He took Emily's glass and dumped the last bit of wine in the sink behind the bar. He said, "Let me get you something else. I mean, that's sad."

"Well, of course it's sad," Stella said.

"No, it's really sad. She looked really hurt. And she didn't look like she deserved it."

"Wow," Stella said. "You took all that away from looking at her." She tried a laugh.

"I was listening pretty carefully." He smiled the same ironic smile she remembered from whenever she'd met him before. "Nothing hurts like having to deal with someone who cheats."

"It's not my fault," Stella said.

"Yeah," the bartender said. "I think you told her that."

Stella didn't say anything. She watched the bartender pour her a new glass of wine.

"I made a big mess, didn't I?" Stella asked.

The bartender slid the glass across the bar and nodded. He said, "It would appear that way."

An hour later Stella was still at the bar. Usually, regardless of the situation she got herself into, she liked herself a whole lot more than she did right then. Because, no matter how she looked at it, she couldn't figure out how to fix all the broken parts of what she had tried to build.

She sipped her third glass of wine. She texted

Emily and said she was glad they'd met and thanked her for coming. She said she was sorry, again.

Keep me posted, won't you? Stella texted. And then ten minutes later: *You will keep me posted?*

Emily did not respond.

"Want anything else?" the bartender asked.

"Could you give me a menu? What's that bacony smell? If I don't eat something right now I'm going to be in even more trouble."

The next day Stella found herself at the morning meeting with a headache and an upset stomach but without a single solution in her head.

"I see we've got our *Canoe* update on the agenda," Helena said as she pawed at the sheet in front of her. "*Canoe* girl? You here?"

The room went into a pause while Helena searched for Stella, who was against the far wall in the back.

Everybody could hear the swift whisper from Melissa Kerrigan: "It's Stella who deals with *Canoe*. Stella Petrovic."

"I'm here!"

"Stella Petrovic, you'll stay after and we'll talk." And another pause. "Stella Petrovic. Hmm. What's Petrovic, anyway? What kind of name is that? Polish?"

"My father's family is from Montenegro. His father changed it to Peterson, but my father

416

changed it back." A lot to say to over fifty people who don't like you, Stella thought. But whatever, it was only one more thing to add to the list of things she hadn't thought about before she said them.

"What kind of work does your father do?" Helena called out.

"He is a plumber." Stella bit her lip. Last time she'd spoken to her dad he said he was spending a lot of time engineering fountains for a project at Duke, so close enough. Garden designer sounded foofy and Helena did not like foofy.

"Really. A plumber who names his daughter Stella. Very sweet. There's a book in there somewhere, that's for sure. My father was from Poland and he sold life insurance policies to his poor Jewish neighbors in Boro Park for fifty years. Dropped dead at his desk with the signed renewal for someone else's policy in his hands, and he always said that's just what he wanted. When I was coming up I thought I had to hide my background but now I embrace it. So does my daughter. We are all working people here, aren't we? Hardworking people."

"That's right," said Lucy Brodsky, vigorously nodding her head.

Helena raised an eyebrow at Lucy and said, "Yes, we are. Okay, let's get on with it. Do we have any general updates?"

"*Dust on the Mirrors, Blood on the Stairs* won

"Um, in fact there's no need to pretend."

"I've turned bigger piles of bullshit into pots of tulips." Helena spoke abruptly, her brown eyes smiling and warm and, in Stella's estimation, betraying her strident tone. Helena liked her! She was sure of it. And then Stella was left to watch Helena's heel twist as she swung around and walked quickly down a beige-painted hall hung with trophy covers, representing books that belonged to her more than anyone else.

At least, Stella thought, they were wittier with each other than Helena seemed to be with others. But maybe everybody felt that way? Maybe that was the gift of leadership? No, Stella was sure that Helena took extra time to focus on her. So Stella had messed up a contest. Hadn't she at least proved she was smart? Wasn't smart valuable?

As she drifted back to her elevator bank, Stella entertained a couple of thoughts: I really like Helena and she likes me. If I can just get through this, I can imagine how she might turn me into a confidante, a young friend who got to listen in on big decisions and who actually had a clue about what was going on in the company. Then she reminded herself of what Sara Byrd had said and wondered how to address the flirtation Helena must have had with Peter when they were kids.

Wait!

She realized that all she had to do was bring Peter to Helena and that would make Helena happy. Why would Helena care about a miserable couple from Brooklyn? She wouldn't! She definitely wouldn't listen to Emily, even if she did show up. And LRB wasted millions of dollars on poorly thought-out marketing all the time! What was the big deal? These last thoughts hit her the way morning thoughts do. Abruptly and with a subsequent coating of satisfaction. Peter was coming to New York. He was just like anybody—he was curious and he would come to a meeting that was, ultimately, about him and his book. Helena wanted to see him and Stella had made that happen. They'd already sold a bunch of copies of *Canoe*. Okay, those were a lot of thoughts run together. But really weren't they just one big sizzling synapse of a thought that was utterly cohesive? Stella stepped into the elevator and smiled.

She whispered, "You're welcome, Helena."

Peter, November 2011

Peter checked into the Algonquin because that was where Lucy Brodsky at Ladder & Rake had put him because he had requested it. He liked the place, and when he visited New York, he tried to avoid deviating from what he already knew. He threw his bag on the bed in a room that faced an air shaft, thought about napping and didn't, and went to read the newspapers in the lobby bar. By then it was late on Wednesday afternoon.

He wanted to see Emily and set things right with her, to apologize at least. For causing the poor young woman any additional pain. Why did he have to be greedy when Stella had first called? Why couldn't he have just moved with Maddie to California without involving himself in all this mess? He thought of Maddie. Maddie had considered going down to New York with him but was too busy packing up her house. He had promised to help out when he returned from New York. But had he subconsciously dissuaded Maddie? Was he really just curious about Helena?

He settled himself in a chair in a corner near the windows and watched an old orange tabby sleep next to a potted palm.

"Is that a new tabby?" he asked the waiter.

"That is Matilda," the waiter said. "What can I get you, sir?" The waiter threw a napkin down on the mahogany side table to his right and placed a brass carousel on it. He looked at the carousel's half-full bowls of peanuts, minipretzels, and potato chips and thought, Hell, I'm on a trip. I'll eat it all.

"Give me a scotch and soda, please. Make it Johnnie Walker Black. I'm staying here at the hotel. Matilda, huh?"

He pulled out his cell phone and looked inquiringly at the screen. He listened to a voice mail from Stella Petrovic who was asking that he please, please call when he arrived in town. She was so much looking forward to the next day's morning meeting. Also Helena looked forward to seeing him. The whole message was jagged, in that tentative and calculated style of speech Stella used. He'd meant to come a day earlier and walk around, maybe visit the Met or the Frick, go to one of the places that Lisa used to like to go. But he'd ended up feeling hesitant to spend more time in New York than he had to, so he hadn't driven himself to the train station until that morning.

He clopped the phone closed. And then he toyed with the phone some more and saw that the message icon hadn't gone away, that his daughter, Belinda, had left a message. He listened to her saying that she hoped he had had a smooth trip to New York and maybe he could visit on his way back, have dinner with her and her partner, Jancy?

He called Belinda and said he'd be there for dinner, probably tomorrow night. He'd call again tomorrow and check in. He missed her and told her so.

Then he called Maddie.

"The packing is going well. I am nearly finished here!" Her voice was bright. He wondered at that since she was not typically a bright-sounding person. "You will be back tomorrow or Friday?"

He said he wasn't sure.

"Peter, I want to tell you how happy I feel now that you have decided to come with me. It is without question the most romantic thing a man has ever done for me."

Her syntax felt odd to him—even beyond her inability or unwillingness to use contractions. But he didn't mention it, choosing instead to just agree with her and then get off the phone. He felt increasingly afraid of Maddie. He didn't want to let her down. He had always hated disappointing people. That had been the paramount good, for so many years, about his life with Lisa. No matter what foolish thing he did, she loved him. He could never let her down. And he had loved that. He had depended on her for that acceptance. He had been lost and fretful before Lisa, and was likely forever lost again without her. And if their relationship had lacked true romance, well, that was a fair trade-off and they both knew it. He settled deeper into the chair, feeling some shame and surprise that it took coming to New York to knock such a simple thought back to the front of his brain.

Maybe getting a little drunk wouldn't be such a bad idea. He took a long sip of his drink and finished the chips and started in on the peanuts. Lisa didn't let chips in the house and Maddie wouldn't want him to eat them either. He felt like an old Hudson Line locomotive pulling into Grand Central for the last time, chugging right into a salt-, carb-, and alcohol-fueled gastrointestinal slump. After ordering another scotch, he called Emily.

"Hello?"

"I'm here in New York." He paused. "As we discussed. If I can't see you with your husband, I will see you alone. Are you by any chance in midtown?"

"Where are you, Peter?"

"The Algonquin, in the bar in the lobby."

"We can meet briefly. I have something scheduled for later."

She would be there in less time than it took to finish another drink. He adjusted his belt buckle so it didn't bite into his stomach. He rustled the newspaper, made sure he could feel his toes waggling in his Rockports.

She was at his side far sooner than he could have imagined. Taller, thinner, than he remembered.

Had it been ten days? Could a woman take on such a haunted look in ten days?

He stood up to say hello but she turned and went away from him. She spoke to the waiter and then found a big brown armchair and dragged it toward him, ignoring the room instead of apologizing, the crowd of business people all oblivious anyway, bent in toward one another and trying to ignore the woman banging into their knees with an armchair. An upright bass player and a piano player began to warm up not a dozen feet from them. She dropped her bag and kicked it out of the way.

"Emily." He chewed his lip and tried to find the personality he'd used with her and her husband.

"I should have asked this on the phone. Before we say anything else, are you seeing me so you can fulfill your obligation to your publishing company?"

"Of course not."

"You're sure?" Her eyes were puffy around the edges, and she seemed funereal in a black turtleneck sweater and black pants.

"I have a responsibility to you. To you and your husband. I signed on to help."

"I wanted to see you. But I think we're through with all the help."

They brought their heads closer to each other and fought the soft chairs to do it. He could see that her lips were newly painted, but dry around the edges.

"What do you mean?"

"My marriage is over."

"Please don't say that, Emily."

"He left me for another woman. You watched him do it." She sunk back into the chair. "Now I understand that he was trying to stay married in front of you. He was fighting himself. But he gave up and I lost him. You saw."

"I have to tell you something." He took a gulp of his drink.

"Please, no more recycled sayings. I love your book. But when you say the stuff in it aloud—I think it's better if the words just stay in the book."

"No, this isn't in the book. Here's the thing. I was happily married. That's true. But my wife, Lisa, she would have been better off if she left me. I didn't give her everything I could have. I was mean when I didn't need to be. I did some philandering. And Eli, if he's not going to give you everything—I'm not saying what happened is okay. I'm sorry about what happened."

"Yes." Emily looked at her shoes. "We already figured that out. You and Eli are a bit alike."

"Ouch," Peter said.

Emily only smiled up at the waiter who delivered her wine.

Peter said, "I can't wait to meet Stella, the young woman who started all this."

"She's quite a character. An editor who can't

even edit herself." Emily took a long sip and held the glass.

"You met her?"

"Yes. She reminds me of how I was right when I met Eli, when I couldn't figure out the difference between my career and my personality. But I'm over that. Look, I figured something out. It's not you that I care about. How could I care about you when I didn't know you? It's the book."

"I'm not the book." Peter smiled but he knew he couldn't hide how sad he looked.

"You sure aren't."

"So you'll go to the meeting tomorrow?"

"I will go. Because that'll be where all this ends." Emily nodded and pursed her lips. "That kind of meeting is important. I'll go in and help shut the whole thing down. And of course reinforce the no-media message."

"No media. That wouldn't be right."

"I really did believe we were a happy couple when I entered the contest. That was honest, I swear. I'm sorry it turned out this way."

"You are not the one who needs to apologize." Peter looked at this beautiful young woman he'd so admired—her dark hair was cut into severe bangs over her eyes but it fell softly over her shoulders. All dressed up and being polite when she should be crying. It was horrible.

"You don't have to look so sad," she said. "I

understand now that he would've left me anyway. All of this only exacerbated it."

"Is that the right word?"

Emily nodded and said, "It is."

"Then I apologize for my role."

"The stories about your childhood are so good. I love the way you wrote them. They've gotten me through some tough moments. The parts that happen in the canoe are quite . . . magical. I know it's not brilliant, but it's become a part of me."

"All that canoe stuff came from someone else, actually." Peter nodded and made a dry noise in his throat. "Not quite lies but like lies, which is far worse."

"Please," she said. "I don't want to keep your secrets. I can't stand it."

She stood up. But he didn't. She looked down at him, and he was honest with himself and realized that there didn't need to be another moment of connection between them. He thought, I'll see her tomorrow morning and then never again. He flashed on Maddie. He'd be back in Millerton late the next evening, after dinner with his daughter. He would help Maddie pack boxes of scarves. Wary, always wary, of disappointing her.

"I'm sorry all over again," he said. "I should never have indulged in all that talk about my book with you."

"When a fan like me gets too close to the source,

I guess that's what happens." She twisted the strap of her bag around her arm.

"So you'll come to the meeting?" he asked, though he was in a haze. Why did he care? And hadn't they already discussed this?

"I wouldn't miss it," Emily said. "Goodbye."

"You have to leave right now?"

"I have to. If I don't, I'm going to be late for a lecture at the Harvard Club. Chelsea Clinton is interviewing some of the first woman fighter pilots from Pakistan and I don't want to miss the beginning."

After he watched Emily go, Peter strolled over to Third Avenue and found the right sort of Irish bar at which to have a burger and beer while sitting on a stool, looking at whatever everyone else was watching on the television. It turned out to be the Rangers game. The food he was eating would hurt like hell in the morning. He was already regretting the trip, ashamed that he meant well but used his intentions as an excuse for his blunders.

"I've got to get up," he said to no one in particular.

But at the same time, he kind of had gotten up, hadn't he? He was trying to help and that was something. He was present in New York and he had reached out to Emily, the contest winner. He was being honest, at the very least. Divorcing himself, at this late date, from the damn book.

He stood outside after he'd eaten, leaned against

a parking meter, fist on chin, watching the cars rush uptown on Third Avenue, thinking, Which direction back to the hotel? He was nobody special. Just an old guy from upstate who needed to do half a day's business in midtown, not feeling the cold weather since it was nothing compared to nights on Lake Okabye.

He thought of the evenings when he and Helena would meet for drinks after work. They would talk about his book and its upcoming publication and toast to what they hoped would be their first big success. Those were wonderful evenings. But even then he worried over what would happen when he left her. And she kept saying that they had their whole futures before them. He loved that expression. He loved that she wasn't afraid to say it. But he knew she loved something that he wasn't, and he didn't want to spend his whole life pretending otherwise. But, was he even right about that? Had he called that one wrong, too? What was he, really? He didn't know.

Now, looking back on the mess he'd made, he felt like such a damned sentimentalist under his cynical veneer. Or, he thought, as he wandered back to the hotel, was it the opposite? Either way, his sentimentalism was tightly threaded through his cynicism. Like a barber pole. On nights like this he could hardly tell where one ended and the other began. How could women stand such disparity in one man? But he knew that somehow, they did.

Stella, November 2011

Ivan wasn't home when she got in and what the hell? Stella really needed him. He was being totally unreachable and she had no idea why. Or was she overreacting and he was just working? She needed to chill out. Her body hurt. Her head hurt. Her brain hurt.

The weirdest part was that at the end of the workday, when her mind was on other things, she had bought a new book. She'd cornered Sara Byrd on the Joan of Arc pitch and the thing had turned out to be sixty pages and an outline of something that only had a veneer of the medieval and really was an analysis of character traits. But it also had lots of cool metaphors about using your sword in a fight and how dating was a battlefield, and she felt the whole thing was a little sexist and it made her want to throw up, but whatever. She liked books about character traits. She'd been aggressive on the phone with the agent and closed the deal. She heard the author was both shy and mercurial. Big surprise.

She was worried about Emily and what she might do, but she couldn't stop thinking about Helena. Helena had become a constant for her; she lived in her dreams and daydreams and fantasies of the future.

Stella really needed Ivan to come and love her and ease her off the path to a sleepless night before the big meeting. The big showdown. But of course she also knew the meeting was only a preamble to something else, something that was possibly really good. Even if the contest was considered a failure, it was still kind of smart, wasn't it? Depending, of course, on how Helena felt. And nothing bad could really happen at the meeting, could it? Nothing ever happened at meetings, at least not the meetings she attended.

She was at her kitchen table drinking rioja, thinking about how she used to listen to Gram Parsons and smoke pot from a tiny white ceramic pipe with her girlfriends and how she missed that part of herself. How far away that was, now that she mostly thought about her career. How much she depended on Ivan for fun, now. And before she realized it, she was reading *Canoe*. It had become her habit to just page around and look for inspirational sentences. She found:

Compromise keeps your canoe steady.
Compromise and you'll never go in circles.

Pop's hand on Bess's back was a promise. They would paddle through the afternoon together.

Everyday love must travel through
my story to you, dear reader.

433

Horrible sentences! Addictive sentences. Undeniable sentences. And there were so many more like them. As if there was a mystery. As if there was a code. She had begun to hope that meeting him would be a huge disappointment. He would be totally fake. Or what would be even worse was if he totally believed in his fakeness. Like a television pastor. Maybe he would have a big diamond ring. Or a fat gold Rolex. Maybe he'd drop names of old famous people he'd once met, like Diana Ross or Joe Torre or Lorne Michaels. She hoped she didn't like him so she could be disappointed and not feel so bad about the darn contest. So she could get back to slowly and obsessively building her career and enjoying what remained of her young life.

She began to read from chapter 9:

Suppers

I caught them kissing once. Bess was going to take hot soup to a friend in town who'd caught a summer cold. Pop was in the nook near the back door, carefully filling his tackle box for some moonlight fishing. I was reading the Hardy Boys: *The Mystery of the Chinese Junk* at the kitchen table and they couldn't see me. But I could see them.

"Bring the boy back some ice cream," he said.
"What type?"
"Chocolate—no, strawberry. Get both!"

She whispered, "Of course I will."

She put the pot she'd been holding on the shelf in the nook, and he gently dropped the lures he'd been handling into the box. They kissed then, as I stayed still, watching.

She placed a hand on his chest and said, "Again."

After they were done kissing for what felt to me like way too long, Bess slipped out the back door and walked down the dirt path to the Pontiac. Pop stood for a moment, still smiling down at his own shoes, and for a second I thought, Sweet old man. To be so happy. And about what? But now that we're deep in these pages, I think that you and I, we understand.

"Come on, Peter. Let's get out on those waters and catch our supper."

"Okay," I said.

Their love was as big and strong as old houses. And I learned one other thing, right then. If you can do nothing else, if you're just running out to visit a friend and do a few errands and life is busy and humming all around you . . . Well, right then, remember to reach back into your home and your marriage. Remember to take good care of those who you love and who love you.

It's okay to set down your paddles and love each other. Your canoe will find its way.

435

Lines like that one reminded Stella of what she had first seen in the book, that had resulted in her making out with Ivan in the parking lot. The sentences weren't horrible. It was stupid of her to think that! After her initial calculations, she'd been seduced, hadn't she? There was truth in *Canoe*. She went to bed and fell into an anxious, sweaty sleep.

"Hi, baby." Ivan kissed the top of her head. His eyes were tired and his hair was standing up, but he smelled good. Already she was breathing slower. Loving him so intensely scared her, but at least she knew enough not to try and stop it. He said, "Want to come in the kitchen?"

"I have to rest. I've got this meeting tomorrow."

"The big meeting! Got your six-shooter?"

"Shut up."

Ivan sat on the bed and unlaced his shoes. She loved the sight of his bumpy spine through his shirt.

"Where've you been, anyway?"

"I was out with another woman who's not you, having emotionally fraught sex. Are you thirsty?"

She frowned at him and got up and followed him into the kitchen. She found the bottle of wine and sipped at it, her head in her hand. He reached out and took the bottle. She smelled herself on him, on his hands and shirt. He was never with anybody else. She smiled at him.

"I'm an idiot," she said. "You were editing film, weren't you? I'm sorry."

"You're a weird monster of a person in some ways, but I love you."

"Will you stay with me, even if I lose this job?"

"Especially if you blow this stupid job!" He laughed. "We could move to Buenos Aires and hang out with cool people. We could eat little plates of chorizo and octopus and then tango till three in the morning."

"I'd be jealous of all the Argentinians if we lived there," Stella said. "Why do I take all this work stuff so seriously? It's just that Helena has me turned on. She's so . . . great. And I won't lose the job. I love the job. So long as this meeting goes okay, I'll be able to do whatever I want."

"When's the meeting?"

"Tomorrow at ten."

They began to walk back to the bedroom.

"Remember not to put your foot in your mouth."

"I am going to keep quiet. You can bet on that."

"Sure you are," he said. She could see him raise an eyebrow and smile at her, even in the dark bedroom. She really did love him. It was something. Or, no. It had begun to feel like everything.

Peter and Emily and Stella and Helena, November 2011

Less than a minute after Peter announced himself to the receptionist, Lucy Brodsky came out to meet him. To Peter, she looked so young that her office clothes clashed with her face. The fabric of her blazer appeared to be more experienced than the rest of her.

"I'm an enormous fan of you and your book." Her handshake was uncomfortably firm.

"Thank you." He met her eyes. She looked away.

"No, really. I give it to all my friends. You wouldn't believe how time-irrelevant your advice is. Or maybe you would."

"I'm not sure . . ." Now that he was in the physical space of the publishing house, he adopted the soft dumb tones he'd used forty years earlier—to get through that odd time. He waggled his eyebrows and tried to look befuddled. This action appeared to make Lucy more comfortable. So he did it again.

She smiled and said, "Please follow me. Our meeting will take place in the Dreiser Room."

She led him past rows of cubicles and then down a long hall to a conference room that was warmer than where they'd come from. They were alone.

"Coffee? Water?"

"No thanks, nothing for me." He walked around the long conference table and leaned against a window frame. He glanced to his left and looked out at a corner of Central Park.

"How do you like these new offices?" he asked.

"These are the only offices I know. I've been here for almost a year and a half, ever since I graduated from Carleton. It's in Minnesota."

"Ladder & Rake's old offices looked much . . . dowdier."

"The offices on Park Avenue? I guess that was before I was born," Lucy said.

"Also there were books around. I don't see any books? Except those ones in the glass cabinets."

"You can't touch those. Anyway, paper books are not very green and Ladder & Rake is a green company these days."

"But—"

"I know," she said, half to herself. "Don't start saying 'but' about business or you'll go nuts." She moved around the room, repositioning chairs.

"Do you work for Helena?"

She straightened and said, "Directly."

Emily Babson came in with another young woman who had on an argyle sweater and a leopard-print scarf and maybe a little too much lipstick. Had they been made to wait somewhere else? That seemed odd. He did his eyebrow waggle again and Emily looked first confused and then angry.

"Sorry, Emily," he said, instead of hello. "And are you Stella?" He walked over and shook both their hands.

Emily said, "It's funny to see you in an office."

"For me, too," Peter said. "I haven't been in a place like this in at least a decade. Maybe even two."

Stella was both shorter and obviously younger, somewhere between Lucy and Emily's age. She kept opening her mouth and then instead of allowing herself to speak, swallowing air. Finally, she said, "It's really great to meet you after spending so much time on the phone. I just think—"

And then Helena came into the room through another door, moving fast and talking.

"Hello, hello, hello!" She looked only at Peter. He was striding toward her before he knew what he was doing. But he knew he shouldn't be so familiar with her. So he stopped and retreated to his place at the window. They hadn't seen each other in such a long time.

"Well, I'm glad we decided it'll just be the five or eight of us or whatever it is. My goodness, this is a big conference room for some little personalities! Stop. I mean the opposite. Let me see your charming faces, all of you."

Everyone in the room looked up at Helena while

she settled into a chair at the head of the table. Lucy immediately sat down to her right. Helena held the silence and Peter was thrown back in time to when they were very young and she had just begun to learn how to do that. Through the combination of yelling and sudden silence she could make any conversation dramatic, so even bringing a glass of water with or without ice to bed would turn into a heated exchange. She was capable of this all by the time she was twenty-four.

"Peter, dear—together again! I find I have to come a bit closer!" She got up and made her way to him. Now that he was invited, he pushed himself off the window and came to her.

He smiled and bent in and they kissed each other's cheeks. How could a person smell of the same light flowery scent after nearly forty years? They couldn't. She did. He glanced at her hand and the diamond bracelets around her wrists, and thought of her infinite ambition, the fortress she'd built for herself up high in an office building. There was a weirdly thick gold chain around her neck. He had been far away for so long. He really had. Her hair was silver-gray now, but her eyes were the same deep brown. Without thinking, he reached out. He wanted to touch her face. But she stepped back, still staring at him.

"You look great, Helena," he said.

"Thank you. I'm happy to see you. I missed you, Peter Herman."

She nodded and sat down again, not at the head of the table but in a chair near the windows. Peter sat next to her. She said, "Now this is what I like. A good solid meeting with just a few people, where we can have an honest and forthright conversation about where we are and where we need to be."

And then everyone leaned in toward Helena and began to talk at once. Peter was overwhelmed by the noise. Could Helena have been who Lisa was referring to when she told him not to just be with Maddie? Could Lisa wish him back to Helena? Yes. His wife could have been that calculated about his life, at the end of hers.

The affair with Helen came back to him as snapshot images, the two of them in bed in her studio apartment on East Seventy-Second Street, followed by her screaming at him in the Lever House courtyard on Park Avenue, when Ladder & Rake's offices were located across the street. It was 1975. They were coming from a lunch with someone and he was apologizing. He kept saying that what they had together was never serious. That he had gone and gotten married and he believed in the marriage. The book could be like a child between them, couldn't it? Something they'd created that should make them feel proud. But no, that was all wrong and she had been furious at him. A child was a horrid simile, especially for a woman who did not yet have one.

Even now, so many years later, he deeply regretted his choice of words.

"Nothing more than a few pokes, was it?" she had screamed.

She carried a stiff almond-colored pocketbook and she hit him with it, smacked him over and over again. And then she fell into him, crying.

"I could love you," she said. Peter knew she meant, I do love you.

He had shaken her off, said he was sorry. He'd walked down to Grand Central and ridden back up to Millerton, hoping like mad she wouldn't be too disappointed in him.

"What do you think, Peter?" she called out, now.

She put her hand on top of his. She wore gold and diamond rings on several of her fingers but she had no wedding band. No doubt she'd divorced a second or perhaps a third time. He smiled at her. Here she was again, after so long, in the seat next to him. And in mere hours, he'd be going back to Grand Central all over again.

"I don't know what to think," he said, falling back on the self he'd fashioned so long ago.

"I think we can rebuild the contest," Stella spoke quickly. "I'm sure we can."

The room's attention focused on her. But she stopped as quickly as she started, perhaps realizing that she had not been asked what she thought. Peter found her engaging to look at. Of course, she was just like Helena. Though Stella was far less shrill and bossy. He imagined Stella's career would be more of a ricochet than Helena's had been.

Peter said, "Stella, you remind me of Helena when she was young. She was lovely, like you. And outspoken! You couldn't get a word in . . ."

Stella opened her mouth. She had turned pale. "I am flattered, of course," Stella whispered.

"We all look up to Helena," Lucy said.

"What about the contest," Emily asked. "I am only here because I want to make absolutely sure it goes away." Peter realized no one had been paying attention to her.

"She's right," Peter said. "It should."

"Can you speak for your husband?" Helena asked.

"Um," Emily said. She looked around. "For this purpose, yes."

"For this purpose?" Helena asked.

"We are separating." Emily nodded. Her cheeks and forehead reddened. But she stayed very still. She said, "Therefore we want to keep our privacy and have nothing to do with any of this. I'm sure you'll agree that this is the right course of action. That's what I've forced myself to come here to say."

"I'm sorry to hear it," Helena said. Her eyes were sad for a moment and then she rolled her neck and looked out the window. Her coral-colored blazer did not shift. "I think we can all agree that our recently separated contest winners wouldn't make for very good television or webisodes. In fact, this result doesn't make for very good anything, does it?"

"I'm not sure any of us were ever going on television, Helena," Peter said. He smiled again at Stella.

"Really, Peter?" Helena asked. "Stella thought you would. She sold me on that idea. In fact, she promised me. Didn't you speak to Stella, Peter?"

Peter looked out at Central Park. He said, "I'm sure I promised Stella the moon and the stars. Whenever someone from LRB calls I say yes, don't I?"

"He did promise me," Stella said. She drummed her fingers on the table. The room grew quiet.

"We'll deal with you later," Helena said to Stella, who went still, again.

"No scones this morning?" he asked.

"We can—" Lucy Brodsky began to get out of her chair. But Helena moved her chin to the left and Lucy sat back down.

"No scones, Peter. We're so busy running around like a bunch of Chicken Littles worrying over you and your book that we don't even have time to eat!" Helena laughed.

"So what shall we do?" Peter asked. "I played my part."

"You certainly did," Helena said. "I knew Stella was lying to me. Making promises she couldn't keep. And we've got your book. Or I should say, we still have it. We already have substantial unit escalation week to week. It's great. Now that we've elevated awareness, the word of mouth will keep it going for a long time to come. I couldn't be happier. And you should be, too, Peter. You wanted a little money. You've got it. We don't mind that we paid you for participating in this catastrophe—that's not the problem."

Peter looked at Stella, who had begun to sink in her chair. She stuck her tongue out and licked a spot between her lips and nose.

Peter said, "Then what is the problem?"

Helena stared at Peter and said, "There are a couple of things I hate. One is betrayal. I hate betrayal. But something I hate even more is working with someone who makes promises she cannot deliver!"

"I don't understand," Peter said. "What promises were made? I'm saying I made them, not her."

"Peter, it is living hell to work with people who promise and then do not deliver on their promises. Living hell. Stella will come to understand that."

"Helena," Peter said. "Please—"

"No." Helena shook her head. "This went too far. Stella took it too far. She doesn't understand how to manage authors, or books." Peter felt the three other women in the room watching him and Helena. They did not move. "We'll take care of the fallout. We can be sure that whatever constitutes the media these days will sling some arrows at good old LRB but we've weathered worse. Twitter and all that. They'll make hay of us. I'll have a talk with counsel later today about how to exit the contest without delivering winners," Helena said. "Now Peter, can we ever expect to see something else from you? Our Stella tells me you hinted at a second book. Or was that one of her lies, too?"

"I'm going to leave now," Emily said.

Helena turned and looked at Emily. "Yes, you can go. We will leave you to your piousy—your privacy," Helena said to Emily. "Please forget us. Enjoy this nice man's book and forget the apparatus behind it. If anyone from the media does get to you, I'm sure you're sophisticated enough to handle it. We are at arm's length from you, as of now. I am sorry about your marriage."

"Okay," Emily said. Peter saw her crying face in two places at once, at this awful business meeting and in the ruins of her crumbling marriage. He stood up and went to Emily.

"I'm sorry, Emily," he said. "I'm so sorry."

"It's not your fault." She walked to the door, stood there, and then turned around, as if she were waiting for something.

"I suppose it's time for me to go, too." Peter followed Emily to the door. "Goodbye, Helena."

He watched Helena stand.

"One more thing," Helena said.

"What's that?" Peter asked. He looked again at Lucy and Stella, both with their hands clasped in front of them and their eyes upraised, silent and expectant as little girls in class.

"Listen." Helena's voice was calmer now. "Your book is not really what we'd call a hit. I've kept it in print all these years without much in the way of sales because I'm nostalgic. Sometimes it amazes even me, what I can do. We'll shut down the contest, as I've said. I'm sorry I encouraged it. I should have said no to this one." She gestured with her chin at Stella. "But I didn't. I let her lie to me."

Stella, who had only been quiet, watching, said, "But I found the romance."

"Did you?" Helena asked. "Well then, that will be your consolation."

Stella only nodded and looked down at the table.

"You kept it alive, all these years?" Peter asked Helena.

"People like it. But people like lots of crap and goodness knows they lose interest and forget and start looking for something new quicker than goldfish. Lucy?"

"Yes?"

"Can you show our guests out?"

"Emily, Peter, please come this way."

"Goodbye Helena," Peter said. "It's always good to see you."

"Keep us updated on that new book, won't you?" But he could see she was frowning, holding back tears. She would not look at him.

"Yes, yes, I will."

He watched her, glancing again at her uncommonly thick gold rope chain—It was like armor, he thought. Such a charming, powerful woman. All these years later and he was still drawn to her, was still walking away from her. He couldn't understand it.

He followed Lucy down the hall. Emily was already at the elevator bank.

"Wait for me, Emily," he called out.

Helena was coming after him.

"Peter? There's just one more thing."

He turned to her. She looked up at him and her eyes flared and if he didn't know her, hadn't known her, he would have thought she was about to yell at him. But that wasn't it. She was gathering enough courage to say something that mattered to her. He loved her eyes.

"You did a lousy job of keeping in touch. You never called."

"I know. I'm sorry."

"I never forget people's promises."

Peter smiled and thought back on the ever-constant love he had with Lisa. He thought back to those evenings with Helena. She had driven him wild and he had ducked the intensity. He had chosen a quieter life.

After a moment, he said, "I was afraid I would disappoint you. I was sure I would."

"You needn't have worried about that."

"Is it too late?"

She frowned. He was astonished at how much he liked the feel of her in front of him, there in the hallway. The way they couldn't quite seem to let each other go, even now. And then she quickly shook her head and went away, down the corridor.

"Well, that didn't go quite as I imagined it would," he said, half to Emily, who was mute, and half to Lucy Brodsky, whose arms were folded tightly over her chest.

"You could start a blog," Lucy Brodsky whispered to him. "Tell the truth about what happened here. We'd all read it. We won't be here forever. This place doesn't rule us."

"Oh?" he said. "Mmm. That's for you to do, isn't it? I'm no blogger. And besides, this place isn't to blame for what went wrong."

And then Peter and Emily were standing on Fifty-Seventh Street, with a blustery Thanksgiving wind and dozens of tourists walking around them.

He took Emily's hands in his. "Emily," he said. "You are going to be okay."

"Maybe someday. What about that awful girl, Stella? She's still up there."

"I imagine that by now she's learned that she doesn't fit in. If she hasn't, Helena will make it even more clear."

Emily got free of him and took a step back. She said, "After a while, when I look back on this, I'll feel that you helped me through a difficult time. You listened to me. You gave me a sweater."

"I didn't do you any good at all."

"That's not true. You were there for me, Peter Herman. You can't deny it!"

From *Marriage Is a Canoe,*
Chapter 11, On Endings

On August twenty-fifth of that wonderful summer, with a single full day left to my visit, I knew I had to break up with Honey. But I didn't want to do a bad job of it and hurt her. So I asked Pop for advice.

We went out on the lake to catch a trout and talk it over. It was already deep into the afternoon when I got up the courage to ask him. The tips of the sun's rays touched the elms across the lake. By then I could paddle us out and so I did that while Pop threaded his rod. When we got to floating, I said what I needed to say, about how much I liked Honey and how I wanted to see her again but that I knew, because of school and the distance that separated us, that I ought to tell her it was over. Even though that's not what either of us wanted.

"Peter, you've got to have endings in order to find new beginnings. Endings are okay. What's not right is treating people badly—no matter if you don't love them anymore. That doesn't excuse you from treating them just as well as if they mattered to you more than anyone else in the world. You know the mark of a true gentleman?"

I did not.

"The mark of a true gentleman is to show the same deference and kindness to the Second Avenue shoe-shine boy as to the Queen of England."

I nodded, never having met either.

"I have never had a break with Bess, but if I were to have one, I would not be unkind to her. No matter what. Now let's look at your own mother. Your mother has had some bad breaks. Let's be honest here. She has."

I only nodded again, because I was still not capable of admitting that my mother had been with a man who abused her. And that that man was my father.

"And there are men she's had relations with in her life—without going into too much detail because you're just a boy, there are men who have not been kind to her and it hurts my heart to say it and I do not like this. I do not like knowing it. But there it is. You see? It won't go away."

My hair had grown long so I was always flipping the front back and I did so then, and maybe that made me look a little prouder or like I had a little more attitude than I actually did.

"You don't want to become like one of those men who treats your mom badly, do you?"

Not for the first time that summer, I swallowed back my tears. I said, "No, sir."

"Then go find that little girl and be kind to her.

Be honest. You're going on back home and won't see her anymore. In life, you have to have endings. She knows that, too. And you shouldn't try to get around them or run anyway. That's a coward's move and in the moment it might feel nice, like it gets your heart beating, to run from a responsibility. But you'll live with that moment of cowardice and you can't brush it off. It's deeper than a sailor's tattoo or a scar from a knife fight. It sits inside you if you don't do the right thing and you can't get free of it. So promise me you'll never shy away from an honest ending. Can you promise me that, Peter?"

"I promise I won't," I said. And the next thing I had to say was said because it had to be. "Are you giving me all this help and advice because of my father, and the way he and my mom are breaking up? I promise I won't end up like him. I don't even like him."

"Don't say that. He's your father. But yes, in part," Pop said. "In part. We can't fix him and set him straight now, can we? All we can do is work on you."

"So I've got to go and say goodbye to her? And just be kind? Just tell her I really like her but we can't go on? That's it?"

"That's right. It is okay to part, and it is okay to end. And you should know that. But you've got to do it honest, and that way you won't have to live with so much regret. Come on, let's go back. The

454

fish aren't biting this late in the day. They're sleeping already. We both know that."

Later, after I'd gone to see Honey, we sat at the kitchen table and ate chicken cutlets with garlic bread and spaghetti with tomato sauce. We drank tall glasses of ice water. For dessert we had a Jell-O mold that was so full of fresh fruit the pink Jell-O could hardly stand the pressure and the weight.

It was nearly eight and the lights were coming on in the houses around the lake. I thought, This is my favorite time of day. Then I thought, There are tons of times of day that are my favorite here. And looking back on that time now, I wish that all of my life could be filled with those soft moments.

If you must put an end to your voyage,
be as kind and honest with each other as you
were when you started out together.

Stella, November 2011

Stella walked into her office a few minutes after nine on Friday morning, which was much earlier than she usually got in, but it didn't matter. She was fired immediately.

She was shocked to discover that she felt no hate for Gina Adams from HR, who arrived with Melissa Kerrigan, who she'd barely seen in days and who she also, incredibly, didn't hate. She didn't feel hate while Gina told her that she would be covered by COBRA for ninety days but that regardless, she ought to get her own health insurance immediately. She didn't feel hate for Melissa, who had come in especially for this event since she normally took Fridays off, to say goodbye.

"Even though LRB considers this a departmental restructuring rather than a firing, the point is that I bear some responsibility," Melissa said.

Gina glared at Melissa while Stella watched. Gina wore a huge engagement ring and Stella had heard that she was going to marry a fund manager and that she'd be rich and that she only stayed in HR at Ladder & Rake because she was a people person. She liked to bring people up to their potential and was likely going to run LRB's HR group someday.

Stella saw that Gina was looking at Melissa and thinking, You're handling this terribly. And she didn't care that Stella saw because as of ten minutes ago, Stella was no longer with the company.

"Can I have some time to pack up my desk?"

"Yes," Gina said. "You can have that time right now."

"Goodbye, Stella." Melissa came forward as if to hug her and Stella reared back.

"The other way, please," Gina said, in a singsong voice. She had her hand on Melissa's arm.

"I'm sorry," Melissa said.

Stella bit down on her tongue so she wouldn't say it was all right. Because she damn sure was not going to absolve her direct superior of guilt.

"I'll be right back with a box for your things," Gina said, after Melissa had left.

"Could I have two boxes?" Stella had her arms folded over her chest. She wanted to say something glib like "And a hug?" but she was afraid it might backfire and she'd cry in front of Gina.

Gina said, "I'll see what I can dig up."

Stella looked around. There were the *Canoe* quotes on her bulletin board. She supposed she'd leave them there. She wanted a bunch of the junk she'd accumulated in her fourteen months at Ladder & Rake but she knew she wouldn't be able to pack thoughtfully. There was a piece of Tupperware on the windowsill that she'd filled with chicken and brought from home. It was clean. She tossed it into her handbag.

A few minutes later, she took a break from dumping random books she would never read into her two allotted boxes in order to use the office phone to call Ivan.

"It's over," she said.

"What is?"

"My job. I was fired."

"What? That's crazy! You love that job and you're good at it. What happened?"

She breathed in. That was it. That was all he needed to say.

"Helena decided that I lied to her. Maybe I did. Anyway, it's just a stupid job," she said. "A job is kind of a stupid thing to love."

"You want to meet somewhere right now?" he asked.

She imagined sitting in a cab with her boxes, on the way home to the place in Astoria that they had sort of backed themselves into, if she was going to be honest. Definitely going to spend some time cleaning that place up. Buy a wine rack. Maybe even build one.

"Stella? Honey?"

"Um. No, I guess I don't want to meet right now.

I don't need to ask you to do that. Call me when you're done working, okay?"

She hung up the phone. She felt older and more tired than usual, a little heavier. She felt like someone else. Who was it? She felt like . . . it was Emily. For a moment, she felt just like Emily. She had believed in someone and that person had hurt her. Wait. She shook it off. She was nothing like Emily. Not right now, anyway. Now she was in love. And what was so bad about being like Emily? She understood that Emily Babson was an earnest person who believed people could be good. There was nothing the matter with that.

She called Ivan back. "I've changed my mind. I need you right now. Can you meet me in front of Ladder & Rake? You can help me with my boxes and we can go someplace nice for a fancy drink."

"Yes, baby. I was just putting on my coat. I'll be right there."

Peter, December 2011

Peter knew he was beginning to get past the contest and its bungled outcome when he started to come up with lines that were so bad they made him laugh out loud: Love is simple and sweet and sour as the lemon-caper tuna sandwiches at Pantomime's.

He figured that he was coming out of mourning and saying goodbye to an awful lot and, further, he imagined that meant he was headed toward something good, soon. On a dark Friday evening, he went and found the zither in the hall closet. He wanted the beautiful thing out of the house.

He walked through the kitchen and down the back steps and all the way to the tip of the dock. He stood in the freezing cold. He watched moonlight glint off the zither's shiny wooden face. There was no sound save the lapping of the water. He held the zither up and stared at it, enjoying the feel of it in his hand. Then he kneeled down and plunged the instrument into the cold water. He held up his empty hand, white and glowing in front of his face.

He had been sorry when he'd returned from New York a few weeks earlier and said goodbye to Maddie. Anjulee had had her baby and it was time for Maddie to go. He told Maddie he wouldn't move out to San Francisco with her after all. He had hoped she would say she had always expected that outcome. But instead, she was deeply surprised and hurt and she would not stop crying.

"I can't keep doing things that are not really my intention," he said.

He thought she might understand. Instead she was furious at him and she had used the fury to propel herself away from him and Millerton, forever.

He had written Helena a short note, asking to see her soon. Whenever you're ready, he wrote. She hadn't written back, or called. He felt it was wrong to push further than that. Though in the past few days, he'd begun to consider reaching out to her again. Soon, he would.

Out on the dock, he told himself he could hear his grandparents. That was possible. Some bits of the book came from them. Some of it was true. Not a lot. But some.

Fifty years ago, where was he? Crying in his room in his parents' apartment on Third Avenue and Sixty-Third Street while they divorced. And then a few weeks later, quietly watching his grandparents go about their lives during those weeks of vacation. They saw him sitting, doing nothing. They told him to go fishing. He was given a pole. Pointed toward the lake. Don't drown, Peter. There was a neighbor who owned a canoe he might use. Though maybe there was a hole in it. They weren't sure. If there was, he ought to learn to patch it—otherwise he'd get wet.

He had managed to patch the canoe himself, using instructions he found in a book in his mother's old bedroom. He'd caught his grandfather's attention once he made the canoe float and the old man had gone out fishing with him a few times. They had talked in the canoe. He had done his best to make Peter feel better. At the end of the summer his grandfather had bought the canoe from the neighbor for five dollars and Peter still had it—the very same one.

Sometimes there had been chicken and vegetables for dinner. Pie for dessert. Other times, when they went to sleep early and forgot about him, he'd made himself a peanut butter and jelly sandwich and sat reading in the kitchen. Just as he might this evening, about fifty years later. They were nice old people. Didn't talk much, but what they did say had been kind, and yes, he'd written down a few things they'd said and some of that had made its way into the book.

At eight in the evening he found that he was still standing there out on the dock. And then he realized he was freezing and turned back toward the house. He saw a car's headlights glint on the lake and heard the crunch of tires on his gravel driveway.

After a few moments of confusion, he rushed up the path to his back porch to see who it was. The car's engine went quiet. Maddie? Henry had told him she left town a week ago, for good, without saying goodbye. Maybe it was Henry? Though he would have called first.

He heard the squeak and bang of his front door opening and closing. He found Helena Magursky standing in the kitchen, leaning against the apron sink. She wore a dark overcoat and her arms were folded over her chest.

"Door was unlocked," she said. "I let myself in."

He stood still and just stared at her. "I see."

"Who'd you expect? Mother Teresa?"

"Sophia Loren," he said with a laugh. "But you'll do. You're more beautiful than she is anyway."

"Please. If that were the case I would have spent my life on yachts instead of in conference rooms. Would've got a nice tan."

He smiled. "You got my note. I'm glad you came."

"I kept meaning to call. But somehow calling didn't quite address it. Took me some weeks to get up the courage to drive here. I don't care about you disappointing me. Too late, like you said. I know what I ought to expect from you. And I've been patient."

Peter smiled and said, "There's nothing in the book about patience. You decided to leave that out? Keep patience for yourself? It's your book, Helena. You know that."

"I think we did put in a bit about patience, actually. But who wants to talk about a book?" she asked. "I meet a guy in a bar and he tells me sob stories about his parents' divorce and a couple of sad weeks he spent on the receiving end of what he imagined might be some wisdom that his grandparents shared with him. I tell him he could get a book out of it and we sleep together. Wonderful affair, too. One of my absolute favorites. We make his memories into a bestseller. We have a nasty breakup and too many years later, here we are."

And then she shut up. And she waited. He kissed her once, deeply, and there was a passion there. They were so close to each other now, listening to the pattern of each other's breathing. Peter couldn't help feeling how it was different than with Maddie.

He pulled back but kept hold of her hand. "I've been unable to stop thinking about you."

"Peter! Didn't I just lay out our awful history? I'm not here to try to go backward in time. I'm here because you wrote to me. I liked seeing you in New York."

He kissed her again, harder.

She said, "It's true you've been on my mind a lot in the past several months. I thought it might be nice to get to know each other again. Neither of us has changed much, so there shouldn't be too many surprises. But don't get me wrong. You can't marry me. You missed your chance for that."

"How'd you know I was all alone up here?"

She laughed and said, "I have my sources. It wasn't hard to find out. What did you think? That I would hop in my car and drive here without knowing what to expect? You think I'm some kind of romantic idiot?"

Peter wouldn't let go of her hand. "Let's go out on the porch for a moment."

Peter took Helena to the inn on Sunday for brunch and to introduce her to Henry, who turned out to be in Hudson for the day. It was gray out, so he had Jenny find someone to make a fire and they sat at the big round table in front of the fireplace. They ordered Bloody Marys and omelets and toast. Peter caught Helena making a face at the wallpaper.

"I should tell Henry to remodel?" he asked.

"I didn't say that."

"Already critical. And you haven't even met him."

"That's my job," Helena said. "I do like the fire."

They watched the fire and then Peter said, "What about the young women? Stella and Emily?"

"Our former editor and her contest winner?

They'll be fine. I fired the one. She kept tripping herself up and banging into things, was what she did. I tried to warn her, but she didn't listen."

"That was mean of you," Peter said.

"No, it wasn't. She'll have another job in two shakes of a lamb's tail."

"How can you be so sure?"

"Stop it, Peter. She was out of control. I told her to find the romance and she made a hash of it. Plus, she lied to me. I know what I'm doing. I only say the opposite of what I mean if that's my intention. Don't attack my character."

"I'm sorry. I shouldn't be brusque."

"Damn right you shouldn't." But he could see she didn't love to talk that way, not to him, anyway.

"You know," Peter said. "My marriage was good. But you're still the only one."

"And I've had a few other relationships, too. Marriages, too. You can bet on that." She raised an eyebrow and winked at him. "My daughter thinks I'm crazy. But she's happy for me."

Peter sipped his Bloody Mary. "We'd better be gentle with each other."

Helena shrugged. "We don't need to be gentle. It's relaxing being with someone who knew you before you knew yourself. We can't possibly harm each other now, can we?"

Peter smiled and said nothing.

"I'll come up here next weekend, too," she said.

"Shake off the week with you. Would you like that?"

"Keep showing up and I'll amend the book for you."

Helena raised her eyebrows. "That would be nice, wouldn't it? But you say that to all the girls."

"I do," Peter said. "But if you'll give me a little help, this time I might actually do it."

Emily Babson, mid-April 2012

Emily took a few months to be entirely alone and then she went out on dates with different men. None of those dates were good. So she stopped and spent more time doing yoga.

And then, after Valentine's Day, once she'd perfected her headstand, she started again. She and Eli agreed to file separation papers. She had thought that would be easy. Instead, it was terribly ugly for a few days after her father suggested she consider the value of her contribution to Roman Street Bicycles. And then it was easy again, once she figured out that whatever her share of Eli's company was worth, it could not be enough to fight over. She suffered the loss of a set of silverware that he said his family wanted. There was an extremely hard night of coming home to find his clothes and the red suede chair she'd never liked gone.

After the holidays, she heard that Eli was as much in Los Angeles as he was in New York. She hoped that he and Jenny were happy together. Well, not exactly hoped. But at least she wasn't trying to learn more about them. She had thrown away that phone bill.

She went on a date with a man named Jesse

Michaelson at the beginning of April. It was a setup. He was a composer who had been Sherry's TA when she was in college. They'd stayed in touch and he had always asked after Emily, who he'd met once, a decade ago. Sherry said he hadn't settled down with anyone for some reason, maybe because he was so self-involved. All that music in his head. But maybe you'll like him, she said. All Emily could think of was how little she knew about music. What would they talk about?

They met outside Carnegie Hall. Jesse had passes for the afternoon dress rehearsal of a quartet from London. They could sit high up in the back where they could whisper. When she looked at him, she thought of a slice of pizza eaten quickly on the street after a cocktail party where there wasn't enough food. Not glamorous, but good. He wore a white, button-down Brooks Brothers shirt that was so old it was furry, and a green tweed blazer. His nose looked big.

"I brought a flask of cider." Jesse flashed the silver vessel, which was in the inside pocket of his coat. "Still warm."

She smiled and wondered how he'd found out she liked cider. They went inside and stood in the lobby. She said nothing. She had begun to tell herself that she was through filling the silences men made. She was not obligated to make them comfortable.

"What was the fallout from the whole *Canoe* escapade?" he asked.

She said, "You are really cutting right to it."

"I am?" he asked. She stared at him. He was wearing docksiders and no socks and she thought he must be cold. He had a sparrow chest. Why were they even on this date? But she tended to hang on until they were over. He said, "I know I don't look like it but I keep up. The gist that I got was that you and the old writer were in love."

"Go ahead." She frowned. "Believe what you want."

"How'd so much information get out? I never understood that part."

"Ladder & Rake didn't do it," she said. "They wanted the whole contest to go away. But somebody found a website that would pay them fifty dollars to prove that we were the winners, me and my ex. And that was a hilarious revelation since there was evidence we'd broken up. So there was something for people to laugh at. There's your answer."

"You're sure you didn't leave your husband for Peter Herman?"

She glared at him before she realized he was joking. She laughed and then suddenly, she relaxed. He wasn't jealous or judgmental. That was a start. And she didn't feel like she had to explain how she'd come to enter and win the contest.

The music was beautiful. There was a cello and she loved the sound of a cello. She was amazed when they began making out in the back of the nearly empty concert hall. She wondered what Peter Herman would think, and didn't understand why she would wonder that, since it was not as if he had any better explanation for attraction than anyone else. Later she would realize it was okay to dwell on Peter, to think of him as just a nice man she'd met, who had tried to help her out during the end of her marriage. She would discover that at the same time she realized that she was still unwilling to live without her several editions of *Marriage Is a Canoe*.

She was at home again, hours later, after they'd eaten cheeseburgers together in the basement restaurant of a hotel down the street from Carnegie Hall, after they'd parted and he'd kissed her. When she was alone, she congratulated herself on not needing to help Jesse with anything, not his career or his ability to make himself understood. Nothing. He had held her hand while they finished their wine.

He called the next day and was sort of funny and confident on the phone, too. His full name was Jesse Edward Michaelson. JEM. She liked that. It was regal without being stuffy.

"I don't think it was such a bad date, really," he said.

"That's awfully kind of you to say."

"Do you want to try again? Maybe on Tuesday?"

"Tuesday," Emily said. "Sure."

She liked Jesse. It would be a long, long time before she could be serious with him, though. There were negatives. He walked much faster than she did. He wore string bracelets on both wrists. But she could learn to stand that. So long as he was never jealous or mean. And didn't cheat. She could feel it, as she imagined walking fast down a city street with Jesse, this possible return to a state of happiness.

The next time she saw him she realized he was taller than her but not so much taller and that his nose wasn't big, it was straight and sort of Roman. He was handsome, but not so handsome that it could get annoying.

"How do you compose music?" she asked.

"Isn't that kind of a broad question?" he asked. "I mean, where do you want me to start?"

"Totally up to you," she said. "But I may as well tell you right now that I do like a man who can give a good explanation."

Peter Herman, Millerton, New York, late April 2012

Peter heard Helena pad down the stairs. He was still in Lisa's study, working on the new introduction to his book.

He called out, "I'm coming to bed. I just need ten more minutes."

"I'm going to make tea. Remind me where you keep the honey."

"In the pantry if there is any—but come in here for a moment. I want to show you the new opening letter."

She came in and put her hands on his shoulders. She read the screen. He could hear her soft breathing and he reached behind to pull her near, pull her arms around his neck so she came down and her chin nestled on his shoulder and he could smell her hair. The closeness he'd discovered with Helena felt tingly and euphoric. It was new for him, the way they touched each other and were slow to move away. He did not know why they were happy together, but did know enough not to question his luck.

"Huh," she said. She straightened up but didn't let go of Peter.

"Well? Does that sound about right?"

"Yes, I suppose."

"Isn't that what's wanted?"

"It's maybe a little sweet. Even for you."

"Is it?" He turned to her and reached up, touched her chin. "I guess it's always been hard for me to tell what's too sweet."

"Don't look sly at me, Peter Herman," she said. "Leave it for the morning. I think I can lop off the burnt-sugar smell of it and get to whatever it is you actually mean. Let me do that before you send it in. We wouldn't want to make a fool out of you."

"Fair enough," Peter said. "I wrote what I meant. But I can wait for you to take a pass at it."

From the introduction to the revised and annotated edition of *Marriage Is a Canoe*, retitled *Love Is a Canoe*, February 2013

Dear Reader:

Perhaps Hank and Bess Latham were not trying to help me understand marriage, after all. Who can help us with that difficult state? I can't. They couldn't either. I was a boy. It was only a summer we spent together.

I'll keep sharing their thoughts and stories. I know they believed that love comes for you. I can write that now, from my advanced age, with my eyes wide open and my head held high. Be open to love when it does come. Don't run from it like a young man from a daunting obligation.

Love is more forgiving than we realize. Love is not so fickle and mean—not as tough as marriage can be. Love is patient. Love is kind. Love can be supple. Love gives you another chance.

Acknowledgments

I must first acknowledge and thank Suzanne Gluck, who pushed extremely hard, for a very long time. She is a force beyond reason. I owe her a great debt. I am grateful to Sarah Crichton for her charm and her wisdom, for her championing and editing. She is a wonder. I am happy to know her and happier still to have been given the chance to work with her.

Many people at WME read and helped with this book, including Laura Bonner, Cathryn Summerhayes, Shana Kelly, Caroline Donofrio, Eve Atterman, and Anna DeRoy. Jonathan Galassi, Jeff Seroy, Kathy Daneman, Dan Piepenbring, Nick Courage, and many others at FSG astonish me with their good humor, their kindness, and their unwavering resolve to uphold the great traditions of publishing. Thanks are due to Rodrigo Corral for reading, for being a good friend, and for giving me a wonderful cover. Joshua Furst, Kate Christensen, Gabrielle Danchick, John Wynne, Harris Schrank, Linda Schrank, and Faith Childs all read and shared welcome comments.

I acknowledge and thank my group at Razorbill, Don Weisberg and the team at Penguin Young

Readers, and Penguin, for making a home for me and for being cool about me taking the time to write and publish this novel.

Lauren Mechling worked alongside me on each page of this book. She is a fine editor and a beautiful writer. When this novel is good, it is good because of her, and when it is dull, the fault is mine. I am grateful to her for helping me to become a better writer. But I am most grateful to be married to her. Also our son, Henry Chester, is really cute.

A NOTE ABOUT THE AUTHOR

Ben Schrank is president and publisher of Razorbill, a Penguin imprint that is home to many award-winning and *New York Times*–bestselling books for children and young adults. Ben is also the author of the novels *Consent* and *Miracle Man*. He wrote "Ben's Life," a monthly column for *Seventeen* magazine, in the 1990s. He grew up in Brooklyn, where he lives with his wife and son.

Center Point Large Print
600 Brooks Road / PO Box 1
Thorndike ME 04986-0001 USA

(207) 568-3717

US & Canada:
1 800 929-9108
www.centerpointlargeprint.com